Old Land, Dark Land, Strange Land

Stories
by John F. Suter

Introduction by Sharyn McCrumb

Cover and book design by Steve Gray

Appearing originally in *Ellery Queen's Mystery Magazine*

: "A Break in the Film", c1953; "When Are People Going to Learn?", c1954; "Your
Word Against Mine", c1955; "The Seeds of Murder", c1955; "Doctor's Orders", c1959;
"The Impossible Theft", c1964; "The Oldest Law", c1979; "The Angel's Hair". c1980;
"The Shades of Death", c1980; "The Power of the Tongue", c1981; "The Unclean
Spirit", c1983; "And They Hauled It Away to the Mill", c1985; "Come Down From the
Hills ", c1987;
"That Man's Moccasins Have Holes", c1987; "Not Alone In Her Grave", c1989;
"No Cradle of Pine", c1990; "The Touch of a Vanished Hand", c1992.

Appearing originally in *Alfred Hitchcock's Mystery Magazine:* "The Stone Man",
c1986, and "Shattered Lamp", c1988.

Library of Congress card number 96-60068

1st Edition

Suter, John F., 1914-

Old land, dark land, strange land : stories / by John F. Suter. Introduction by Sharyn
McCrumb.

ISBN 0-9651108-0-X
1. Mystery and detective stories - West Virginia. 2. Uncle Abner (Fictitious character) I. Title.
813'.5'4

Contents

Introduction to the Short Stories of John F. Suter

By Sharyn McCrumb

John F. Suter has been one of the mainstays of the mystery short story for more than forty years, appearing in anthologies with such luminaries as Raymond Carver and Eudora Welty, and winning a number of awards from *Ellery Queen's Mystery Magazine* for his thoughtful character studies of rural life, past and present. He is published on every continent except Antarctica.

Suter is a "writer's writer." His beautifully crafted, well-observed dramas of crime in Middle America have earned him high praise from readers and editors alike, and a continuing place in the pages of *Alfred Hitchcock* and *Ellery Queen's Mystery Magazines*, where his stories have appeared regularly since his debut in September, 1953, with *A Break in the Film*. That first tale of betrayal and murder, set in a run-down movie house remembered from his youth, won a Queen Special Award for the author, and began a wonderful working friendship between Suter and Ellery Queen himself—or *themselves*, as Queen was the pseudonym of Fred Dannay and Manny Lee.

John F. Suter was born in Lancaster, Pennsylvania, in 1914, moved to Charleston, West Virginia, ten years later, and he is still there. He received a degree in chemistry from Franklin and Marshall College in Lancaster, and worked as a research chemist at Union Carbide for thirty-six years. Suter's crime fiction also profited from his scientific training: in *The Seeds of Murder*, he considers hypnosis and the criminal mind; *The Stone Man*, is exact and convincing in its details of masonry; and the solution to *Not Alone in Her Grave* depends on careful observation, deductive reasoning, and a familiarity with farming.

John F. Suter is a member of the Mystery Writers of America, twice serving as a judge for the Edgar Awards, and the Crime Writers Association of Britain. He has been married for fifty-eight years to Pauline Thomas of Charleston, and they have three children, nine grandchildren, and four great-grandchildren.

Suter is perhaps best known for his two series of mystery short stories. The "Uncle Abner" series is a continuation of the adventures of a character created by Melville Davisson Post. Uncle Abner, a frontier sage in what is now West Virginia, used Holmes-like methods of reasoning and observation to solve crimes in the days when Appalachia was the West. Suter examines this same setting in modern times with his characters Arlan Boley and Sheriff Warren McKee, who use practical knowledge in much the same way Uncle Abner did to solve crimes in their small community.

One of the great distinctions of Suter's work is its originality of setting in a genre where the mean streets of the generic Big City are considered the proper place for detection. Virtually all of John Suter's work is set in rural West Virginia, or in the small town milieu where ordinary people commit crimes for gain or revenge. You will find no gangsters, drug lords, or hard-drinking private eyes in Suter's work; instead, meet folks that remind you of people you know—except that their problems or temptations got the best of them. There is a realism and an honesty of observation present in these stories that makes them snapshots of American life, as well as entertaining puzzles of detective fiction.

In *No Cradle of Pine*, and *Your Word Against Mine*, Suter examines crimes against children. *Not Alone in Her Grave, And They Hauled It Away to the Mill*, and *Come Down From the Hills* reflect Suter's interest in crimes committed for (and against) the land. He has a deep understanding of the importance of land to the common man, both historically and in modern times. Many of the plots in the Uncle Abner series arise from disputes about land ownership, or from the killer's coveting a parcel of land belonging to the victim: (*The Power of the Tongue, The Angel's Hair, The Unclean Spirit, The Oldest Law*).

In a genre with an increasing emphasis on the novel, and an ever-shrinking market for short stories, John F. Suter has remained a constant, a shining planet for four decades, crafting his well-written, meticulously observed slices of ordinary life into gems of crime fiction, and helping to sustain the short story as an art form for those who love the tale well told.

Read on. You are in the hands of one of the best.

—Sharyn McCrumb

AUTHOR'S PREFACE

Let's face it: there's no way to follow Sharyn McCrumb. I won't even try.

The use of some fact is present in nearly all of the stories I do. There's a lot of lore in them. If you want to know some of it, drop me a line. Reply guaranteed. Or, if a get-together is within reason, we could manage that.

A word or two is in order about the characters of two different series of stories chosen for this book, Boley and Mckee, and Uncle Abner.

The Boley-McKee series was originally intended to be only one story, *And They Hauled It Away to the Mill.* However, *Ellery Queen's* asked for more, so I agreed, providing any West Virginia dialect would not be touched. Obviously, my request was honored. Boley is a composite of two real persons who own heavy equipment and sell their services to the less-affluent persons of the county. He resembles a physically larger old friend of mine. McKee is an intelligent sheriff, possible more honest than some West Virginia sheriffs.

Uncle Abner was the creation of Melville Davisson Post, of Harrison County, West Virginia. Post lived and wrote in the late 19th and early 20th centuries, and was, at one time, America's highest paid short story writer. His novel *The Mountain Schoolteacher,* was nominated for a Nobel Prize. He is most remembered for his "Uncle Abner" stories, of which he wrote twenty-two.

Abner is a bachelor cattle-breeder, who is deeply religious and sees the hand of God everywhere. He is a giant of a man who shirks no important physical confrontation. The stories Post wrote about him are considered by many knowledgeable people to be second only to Poe's mysteries.

Many years ago, Fred Dannay, an influential editor and half of the team that was "Ellery Queen," mistakenly characterized Abner as a Virginia Squire of the Jeffersonian period. Actually, on internal evidence, the stories were set at least twenty years later than Jefferson's death in 1826.

In the mid-1970's, Bob Mills, agent for the Post estate, sent me four short stories and an unfinished novel, asking me to complete them. I found the unfinished novel hopeless and quickly saw that Post had already converted three of the stories to "Colonel Braxton" tales. Colonel Braxton was another of Post's characters, appearing in stories in the late 1920's. The final story, involving a streetcar accident, was relatively modern and had never been completed for sale.

The news that there were no new "Abner" stories disappointed several people, including Fred Dannay. I suffered severe writer's block until I saw that the way out was to write a "new" Abner story of my own. I did this with *The Oldest Law,* reprinted in this collection.

The success of the story led me to realize that a vast, rich, untouched period of American history was there to be quarried. Untouched because most American history books cover only events influencing and leading up to the Civil War.

So I wrote two more "Abners," opening up and expanding the sage, his nephew, Martin, and the rest of the basic characters with events beginning in 1837 and going on through the 1850's. Nearly all fifteen of my "Uncle Abner" stories contain some authentic, unnoticed historical fact, such as the emergence of silk in 1837. Five of these new Uncle Abner stories are in this book.

I have been fortunate to be associated with a number of good editors: Fred Dannay and Manny Lee (Ellery Queen), Eleanor Sullivan, and Janet Hutchings, all of *Ellery Queen Mystery Magazine*; Cathleen Jordan of *Alfred Hitchcock Mystery Magazine*; Ed Gorman of *Mystery Scene*; and Jack Adrian, British editor for many of my stories.

My further good fortune is that I have encountered good teachers, professors (some whose classes I wasn't taking), good classmates, and a kaleidoscope of interesting people, among whom are my supportive and still-expanding family.

1

Doctor's Orders
(1959)

This is the author's most reprinted story. It has been used in the classroom to lure reluctant readers.

The pain. The pain is everywhere. No, not everywhere, but I throb in the places where there is no real pain. And now it is only an ache and an exhaustion, but it seems as if there is no time, no space, nothing but this. But I am a little stronger than I was. So little. But I am stronger. I have to get well. I intend to get well. I will get well.

"Mr. Shaw, I think she'll come out of it all right. As you know, it was either your wife or the baby, for a while. But she's improved, I assure you. Of course, there will always be that weakness which we can't correct."
"I understand. Just to have her well again is all I care about."

I had better open my eyes. Jeff isn't here. I can't sense him. But I can stand the white room now. I no longer have a wish to die. Even though he didn't live. I could grieve and grieve and grieve, and I wanted to when Jeff first told me. But there is no strength in that sort of grief. I will get well.

"You did tell her the baby died?"
"Yes, Doctor. It was hard for her to take at first. Very hard. Then I told her that it had been a boy. That pleased her, in spite of—of what happened."

There. The world is back. So much sunshine in the room, so many flowers. I wonder if Jeff—

1

"Did you tell her that the child is already buried?"

"Not yet. If you're sure that she's stronger, I'll tell her today."

"You don't think she'll hold it against you for going ahead with the funeral, Mr. Shaw?"

"Jessie is very level-headed, Doctor. She'll understand that we couldn't wait. And—if you don't think it's out of style to say so—we love each other."

I'm sure Jeff has done whatever is best. If only it—he—had lived until I could have seen him . . . How long have I been here? Where is Jeff? Is he being sensible, as I begged him to be? Is he at work, so that he won't endanger his job, the job that's so important to him? Oh, I do love him, and I so want to give him fine children.

"Perhaps, then, Mr. Shaw, it would be better for you to tell her the rest of it than for me to do it. It might be easier for her to believe someone who loves her. Sometimes the patient thinks the doctor doesn't know as much as she herself does."

"That part won't be easy."

I hope the children will look like Jeff. I'm not ugly, but I'm so—plain. Jeff has the looks for both of us. That's one of the reasons they all said he was only after my money. But he's refused to let me help him. He's independent. He keeps working hard managing the sporting goods department, when neither of us would ever have to work again, if we didn't want to. I must get well, for his sake. I will get well.

"Easy or hard, Mr. Shaw, it has to be done. Someone has to tell her. It will come best from you. She must never try to have a child again. Never. It will kill her. Make no mistake about it—having another child will kill her."

"I'll take the responsibility, Doctor. You needn't say a thing to her. I think I can convince her. Perhaps I can even persuade her to move away for awhile, so that old associations won't keep haunting her."

2

I'm glad that I made my will in Jeff's favor before I came to the hospital. He doesn't know about it, and it wasn't necessary, as it turned out. But I'm glad. He's been so good to me that now I'm sure of him . .
.

The door swung inward, silently. She turned her head, slowly, and a tired smile crept across her white face. A tall young man with crinkled blond hair was in the doorway.

"Jeff."

He was at her bedside, kissing her palm. "Jessie."

"Jeff, I've been lying here thinking. Everybody has trouble of some kind or other. We can overcome this. I'm going to get strong, fast. Then we're going to have another baby, just as quickly as we can. Aren't we?"

He smiled proudly. The truth was exactly the right answer.

"We certainly are, sweetheart. We certainly are."

2

The Angel's Hair
(1980)

The second Uncle Abner story was the first, chronologically. It was the subject of a double crostic in "National Review," covering a quote from the text, the title, and the author's name.

S ometimes when I read the Book of Job, I find my memory pushing Job aside in favor of my Uncle Abner. My uncle was never tormented in the way that poor old man was. My feeling is that the Lord would never have issued to Abner the mighty series of reminders of His majesty which he did to Job. Abner already knew them all and honored the Lord for them.

Yet, a romantic man he was not. He was aware of the colors of the autumn leaves, but it was because they told him something: the identity of each tree. He knew the odor of violets and sweet clover, for these identified the plants.

Most of all, he respected the insignificant, for the Lord was as infinite in patience as He was mighty in colossal works.

When I was only seven, my mother took me with her to visit a cousin who lived a short day's journey from us toward Ohio. She had promised the woman, Sarah Harrison, that she would spend a week caring for her and her household when the Harrisons' first child was born. I had to go, too, for my father had skill enough to fend for himself, but little in caring for a seven-year old.

It was mid-February and biting cold when we alighted from the stage just over a mile from the Harrison farm. The journey had been bumpy, over many a frozen rut. Often the road passed cliffs hung top to bottom with huge icicles, and small waterfalls were locked in irregular, bulgy, glassy sheets. Snow lay unbroken on fields and hillsides.

Now, a week later, a change in the weather had come, but not everyone at our cousins' welcomed it.

"There will be no more skating on the pond after tomorrow, if this warm spell holds," said Cousin Levi, Sarah's brother, coming into the kitchen through the back door. He hung a pair of skates on a nail in a far corner. "I'd best get it out of my system for this winter."

Sarah's husband, Adam, interrupted his conversation in the sitting room. "More'll get done around here when that happens," he said, raising his voice.

His visitor was my Uncle Abner, who had come here on his way back from a farm on the Ohio. He had been inspecting some pigs he was considering buying, and he had stopped to accompany my mother and me home.

"I have mixed feelings about a thaw," I heard him say. "A good thaw and at least one more hard freeze, and the ground will turn that much easier."

"That it will," my cousin agreed.

"On the other hand," Abner went on, "there might be mud under the coach wheels when we go home day after tomorrow. It might be a hard pull at times."

My mother and Cousin Sarah made no attempt to enter into the conversation. Sarah was nursing my little cousin, Jonathan, while my mother busily peeled potatoes for dinner.

I did not like the change in the weather. The snow was disappearing fast, and there were little pools of icy water all over the yard. I was not allowed to play outdoors under such conditions.

I envied my Cousin Levi. He sounded as though he enjoyed himself. I hoped that I might be like him when I was 22, his age. Just now, all I could do was sit and listen. Most of what I heard was family history between the women. I could make little of what Uncle Abner and Cousin Adam said to each other.

Cousin Levi loosened his rust-red woolen scarf, then reached into one of the pockets of his heavy coat. He laid an object on the kitchen table. "Look at that," he said, and went to hang up his things in the back hall.

My mother and Cousin Sarah both rose from their chairs to examine the thing. I put out a hesitant finger to touch it. "What is it?" my mother asked.

It looked like a rock, but it was all glittery. I had never seen gold, but the descriptions I had heard fit this object. It was yellow, and it threw back light when it was turned.

Only one thing about it had never been described. It looked like a collection of square and rectangular cubes sticking out in several directions.

"Gold?" asked Cousin Sarah.

"It's gold," I said, positive now that someone else had voiced it.

Levi came back and picked up the object. "Let's see what the rest of them say."

He took the thing in to the men. I went to the doorway to watch as he handed it around.

My uncle lifted the object in his hand. He shook his head.

"I have never seen such a thing," he said, pulling at his bushy beard. "I have handled gold, but it had already been made into coins or other objects. I have no idea what the crude ore resembles." He passed it to Adam.

Cousin Adam was 24 and big enough to have given Abner a hard contest if the two of them had ever come to blows. He was broad-shouldered and thick-armed. One could almost imagine him plowing a field alone, if his horse or mule were too sick to pull.

The lump of ore seemed tiny in his huge hand. "Gold," he said. "It must be gold. Where did it come from? Did you find much of it?"

Cousin Levi chuckled. "You know those two tracts of land that were willed to us, one to Sarah, one to me? On mine there's a deadfall of old trees and bushes up against a ledge. I was clearing it away, and I found a hole going back under the ledge. I kindled a pine knot and crawled in. I found this and a lot more."

"Then we'll be rich," Adam said, fingering the ore.

Levi chuckled again. "I might get us a little money from it, but not in the way you think. No, that's not gold. I once saw a piece of it owned by an iron miner from Pennsylvania. He says it's a form of iron, and they call it fool's gold."

Uncle Abner listened with interest. "I have heard others speak of it, but this is the first I've seen. You think you can get money from it? How—by mining iron?"

Levi shook his head. "It does not look that abundant. But have you ever heard of the lost Indian silver mine? They say it's in these hills somewhere."

"Yes," my uncle said, "and I neither believe nor disbelieve in it. However, I choose to get my living from the top of the earth, not from deep inside it."

"I might look for it for a little while," said Levi, "if I had an idea where to try." He turned to Adam. "Right after I came away with this, I encountered Eli Rumbaugh. He believes in the mine. They tell me he's been obsessed for years with wanting to find it himself. I told him that I had found it, but that it was gold, not silver. He wanted to buy my land, right away."

"Did you agree to sell?" Adam asked.

"No," grinned Levi, "I told him that I would not sell in my lifetime. He might make Sarah an offer if I should die, since it will go to her, but I could never bring myself to give it up."

"If it were truly gold, you would be a fool to sell," Uncle Abner said.

Levi shrugged. "Eli claimed that it would take money to develop it. He would be able to take that risk. There is some truth in that."

"Does he know that you think this is not gold?" Adam asked.

"No, I have let him continue to believe in the mine," Levi replied.

"Then," said Adam, "if it should be gold, you have wealth. I am not convinced that it is iron, in spite of what you say. But, if it only looks like gold, sell him the land, anyway. You could get a good price if he thinks it is valuable."

Levi shook his head. He had a shock of pale yellow hair, and some of it fell close to his eyes. "I can't do business that way."

Cousin Sarah was listening to the discussion, and it was plain, even to me, that she could sense an argument.

"Ah," she said, "all of that is underground, where it's dark and damp. Let me show you a real treasure."

She went upstairs, where I heard the sound of a chest being opened and closed. When she came back, she was carrying a piece of cloth. She handed it first to my mother.

The cloth was rose-colored, and it shimmered. My mother saw my curiosity and let me touch it gently. It was soft and exciting to feel.

"It is silk," Sarah murmured, as she passed it around carefully. "Cousin Jane Hall sent it to me as a present, to make a dress. She would not tell me what it cost, but I did learn that it is expensive."

"Where did she get it?" my mother asked.

"There is a mill in New England making the cloth," Sarah replied. "I have not heard where they get the thread. They say it had to come from the Far East."

Adam looked at Uncle Abner and smiled. "Imagine—they say that a worm produces the threads. Do you believe that?"

"The Lord has let us learn to get flax from a plant and wool from an animal," my uncle said. "It is no marvel to me that He has permitted a worm to give us such a thing."

Sarah detected a loose thread on the face of the cloth. She gently lifted it away and held it up. "See how fine it is!"

My mother touched it. "It is like an angel's hair," she said.

While all the men were looking at the thread, I asked Cousin Sarah, "What will you do with the angel's hair?"

"I don't know," she laughed. "It is too small to use." She saw my eagerness and smiled. She was already a pretty woman, fair as her brother. The smile turned her, for an instant, into the angel of my imagination. "Here," she said, putting the thread into my hand, "you may have it, Martin. Dream of heaven when you go to sleep."

Until just before bedtime I played with the two things: Levi's shining rock and the shimmery thread. In the end, my mother's urging, backed up by my uncle's gruff discipline, sent me off to bed.

But I did not take either plaything with me. I left the rock on the kitchen table. With the perverse illogic of small boys, I wrapped the silk thread around the blade of one of Levi's skates.

The next day was fair and mild, and the thawing continued. As I had feared, I was not allowed to go out. The morning was slow for me because I got little attention from anyone. Adam was out hacking brush somewhere, heaping it up in piles for burning when early spring came. My mother and Sarah were busy with housework and the baby. Uncle Abner had borrowed a horse from Adam to look at more pigs, at Adam's suggestion.

Cousin Levi might have given me a few minutes, but I did not know where he was. He was sleeping in a corner of the barn's hayloft while Uncle Abner was visiting, but I was not allowed to go even that far from the house. Besides, his skates were gone, and I supposed he had gone to the farm pond for one more time.

Shortly before noon I heard the sound of hoofs picking carefully through the mud. In a few moments I heard footsteps, the sound of the bootscraper being used, and Uncle Abner opened the kitchen door. He merely looked in.

"Sarah," he said in a tone of urgency, "is Adam here?"

She glanced at the clock. "He should be coming in at any minute. Is something wrong?"

"Perhaps," my uncle replied. "The ice is broken on your pond, as though someone had fallen in. It will take at least two of us and some boards to find out."

"Levi!" she cried. "It couldn't be Levi. He sometimes takes ventures, but he always knows what he's doing."

Abner could see that she was of no help, so he said, "I must look for Adam, or some other help if any should be near." He closed the door.

I went to the window and watched him walk to and fro, looking to see if Adam were in sight. Evidently this was fruitless, for he went through the yard to the front. There his luck was better. A tall thin man was just passing on horseback.

"I need help," I heard Abner say. "Come with me to look for boards in the barn."

"I'll help anyone," the horseman answered. "Could you tell me why?"

"Certainly," said Abner, "someone might be drowning. Come in quickly."

He opened the gate, and the man rode in, heading for the barn as fast as the horse could safely go on the slippery ground. He had dismounted and was tethering the horse when Uncle Abner caught up with him.

All of us were now watching as the two men disappeared into the barn. I could see Sarah craning her neck in an effort to get a glimpse of Adam, if he should be coming.

At the end of several minutes Uncle Abner and the thin man emerged from the barn. Each of them carried two long planks. They started toward the pond, which was in a small pasture west of the house. The pond was back from the road about a hundred yards. Adam allowed anyone to skate on it who wished.

Abner and the other man had not gone far when Sarah called to them. "I see Adam coming. Shall I tell him anything?"

9

Abner turned about. "Have him bring rope and a hook, if he has one."

I ran upstairs, where I would have a better view. I saw my uncle and the other man pick their way carefully, for their burden was awkward and footing was treacherous. In a few minutes I heard Sarah calling to Adam, giving him Abner's message.

Uncle Abner and the thin man reached the pond. I could see the hole he had mentioned, a little bigger than a man, several feet out from the shore and exposed to the sun from the south. I observed Abner putting down his boards, then the other man did the same.

Now Abner picked up one plank and slid it carefully along the ice until the center of the plank was opposite the hole, with half of the wood protruding onto the solid ice. He then did the same with another plank on the opposite side of the hole. When this was done, the thin man crawled along one plank pushing a board, then laid it across the ends of the first two at right angles. He did this again with his second board, forming a square of planks around the hole.

When the thin man was finished, he inched carefully along each of the planks in turn.

"He's looking for someone under the ice," my mother said, behind me.

The thin man shook his head. Uncle Abner turned and looked our way. He had no need to take a long look. Adam, running as best he could, was almost at the pond carrying a coil of rope with a hook on the end.

Uncle Abner held out his hand for the rope, but Adam shook his head. He motioned to the other man, who hesitated, then came back to shore.

"One of them could dive in," my mother said. "Adam has told me the pond is shallow. But it would not be safe. The water is too cold."

I was too young then to realize that extremely cold water would do more than make one shiver badly. I could not know that anyone who had been in the pond that long would never come out of it alive.

Adam inched out on one of the planks, carrying the hook and some of the rope. Uncle Abner and the other man held the rope's other end. When Adam came to the hole, he dropped the hook into the water and let the rope run through his hands until it went slack. The he pulled it up about a foot.

Slowly and carefully Adam worked his way along the boards. He was about halfway along the second side of the square when he stopped. He began to work the rope from side to side. I heard him shout something to the others. Finally, he pulled straight up on the rope. Clearly, it was not easy to do, but he was doing it.

At last, something dark came up from the black water. It looked like a man.

"Martin," said my mother, "turn around. You have seen all that I think you should see."

Frustrated and curious, I tried to slip away to downstairs, where I might not be noticed, but my mother kept close watch on me.

"They have taken him to the barn door," she said finally, "and laid him in the sun."

"Who? Who is it?" I asked.

"Your Cousin Levi," she answered, and began to shed quiet tears.

Downstairs, Sarah gave an anguished cry and called to my mother to watch the baby. So, in the confusion, I managed to put on my boots and coat. I crossed the yard while Adam, whose clothes dripped water, was holding Sarah back.

I could not see much, for Uncle Abner was examining Levi for signs of life and talking to the thin man. Adam and Sarah were also in the way. I could only see Levi's feet. He must have been trying the ice one last time, for he was wearing his skates.

"He is dead," Abner said finally. "Look, here is a large bruise and cut over his left ear. He must have hit his head on the ice when it broke. That is why he could not pull himself out and escape drowning."

Sarah began to cry uncontrollably. Adam managed to lead her to the kitchen door, where he called to my mother. She came and took Sarah inside.

Uncle Abner straightened and turned around.

"Martin!" he said in surprise. "What are you doing here?"

"I wanted to get the angel's hair," I said, looking for an excuse.

"The angel's hair? What do you mean?"

I stooped at Levi's foot. "I wrapped it on his skate last night."

11

My uncle frowned. "So you did. I saw you. Let me get it for you."

He knelt and gently untwined the sheer thread which still encircled the skate. He held it up and examined it.

He stood up, looking first at me, then at the thin man, who reminded me of a woodpecker with his red hair and sharp nose. "Martin," he said, "this is Mr. Rumbaugh. Go into the house, both of you. I must go to the pond for a moment. And Martin—tell Adam not to remove his wet things until I return. Rumbaugh, tell the others to stay inside.

When Rumbaugh and I went in, Sarah was outraged that Abner had permitted Levi's body to remain where it was.

"He doesn't care!" she cried to my mother. "He's Rufus' brother, not yours. No wonder he doesn't care! He's mad! He doesn't even want Adam to put on dry clothes."

"Levi is as much my cousin as you are," my mother replied quietly. "Abner does not always show his reasons early, but he is neither heartless nor a fool. Wait before you denounce him."

Wait we did for what seemed a long time, but probably was not. Seconds are minutes to a child, and minutes are hours.

At last Abner returned. Before he came into the house, he went to the barn. He reappeared in a moment or two, then came into the house.

"Finally!" Sarah cried. "Will you let us now bring him in and wash him?"

"It is not for me to stop you," Abner replied, not unkindly. "However, do you want me to determine his murderer?"

There were shocked exclamations from everyone. Why, I wondered, should one person kill another? Was it like the Bible story of David and Goliath? But Levi should have been David! He should still be alive!

Abner walked around the room studying everyone except me. He did not even except my mother.

"You have no cause to say such a thing," Adam growled as Abner came to him. "He was a fool to go out on rotten ice, and it broke under him. He hit his head, and he drowned."

"That is the appearance of it," my uncle replied. "He might have drowned, it is true. However, he was hit on the head before he went into the pond. The ice was broken before he went into the water, and he never went out on it on this day."

Rumbaugh heard all this with interest. "You speak as though you saw it all. How is it you did not intervene? Or were you the one who did it, now trying to throw suspicion somewhere else? Or is it all a made up tale?"

"Rumbaugh, you ask many questions," said Uncle Abner. "I can reply to all of them with two answers. I saw none of this, because I was not there. It is not a made-up tale, because the one who killed Levi forgot one of the simplest of God's rules."

"Oh, you are a prophet, then," Rumbaugh said, with a smile. "God reveals things to you."

"God reveals to any man who looks and understands what he sees," Abner said. "I was not there, but I saw the truth."

"You saw what took place?" Rumbaugh asked.

"I saw what did not take place," Abner said.

"That it was not an accident?"

"That, above all. But first I saw that Levi's murderer had overlooked a rule which even Martin knows: sharp edges cut."

"Abner," Adam said, a puzzled look on his big face, "there were no cuts on Levi."

Uncle Abner shook his head. "That was not my meaning. If your brother-in-law had skated on that pond today, he would have left fresh cuts in the ice. In this sunshine they would have water in them. There is a thin sheen of water on the entire face of the ice, but there are no skate marks."

"That is hardly proof," Rumbaugh said, scratching his thin nose. "He was a high-spirited young man. Perhaps in foolishness he sprang from the bank onto the ice, and it broke."

For a moment it looked as though Uncle Abner's patience was at an end. However, when he answered, it was in level tones.

"At such a distance he would have needed a fast, running jump to make such a leap onto the ice. He could not do it from muddy ground."

"But there is only your word about the condition of the ice," Rumbaugh said. "By now the sun has melted so much surface that we could not verify it. What made you invent such a tale?"

"It was not invented," Abner said sternly. "It was directed to my attention."

Rumbaugh's sandy brows rose. "By divine revelation?"

"By an innocent child," Abner replied. "By my nephew, Martin."

"A child's fantasy?" sneered Rumbaugh.

"Not a fantasy," my uncle said. "The absence of cuts on the ice was the second overlooking of God's simple rule, that sharp edges cut. Martin showed me the first."

Uncle Abner reached into his pocket. "With this." He pulled out the silk thread and stretched it to its length.

"Last night Sarah showed us this thread and gave it to Martin. Before he went to bed, he wrapped it around the blade of one of Levi's skates. When we pulled Levi from the pond, the boy found the thread still on the skate, *uncut*. It could not have resisted even one stroke of the sharp skate."

"Then he *was* murdered," Sarah cried. "Who could have done it?"

"I believe I can find out," Abner said.

Adam gave a slight sneeze. "I'd like to change from these wet clothes," he said.

He had been standing ever since he had come in, and there were damp spots around his feet. I glanced at Eli Rumbaugh, but he was wet only at the ends of the sleeves of his heavy coat. He must have carried either Levi's arms or his feet. His only other signs of disarray were a spot of mud on the tail of his coat and a rusty-looking bit of wool caught on a button.

None of us spoke until Adam had changed. He came back wearing work clothing much like he had removed.

"Now Abner," he said, "why should anyone want to kill my brother-in-law?"

Adam laughed without humor. "Greed? He owned little. He got by, with the work he did for me, but that was no more than he had to."

"He had land," said Abner.

Adam laughed again. "Land? Put his little bit and Sarah's little bit together, and you still couldn't raise a ruckus, let alone a decent crop."

"His land had something that two of you wanted—a possible Indian mine," Abner said.

Adam shook his head. "That! You heard him say, himself, that it was worthless. I even think you believed him."

"I did believe him. I am not so sure that you did. Was it gold he showed you, or wasn't it?"

"Why," Adam blustered, "it wasn't."

Abner's voice grew stern. "And if it wasn't, it might still be sold to Rumbaugh for the real thing, you suggested. Levi would not do that. Even so, it could still be done, if your wife owned the land. She is her brother's heir."

Adam's face grew red, and his huge fists bunched. "I'll call you to account," he growled.

Uncle Abner did not even pale. "You were not the only possibility, Adam."

"There might be many possibilities," Rumbaugh said. "I am glad to have the warning about the worthless mine."

"I regret that you did not find out sooner," Abner replied. "You were not given the chance we had to doubt the ore specimen. I am told that the legend of the mine is real to you. You could not bear to have it in the hands of an irresponsible young fool. A fool, because he could not develop the thing, and because he would not sell to someone who might do it properly."

Abner indicated Adam and Sarah. "You, too, might consider that it would be easier to buy the land from surviving owners. Adam is a successful farmer. He would know that a man of greater means could develop a mine easier than he could. Sarah, as owner of the land, might be persuaded by him to sell to you. To bring this about, you would first have to remove the stubborn fool, Levi."

"This story is as strange as the one you told about Adam," laughed Rumbaugh. His eyes were bird-bright.

My uncle ignored the remark. "It might be that you intended no murder when you came by and saw Levi at the barn door with his skates. What caused it? Did you hit him when he gave you the ore again and told you it was worthless? Did you think he was lying, to make you forget the mine?"

"I intended no murder because I did not kill him," Rumbaugh said. "Your questions are useless."

"The questions may be useless," Abner said, "but those answers are not needed. You did hit Levi with the rock. I found it in the barn, bloodstained. You did put the skates on him and throw him into the pond. You were about to leave when you saw me in the distance, and you led your horse out of sight of the house. You then rode along the road and let me get you to help me retrieve Levi's body."

"I have heard many marvels from preachers," Rumbaugh said, "but none can match the ones you have been inventing here."

It was remarkable that any man's eyes could meet the stare which Abner gave Rumbaugh. "The marvel is that nothing is invented. The greater marvel is that a tiny thing has betrayed you."

Rumbaugh had met Abner's stare and continued to do so. "What would this marvel be?"

"A thread," said my uncle.

"I did not put the thread on the skate," Rumbaugh said. "Your nephew did."

Abner turned to Adam. "I am going to the door. Do not let this man leave."

He opened the kitchen door and reached to a peg outside. I heard him wring water from something. He came back carrying Levi's muffler.

"The man who threw Levi's body into the pond had to carry it there," he said. "Levi was wearing this. Hold out your arms, Rumbaugh."

The thin man obeyed my uncle's command.

"Your sleeves are wet from helping to carry the body back," said Abner. "The rest of your coat is dry. If this muffler had touched you on the way back, it would have left a wet mark, or if it had shed any part of it, that part would be wet. Neither you nor Adam had anything on your clothes where you were wet."

He held out the muffler in his great hand. "Look at the color of the threads. Red as rust. Nearly as red as blood. If this cloth had lost any part of itself while Levi was carried from the barn *to* the pond, it would be dry."

Abner reached out with his other hand and clutched Rumbaugh's coat. "You are betrayed by a tiny thing, Rumbaugh. A tiny thread, red as rust. A *dry* thread."

Wrapped around the button encircled by Abner's hand was a thread. It matched the ones in Levi's scarf.

3

The Power of the Tongue
(1981)

The curious reaction to the census recounted in this story actually happened, though not in West Virginia.

A shadow lay over the land.

When such a thing happens, and the people cannot see what casts the shadow, they sometimes invent strange and surprising causes for it . . .

An unusual act of defiance of our national government drew my Uncle Abner and my mother into a matter that neither liked. It was not the act of defiance itself that brought this about, but one of the principal reasons for it.

The year was nearly half over, and it was already clear that it was another in a string of bad years. It was hoped that the presidential election would bring a change for the better.

It was also the year for the census. The government man, a Mr. McHenry, was at our house asking his questions. Knowing that he would be there, Uncle Abner had ridden over, to save time for both himself and Mr. McHenry.

Because my father was no conversationalist and my uncle often preferred to listen, my mother addressed our visitor as he was finishing his questions. Perhaps, being closer to his size than these big men, she wanted to put him at ease.

"Mr. McHenry, do you find this work difficult?" she asked. "Do the people answer you willingly, or are they hostile?"

The census taker looked up from his writing. He was a man of ordinary size, plainly dressed, with green eyes and an abundance of freckles.

"The work has only begun," he answered, "and this is my first time. However, it is not a good year to be doing it. There are many who think it a waste of the government's money. They prefer to put it off another ten years."

Uncle Abner pulled at his brown beard. "I wonder if they are the same persons who are greedy for every penny of foreign money they can borrow to spend on some wild, shaky investment?"

The census man shrugged. "I'm unable to answer that. There was such talk in Wheeling, where I live, but it was rumored to have come from Washington."

Both Abner and my father snorted.

"However, I had scarcely begun to work in this county when I encountered the strangest opposition I have ever heard," McHenry went on.

"In this county you might hear anything," my father remarked. "What was it?"

McHenry arranged his papers neatly. "Are you acquainted with two families named Stoneman and Bowers?"

"We know who they are," Abner replied. "I am not acquainted with Jonathan Bowers, but Abel Stoneman's cattle have sometimes been in the same droves with mine."

My mother, a small woman, was following the conversation with the attentiveness of a sparrow. "The Stoneman family is a large one," she said.

"Then you know that these two families are the total population of a small hollow in the southwest part of the county," McHenry said. "I intended to list them among the first, for convenience. As it was, I did not even get to see them."

"What prevented you?" Abner asked.

"Abel Stoneman. He was sitting on a horse at the mouth of the hollow when I arrived. He had guessed who I was, and he refused to let me pass. He said that both families wished not to be counted in the census."

He had our attention. Even I, who had almost no concept of the many interests of our national government—I was only ten—wondered at the thought of its being challenged by anyone.

"Did he give a reason?" my uncle queried.

"He did. He reminded me that King David numbered his people and angered the Lord. In punishment, seventy thousand Israelites died before David's atonement was accepted. With this bad year upon us, these two families fear that it might happen again. They want to avoid the Lord's wrath if it does."

It was clear that Abner had not expected an answer like this. He was thoughtful. "What did you say then?" he asked.

Before McHenry could speak, there was a sound of hoofs and wheels. They slowed to a stop before the house, and I ran to see who had come.

"It's Squire Randolph's gig," I called back from the doorway.

"Then I'll let him tell you the rest," McHenry said. "I only told Stoneman that I'd have to think on his refusal. When I returned here, I took the problem to Squire Randolph."

Randolph came to the door blotting perspiration from his forehead with a linen handkerchief. He greeted me with his usual effusiveness and seemed especially interested to see McHenry. He sat down carefully, fussing with his coat.

"I came hoping to find Abner, and here you are too, McHenry," he said. "It will save both of us some time."

He looked at the rest of us. "Has McHenry told you of the absurd thing he has encountered with the Stoneman and Bowers families?" When we assented, he continued, "Superstition! They'll be burning witches again before we know it!"

"What these families believe is misguided, but it is not superstition," Abner said. "Did you come here to ask me to tell that it is?"

"No, no," Randolph protested. "I want to discuss something Stoneman has raised, but it might not be related to McHenry's problem."

"What have you done for Stoneman?" my uncle asked.

"I tried to put it in the hands of those who should be of most help. I asked Bronson, then Adam Bird to talk to those people." Randolph turned to McHenry. "Both of them are circuit-riding preachers. Bronson is a Calvinist, Bird is a Methodist."

"One of them must have failed if you sent two of them," Abner remarked.

"Both of them failed," Randolph said. "Bronson went first. He said he tried to persuade them by pointing out that the people of Israel were numbered after that without coming to harm because of it. They turned him away."

"Bronson is an intelligent man," my father said. "People don't always take to that kind of man."

"Adam Bird is no less so," Uncle Abner said to him. "Bronson tries to persuade. Bird attacks sin and will not be turned aside. The two of them are different."

"Nonetheless, Adam Bird could not change their minds, either," Randolph cut in. "He did achieve something, however. They did say that they feared a sin of their own might work against them."

"Did he find out what that sin was?" my father inquired.

"No, even though Bird offered his help, they would not tell."

"It has to be the death of that boy, Isaac Stoneman," my mother said. "Although," she went on, "there's enough sin in how they married off that Bowers child to him, without adding in the boy's death."

McHenry's eyes gleamed with interest, but my uncle had a question for Randolph.

"Did Jonathan Bowers tell Adam Bird that he might talk to McHenry if he were approached separately?"

Randolph considered. "Bird made no mention of such an offer."

"Abel Stoneman is serious in his stewardship," said Abner, "but he is the master—that must never be questioned. His will must be obeyed by his family, his livestock, and his dogs. Some have said he is greedy for power. If that is true, neither Bronson's reasoning nor Bird's emotion could ever change him. If he changed, he would be yielding power to them."

My father looked at him and cleared his throat. "What about Bowers and how he got his land?"

"Rufus, that is only hearsay," my uncle said.

My mother spoke directly to McHenry. "All we know is gossip and rumor. It is a fact that Jonathan and Lydia Bowers and their daughter, Rachel, came to this county only a few months ago. They wanted to buy land, and Jonathan Bowers tried to purchase sixty acres from Abel Stoneman. He could not meet Stoneman's price. But he did get the land."

The census taker leaned forward. "How?"

My mother glanced at the three other men, then went on. "That is not known. There is talk that he got it for consenting to the marriage of his daughter, Rachel, to Abel Stoneman's boy, Isaac."

McHenry shrugged. "That is not unusual."

"No," my mother agreed. "Even at fourteen, Isaac was of legal age. But Rachel Bowers was not. She was only twelve, and her marriage was allowed only by consent."

"Some would say that she has lived a fourth or a third of her life already," said Randolph.

"Your own Betty is well past that," my mother reminded him. "Have you thrust marriage upon her?" She looked around again. "Rachel Bowers was only a *child*, and that is where the sin in those two families lies!"

Before anyone could answer she went on: "To make it worse, they say that the Stoneman boy was every bit as overbearing as his father is. That's no way for a child to begin a life!"

Not one of the four men ventured to answer her. Randolph looked distressed. A widower, he was all too conscious of his responsibilities to his own daughter.

Finally, he nodded toward my mother and spoke to my uncle.

"Abner, I need your help, and it has to do with these very families."

"If neither Bronson nor Bird could persuade them, I would be no better," Abner said.

"That is not it," Randolph replied. "It relates to the land Abel Stoneman gave Isaac and Rachel as a wedding gift. Ten acres. He wants it back."

"Is there a deed on record?"

"There is."

"To the boy alone, or to the two of them?"

"To both of them."

"Then, even though the boy is dead, Abel cannot get it back. Surely you know that better than I," Abner said, with a mild rebuke.

"It is more than that," said Randolph, twisting his great carved ring.

"I am sure that you speak in riddles to some of us," my mother interposed. "We may be as ignorant of these things as Mr. McHenry is."

Randolph momentarily seemed taken aback. Then he inclined his head to my mother. "I had no wish to be discourteous. The root of the matter is that the girl, Rachel, killed her husband, and his father witnessed it." He shifted in his chair. "When the boy, Isaac, married the Bowers girl, his father gave them a small house, a barn, and ten acres of land to make a start. Two months ago these children were in the barn just at dusk. The girl was holding a lantern for the boy, and she displeased him in some way. He struck her violently—I have heard that she still bears the mark. In return, she threw the lantern, hitting him. It then fell into the straw at his feet. He was in flames almost at once, and the barn was afire very quickly. Rachel, herself, escaped by running out."

"The boy's father witnessed this?" McHenry inquired.

"He was on his way to see them, and had almost reached the barn when it happened. He rushed to save the boy, but the flames were too fierce."

"What of the livestock?" my father inquired.

"There were two cows and one horse in their stalls," Randolph answered. "The boy was in the center of the barn, and the stock was along the sides. Stoneman got them out unharmed."

"When is the girl to be tried?" McHenry asked.

Randolph seemed distressed. "Perhaps never. And this uncertainty is at the root of Stoneman's determination to get the land again."

"I have heard that the child had a breakdown," Abner said. "Is that true?"

"It is," Randolph acknowledged. "It seems that she has never recovered. How could she be put on trial?"

"They say that she sits in a chair all day, staring," my mother said. "She never speaks, and she seems unaware of anyone."

"And that is Stoneman's argument," Randolph said heavily. "Because of her condition, he says she is incompetent. If that can be established, he will get back the land."

My uncle had been frowning ever since Randolph had described the tragedy. "It is a matter of reality," he said, without addressing anyone.

"You mean, does the girl understand reality?" Randolph asked.

"No," said Abner. "The reality is that Jonathan Bowers had control of seventy acres of land. Sixty acres are his, and he is overseer of ten more for his daughter. Stoneman grudges him the sixty acres, and the thought of the extra ten is intolerable."

"That does not enter into what he has asked of me," Randolph said. "He wants me to have the child's competency investigated. Would you do it?"

Uncle Abner stared in surprise. "I? Surely this is a matter for Storm. He is a doctor. Or Bronson or Adam Bird might judge the thing properly."

"You have had ten years observing your nephew Martin," Randolph answered. "Your judgment of him has not been as uncritical as his parents' has."

Abner was silent, considering this assessment. Finally he looked at the clock, then he said: "It is a great responsibility. If I accept, I must go at once to the courthouse to inspect the two deeds given by Abel Stoneman. But my acceptance is based on one condition."

"Name it."

My uncle shook his head. "You are not the one to agree, Randolph." He turned to my mother. "Miriam, I will go tomorrow, but only if you go with me. It may be that your judgment is more reliable than anyone's"

Astonishment and confusion were plain to see on her face, but she quickly composed herself. "Why Abner—" she began. Then she raised her chin. "Yes. I will go with you."

I watched as Uncle Abner readied our buggy the next morning. I was not permitted to go with him and my mother, but I knew that the trip would be discussed in detail. Besides, it promised to be a warm summer day, and I had other things which interested me more. When the horse was finally hitched, my uncle came into the house. He spoke first to my father.

"Rufus, I studied the deeds that Stoneman gave Bowers and those children. They are clear and uncomplicated. In the deed to Bowers, however, one thing caught my attention. Stoneman reserved the water rights on a small stream."

My father reflected. "He wants to be sure that his cattle will not go thirsty in a dry season."

"Perhaps." Abner turned to my mother. "Miriam, if you are ready—?"

She arose. "I am."

As they went to the porch, Uncle Abner said to my mother, "Miriam, do you recall that Isaiah saw the Lord when King Uziah died and feared to speak because of an unpurged sin? If you do, you will remember that a seraphim touched his mouth with a live coal and purged that sin, and Isaiah spoke."

She turned her head toward him. "I sense what you mean. Surely you don't intend to burn that child's mouth?"

"No," he answered. "No man should pretend to a power that was not given him. But if you will say to that girl what I suggest to you, her lips might be unsealed."

"Then suggest," she said.

He helped her into the buggy. "We can discuss that as we go. It must be done carefully."

In the hills, hollows take many shapes, depending on the sculpture created by water. The hollow where the Stoneman and Bowers families lived was a broad U. The slopes above the small stream were gentle and better suited to farming and grazing than some other locations in the county.

As Abner turned the buggy from the main road into the hollow, he studied what he saw. The head of the hollow was nearly half a mile farther on. A large gray frame house with a wide porch commanded the area from a height of approximately a hundred feet. Several large oaks shaded it from the front. It was flanked by a number of cedars erect as grounded spears. It was Abel Stoneman's house.

Small outbuildings were scattered behind the house, but the barn and stable were along the slope to the left, as one faced it. Orchards, pastures, and crops advanced from the barn along this arm of the U. The center of the other arm was occupied by a small house and the ruins of a burned barn. The outer end of this hillside was the holding of Jonathan Bowers.

Abner had no need to urge the horse to climb a hillside. Bowers' dwelling was at the level of the road, facing south. Stoneman's large house faced east. Bowers had not built new when he bought his land. His was a story-and-a-half log house where Stoneman's family had once lived.

Abner had scarcely pulled the horse to a stop when Bowers came around the side of the building. He was a small wiry man in patched but neat clothing. It was clear that he did not know his visitors.

"If it's Stoneman's you want, you'd best go on," he called to Abner. "This is the Bowers' place."

"Then there is no need to go farther," Abner replied. He introduced my mother and himself. "We came to see you and your family."

Bowers looked at him thoughtfully. "Are you more people come about that census matter?"

"No," said Abner. "I have heard of it, but I am not involved."

"Step down, then, and come inside," Bowers said.

The interior of the house had been changed very little since it was built. The main room dominated the entire western end, with no ceiling but the roof. The eastern end had an upper loft for sleeping quarters, reached by a ladder. The hearth and kitchen were under it. A small, summer wash house and the toilet were behind the house, at the end away from the well. A small barn was farther to the right.

When Bowers showed my mother and Uncle Abner through the front door, his wife came out of the kitchen, looking inquiringly at her husband. She was much of a pair with him, but more faded and showing more gray in her hair.

Both my uncle and my mother were civil when they were introduced, but their attention was caught by the other person in the main room.

She sat in a cane-bottom rocker, staring out of the front window. The chair never moved. She was dressed all in black. In spite of the heat, the collar of the dress was high at the throat, and the sleeves were long to the end of the wrists. Her mother had done the girl's deep honey-colored hair carefully. It and her staring blue eyes were all the color she had.

25

Bowers cleared his throat. "Our daughter, Rachel."

My mother leaned toward Lydia Bowers. "Is she always like this?"

"Yes."

Abner looked around. "Does she always look from the same window?"

The girl's mother was surprised. "No. She looks from all of them—except the west one."

Uncle Abner walked to the west window. The view covered the small wedding-gift house and the burned barn. Beyond lay the head of the hollow and the large Stoneman house. He made no comment. Instead, he turned to Bowers.

"Could we step outside?" he said to the short man. "The women would be more at ease without us."

He drew my mother aside even as Bowers was agreeing. "Speak to her alone, if you can. Tell her the thing I suggested," he said in an undertone. "Also," he added, "try to get her to change her dress."

"Would you show me some of your place?" Abner asked Bowers as they went through the front door again.

"I'm just getting started," Bowers said. "You'll have to overlook much. I only have five cows, two horses, and two pigs. A few chickens."

"Are your cattle for milk or beef?" my uncle asked.

"A little of both. Mostly for us. Later I want to raise more beef cattle."

"How is your water supply?"

Bowers paused and looked at him. "You have not yet told me why you came here."

"Randolph asked me to come," Abner said. "Stoneman wants the land returned that he gave his son and your daughter as a wedding gift."

"I see. Rachel is thirteen now and of legal marriageable age. She has her own rights."

Abner said mildly, "That is not in question, and I suspect you know it."

Bowers sighed. "Yes." He turned away. "You asked about water. Let me show you."

26

He led the way to where the bed of a small stream wound down the hillside between his land and the small holding Stoneman had given the children. Although the dry part of summer was still weeks away, no water flowed or even remained in small pools in the watercourse.

"This run is dry," Abner said. "What happened to the water?"

"It begins on Stoneman's land," Bowers said. "He diverted the water to make a pond for his son's stock."

"Your own stock needs water," Abner said. He must have known this when he sold you the land.

Bowers looked at him without expression. "He made no excuse to me when he took my stream."

Abner looked about. "Your stock are still here. Where do they drink?"

The short man smiled. "I tapped into a spring on my own land and got enough water to supply drinking troughs. Besides, as Rachel's father, I look after her interest in her own property. I can't let that pond go to waste."

"What about your family's needs?"

"We have a well near the house."

Abner considered the other man. "You are not easily defeated, Bowers."

A shadow of a smile came and went on Bowers' face. "Not often. But," he said, nodding toward the house, "I am not one to challenge the justice of the Lord."

Uncle Abner stared along the hillside to the ashes and blackened timbers of the barn. "Nor am I," he said. "But I will stand against any justice wearing false clothing."

He raised his big hand. "Let us go to your daughter's land, Bowers."

As the two walked across the modest pasture toward the small house and the blackened remains of the barn nearby, a man strode up the slope to meet them. He would have filled any ordinary doorway, and he could have been taken for the Devil's brother, so burned was he by wind and sun.

"Hello, Stoneman," Abner said.

The other man raised his head, and his eyes, black as fresh-cut coal, gleamed.

"Abner. Why have you come to this place?"

Abner took his time in replying. He noted that Stoneman's gray shirtsleeves were rolled up, showing the man's muscular arms furred with coarse black hair. He look hard at the whip coiled on the man's belt.

"I was asked to come," he answered, finally.

"Is someone interested in buying cattle? Are you to report the worth of my stock? You are known for a fair man." A new thought struck him, and his expression hardened. "Or did that government man send you?"

"My only dealings with McHenry are my own," Abner replied. "I am here to do an appraisal for Randolph."

"An appraisal?" The man hooked a hand in his belt and laughed. "Then you know I want this land back. But—an appraisal? Does Randolph expect me to pay a tribute to the person who has already taken my son's life?"

"No," said Abner. "If your land is returned, the justice of your claim will be acknowledged."

"Then why are you to appraise it? Does someone hope to buy it?"

"It is not the land that I was asked to appraise," replied Abner. "It is the child."

Stoneman looked at him in disbelief. "You? Why, then, I am as-sured of a favorable decision. You could never be swayed by a pretty face if there is only emptiness behind it."

Abner made no attempt to counter. "My sister-in-law, Miriam, came with me. She is examining the child."

"Then it is her answer that I need."

"It is the answer of both of us that you will get," Uncle Abner said, "but before I can reach mine, I must see your son's barn."

Stoneman shook his head. "The barn? You would need to be Joseph or Daniel, a reader of visions. There is no longer a barn. Even some of the ash has been washed into the ground by the rain."

My uncle spoke calmly. "I know that the spot is one that is most painful for you, Stoneman, and I have no wish to add to that. I am going there, and I asked Bowers to come with me."

The large man would have spoken, but he changed his mind and stood aside. Abner and the short man walked past him to the ruin.

Bowers gestured. "It is still plain how it was built, with the long way going along the slope. The stalls were at the ends. Barn doors front and back. Hay loft over the middle section."

Abner studied the charred timbers which lay in disordered heaps at each end of the ruin. "I am told that Stoneman witnessed the start of the fire as he approached along the road. Then the front door must have been open."

"That's true."

"The fire blazed swiftly," Abner went on. "It must have been in the center of the barn. That part is gone completely. The back door must have been open, then."

"That is true," said Stoneman's voice, from behind them. "How did you know?"

Uncle Abner did not turn. "It happened at twilight, I am told."

The large man stepped to his side. "It did."

"At twilight the warm air of the day rises up a slope, and the cool air sinks to lower ground along that same slope. There is usually a breeze. With both barn doors open, this breeze would pass through and fan a fire."

Bowers spoke up. "It was more than a twilight breeze. It was the wind ahead of the rain. The rain came in time to quench the fire at the ends of the barn."

"But not in time to save the boy's life," said Abner. "Were you a witness to this, Bowers?"

"I saw only the last of it. I was out bringing in a stray cow when I saw the blaze and Stoneman driving the stock to safety. Then the rain came. A hard rain."

"Where was your daughter?" Abner asked.

Shame crossed Bowers' face. "She was cowering outside the barn, at the back corner towards our house. She was much as you saw her today."

Abner glanced at the heaps of blackened wood on both sides of him. He turned to Stoneman.

"Was it hard to get the stock out? Did they leave willingly, or did you have to drive them out?"

"A frightened beast does strange things. You are right," the large man answered. "This time they knew what to do when they were

29

turned loose. All the same," he added. "I encouraged them. With this very whip."

Abner looked down at the whip. "I judge that you find that a help in many problems. Might I see it?"

Stoneman detached the whip from his belt and handed it over. "There is never any doubt when that talks, Abner."

My uncle examined it without uncoiling it. The lash was stout braided leather, with an iron-hard knot at the tip. The butt was nine inches long, two inches across at the base, leather wrapped, and heavy.

Abner tapped the butt against his palm. "It has a lead core," he remarked.

"Protection," Stoneman replied. "I could stop a bull with it."

"You fear the angel of the Lord, Stoneman," Abner said without emotion. "If he comes to smite you, will you smite him first?"

The large man's tan deepened. He made no answer, but held out his hand for the whip.

Abner seemed not to see the hand. Instead, carrying the whip, he walked to the rubble on the side toward Bowers' house. A dull gleam showed beneath one of the burned timbers.

Stopping in front of the half-visible object, he reversed his hold on the butt of the whip. Grasping the timber with his left hand, he raised it. He raked out the metallic object with the butt of the whip.

It was a four-sided tin lantern.

"That was the lantern the girl threw at Isaac the night of the fire!" Stoneman exclaimed. "I have not seen it since."

Abner carried the lantern and the whip out of the ruin. He wiped the whip clean in the grass and handed it back to Stoneman, then began to examine the lantern.

The light was square-sided and flat-bottomed, with a peaked tip capped by a ring. Openings were cut in the tin sides to let light out. One side was a hinged door, firmly latched.

Abner unlatched this door and looked inside. In the center of the bottom was a candle holder. Around its base were a few blobs of hardened wax. There was no candle, nor even the stump of one.

He turned to Stoneman. "Soot and ash must have concealed this from you, and the rain has washed it clean enough to reveal it again. Do you want to look at it?"

"Not even once!" the large man snarled. "It cost my boy his life. Better if the fire had melted it down to shapeless metal!"

Abner studied him. "Yes, Stoneman, I agree with you. It should have been melted."

He turned away.

"Now, let us all go to Bowers' house and determine what to say to Randolph."

Lydia Bowers, her daughter Rachel, and my mother were still seated in the same room when the men returned. There was one difference: the girl was wearing a dress better suited to summer, but she had a shawl around her shoulders. The ends were drawn down to cover her arms.

Abner introduced Stoneman to my mother, then all three men seated themselves. My uncle rested the lantern on his knee.

Stoneman looked around the room, then addressed Uncle Abner. "Now I am to hear what you will suggest to Randolph, am I? You must find in my favor. I see nothing changed here."

Uncle Abner turned to my mother. "Were you successful, Miriam?" he asked.

She gave him a grave smile. "In every way."

"Then I can summarize for both of us."

He now looked at the girl's father. "Bowers, from the moment you found your daughter cowering outside the barn until now, has she ever spoken?"

The short man shook his head. "Not one word. She has been unable to feed herself or care for herself in any way."

Stoneman interrupted. "She was cursed by God for what she did. She will never be able to care for that land again."

"You speak strong words," Abner said. "I am reminded of the man of old who said that death and life are in the power of the tongue. I think that I must test the truth of that."

He looked directly at the girl. "Rachel. My sister-in-law is a good woman, and she has never spoken anything but the truth. I know that she told you something. I am here to tell you to believe her."

Stoneman interrupted once more. "Have you been trying to put words into that girl's mouth, Abner?"

"If I am to believe you and Bowers, that would be impossible," my uncle said. "You say she is cursed and unable to speak." He addressed the girl again. "Is that true, Rachel?"

For the first time the girl blinked and color came into her cheeks. Her lips parted. Her voice came, at first a withered and unused thing.

"That—is not true. I have always been able to speak."

Amazement and shock were plain on the faces of the Bowers and Stoneman.

Uncle Abner held up his great hand. "There is much you have to tell, but I must ask you to be quiet for a while. I must talk to your father."

"Bowers," he said, "I have read the deed Stoneman gave you for your land. What is set down is simple and uncomplicated. I want you to tell me what was not set down."

The short man appeared to be still dazed. "Not set down? What do you mean?"

"I have heard rumors of an unwritten bargain," Abner replied patiently. "It is for you to confirm or deny it."

Bowers turned uncomfortably in his chair. "I don't know what you heard, so I'd best tell you what did happen. Stoneman's boy wanted to marry Rachel, but she wasn't of age. Stoneman offered me the land at a price I could pay if we'd consent to the marriage."

Stoneman's thick eyebrows drew together. "There was nothing illegal or underhanded about that, Abner. I remind you that Bowers' land is not the issue."

"It would not seem to be," said Abner. "For now, let me only remark that, no matter how you clothe the act, you bought your son a wife."

"And a sour bargain it was!"

"Bowers," my uncle went on, "in his deed to you, Stoneman reserved the water rights. You have shown me how he has exercised those rights. Your stream bed is dry."

"Did you see what I did?" Stoneman barked. "I used that water to make a pond for my boy's stock. I was entitled to do that."

"You were," Abner agreed, "although you could have diverted only half the flow, and let Bowers use the rest. You are not a compassionate man, Stoneman."

"My own children come first," the large man growled. "When my other children need help, they'll get it, too."

"Perhaps I deny you credit," Abner said. "We are told that this girl has sinned. You would seem to accept this sin as your family's, also."

"It is a responsibility older than any of us," Stoneman said.

"You know what you do," my uncle observed. "Before we leave, I believe that it will be known to all of us."

Then his tone changed. "I am told that you are a harsh man, Stoneman, that it is your will, and only yours, that holds good, even down to the least creature on your land."

Stoneman drew himself up. "Have you ever known me to deal in any livestock that a man would be ashamed to offer another man? Are my cattle gaunt? Can you count the ribs on my pigs?"

"That has never been said of you."

The large man's hand rested on the butt of his whip. "The Lord gave man dominion over every living thing, and I live by that!"

"In all things?"

"In all things!"

Abner turned to the girl, and his tone changed. "Rachel, there are other rumors to lay to rest. You were married to Isaac. There are stories that he was a bully. Is this true?"

Her eyes flashed. "That is not true. He was always kind to me. I loved him."

"Loved him!" Stoneman snapped. "A strange love that takes the life of the other. You can speak, girl, but it is a mad thing speaking!"

Abner's voice was quiet, but it commanded attention. "Rachel, what did Miriam say to you that unsealed your lips?"

She kept her gaze fixed on her father-in-law. "She told me that you would give me your word that my father could not legally be forced to return his land."

"But I did not ask for his land!" the large man shouted. "I only want back the land I gave my son!"

"Do you?" said Abner. "Rachel, it is time now to tell what happened on the evening of the fire." Seeing her hesitate, he said, "It is better to tell the truth."

She sat up straight and began to grow into a woman. "It was getting dark fast, and Isaac said that rain was coming. He was tired and thought he had dropped his awl in the barn, when he was working on some harness. He asked me to light the lantern and hold it while he looked for the awl.

"When we got inside the barn, we found his father there. He had been examining the cows and the horses, and he was not pleased. He began shouting at Isaac, saying he was neglecting his animals. It wasn't the way he'd been taught. Isaac tried to answer, but his father slapped him to the floor. He uncoiled that whip and was going to use it. I couldn't stand that, and I held the lantern in his face.

"Then he stepped back and lashed me around the neck and shoulders with the whip. I fainted and fell to the floor.

"I heard Isaac shouting, and I opened my eyes again. The lantern still burned, but it was beside me, and the rest of the barn was dim. I am certain that Isaac was fighting his father. Then that man reversed his whip and struck down Isaac with the butt."

"Isaac was fighting because of you?" Abner asked.

"Yes. I know he was struck down, because I fainted with fear. The next I knew, I heard the door of the lantern being opened. I saw that man reach down and take out the candle. He closed the lantern again and dropped it. Then he tossed the candle into a heap of straw in the middle of the floor.

"I didn't know what was under that straw until it blazed up. When I saw, I got to my feet and tried to drag Isaac out, but I only got burns on my arms, and I couldn't do it.

"But he was still there, getting the livestock out. When he was finished, he came back and pulled me from the building. Then he said, 'It was an accident that killed my boy. If you tell any other story, I'll take everything your father owns.'

"He walked away and left me in the rain.

"I knew what must have happened. I loved Isaac, but I couldn't bring him back. I love my father, too, and I couldn't see him ruined. I started to pretend to be what you saw."

Stoneman leaped to his feet. "She is possessed! No sane child would accuse a father of burning his own son to death!"

"Let us expose that unclean spirit then," said Abner, his voice grim. "Rachel, remove your shawl and lay it in your lap."

Slowly the girl slipped away the shawl, exposing her neck and the tops of her shoulders.

Abner rose and bent over her.

"Stoneman, see this scar across her left shoulder and around her neck. It will match the end of your whip. Look—here is where the knot tore the skin."

The dark man's rage was tempered. "Very well, Abner. I did give her a taste of the lash, when I found that she had cost my boy his life."

"After you tried to drag him from the fire?"

"Yes."

Uncle Abner touch the girl's shoulders. "Lift your arms, child."

She raised her arms, showing the ugly, tortured flesh of recent burns.

"She has said she tried to drag your son from the fire, but only burned her arms. I see burns on her arms," Abner said, pointing. "Where are your scars, Stoneman?"

"I was wearing a heavy shirt, and it protected me," Stoneman replied.

He started toward the door, then paused. "I see that you have made up your mind against me, but if you try to spread this pack of lies, I'll drive you into the ground!"

"That you will not!" Abner thundered. "Her story fits all the way. The lead in your whip would kill an ox. What chance would it give a young boy? You killed him, whether you meant it or not. Then you burned his body to conceal the wound, and you tried to place the burden on a child."

"Saddle up, and ride in to confess to Randolph!"

"I refuse your wild demand, Abner," Stoneman said grimly. "It is a saner tale that she threw the lantern when my boy slapped her than the one the two of you have patched together."

"It would be," said Abner, "but for one thing. You overlook the lantern."

He lifted it from his side, where he had dangled it.

"I found the lantern, not in the middle of the ruin, where the fire was hottest, but at one end, where the rain saved part of the timbers."

Stoneman's lip curled. "It was kicked there by a cow or the horse."

"It is also where this girl could have fallen. That is only one thing. Where is the candle?"

Again Stoneman was disdainful. "It was consumed by the fire."

"Yes," said Abner, as though considering it, "a fire as hot as it must have been would have consumed the candle.

"But," he said, and the other man seemed to shrink as he spoke, "you will stand before Randolph unless you can explain why so hot a fire did not also consume these blobs of wax in the bottom of the lantern!"

"Stoneman, I can understand why you refuse to be counted. The Preacher said it better than I:

'That which is wanting cannot be numbered.'"

4

The Shades of Death
(1980)

This Uncle Abner story is one of several John F. Suter stories to be used in a classroom. Students in Western Maryland were surprised that anyone would write about their part of the world.

It was the only road of its kind ever constructed wholly by the government of the United States. It was called the National Road, and it stretched first from Cumberland, in Maryland, through western Pennsylvania to Wheeling, in western Virginia, then later to Vandalia, in Illinois. It opened the frontier to development as nothing else had done.

It was also, in places, a peril to the unwary traveler, who stood to lose either his property or his life. The Indians were gone, but the savages were not. Abner had been warned against traveling alone as he made his way west toward Wheeling from Baltimore. He replied simply that he was never alone and went on his way.

It was after he had descended the western side of Little Savage Mountain in western Maryland that his confidence was put to the test.

He was in a giant's steeplechase of great mountains, narrow valleys, and turbulent streams, and dark had come upon him before he had reached the tavern where he intended to sleep.

The night sky was pale with the blaze of stars, but as Abner's great horse went forward, a thousand ragged fingers against the sky began to obscure the glow. It was not long before it was completely black overhead, and Abner sensed that he was in an immense grove of trees. From the scent in his nostrils, he knew they were pines.

He had heard that this was a twilight place by day and blacker than the night after sundown.

Yet the gloom was not absolute. A short distance ahead a fire was flickering by the side of the road.

Abner rode on until he had almost reached the fire, on his right. Suddenly a dark figure stepped from the opposite side and stood squarely in his path.

"Pull up," a harsh voice said.

Abner reined in the great chestnut. "By whose authority?" he demanded.

The man before him lifted a rifle. "The best authority anywhere."

In the flickering light cast by the fire Abner could see that the muzzle of the rifle was not pointed at him. It was aimed between the eyes of his horse.

"Very well," he said.

"Get down," growled the man with the gun.

Abner dismounted carefully.

"I'll take your gun," said the man in the road.

Abner handed over his own rifle. In a sudden flare of the fire he could see a grin on a bearded face.

"What now?" he asked.

"Go over to the fire," the other man said. "I'll bring your friend." He suddenly gave a piercing whistle.

When Abner reached the fire, he saw a second man seated by it on a log. This man was drinking from an earthen mug. He stopped after finishing a swallow and spoke around the rim of the mug.

"Who's this come to visit?" he asked the man with the gun.

"I'll leave that to you to find out," the first man said. "Get his papers and look."

"Who are you, friend?" the man on the log asked, setting the mug beside him.

"I would tell anyone who is qualified to ask," Abner replied. "I doubt that you are."

The man at the fire stood up with assurance. "Oh, I think we are. Your papers."

Abner hesitated. The man with the gun hawked and spat. "You still need a horse."

Without a word Abner handed over his note case. The second man took it and removed the contents quickly.

"Could be we could make us a little money easy, if we go over him good," he remarked to his partner. He examined everything in turn. "Sold a bunch of cattle in Baltimore, huh?"

He looked up. "You know what came our way? A western Virginia snake-eater!"

Both of Abner's ambushers laughed loudly.

"You would be Pennsylvanians, then," Abner said evenly.

"Gave ourselves away, did we?" the second man said. "Not that it matters. Here."

He had stuffed Abner's documents and paper money back into the note case. He handed it back.

"You needn't worry about your money," he said. "You come from the direction of Cumberland. Where you bound—Wheeling?"

"Yes," said Abner, "but not tonight. I had hoped to reach Tomlinson's, at Little Meadows."

Although the man at the fire seemed more relaxed, his partner was not. His gun was still aimed at the horse.

"You might or might not make it," he said. "There are things to be done here before we can turn you loose. Where's the stage?"

"No stage is coming through from the east tonight," Abner said.

"How do you know? Are you a company agent?" asked the first man.

"I am only a traveler," Abner replied. "What is this place?"

There was no grin on the first man's face. "We are on the edge of the Shades of Death."

"I had thought so," said Abner. "A notorious area. There were massacres here, they tell me. They also tell me that stagecoaches are often plundered in this place."

"So they say," growled the man with the gun.

"There will be no stage tonight," said Abner, "because the eastbound coach was waylaid last night in this area. It was not a good trap, for the driver crashed through the barricade. He and the four passengers escaped unharmed."

The second man listened carefully. "What has that to do with today's westbound stage?"

39

"Shots were fired, and the guardsman was killed. He was to return from Cumberland today, but there is no replacement yet."

The man with the gun nodded. "And they won't try it without a guard."

He spoke to Abner. "One of us may be all we need to watch the road, then. Come along."

He took a pine knot from the fire and gestured to Abner to lead his horse.

"Go on," he said. "The way you were heading."

They proceeded in silence for several minutes until the road rounded a small bend. The light of a larger fire showed through the trees, and voices could be heard.

Finally, as he and his guard approached the second fire, Abner could see three wagons drawn up in an open area beside the road. Two men stood beside the fire talking. A third man was lashed to a tree, his hands behind him around the trunk.

The wagons were not all alike. Two were of the Conestoga type commonly used to haul cargoes over the road. The third was a covered flat-bed farm vehicle. A six-horse team was hitched to each of the three.

The men by the fire stopped talking and looked up as Abner and his captor came toward them.

"That you, Reese?" one of them called. "Who's with you?"

"A man from western Virginia," Abner's companion answered. "On his way to Tomlinson's, he said. It could be true."

"He'll be a little late gettin' there," the questioner remarked. "We can use him. He can spread the word about what we'll do to sharp-shooters from now on."

"He says there'll be no stage this way tonight," Reese said. He repeated Abner's information.

The two men by the fire were dressed warmly, but differently. One , a short burly man with a straggly beard, wore buckskins and a knitted cap of gray wool. The other, who had done the talking, wore dark woolen trousers, a navy-blue woolen hunting shirt, and a large cape trimmed in red. On his head was a wide-brimmed yellow hat. Both men wore much-used boots reaching nearly to their knees.

The man in the yellow hat addressed Abner. "Is it true what Reese says?"

"That was the talk in Cumberland when I left," Abner replied.

"And the guard was killed? That's bad."

"It is thought that he was killed," Abner said. "The driver saw him fall from the seat while shots were being fired. He did not run after the stage."

"Even if he wasn't killed when he fell, the bandits wouldn't let him live to tell about it," the man in the hat remarked. "Especially if they hadn't got anything."

He pulled a long thin object from beneath his cape and held it out to Abner.

"Stogie?"

When Abner declined the smoke, the man put it into his own mouth.

He pulled a burning twig from the fire and lit the cigar. The light of the flame showed a clean-shaven raw-boned face. Its most noticeable feature was a large nose which had been broken and reset slightly to the left.

"Dillon, better see if the tar's thin enough," he said to the man in buckskins.

Abner looked around. A large copper kettle was set on stones at one side of the fire, with some of the shorter burning stubs beneath it. A smell of pine tar drifted across his nostrils momentarily.

Dillon thrust a stick into the kettle and withdrew it. The end was dark and gummy.

"Not runny enough yet, Owen," he said.

"It will be, in time," the man in the hat said. He turned to Abner. "When that happens you'll see some justice done."

"Whose justice will that be?" asked Abner.

The man before him drew on his tobacco. He laughed. "Wagoner's justice."

Abner addressed him in an even tone. "Justice is a thing of God, sent down to be dispensed by men who try to measure mortal frailty against the will of God. Law is its chief component, whether that law is divine or written by man. What law has he broken?"

"The law of survival," the wagoner answered.

"Whose survival?"

"Ours."

Abner made no answer. He stood straight as one of the tall pines surrounding them on all sides. He faced the man, Owen, with a steady stare.

"You doubt me?" the wagoner demanded. "There are four of us here, Dillon, Reese, Hamilton—up the road—and me. We work hard at what we do. We're out in all kinds of weather, haulin' the freight over these mountains. We earn every fipenny bit we get.

"Now, these farmers up and down the road: when freight rates are low, you never see one of them haulin'. Not one. But let the rates go up, and they turn up like maggots in fly time. They get to the commission house before we do, and they make more miles a day than we do. Sharpshooters, people call 'em. What I call 'em is something else!"

He crooked a finger at Abner. "Let me show you something."

With Abner following, he walked to one of the Conestogas. He stopped by one of the wheels and rapped the iron with his knuckles.

"Mark the width of that tread," he said. "A good four inches. Makes a good sturdy wheel. More important, it spreads the load on the stone base of the road."

He moved away and walked to the flat-bed farm wagon. Again he stopped by a wheel and rapped the iron.

"Here's your sure mark of a sharpshooter—a narrow rim. Not so much drag on the wheel, but it works on the stone base of the road like all the imps of hell pounding with sledgehammers."

"Is that your evidence, then?" asked Abner. "The width of a wagon wheel?"

Owen grinned without humor. "No, by God! There's more, and I'll show you when the time comes!"

"It would seem that the man needs someone to defend him," Abner said.

"You can have that task," Owen answered. "But I know how it'll end. The tar'll be thin enough soon. We have no feathers, but there're more than enough pine needles."

He started to walk toward the fire. Over his shoulder he remarked, "We were a little short on tar, but we made it up from this one's own tar pot." He laughed. "If his wheels get dry at the hub, he can always scrape some off himself and use that."

"Some of his own tar, did you say?" Abner asked.

"I did," Owen answered, laughing again. "We wouldn't want to do part of a job, would we?"

Abner looked over at the man tied to the tree. "I see no harm in freeing him," he said.

The broken-nosed man studied him. "And if he breaks away?"

Abner was already striding toward the tree. "I offer myself in his place."

None of the three wagoners made any move to interfere as Abner went up to the captive.

The man was dressed all in plain gray wool, except for a pair of boots which seemed newer than those the wagoners wore. His head drooped forward on his chest. The wide farm hat that he wore had slipped down to his eyes, making it difficult to see his features.

Abner removed the hat. He noticed that a bandanna had been stuffed around the inner rim. The cloth was soaked with sweat.

"Look up," he said to the captive, "and have no fear. I intend to speak for you."

The bound man raised his head. His fleshy face was bordered with thin sidewhiskers. His eyes were wide. His dark hair was matted and damp.

"Your intentions are good," he said to Abner in a hoarse undertone, "but it might be better to let them tar me and get it over with."

"Why do you say that?" Abner asked in surprise.

"How do you know that this is not the gang that tried to ambush the stage? Tarring is the least of what they might do."

Abner pondered this. "They have shown no signs of that. Why do you think this might be true?"

"Because I came through here with my wagon, heading east, just after the stage escaped. I pulled in and hid behind some of the smaller growth as the gang rode off."

Disbelief was written on Abner's face. "They rode away in Conestogas?"

"No, but they could have left the wagons somewhere to the west while they came to ambush the stage."

"I see," said Abner. "What is your name?"

"Nathaniel Grimm. I'm a farmer."

Abner gripped his shoulder. "I came to untie you, Grimm. See that you don't run away."

Grimm turned his head as Abner walked around the tree. "I have four small mouths to feed beside my wife's and mine. Be careful what you do!"

Abner made no reply, but busied himself with the rope. It was skillfully knotted and did not come free easily, but at last it yielded.

He leaned down to take the last turns from Grimm's wrists. "It would be wise to rub your hands when they are loose," he said.

As the rope came free, he grasped one of Grimm's hands. It was plump and sweaty and the skin felt slippery and cold, either from the night air or from diminished blood supply.

"Look to your hands, Grimm," he said, gathering the rope.

He walked in front of Grimm again and picked up the hat. The bandanna fell out as he did so. He stuffed the bandanna into Grimm's right hip pocket and started to set the hat on the man's head. Grimm stopped rubbing his hands and took the hat.

"My head's too wet," he said. "I'll let it dry before I put this on."

Abner led Grimm to Owen, "Before I speak for this man, you must know two things. First, the Northwestern Turnpike goes through the area where I live. I know about sharpshooters, although I have never been one. Second, I am a farmer, myself."

"You stating a bias, are you?" Owen asked.

"No," said Abner. "I want you to know that I am not acting out of ignorance."

"Fair enough," said Owen. "To show you that we are not doin' that either, I suggest that you look at the contents of his wagon."

Abner gestured to Grimm to be seated on a pine stump near the fire. He walked to the flat-bed wagon and drew back the canvas cover. The man in buckskins appeared beside him, holding a blazing pine knot for light.

The cargo in the wagon was a mixed lot. Nearly half of it was shingles. The rest was an assortment of kegs of cut nails, several copper kettles, a variety of kitchen utensils, a bale marked calico which felt as though it contained a number of bolts of material, and six large boxes marked Oysters. A shovel was wedged against the side of the wagon, its blade damp and dirt-stained and containing a blotch of gum with some pine needles sticking to it. A pewter mug crusted with dried residue of cherry wine was thrust into a space between some of the nail kegs.

Abner looked at everything. Nothing in the cargo seemed unusual. The lid of the top Oyster box was not fastened tightly. It could be raised easily, as though Grimm had been helping himself at stops. Some strands of wool were caught on projections of the sideboards, but Abner had not expected to find a meticulously clean interior.

He replaced the canvas and walked to the front of the wagon. The six horses stood quietly, covered against the chill by bearskin capes. Abner looked at each animal in turn, observing its condition. All appeared to be well-tended.

One beast, the right wheel-horse, had a pair of saddlebags over its back. Abner opened these. Each one had a collection of small items for a woman and children. Some paper money and coins were in the bottom of both.

Abner closed the bags and replaced the cape on the horse. He walked back to the fire, where the wagoners and their captive waited. "Owen," he said, "I think you will save your tar. However, state your case."

The man in the yellow hat removed the stogie from his mouth and pointed it at Grimm.

"My case is his story, and I'll let him tell it. You—what do you say you are, and where are you from?"

Grimm looked at Abner. "I'm a farmer, and I'm from north of Grantsville, between this road and the one farther north that runs to Pittsburgh."

"What are you doin' over here?"

Grimm swallowed. "I took a load of whiskey—my own—to Cumberland and sold it. Then I bought a wagonload of stuff we needed or wanted and started back. I met up with you at this place."

"Wait," said Abner. "Where is Grantsville? How far is it from Cumberland?"

"It's just west of here, in Maryland," Owen answered. "From where he says he lives, it might be around twenty-five miles. His road turns off just before Grantsville." He smiled coldly at Abner. "That was a good question—for us."

He addressed Grimm again.

"When did you leave home?"

"About two yesterday afternoon. I kept going until I came to Tomlinson's. I stopped there and watered the team some. I went in for a mug or two and a bit of food, then I moved on."

"And you came to the Shades of Death just after the holdup failed," said Abner.

Grimm closed his eyes and slumped forward. He had been gaining confidence, but it deserted him again.

Owen spat into the fire. "He didn't tell us that, by God!"

"Would it change your thinking?" Abner asked.

"Yes, but not in the way you hope."

The wagoner stared at the prisoner. "So your story, then, is that you came through here—when?"

Grimm choked, then managed to speak. "Early dark. It was hard to tell in here. You know that. And I didn't see anybody—to make out who they were, that is."

"Didn't you now!" Owen said. "What you saw or didn't see is no concern of mine. But you say that you took a wagonload of whiskey from here over Little Savage, then Big Savage, then down by Braddock's Run and Wills Creek into Cumberland. By night. Then you sold your whiskey, loaded up, and came this far before dark today."

"I did."

Owen snorted. "Nobody, not even a sharpshooter, could do what you claim. I say you did something different, and I'll prove it before we're through."

Reese no longer held the gun on Abner's horse. He cut into the conversation. "Owen, he could have done it."

"I did do it," said Grimm. "I unhitched at Coonrod's, on Big Savage, gave the team a little feed, and got a short nap. I got up again, hitched up, and went on." As an afterthought, he said, "I was lighter by one keg. Coonrod's bought it."

46

Owen glared first at Reese, then at Grimm. "I thought I'd have to prove this to just one man. But if I have to do it for every man in these parts, I will!"

He reached under his cape and brought out a folded paper.

He handed Abner the paper. "Open that and read it."

Abner took the document close to the fire and read it carefully.

"Well?" rasped Owen.

"It seems to be a receipt, made out to Nathaniel Grimm," said Abner.

"Yes, from McKaig and Maquire's in Cumberland. That's a commission house," said Owen. "But is it for whiskey?"

"No," said Abner, "it listed 5,000 pounds of wool, at two dollars and a half a hundred for hauling."

"You see," said Owen. "He lied. He claims whiskey, but the receipt says wool. And we got that right out of the wagon, stuck in the bottom of a nest of kitchen pots."

"This proves nothing," said Abner.

"What do you mean?" demanded Owen.

"The date is a year old."

Owen stepped to Abner's side and snatched the paper. He studied it, then thrust it back at Grimm.

"Very well," he said. "I'll grant you the date. But he could have been sharpshooting more than once, I say. Now, I'll tell you what I think about your Nathaniel Grimm. He probably is a farmer. All the sharpshooters I've ever met are. But he doesn't live where he says he does. He lives farther west, at least beyond Uniontown. In spite of you and Reese, I say he couldn't have done what he says he did in the time he had."

Owen once more recounted the territory Grimm claimed to have covered, pointing out that it was mountainous, with many steep grades. He also pointed out that a heavy front the night before would have made the road surface slippery and difficult, especially for a lone driver, even if he walked by the left-front wheel, as was common in difficult situations. He launched into a discussion of braking methods for a heavy cargo such as whiskey. All of this, he said, would have slowed Grimm too much for the time interval.

"I'll just call your attention to two things," he said to Abner. "Then I'll shut up. You looked in the wagon. You saw six boxes of oysters, I know. Maybe you also saw a pewter mug with wine stains on it."

"I saw all of that," said Abner.

"Good. Those are the things which give him the lie, even if you think he could have done everything he claims. The oysters—do you think a farmer and his family will eat six big boxes of oysters before they spoil, even if they are salted? A man and his wife and four small kids? They'd be sick of 'em before they'd be through two boxes. But there's a big hotel in Uniontown that sells every oyster they can get, as fast as they can be supplied. Uniontown's a good distance beyond where he says he lives. So he's running for business, not for himself."

"I was not aware of this," Abner conceded.

Owen touched a finger to the brim of his yellow hat.

"You are an honest man, then. This thing might work out as we want without an argument."

"It might," said Abner, "but you have still not produced a critical, unarguable fact."

Owen's face showed extreme unbelief. "An unarguable fact? Do you live by a thirty-hour clock? I tell you, you and this rascal had better live by one, for one's needed to account for what I'm about to say!"

"Say it, then," said Abner.

"You say you saw the pewter mug with the wine stains," Owen said, with a sardonic grin. "You'll not deny the stains ain't old and crusty?"

"They seemed fresh," Abner agreed.

"They were! And there's only one place on this road that has pewter mugs—Cheney's. It's on the east slope of Big Savage, between here and Cumberland.

"Now, if there's a pewter mug in that wagon, and it has fresh wine stains on it, that means this conniving rascal stopped there sometime this afternoon to lift a mug or two, and rest his team, as well. That would cut his time on the road even more."

"It would," Abner agreed.

"Add it up, then," Owen said triumphantly. "He has to start farther west, to get that order for oysters he's to deliver. This means that he's not even close to here when the stage was ambushed. He came through here a lot earlier, and he heard about it in Cumberland before he started back. He hoped he could use it to change his times and places if he ran into anybody like us. We just saw through it, and he won't get away with it."

He stopped and stared at Abner. "I don't hear you interrupting in his defense."

Abner's voice was not contentious when he answered. "You overlooked something, Owen."

Owen eyed him with suspicion. "What?"

"The tar pot. No farmer would set out on a trip longer than the one Grimm says he was making unless he carried a full tar pot, to make sure his wheels were greased."

Owen's look of surprise changed slowly to a broad grin. "We do the same. His tar pot was full, too. But," he said, "you go against yourself. It's a point for us."

"No," said Abner, and it was clear that he was certain and unswerving, "I told you that he is innocent of what you think, and he is."

"But everything about that wagon says he's guilty!"

Abner faced Owen as Moses might have faced Pharaoh. "You reason well, Owen, but you could only convict the wagon. You have not built a case against the man."

Owen's mouth opened in surprise and bafflement, but he said nothing.

"You have made a serious mistake," Abner went on. "You can be pardoned for some of it, for you and I had not yet met when you first built your theory. All the same, you have let timetables and the complexities of freight hauling blind you. You have forgotten two fundamental things."

"Not if they have to do with driving wagons!" Owen retorted.

"One of them is universal," Abner said. "The other is a primary thing in your work."

The wagoner hurled the remnant of his stogie into the fire. "I don't believe it. Name it."

"How to handle a wagon."

Owen laughed scornfully. "Reese—Dillon—did you hear that? You think I've forgotten how to handle a wagon?"

The other two wagoners chuckled in derision. "Tar oughta be hot enough, now," Dillon smirked. "Looks like we'll be a-usin' it."

Abner resumed speaking, as though he had the agreement of his audience. "The wagon's story is false, as I have said. However, I believe that one thing in it points to the truth, and another might reveal the complete truth."

"What thing do you accept?" demanded Owen.

"The shovel."

"The shovel? To dig the wheels out of the mud or throw gravel on a slick spot? Show me what good it is in proving this man's not deserving of being tarred!"

"I will," said Abner, "but first I must point out to you one of the two things you have forgotten: did you investigate to determine that he is Nathaniel Grimm?"

"There's things in the wagon with his name on 'em," Owen replied.

"And in the saddlebags," said Reese.

"Again, you are judging the wagon and the trappings, not the man," Abner said. "Nathaniel Grimm might be a sharpshooting farmer who lives and operates from somewhere near Uniontown, on the basis of what the wagon says. But this is not Grimm."

"Who is he then? His partner?" Owen asked.

"I think not," Abner replied. "Grimm's partner would be a farmer or a wagoner. This man is neither."

"The shovel told you that, did it?" Owen snorted.

"No," said Abner, "the shovel hints at something which is yet to be proven."

"What would that be?"

"That you should forget tarring a competitor. That instead you should deliver a murderer to justice."

Consternation was plain on everyone's face except Abner's.

"He killed somebody? Who?" Reese asked.

"I believe he killed Nathaniel Grimm," Abner answered. "I believe he waylaid Grimm near this spot, killed him, and buried the body. The dirt on the shovel is still damp, and the blade has pine gum and needles clinging to it."

"A case could be made against that," Owen remarked. "Let's hear the rest of it. Who is he? Why should he kill Grimm?"

"I believe him to be the stage guard," Abner said. "He fell from his seat during the ambush, I was told. Suppose he had been entrusted with a sum of money to deliver? There was talk of that in Cumberland, but it was not known for a certainty. If he were a scoundrel, he might have pretended to be shot, in order to disappear with the money."

"There was still the gang to avoid," Owen pointed out.

"That is true," Abner admitted. "I could not tell you how that was done, unless he escaped while the rascals were trying to catch the stage. A dead or wounded guard would not concern them. Live and moneyed passengers would."

"You say he killed Grimm," Reese said.

Abner nodded. "I believe that. He would have done it to get the wagon, or, at the very least, a horse. He had to get away from here with his money."

Owen turned to the man in buckskins. "Dillon, you still got his gun?"

Dillon reached into his shirt. "I do." He drew out a pistol and handed it to Owen.

Owen passed the weapon to Abner. "We would have returned it after we'd finished with him."

Abner sniffed the barrel of the pistol.

"It has been fired recently."

"I noticed that," Owen agreed, "but that could mean anything. The only money we found was that little bit in the saddle bags. If he stole money, where is it?"

"It is certainly hidden," Abner said, "but not too well hidden."

"You seem pretty sure of that," Owen retorted.

"I am," Abner said. "When I first talked to this man, he begged me to let you tar him. He feared that you and these others were the gang who ambushed the stage. I believe that he spoke what he thought was the truth. He was willing to accept shame and mild torture to distract you from looking too closely at his things. What would that gang have done if they had found the money?"

Owen stood straight before Abner, and his eyes gleamed on either side of his bent nose. "He could be right. Have you thought of that?"

"Yes," said Abner. "I also remembered that your men touched not a penny of my own money."

Owen touched his yellow hat again. "A fair man, that you are. Well, then, if his money is not well hidden, where is it?"

Abner made no answer. Instead, he strode to the flat-bed wagon, reached inside, and grasped one of the oyster boxes. With one smooth heave he lifted it out.

As Abner was carrying the box to the light of the fire, the man in buckskins saw what he had done. He walked to one of the Conestogas and opened the box beneath the driver's seat. He removed an iron pry bar and handed it to Abner.

Abner thanked him. "The box has already been opened," he said, "and it should be easier to reopen." He set the bar between the lid and the side and applied leverage.

There was a groan of nails, and the lid came free. Abner lifted the box and emptied the contents to the ground beside the fire. A heap of oysters and salt built up. Abner raked this heap with his foot.

A leather bag, closed tightly with a drawstring, emerged from the midst of the oysters.

Abner lifted the bag and set it on the end of the box. He carefully undid the string and spread the neck of the bag. Then he tipped it and poured out the contents slowly.

A shining pile of gold coins glistened by the light of the fire.

The three drivers crowded around.

"Double eagles," Reese breathed.

"More'n two hundred, I'd guess," Dillon said.

"At least four thousand dollars, then," Owen concluded. "That would seem to show you're right, mister."

He stood for several minutes, thinking. "Closest place to a sheriff is on west of here, at Grantsville. We can put him in his wagon and let Hamilton come back in here and drive it to Tomlinson's, with you. Let him leave you and this murdering rat and the money there while he goes for the sheriff. The rest of us will stay here and look for the body.

There was a sudden movement. The prisoner thrust himself forward. "Wait!" he shouted. "Now you are mistaken!"

Everyone paused and stared at the fleshy man.

"You were right the first time," he said excitedly. "I am a farmer. I am a sharpshooter now and then. I admit it."

"And the money?" Owen demanded.

"I have had a bank account in Cumberland. I closed it out, and I'm taking the money to a bank in Uniontown."

There was silence as the group considered this statement.

Finally Owen looked at Abner. "What do you think? It could be true. Do we turn him over to the sheriff and let him find the truth about this, or do we give this one his tarring and let him go?"

In his excitement the prisoner had let his hat fall. Abner picked it up.

"I find it strange, Owen," he said in severe tones, "that we have a man before us who claims a wealth of gold. Yet he must be a poor man, for he cannot afford to buy his own hat."

Before the prisoner could protest, Abner set the hat on the man's head. It was too large, and it slipped down until it rested on his ears.

"There is no bandanna in it now to make it fit," said Abner.

"He had lost his hat, and he took one from Grimm's body!" exclaimed Owen.

"Yes," said Abner, "and if you still doubt that he is not Grimm, I remind you that you have forgotten the bitterest lesson of driving wagons."

"I have forgotten nothing about driving a wagon" retorted Owen.

"You have, indeed," said Abner. "If you had not, you would never have held this man for a sharpshooter. Look at his hands. Feel them. They are fat, and the flesh is smooth and soft. Where are the calluses? Where, at the very least, are the blisters which come from handling the reins? He does not drive wagons.

"These are not the hands of Esau. They are the hands of Jacob!"

5

The Unclean Spirit
(1983)

*Uncle Abner's prescription for this spiritual crisis was based on an
actual event in the mid-1800's.*

James Blackburn had been slain for a little while before my
Uncle Abner returned from a nine-day absence.

In the yard before our house was a large sandstone block to
assist in mounting horses. I was sitting on it in the pale morning sun
of early November, listening to the tumultuous chatter coming from
the trees several hundred feet down the road. A vast flock of star-
lings, bound south, had just settled in the branches. There were
hundreds of the noisy things, perhaps as many as a thousand.

Suddenly there was a sound of pounding hoofs on the road, and
the birds rose to the sky like a vast black fabric caught in a rising
wind. Hard on their taking wing came a wagon drawn by a pair of
grays driven by a big, lean man in gray.

The driver gave me no hail. I could see little of him, for his head
was down, the broad brim of his flat-crowned hat flopping as he
passed. Although it had not rained for several days, I glimpsed great
spatters of dried mud on his cape and his hat.

Just as he passed, he raised his head and I caught sight of wildly
staring eyes and a mouth gaping in a tangled black beard. I was rigid
with astonishment. I had recognized the team, and suspected from
the driver's figure that he was Luke Chapman, but the face was so
contorted that I thought I must be mistaken.

Then the team was gone and the birds began to settle. They had
scarcely put their feet down when they rose again. From the direction the wagon had come, a buggy drawn by a red roan was ap-

proaching at a brisk pace. Its driver was the old Calvinist preacher, Bronson. From the opposite direction rode my Uncle Abner on his great chestnut. They had met in front of our house. Both men reined to a halt.

"Good morning, Bronson," Abner called. "Chapman drives as though he were pursued by a fiend. I did not expect to find you behind him."

"Fiend there may be," the old man replied, "but it is within, not behind him. Or so he says."

I saw my uncle's head come up in interest.

"Indeed," he said in wonderment. "Why does he say that? Do you agree with him?"

The old man shifted on his seat. He regarded Abner from beneath bushy white eyebrows. His voice was harsh when he answered.

"Has nobody told you?"

"Nobody has told me anything," my uncle said. "I have been gone to Ohio for nine days, and I only returned last night."

A small breeze ruffled Bronson's thick shock of white hair. "Many days ago, Chapman began to act strangely. When he met anyone, no matter who or where, he shrieked and cursed at them. He grew unkempt, and his clothes became stained and mud-spotted. His beard was flecked with spittle. His speech was incoherent and filthy."

Abner frowned. "Has he taken to drinking heavily?"

Bronson shook his head. "No, and I must be on my way. I met him on the road but a short while ago, driving as you saw him. He pulled to a halt, laughing wildly, and shrieked 'Do you know I have just killed Blackburn? I'm going to bring him in! Give me a reason and I'll kill you, too!' "

Abner's eyes widened. "James Blackburn?"

"I suppose," the preacher answered. "When he said that, he beckoned me closer and said in a calmer tone, 'You know me, Bronson. I wouldn't harm you, but *he* would. He did this, not—' Then he drove away, slapping the reins in a frenzy."

"There has been bad blood between Chapman and Blackburn," my uncle said. "Who is *he*?"

The old preacher stiffened. "The unclean spirit that possesses Chapman. Who else could it be?" He stirred restlessly. "I must be after him to see—"

Uncle Abner had noticed me, I knew, but he now acknowledged me for the first time. "Martin," he called, "you might be useful! Bronson, let the boy go with you. I can accompany you, as well. Who can say what Chapman intends?"

As I climbed in beside the old preacher, I reflected that my mother would have opposed my going. Yet, I had once faced Dix, a murderer, and in the company of my uncle and the commanding old preacher I had no fear.

"Have you ever met with an unclean spirit before?" I asked the old man as we went along.

"Never," he admitted. "I have followed the trail of the devil many times, but this is the first of his creatures I have actually met."

"What are you going to do?" I queried.

"I intend to cast him out," he replied.

I might have pursued this further, but Uncle Abner, riding close beside us, had heard the questions.

"Bronson," he called, "you say that Chapman—or this thing which controls him—spoke of killing Blackburn?"

"He did."

Abner reflected. "That is strange. You know Blackburn as well as I do. Would you think a devil's minion would destroy a follower of his own master?"

"There is guile of the serpent here," the old man replied. "The answer is yet to be seen."

At this, Uncle Abner nodded and rode ahead.

As we followed at a slower pace, I continued to question Bronson.

"My uncle says that Chapman and Blackburn don't like each other," I said. "What is the reason?"

"The trouble comes from Blackburn's father," the preacher replied. "In his last years he was nothing like his former self, and he swore that his neighbors had robbed him of some of his land. In his mind, the Chapmans and the Tylers were those who had done the thing."

"Was any of this true?" I asked.

"Not even his son, James, thought that it was."

"He might have been trying to get more land," I ventured.

"So it was thought," the old preacher agreed. "He never got an extra foot. The only person he ever convinced was his son James. It is said that the old man made his son give him a deathbed promise to take back the land."

I had never heard of this. Bronson saw my surprise and went on, "For a long time after his father's death, James Blackburn did nothing. Then, over the last two years, he began to move against Chapman and Tyler."

"What did they do when he accused them of being on his family's land?"

"He made no accusations. He cut the trees that marked the boundaries and put snake fences inside the land they thought was theirs."

I was about to inquire about action by the law when Uncle Abner came riding back to us.

"He was seen driving on the road to Scout's Rock!" he called when he came up to us. Then he turned and rode on ahead again.

Scout's Rock was a stony outcrop overlooking the river. It thrust up from a dense patch of woods and ended in a sharp cliff on the upriver side. At the foot of the cliff, a small ravine led between two hills to the river. On the hill opposite Scout's Rock, at a lower level, was a smaller, unnamed cliff. Paths went through the ravine to the river and up through the weeds and brush to each of the cliffs.

On the road at the end of this ravine we came upon Chapman's team, tethered to a sapling. Nearby was Abner's great horse. Nobody was in sight, but voices could be heard, coming closer. The conversation was punctuated with wild laughter.

At last three men came slowly along the path. Two of them were big men—Chapman and my uncle—carrying the body of a third big man. A smaller gray-faced man with a permanently cowed look followed slowly behind them.

There was no mistaking that the man they carried was dead. No live person's neck lolled at such at angle.

Chapman was carrying the man's arms and addressing Abner, who had the feet.

"Yes, I killed him," he was saying. "How many times must I tell you I did, Abner?" He gave a peal of wild laughter. When it subsided, he said, "I cast him down from a great height—I did, I did! You saw it happen, Tyler. I did it, didn't I?"

"I saw it happen," the small man said in a low voice.

"I found you trying to move his body from the rocks where it hit," Abner said. "It appears that he fell from the cliff. Did you pick him up and throw him over? Did you push him?" He spoke over his shoulder to Tyler. "Did you see either of these things happen?"

"He did not!" Chapman yelled. "I did neither of those! *I*—have greater power! I have only to level my finger and strike a man down—any man! That is what I did to Blackburn! I struck him down and he fell!"

Abner's tone became less demanding. "Let's get him into the wagon and lay him down. Then we can look at him better."

Bronson stepped down from his buggy. "I have a duty to perform." He was looking at Chapman.

"Later," said Abner. "The one you want will not hurry away."

Chapman's laugh became more of a chuckle. My spine grew cold from my neck to my hips.

Together, Chapman and my uncle laid Blackburn's body in the back of Chapman's wagon. I looked on in curiosity. I had no fear of Blackburn; the man could not harm me. Abner straightened his limbs and studied him. He was a big man, with thick brown hair. The tip of his nose had a pronounced upturn, and his upper teeth protruded slightly. His staring eyes were dark brown. As I watched, Abner gently closed the eyelids.

"There is nothing to see but the fact of his death," my uncle remarked. "Before he came here, he had been at his pigsty. My hands tell me that." He wrinkled his nose.

He stopped to pull a handful of the wildgrass at the side of the road and wiped his hands. "Only his boots are stained," he said. He gestured toward the man's heavy gray-wool trousers. "See how clean his trousers are and how untorn. No branches or bushes broke his fall from the rock."

He looked at Chapman. "Where did you direct this power of yours? At his head? At his heart?"

Chapman laughed again. "At his head? Hardly. There was nothing in it. At his heart!"

Uncle Abner opened the man's coat and shirt, then his underwear, and looked at the skin. "He is unmarked," he commented.

"Of course," the demented man cackled. "You do not know the limits of my power."

Abner turned to the small man. "Tyler, did you see this happen as Chapman claims?"

The gray-faced man was already wearing a heavy woolen cap. He pulled nervously at it with grimy fingers. "Yes, I did, Abner. I was up on that other rock and I looked acrost and there was Blackburn—"

"What were you doing there?"

"I was comin' back from stayin' overnight with my cousin Walter when I noticed Blackburn headin' into the woods. I wanted to talk to him about his fences. I was too far back to see which way he went, so I took a guess. It was the wrong path."

"You saw him on the rock," my uncle prompted. "What was he doing?"

"Why—jest standin' there. Then, all of a sudden, he staggered like he'd been hit. Next thing, he'd fell over the cliff."

"Where was Chapman when this happened?"

"He was nowhere in sight. Then, jes' when Blackburn fell, he showed up at the very back of the rock, maybe ten-fifteen feet away."

"Could he have pushed Blackburn in any way? Hit him with a rock?" Abner questioned.

The small man shook his head. "I don't see how he could have pushed. And I didn't hear anythin' hit."

Uncle Abner turned to Chapman. "You are going to bring the body in? Where?"

Chapman's eyes gleamed, and he grinned, but he did not laugh. "To Thaxton."

My uncle was surprised. "The sheriff?"

"Why not? Isn't he good enough for you?"

Chapman's question was indeed pointed. Thaxton's predecessor had been a thief, and Abner had exposed him.

"I am not one to judge him. I believe he is a good man," Abner replied. "However, you or the thing speaking through you has a fine regard for the law. Strange that an unclean spirit should be a contrite one."

His only reply was another grin.

Uncle Abner spoke to the small man. "You will go with him, Tyler?"

"Yes. He wants a witness. I'll jes' follow along on my horse." He indicated a bay mare tethered farther along the road.

"Start, then," Abner said. "I have something to say to my nephew before I come."

When the wagon began to move, my uncle came over to us. "Bronson," he said, "be patient until Martin does something I want him to do. Then bring him to the sheriff's office."

"Now Martin," he went on, "I want you to listen carefully and do exactly what I ask. When it is done, you will come in with Bronson."

Perhaps half an hour later, Bronson stopped the buggy in front of the courthouse. The building's white-plaster pillars were subdued in the pale sunlight.

The old preacher and I went around the building to the rear. After Smallwood's rascality, it was decided to put the sheriff's office in a public place instead of his own house. It was there where the new man, Thaxton, might be found.

I knew that the others were still there, for Chapman's wagon and Abner's chestnut were behind the building. The body was still in the wagon, but someone had thrown a cloth over it.

There was a hubbub of voices coming from the small office as we approached. Then I heard Tyler speak.

"I can only tell you what I saw. I was on the other side of the ravine. I had no part in it!"

"But—" said a voice not yet familiar to me. It was Thaxton, as I learned.

"You can hardly be faulted, Thaxton," I heard Uncle Abner say. "You are being asked to believe that Chapman has confessed to murder—but that a creature from Hell, hiding within him, is the real killer."

"You put it clearly, Abner," Thaxton answered.

Bronson put his blue-veined hand on the latch and opened the door. There, behind a battered oak table sat a blocky man with spiky black hair and a short, wiry beard. His slate-gray eyes glanced in our direction. So did the eyes of everyone else standing in the crowded little room.

A look of surprise crossed Bronson's face, and one must have been on mine, too. Among those standing around Thaxton was Adam Bird, the other circuit-riding preacher, a Methodist.

Neither Bronson nor Adam Bird was a young man. Bronson was the older. Each of them regarded his calling with utmost seriousness. Neither would have compromised with the Devil. Yet they were not alike. Bronson attempted to appeal first of all to reason, assuring his listeners that their destiny lay in the ways of the Lord. His dogma was called upon when he mounted any crusade against wickedness. Adam Bird, on the other hand, was more practical and adaptable. He chose to strike for the emotions. His favorite tactic was an attempt to overwhelm his opponent. When Bronson saw him, he ignored everyone else in the room.

"What do *you* here, Adam?" he inquired, with a side glance at Chapman.

"I came to ask Thaxton to let me see Howard, who is his prisoner for drunkenness," Adam Bird replied. "It seems that I have walked into something that concerns us both."

"I have my intentions to deal with it," Bronson said.

"I have never doubted your competence," Adam Bird assured him. "I do offer my help. Have you ever faced an enemy such as this one?"

"No, but I have no fear. Did the Lord not assure the children of Israel, through Moses, *I will be an enemy unto thine enemies?*"

Uncle Abner was listening to the two old men. Without drawing attention, he stepped to Thaxton's side and bent over.

"There is nothing in this for you, Thaxton," he said in a low tone. "Let us go outside for a moment."

The sheriff got up quietly and squeezed to the door. Abner followed, motioning me to accompany them. None of the others came after us.

"Thaxton," said Abner, when the door had closed, "let us look at Blackburn again."

He walked to the wagon and threw back the cloth which covered the body.

I had seen enough of Blackburn. I leaned against the nearest hitching post and stooped to pull some of the beggar-lice from my trousers. I had gathered a generous collection when I was carrying out my uncle's errand at the cliffs. Even though the twin prickles of these small, tapering brown seed cases were not painful, they were a nuisance.

At Uncle Abner's suggestion, Thaxton was peering at the body.

"Look at his neck," my uncle was saying, lifting the shoulders gently.

Thaxton bent over. "Splinters. He must have fallen on a branch."

Abner lowered the body. "Splinters, indeed. Now, look at him well."

The sheriff studied slowly and carefully, then shook his head. "I must be blind, Abner. I fail to see what you mean."

"You will see it," Uncle Abner said. He looked over at me. "Leave that for later, Martin, and come over here."

I obeyed, but stole a glance at Blackburn. I saw nothing I had not seen before.

"Thaxton," Abner said. "This is my nephew, Martin. Observe him. Tell me what you think of him."

I was all of thirteen, and I had always had my uncle's affection and trust, but this was the first time I had known him to show pride in me.

The sheriff looked at me. "A fine lad. I can see you've been in the woods. Did they call you away from inspecting your rabbit snares, Martin?"

Before I could answer, Uncle Abner intervened. "I had set him on a different game trail."

The sheriff was interested. "Indeed. Did you have any luck, boy?"

My reply was cut off again. The door of the office opened and the four other men came out. Bronson strode over to us, his deep-set eyes gleaming.

"Thaxton," he said in a commanding tone, "this man has turned himself in as a murderer. You can arrest him, but you surely would be arresting an innocent man. He was merely the helpless tool of the creature possessing him. You know this as well as I."

The sheriff gave back his stare. "How can I turn him loose? I hear that he even threatened to kill you."

Bronson quivered with indignation. "There is a place for the mad, but it is not the gallows. Would you have him die and be carried off by a fiend?"

"No," the sheriff conceded, "but the law insists that I arrest him."

"That is unnecessary," Bronson argued. "I shall drive this thing from him. Then let us see."

Thaxton shrugged. "It could do no harm."

Bronson dipped his head in acknowledgment and walked back to the group. He grasped Chapman by the arm and drew him well out into the yard away from everyone else. To my surprise, the demented man grinned but offered no resistance.

Bronson faced him. "You—*that other*—what is your name?"

Chapman, with an idiotic look on his face, shook his head. He spoke no word.

Bronson took a small Testament from his pocket and held it in his left hand. He reached into his coat and drew out a small wooden cross. He faced Chapman with the book and the cross.

"Know that our Lord, when He has risen, bestowed the power to cast out unclean spirits upon anyone who believed and involved His name," the old preacher said in a steady voice. "Therefore, in the name of Jesus Christ, I command you who possess the body of this mortal, Luke Chapman, to come forth."

Nothing happened. Chapman stood like a wooden image.

"*Do you hear me?*" Bronson demanded, his voice louder. He thrust the cross before Chapman's staring eyes. "*Come forth!* "

This command, as had the first, produced no result.

Bronson stood still. It was plain from his face that he was uncertain as to how to proceed next. He looked to the sky and his lips moved silently. He lowered his head and avoided looking at us.

Then old Adam Bird stepped forward. He was big and arresting, and it was plain that nothing would stay him. He was like a prophet of old, even to the mark the land left on him, the dried mud on his boots.

At first, his approach was mild.

"Bronson," he said, laying his hand on the other preacher's arm, "do not be downcast. We are brethren, as our Lord said.

"Why," he went on, "nowhere is it written how you or I should do what must be the right thing. But you failed to complete the matter."

"Where did I fail?" asked Bronson.

"You gave him no place to go."

Bronson straightened, but Adam Bird tightened his grip on his arm.

"This might be dangerous," he said. "Let me do it."

He took the book and the cross from Bronson and turned to Chapman. He let go Bronson's arm and gripped Chapman's.

With no resistance from Chapman, Bird led him to one of the grays in Chapman's team.

"Now," the preacher said, "you thing of Satan, whoever you are, I offer you this beast as a refuge. Will you accept?"

His answer was a high-key titter from Chapman.

"Is that agreement?" Bird asked. "It may be. Let us see."

He uttered the same command in the name of the Lord that Bronson had. "Now begone to this beast!" he said in conclusion.

The animal stood unmoved, its attitude unchanged.

Chapman laughed a short, discordant laugh.

The preacher glared. He shook Chapman's arm fiercely.

"I fear no devil!" he shouted. "I would offer myself as a prize for you to take, if you could. But I know that if you failed, you might even take that innocent boy before we could prevent it. *But know this*—I intend to stand before you and command you until you come forth and enter this beast!"

A guttural chuckle came from Chapman, but the horse remained placed.

The old preacher stood in helpless fury.

Then, as he gathered himself for another attempt, Uncle Abner stepped forward.

"It might be beyond the strength of both of you," he said. "Let me try something different."

Adam Bird looked at him in wonder.

"Have you cast out devils, Abner? Remember, it could fall on you and overcome you, even as the seven sons of Sceva were overcome."

"I think that might not happen," Abner replied. "However, the risk is mine."

Adam Bird stood back, and Uncle Abner beckoned to Chapman. "Come with me."

"Here," Thaxton retorted. "This man is in my care. You can't take him away."

"Consider me your deputy, then," my uncle answered. "Trust me. He will be returned."

Misgiving was plain on Thaxton's face, but he subsided. He watched as Abner pointed a direction and Chapman walked to his bidding. I had not been told to remain, and I followed. The two preachers took a few steps, but a wave of Abner's other hand stayed them.

We walked from the rear of the courthouse, then continued straight on, along another road. I knew that Uncle Abner would not go far. I felt that he wanted an end to this business.

I was right. We had gone only a few hundred yards when we came to a modest, two-story frame house painted white. I knew the house. It belonged to Doctor Storm.

We knew that Storm was there, for his horse was tethered near the house. He responded quickly to Abner's knock, which meant that he was not treating anyone.

His mouth quirked behind his wispy beard as he saw the three of us.

"Well! Which of you is the sick one?" he snapped. "None of you looks it."

"Perhaps Chapman is," my uncle answered. "We need your help."

The old doctor ran his hand through his graying reddish hair. "Come in, then."

Storm's office was on the left side of the hall as one entered. He lived in the rest of the house—alone, except for a black housekeeper who came daily to cook and clean for him.

He stood aside as we entered the office, bare except for a desk, two chairs, an examining table, and an instrument cabinet. The

65

floors were dark from oil. We had scarcely passed the door when his nose wrinkled.

"Pah," he snorted. "One of you has been in a pigsty."

"None of us has," Abner said. "My hands were on the boots of the man who had."

"Then go to the back porch and wash them," Storm ordered. "I can think better without distractions."

Had I been my uncle, Storm would have been reminded that, as a doctor, he would have endured far worse things. Abner was not so tactless. He went to wash.

When he came back, Storm looked sharply at Chapman, who was in the chair. "Now, then, man," he said, "what seems to be the matter?"

Abner intervened. "Perhaps I had better tell it."

He proceeded to give a shortened account of the things that had happened. Storm listened intently. When Abner finished, Storm showed his teeth in a twisted grin.

"So Thaxton wants him, does he? What's the charge—harboring a criminal?"

My uncle's only answer was to stare at him from beneath his bushy brows. Storm cleared his throat.

"Very well, Abner. No harm done. However, indulge me. Where does a doctor enter this case?"

"In a moment," Abner responded. He turned to the demented man. "Chapman, you tell us that an unclean spirit lives in you."

Chapman threw back his head and laughed wildly. Storm started in his chair, but settled, observing the man closely.

Abner leaned close to the laughing man. "Chapman! The Chapman who knows me well! Do you want to be free of this thing?"

The laughter stopped, and Chapman whispered hoarsely, "Yes!" Then he began to chuckle.

"Where does it live in you, Chapman?"

Again the hoarse whisper. "Everywhere."

Uncle Abner glanced quickly at Storm, then concentrated again on Chapman.

"It can only be everywhere in you if it lives in one place, Chapman. Your blood."

Chapman stopped chuckling. He seemed to be listening warily.

"Then, if Storm bleeds you, you should be free." Abner turned to Storm. "Do you agree?"

"It is my custom to withdraw a quart and a half," the old doctor said. "That should do it. If we want to be certain," he went on, "I could also purge him."

"No, no, no!" Chapman exclaimed. "The bleeding should be enough!"

Storm measured him with a look. "That reaction, at least, is normal."

He arose, addressing Chapman as he did. "Take off your cape and roll up your left sleeve." While the man obeyed, Storm opened the cabinet and took out a brass bowl and a razor.

He first placed Chapman's arm on the arm of a chair, resting on the bone. Then he put the brass bowl beneath the forearm, touching the flesh. He bent over the arm, studying the flesh a short distance from the elbow, toward the wrist. When he was satisfied, he opened the razor and made a quick, short slash across the skin.

A thin thread of red sprang forth on the surface of the flesh. As the seconds passed, it swelled into a thin stream and began to inch down toward the bowl Then it flowed even freer and went steadily into the bottom of the bowl.

I watched with fascination. I wondered if the growing red pool would heave—or roll—or bubble—with the contortions of the demonic thing.

It did none of these things. It increased quietly.

Dr. Storm broke the silence. "I'll return in a moment." He left the room.

We stood watching the blood accumulate in the bowl. In a few moments, Storm came back with an old bucket stuffed with corn husks. He gave us a crooked smile.

"As I remember, swine were once involved in a situation like this." He peered into the bowl and grunted with satisfaction. He reached into his instrument bag and took out a needle and some stitching. Before we could concentrate, he went to work and closed Chapman's wound with a few quick stitches, then wiped it with a clean wet cloth he had brought in with him.

Chapman started to lift the bowl, but Storm took it from him and emptied the blood over the husks in the bucket. He held the bucket out to my uncle.

"Here, Abner," he said, "give this to your pigs."

Uncle Abner made no move to take it. He seemed to be looking for words to answer the old doctor.

"I know you raise some pigs to sell," said Storm. "I was reminded of it when you didn't get all that smell off your hands. You still seem to have it."

Abner began to speak, then changed his mind. He began again, addressing Chapman.

"How do you feel now, Chapman?"

I saw now that the man had changed. His eyes no longer rolled, his breathing was slow and steady. He answered Uncle Abner in a quiet tone. "I think I'm myself again, Abner. I thank you. You, too, Storm."

Abner gripped his right hand. "You will be weak after losing your blood, Chapman. Let me help you stand. You must now go back and make your peace with Thaxton."

Chapman rose very slowly. "It was a terrible thing that was done to Blackburn, Abner. But Thaxton must surely see that I was only an unwilling tool. Nobody could doubt it. Even if I had no witness other than Tyler—"

"Yes, Chapman," said Uncle Abner, "Tyler, Bronson, Bird, Martin, Thaxton himself, and—" he swung around "—Storm. These should be witnesses enough for any man."

"I am humble before them," Chapman said.

"And humble you should be," Abner said. "Some of God's own humble things will bear witness, also. Put on your cape, Chapman."

The sheriff was standing by the wagon when we returned. At the sound of our voices, Tyler and the two preachers came out of the office.

"Well, Chapman," said the sheriff, "are you one man or two?"

"Only one."

I looked at Chapman again. He was still as calm and ordinary as he had been in Storm's office after losing his blood. In the sunlight, his boots were stained and his cape and hat still had spots of dried mud, but he had smoothed his hair and his beard. His clothing was not in disarray, as it might have been. Even coming from his own backyard or the woods, he would have looked worse.

Storm came forward. "The other one is in here." He held out the bucket.

Thaxton was perplexed. "I wish that Squire Randolph were here. I have a man who killed another, but he vows that one of Satan's creatures used his body to do it. Now that creature no longer controls him. Can I arrest him or not?"

He looked at the two preachers, then at Abner, and finally at Storm.

Uncle Abner was the only one to speak. "You can," he said gravely.

Adam Bird straightened. "Abner! Does this mean that you deny the presence of devils and unclean spirits? Do you defy the written testimony?"

"No," Abner replied. "It is plain that the devil exists. Chapman is proof of that. I am sure that the rest of those creatures are with us, as we are told. But we overlook the myriad instruments of good around us."

"I was seized by that thing, and it does prove the devil exists!" Chapman exclaimed. "Yet you want me arrested!"

Uncle Abner ignored him. He motioned to Storm and drew him to the body in the wagon. As he had done for Thaxton, he lifted Blackburn's shoulders. "The neck," he said.

The old doctor examined Blackburn professionally. "I see," he said finally. "Broke his neck. But that is not what you mean."

Abner put the body down and faced the rest of us. In a few sentences he reviewed again what we had been told about the killing.

"Why do you repeat, Abner?" Thaxton asked impatiently.

"To fix your mind on what was said," my uncle answered calmly. He walked over to Chapman.

"Why did you kill Blackburn?"

Chapman groped for words. "Why, Abner, who knows why an evil spirit does things?"

"Was it because the man was forcibly moving in on your land and Tyler's?"

"It could have been."

Abner seemed confronted by an enigma. "A strange demon that would right human wrongs."

Chapman shrugged.

Tyler had gone almost unnoticed until now. He spoke up. "Likely it was to cause trouble just as we were to go to law over that land."

Abner was genuinely surprised. "I had heard the stories about Blackburn and his father, and I was puzzled when neither of you challenged Blackburn. I see."

He stood in thought, then raised his head. "Let us put that aside and consider other things. This morning when I helped bring Blackburn's body to the wagon, I left my nephew Martin behind to observe several things. Let me ask him what he saw.

"Martin, you went to the ledge opposite Scout's Rock. It is lower than the place where Blackburn fell, is it not?"

"Yes."

"If Blackburn stood at the edge of the rock, and you were on the other ledge, do you think you could have seen someone push him?"

"I think so. It's not so much lower."

"He was thrown down by a power of that thing I had in me!" Chapman interrupted.

My uncle ignored him. "If a stone had been thrown, it could have been heard by Tyler. Martin, if a long broken branch had been used to push Blackburn, could it have been seen?"

I nodded. "Yes. The rock is bare for fifty feet in every direction. The branch and the man using it could been seen."

Chapman cut in once more. "Your memory is short, Abner. I was among the trees when I directed him to fall."

"What I say is not against your account," Abner said. "I am merely looking for the source of the splinters."

Chapman stopped, his mouth open. "Splinters?"

"In the back of his neck. Thaxton has seen them. Storm has seen them. I observed them when we moved the body."

Chapman laughed. "He fell on some old dead wood."

"No," said Abner. "There was none. There were only rocks where we lifted him."

There was a silence.

Storm returned to the body and turned it over with some difficulty. He took a knife from his pocket and probed the back of Blackburn's neck. In a few minutes, he came to each of us in turn, showing the contents of his hand, four large splinters, blood-stained at one end.

"Weathered wood," the sheriff said slowly.

"Weathered as a fence rail," Abner remarked.

Thaxton sighed. "There are plenty of those around."

"Especially at Blackburn's pigsty. Isn't that possible?" my uncle asked.

"It's possible," the sheriff answered. "Why there?"

"Because I believe that that is where he was killed. He was taken to the ravine afterward."

"He fell from the rock!" Tyler exclaimed. "I saw him!"

Uncle Abner paid no attention to the small man. "When I helped to carry Blackburn from the ravine, I took on the smell of pigs from his boots. Storm later made me wash my hands. After that Storm accused me of not cleaning myself thoroughly. But I had."

He confronted Chapman again. "There was one other source of the stench. You had carried Blackburn under the arms. It was not on your hands. It was on your boots."

Chapman scorned this. "Most of us have pigs."

"Yes," Abner agreed. "I raise some myself, to sell in Cincinnati. But," he said, his voice lashing the other big man, "I have yet to see a pig on your land!"

He had only begun.

"Take off your boots, Chapman, and let Thaxton see them!"

Before the man could react, Abner's big hand shot out and grasped Tyler.

"Possession, indeed! There was no need for such a thing when not one but two of Satan's followers were at work! The entire thing is a series of lies. Blackburn was not killed by a fall, he was killed by a blow with a section of fence rail. The rail might still be on the ground at the pigsty."

He shook Tyler. "Because Chapman pretended for days to be demented, it was a planned act. All that you were asked to do was bear false witness, but that might have been enough."

He shook Tyler again. "No demented man had any part in this—not even Blackburn's father. Because he was old and sick, his own son doubted his stories against you and Chapman. When he began to see the truth and take direct action, you thought he had to be killed."

He marched Tyler over to the sheriff. "You'll have two after all, Thaxton, but not in one body."

Thaxton was awed. He already had a firm grip on Chapman.

"All this because of some splinters and a smell of pigs?"

Uncle Abner shook his head. "Even less things than that. The instruments of good that I mentioned bothered me in addition to the things he has described." He walked to the wagon, pulling Tyler with him. Then he beckoned to me and to Thaxton, who came with Chapman in his grip.

"Martin, on the end," Abner directed. "Then the body, Chapman, and Tyler."

When we were aligned, Abner addressed everyone present. "Now, begin with Martin and observe the workings of those of God's things that are all about us."

Storm sniffed. "I only see a good example of an ordinary boy, one dead man, and two rascals."

"Is there anything you cannot find anywhere?"

"The boy's been in the woods," the sheriff said. "He's scratched from briars and his clothes are snagged. His pants are covered with beggar-lice. Something I *can't* find?"

Comprehension began to come into his slate-gray eyes. He gave a long, searching glance to the body, then to Chapman and Tyler. He did not need the guidance of Abner's pointing finger.

"The boy was in the woods where everyone else was supposed to have been, even Blackburn. Yet he's the only one with snagged clothes, scratches, and beggar-lice."

Adam Bird cleared his throat. "Abner, I believe the very stones would speak to you."

My uncle pulled at his brown beard. "You have given me too much credit, Adam." He stooped and pulled one of the beggar-lice from my trousers.

"The plant is a weed," he said, "and it trusts its seed to this to multiply. An insignificant thing, and a plant that is worthless to us."

He touched the two prongs of the prickles. "Can anything so persistent be worthless?"

He was looking at Chapman and Tyler, his voice had a chill that even the November air lacked.

"I think not."

6

The Oldest Law
(1979)

The first of the Uncle Abner stories is the last, chronologically.

I t was a time of change. We could not fail to reap benefit, many said. My Uncle Abner agreed, but he would not say if only good would result or if troubles might come which would outweigh the good.

I tried to get him to discuss it as we rode our horses to get Thomas Harper, the County Clerk, just before dawn that morning early in spring. The railroad already passed through Wheeling, to the north. Now a spur was to be laid through our area, eventually reaching the Ohio River, to the west. This would permit cattle to be taken to the big markets without losing weight on a drive. We could ship out coal, timber, and grain. I found it exciting when I thought of it.

But when I wanted to talk of these changes that morning, Abner merely said, "Rufus depends on you now for much of his farm work. How will these things affect that?"

I had grown into this responsibility, even as my father grew older, but I had not foreseen the things which were coming. I said as much.

"We must consider each thing as it comes," said my uncle. "We should now be considering why Randolph asked me to meet Harper very early and ride with him to the courthouse."

I had no answer. My uncle had asked me to come with him because he knew that the soil was still too wet to turn and that my father could easily handle the other work. If Abner had not divined Squire Randolph's purpose, I could not.

Few people were stirring along the road, although the sky was paling rapidly. The only activity we saw was at Randall Dorsey's blacksmith shop. The forge already glowed, and a steady clanking sounded. There were two of our neighbors waiting outside the shop and one was inside with his horse. Three others were turning away.

Although the white in my uncle's hair and beard was now more noticeable, Abner still seemed as one who might have been moulded in that very forge, or another like it. The chestnut he rode could almost have been sired by the great horse which had been his companion when I was a boy, so that the pair seemed to present an unchanging picture.

My uncle glanced across at me. "Randolph could expect to meet Harper this morning at the courthouse. He has been unable to see the man at all for two weeks, for Harper has been in Pittsburgh. His return was expected late last night. Yet Randolph wants me to meet him early and ride with him to the courthouse. Why?"

I shook my head, but I felt that no answer had been truly expected.

"Something has happened while Harper was away," Abner said, fixing his eyes on the road. "And Randolph does not want him to talk to anyone who has a hand in it before he does. That must be the way of it."

It was not a long ride to Harper's place. He had a modest acreage of several pastures, some timber, and a small section of hilly land bisected by a steep ravine. Since Harper was the County Clerk, he farmed little, contenting himself with a few beef and dairy cattle and some poultry. His house was a neat, white-painted, two-story frame which sat close to the road.

We tethered our horses, Abner's chestnut and my roan gelding, where they could drink from the wooden trough near the barn. At the front door of the house Abner's knock was answered by Margaret Harper, a short, stout woman with plain features.

"Why, Abner!" she said in surprise. "And Martin. It's early for you to be out. Do you want to see Tom?"

"If we might."

An apologetic look crossed her face. "He's not in. One of the cows must be out and has strayed up onto the hill. He's gone to bring her in. Will you come in for coffee until he comes back?"

Abner seemed not to have heard the invitation. "Does he often have this trouble?"

"Why, no. Almost never. Tom was amazed when he heard the cowbell back on the hill a while ago."

"So should I be. Tom builds good fences." Abner turned to me. "Martin, you and I might ride up to help bring that cow in."

As we rode away from the yard toward the hill, I could hear the irregular tonking of the cowbell in the distance. There was something odd about it, and it made me frown. Then I realized: it neither came closer nor went further away. The beast might be grazing, of course, but where was Harper?

I started to mention this to my uncle, but he was glancing intently at the ground, which was soft. I looked down and could see the hoofmarks of Harper's horse, but that was all.

There was morning mist as we approached the hilly tract. A small pond lay at the foot of the hill, and white vapors from the water had spread up the slope and into the ravine which flanked the right side of the hill. The sun, just rising at the hill's top, made long, slanting shafts in the mist in the places where the trees let it shine through. Down in the ravine I could hear the piping of the peepers, the tiny frogs of early spring.

As we urged our horses carefully through the dead brush, Abner shook his head impatiently.

"A strange cow which makes no sound but the clanking of its bell. Why do we not hear Harper or his horse? See, they came this way."

We mounted higher until we were more than a hundred feet above the bottom of the ravine. Then the mist thinned to mere wisps, and I could see empty wood before us. There were only the spruces, the sweet gums, the maples, and the stalks of the brush, all bare and leafless. The spruces alone were green.

Then I saw that the woods were not completely empty. Ahead, to our right, a horse stood, its saddle empty. There was no cow, although I could still hear the bell. It was very close.

"The cow—" I began.

"There is no cow," said Abner, raising his right arm. "There. Look up."

I stared where he pointed. Near where the horse stood there was a ledge or rock, at the edge of a straight, high drop into the ravine. A silver maple grew by the left side of the ledge, one long branch extending over the rock. Attached to the branch above the center of the space was a cowbell, sounding when the gently morning breeze stirred the branch.

I started to urge my horse toward this strange thing.

Abner's massive hand closed on the gelding's bridle. "Wait," he said. "Where is Harper? And look at his horse. It only stands on three legs."

He turned his head this way and that, then faced the ledge.

"Harper!" he called.

There was no answer.

He dismounted and walked slowly toward the horse, a young bay stallion. I saw that he was right—it did, indeed, favor its left foreleg. I saw, too, that Abner paid less attention to the horse or the bell than he did to the ground. He stooped once and picked something up, examined it, and carefully put it into his pocket. Then he walked to the ledge and looked down into the ravine.

"Harper!" he called, as before, then waited. Again there was no answer.

He turned aside and walked to and fro near the ledge. Once again I saw him pick up something. Finally he walked to the side of the horse and began to soothe it.

"Now come here, Martin," he said. "I want you to look at this animal's hoof while I hold his head."

I dismounted, tethered both our horses to a nearby beech, and came to the stallion's side. The beast was distressed, but Abner had quieted it and was holding it firm.

I raised the bay's left foreleg carefully and gripped it much as Randall Dorsey, the smith, might have done. When I looked at the hoof, the reason for the horse's lameness was clear. A pronged piece of metal protruded from the tender part of the foot, and the hoof was bloody.

I told Uncle Abner about the curious thing I had found.

"A caltrop," he said. "A Devil's tool, in this case. I thought you might find it. Now, Martin, you are strong. Take my glove, then grip the prongs and pull hard."

He passed his right glove, of heavy leather, to me. I donned it, reached down to grip the protruding metal, and pulled with all my

77

strength. The bay would have plunged with the pain had my uncle not curbed him. The metal object came free, and the bay grew quieter.

I examined the thing. It was of iron and consisted of four prongs so arranged that no matter how it fell, three prongs would rest on the ground and the fourth would project upward. The points were almost needles, and the edges were sharp. Each prong was between one and two inches long. Three of the prongs were bright; the fourth was bloody.

I held it out to my uncle, who glanced at it briefly and put it into his pocket.

"I picked up two more," he said, his voice wrathful. "Now, look at the bell. It hangs just higher than a man can reach, even sitting in his saddle. Harper would want to cut down the bell, else how would he know when a cow really was out? He would ride to the ledge and raise himself in his stirrups. On the ledge would be three of Satan's instruments, placed where the horse would be sure to step on one. Then—"

He turned and began to lead the bay gently toward our own horses.

"Martin," he said. "Get the bell. Then we must go down to the ravine."

We were both silent as we came to the courthouse, with its white plaster pillars, later in the morning. I had completed the unpleasant task of carrying Thomas Harper's body back to his house across the front of my saddle. My uncle, after leading the lame bay to the barn, had taken the burden of telling Margaret Harper how we had found her husband. Both of us were in a somber mood.

We had just tethered the horses when I looked up and saw Squire Randolph coming down the steps of the courthouse. He moved slower nowadays, and there were pouches under his eyes. He still cherished his affectations, but he had lost none of the respect he still commanded as a Justice of the Peace.

"Abner," he called, "did Harper not return? Or is he following you?"

My uncle looked up, his eyes as bleak as January sky.

"Harper did return. He is at his house, but he will not be following us. You asked me to find him this morning, and we did. We came upon his body at the foot of a small cliff in the ravine on his land. His neck was broken."

"Did you see anyone else?" Randolph asked.

"That is a strange question," Abner replied. "We did not, although it was clear that he had been led into a trap. A fall killed him, but that fall was planned."

Randolph's face was heavy with sadness.

"Harper was needed to help settle a case. The disputants are in my office now. It would seem that one of them might have caused this terrible thing. I had foreseen interference, and I asked your help. But you saw nobody."

Abner seemed to grow taller.

"Randolph, I think we should talk to these people. It is true that we saw only Thomas Harper's body, but the image of his murderer's mind was all around."

Randolph nodded. "Mr. Emerson says there is no den in the wide world to hide a rogue. How does he put it? 'Some damning circumstance always transpires.' "

Abner was beginning to mount the steps. "He had only to look to Adam and Cain for his examples." He glanced sidewise at Randolph. "This morning someone attempted to ignore the oldest law. If that person is in your office, we shall know it."

There were three persons already seated at the big oak table when Randolph, still puzzled by Abner's last remark, showed us into his office. Two of them I knew; the third was a stranger.

Everyone knew Randall Dorsey, the blacksmith. Not only his chair, but the room, seemed too small for him. He had removed the superficial grime of his trade, but his horny hands were gray with ground-in dirt. Flying sparks had singed his brown beard in spots. His eyes seemed to have carried some of the banked fire in his forge with them.

At his side sat his sister, Anna Blackhurst. She was in her mid-forties, but the widow's black she wore detracted in no way from the appeal she had for any man who ever saw her. Her figure had scarcely thickened. Her auburn hair had no gray, and it had barely darkened. Her milky skin was unlined, and her green eyes were clear and penetrating.

For us, her neighbors, she had been the preserver of tales and legends as far back as my memory went. She could summon up for children the fairies, the elves, the leprechauns, and the gnomes. Frontier history was as familiar to her as her next-door neighbors. The Indians themselves knew no more of their lore than she. I still remembered the day when she shocked many women by appearing at school in buckskin shirt and trousers. She was recreating for us the famous exploit of Anne Bailey, when that frontierswoman rode through nearly 100 miles of hostile country for ammunition when Clendenin's Fort was besieged. All the same, Anna Blackhurst never completely won back her standing in the community.

As a Justice of the Peace, Randolph often settled disputes of many types. When the issues were beyond his jurisdiction, he acted as a sort of Special Commissioner of the Circuit Court. As such, he lacked a judge's authority, and his decisions could always be appealed. He was known, however, to be able and fair, and few appeals were taken. This reduced the number of Circuit Judge's cases, and he could dispose promptly of litigation requiring jury trials.

Randolph waved a hand. "You know Mrs. Blackhurst and Randall Dorsey, Abner. This young man is a stranger. Let me introduce you to Nathan Dillworth."

My uncle looked at the young man curiously, and no wonder. Ephraim, the oldest of the local Dillworths, operated a busy still, among other things, and he was no better than he should be. The Dillworth most remembered was Lawrence. His greed for land had twice led him to clash with Abner. The second clash had ended in his hanging for murder.

The young man stepped forward. "I might be unfamiliar to you all, but my roots are here. My father was Gideon Dillworth."

Abner nodded in recognition. "I remember him. He left here for Baltimore nearly twenty years ago. He had a wife and a small boy. He was a sign painter, I recall."

He studied young Dillworth, who was tall with thick, black hair and a sweeping mustache. He was lean and appeared to be keeping a ferocious strength in check. His most striking feature was a hook which had replaced his left hand.

"And what do you do, Nathan Dillworth?" Abner asked.

"I was a cavalryman until my horse fell on me and crushed my left wrist," Dillworth said. "Now I am an actor."

"Were you ever sent to fight Indians?"

Dillworth laughed. "I have never seen an Indian. The accident happened when I had just finished training."

Randolph clucked with impatience. "And we are attempting to settle a matter of land ownership. Shall we be seated?"

When we had taken our places, Randolph placed two folded pieces of paper before Abner.

"Here are two deeds to a piece of property," he said, settling back in his chair. "Read both and tell me what you think. Be sure to examine everything."

I could tell that Abner considered protesting that he was no lawyer, but he said nothing. He knew that Randolph valued his opinion.

He read slowly and carefully. When he had finished both documents, he placed them side by side and glanced from one to the other. Finally he turned them over and examined the writing on the back of each.

"These deeds are both drawn to the same piece of land," he said finally. "They were drawn about fifteen years ago. The property is a tract of two hundred and fifty acres, sold by Oliver McCoy. One deed is made to Gideon and Flora Dillworth. The other is made to Richard and Anna Blackhurst. Yet one deed must be worthless, for the two are identical."

"Not quite," said Randolph.

Abner looked again at the papers. "Not quite, that is true. The Dillworth deed is dated three days earlier. In all other respects, the documents are twins—the same lawyer, the same notary—why, even the recorder's statement on the back as to the number and page of the record book is the same.

Randolph stroked the sagging flesh along his jaw. "And that is impossible."

"Not entirely," Abner said. "Oliver McCoy could have bilked Richard Blackhurst, who was given the later deed. This is unlikely. It was not in McCoy's nature to do this. Besides, the fraud would never have passed Morgan Roberts, his lawyer, or Morgan's clerk, who made out the papers and notarized them."

He looked hard at Randolph. "What does the record book show?"

Randolph sighed. He picked up a large ledger-type of book which was in front of him and opened it. Without a word, he pushed it to Abner. My uncle consulted the deeds for a page reference, then glanced at the book.

"The page is gone!" he said. "It has been cut away with a sharp edge. It might never have been missed until a time such as this came."

This provoked Randolph into a summation of the situation as it stood. One of the deeds had to be false, but it was difficult to say which one. The later dating of the Blackhurst deed might make it suspect, but the Dillworth deed might have been dated earlier to throw suspicion the other way. There were no witnesses to testify one way or the other. Oliver McCoy, his lawyer, and the law clerk were all dead. The dead law clerk was shown as notary on both deeds. The fact of fraud had been established by the missing page from the record book.

"That is why I wanted to talk to Harper," Randolph said. "He had a prodigious memory. He might have recalled whose name was on the copy in the records. He might even have remembered who asked to look at the book. That person could have removed the page."

The table vibrated to the slap of a heavy palm.

"There was no fraud done by our family," growled Dorsey. "My sister is as honest as anyone here. So was her husband while he was alive."

He turned to his opponent. "Dillworth, I don't know you. I did know your father, and I had thought well of him. Now I think he was cut from the same cloth as some of the others of that same name."

Young Dillworth paled. "You can never support that."

The smith leaned forward. "Your father was a sign painter. He could have had the eye and the hand to be a forger. And he came back here once, fifteen years ago. He could have cut that page from the book then."

Dillworth's jaw was set. "My father had the honesty you claim for your sister. As for Blackhurst, I have been told by many of your neighbors that customers in his store had to be wary of short weight and scamped measure when he was alive."

Anna Blackhurst's eyes flashed. "You defame a man who cannot defend himself."

"My father has no better defense against your brother," said Dillworth, indicating the smith. "And my mother's a widow, like you."

Dorsey raised his hand to thump the table again. Dillworth saw it, and brought his own left arm down so the hook at the end of it cracked sharply against the wood. My uncle's mouth tightened in displeasure at such tactics.

Anna Blackhurst smiled ruefully and dropped a handkerchief on the surface of the table. "But it is such meager land. Why should my husband have risked going to prison over it?"

"My father knew there was coal under it when he bought it," Dillworth replied. "He always said that its value would increase. I have learned, in Baltimore, that the railroad will pass within a quarter mile of the property. The coal will now be more valuable because it will be easier to transport. What my father knew, Blackhurst could have known."

"My husband's judgment was poor," Ann Blackhurst said. "He bought land for the sake of owning it."

Dillworth turned to Randolph. "You spoke of Harper, the County Clerk. Where is he? If he could help, he should be here."

Randolph made no reply. Instead he gestured to Abner.

My uncle reached into his pockets. "Two of us have seen Harper this morning—Martin and I," he said. "Before we discuss that, let us all look at these."

He set on the table the cowbell and the three sharp-pronged objects. The point of one of these was still stained with the blood of Harper's horse. The other two were clean, bright metal.

Dillworth leaned forward and drew one of the pointed things to him with his hook.

"Caltrops," he said wonderingly. "Where did you get them?"

My uncle was watching him, and a flicker of surprise crossed his face. "You recognize these things?"

83

Dillworth pushed it from him. "A cavalryman should know them. Many a charge has been undone by these wicked things. It is said that Napoleon met with them, to his cost."

"Not only Bonaparte," Abner said. "Thomas Harper encountered these four objects this morning and paid for it with his life."

Amid shocked exclamations, he went on:

"At first light, someone hung this bell on a branch, to lure Harper into looking for a stray cow. It was hung at the edge of a small cliff. To complete the trap, these Devil's tools were strewn near the bell where a horse would step. Harper's horse did step on one. The blood is still to be seen. Harper was thrown over the cliff. His neck was broken."

There was silence at the table. It was plain that everyone remembered what Randolph had said about Harper's memory and knew what the murder implied.

Anna Blackhurst broke that silence. "I propose a test. Squire Randolph, will you send for a candle?"

Randolph rubbed the side of his nose, where the tiny broken blood-vessels showed. "To what end?" he asked.

The widow's green eyes flashed. She stretched out her right hand, slender and graceful, but clearly strong. "Let us have a trial by ordeal. Mr. Dillworth and I, as the Indians would do. I am willing to expose my good right hand to the flame to prove my innocence. Is he?"

Dillworth went pale. "You know well that no man would face a woman in such a test."

"There is no need for such foolishness," Abner said sharply. "By ignoring the oldest law, Harper's killer has stepped into plain view."

Randolph cleared his throat. "That is the second time you have referred to a law which escapes me. A Virginia law? Something carried over from England? The Sixth Commandment? Or the Tenth?"

"All those might be involved," replied Abner. "The Sixth and Tenth Commandments are, I am certain. As to the rest, I do not know. The law which I mean is older than any of these."

"It goes back to Adam, I suppose," said Randolph.

"It is older than Adam."

"Impossible!" Randolph snorted. "There is no law named before the commandments made to Adam."

"It is not named, that is true," Abner agreed, "but it is written in everything which was created. Think, Randolph: the Lord decreed that mountains should crumble, rocks should break, the sands of the desert should powder, all living things decay. From all this came the dust. From this dust Adam was formed. Now do you read the law?"

"It is still unclear."

"Once again—it is stamped on every created thing and cannot be broken. This is the law: all things must change."

Randolph nodded. He could not fault Abner's explanation. "And by naming Harper's murderer you will also name the forger?"

"By no means," said Abner. "The forger is different. I suggest that the forgery was done by Morgan Roberts' law clerk. No other person could have had the original document long enough to do it. No person here could have produced the necessary form for the deed."

"Morgan Roberts—" Randolph began.

"Had no motive," Abner finished. "He was an old man, and the land involved seemed of little value. Where was his gain?"

"I can hardly remember his clerk," Randolph reflected. "McGraw. Joseph McGraw. A sickly man. He died young. He had few attractive qualities while he lived."

Abner turned to Dillworth. "Dillworth, why did your father leave here for Baltimore?"

The ex-cavalryman was surprised. "To earn a living."

Abner stared at him. "That completes it."

He gestured toward the three caltrops. "That law decrees that everything must change. What are we told in the Sermon on the Mount? Lay not up for yourselves treasures upon earth, where moth and rust doth corrupt. What, then, is rust?"

His question brought only silence.

He answered it himself. "Rust is nothing but the oldest law at work. Now, look at these three of Satan's instruments. One is stained only by the blood of Harper's horse. The other two show not the faintest blemish, not a pinpoint of rust. All are newly made."

He turned to young Dillworth. "Dillworth, when you showed familiarity with these things, I became unsure of the picture which had formed in my mind. There were things which stood in your favor, but you could have brought these objects with you. Even so, they would have shown rust somewhere, if only faint blackening."

Dillworth made no answer. He lifted his good hand and let it fall to the table.

Randall Dorsey started to rise from his seat. "There's no man's blood on my hands, in spite of this made-up law of yours!"

"No, Dorsey, I don't believe there is," said Abner mildly. "You could not have been at Harper's place this morning. Martin and I both saw you hard at work when we passed your smithy."

Anna Blackhurst laughed, and I could hear nothing but music in it. "Then you must be saying that I did all the scheming for the land, that I stole out in the last shades of night to take a man's life. Abner, I must remind you that it is not I with theatrical connections. I am not the one skilled in pretending."

"You have many skills," Abner said gravely. "You know the ways of the Indian, and you know the ways they have been fought. How would Dillworth know, when he was raised in Baltimore?"

"You become more confusing, Abner," she laughed. "First you talk of old laws, then of Indians."

"It is simple enough," Abner said sternly. "You heard how Harper died. The ruse with the bell is a redskin's trick to lure a settler from his cabin. The settlers, in turn, used the deadly steel tares to penetrate the moccasins and cripple prowling enemies. You knew these things. I have heard you tell of them."

I, too, heard her voice talking of them, in the days I carried a wooden hunting knife.

She raised her head and thrust out her chin. "Who paid Joseph McGraw to forge a deed to the land? Dillworth's father had money. I had none."

"Dillworth's father had little money," Abner replied. "Why did he go to Baltimore? Only ten minutes ago I was told 'to earn a living.' "

Abner's presence suddenly seemed to increase, dwarfing even Randall Dorsey's.

"Joseph McGraw was an unloved man. And not all payment is in money. If you want an example, I give you Delilah."

Still she did not yield. Reaching out she swept the caltrops the length of the table. "Still, to prove your ancient law, you must say that I made these things. That is impossible."

"Then I have a question," said Abner. "Is your brother Tubal-cain or Cain?"

Dorsey suddenly shot to his feet. His voice shook. "Cain I am not! I said that no man's blood is on my hands, and that is true. She said she wanted them to show in school, and I thought it was the truth. I always believed the deed to the land was a true one, but I will not defend murder."

He looked down at Abner. "I made the caltrops for her. Yesterday."

7

And They Hauled It Away To The Mill
(1985)

This is the first Boley-McKee story. Timber piracy was common in the West Virginia forests at the time this was written. (1984)

When Arlan Boley pulled into his carport and switched off the engine, he heard the chainsaw.

The car radio had been on when he left the paved road, drove down the short gentle grade on his gravel lane, and turned onto the level bench of the hill where his house stood. A country baritone was singing an old tune.

"Oh, they cut down the old pine tree
And they hauled it away to the mill-"

Boley cut the radio switch and the ignition switch in quick succession as the car stopped in the center of the port. He started to close the car window when he heard the saw.

His wife, Geneva, heard it too. She turned toward him. "Sounds like someone's cutting timber over at Gilbert's."

The two children in the backseat started to talk. Boley held up his right hand. They subsided.

"Not so sure it's at Gib's, " he said.

His wife's brown eyes widened. "Over here?"

Boley made no direct answer. He turned to his eleven-year-old son in the back seat. "Carl, hop out there and look down our road into the woods. See are there any fresh tracks from heavy equipment."

The boy, whose body was just beginning to string out, jumped from the car and ran back to the point where the drive had turned toward the house. His sister, Martha, two years younger, popped from the other side of the car and ran after him. Boley went to the trunk and began to unload suitcases. Geneva stepped to the back door of the house and unlocked it.

The children came running back.

"No tracks, Dad," Carl shouted.

Martha put a period to it. "Not one."

"It must be over at Gilbert's," Geneva said from inside the screen door.

Boley handed the children their bags and picked up two others. His broad, heavily tanned face was set in thought. Then he shrugged and went into the house, a three-bedroom frame cottage.

He was a man just under six feet in height, deceptively lean until it was noticed that his shoulders were unusually wide and his muscles were like wire rope. He had crinkly blond hair, which he had passed on to his children.

His wife was holding the door open for him. As he passed her, he muttered, "Can't help but think that we came home from the Fair too soon. We wouldn't usually be home until after dark." He looked across at her. "Maybe it's a good thing."

Geneva looked up at him, her brown eyes slightly troubled. Her mouth, usually stretched in good humor, was sober. She pushed distractedly at her light brown hair. "Bill and Janet could hardly put us up the second day this time," she said. "Not after that call last night saying that her mother was rushed to the hospital at Clifton Forge with a heart attack."

It was their custom each August to attend the West Virginia State Fair near Lewisburg, in the southeastern part of the state not far from the Virginia line. Although they lived only an hour's drive away, they made a two-day holiday of it, staying with Geneva's brother and his wife in Ronceverte, near the fairgrounds. This year, they had to come home late in the morning of the second day because of the crisis in the other family.

Boley carried the bags into the bedroom. Been doing this like clockwork, year in and year out, he was thinking. He began to change into a blue shirt, jeans and work shoes. You can count on us not to be here, he said to himself.

Geneva appeared in the bedroom doorway. "What would you like for lunch?"

"Go ahead and fix for you and the kids," he said tying a shoe. "I'll throw together a sandwich or two later."

"You're going to have a look, " she said, making a statement.

"I have to know," he answered.

"Don't get into anything."

"Not if I can help it."

He went out of the house and along the hillside to his toolshed. He unlocked the door and stepped inside. A pair of walkie-talkies was on a shelf close to his hand. He picked them up, locked the shed again, and returned to the house. He handed one instrument to Geneva.

"Turn it on about five minutes after I leave with the jeep," he said. "I'll call in, one way or another." He grinned. "I don't think you'll have to come to my rescue."

He kissed her lightly and went out the back door again.

Boley owned a seventy-acre tract of land on a paved secondary road. The shape was like a wedge truncated and rounded some distance before it reached a point. The paved road, which was populated at only about eight families per mile, rounded the smaller end of the tract.

About twenty acres of Boley's land formed a grassy semi-circle from the road down to a small run at the bottom of a 300-foot gentle slope. Looking downhill, the house, Boley's equipment, and his outbuildings were on the left. The house faced away from the road. Where his lane turned to the house, a dirt road went on, straight down through the meadow to the run, crossed on the culvert, and went up into woods on the steep hillside, which formed the larger part of his acreage.

Boley went from the house to the level, graveled section where he kept his equipment under a protecting roof supported by pillars. Starting with a sturdy old tractor years before, he had built up an impressive collection of bulldozers, tractors, end-loaders, and miscellaneous farm equipment. He made a good living doing heavy work of several types for small farmers who couldn't afford the machinery. He employed no permanent workers—there were always enough teenage youths willing to hire for single jobs.

He made no attempt to farm his own land. He used the grassy meadows for hay, a cash crop he easily sold to horse breeders or to farmers who came up short. He also had two other hay fields on level patches in the acreage across the run. These were screened from general view by the woods which covered most of that hillside. Near his house was a small garden and some fruit trees. His wife worked the garden, as well as cutting the grass around the house with a riding mower.

Boley looked inside his jeep, which was parked facing the lane. He stared at the miscellaneous tools behind the rear seat.

Loggers, he thought, can be touchy.

He went into his toolshed, unlocked a cabinet, and took out a carbine. He wasn't a violent man and only used the gun for hunting. However, he felt that it might be useful. There were shells in it, he knew, but none was in the chamber.

He carried the carbine to the jeep and carefully laid it on the floor of the front seat, not far from his right hand, after checking that the safety was on. He wondered if Geneva had seen him take the gun. She would worry, but it couldn't be helped.

Boley switched on the motor, wondering if the timber cutters would hear him coming. Except for an occasional car on the road, the usual sounds were only those made by the birds or an infrequent small plane or helicopter checking utility lines. An ordinary radio or T.V. could sound like a theater performance or a stadium crowd. He hoped that the saws would drown his approach.

He drove away from the house and turned down the slope toward the run. Even at this time in mid-August, the run contained ample water. The annual period of violent thunderstorms had ended not many days earlier. Boley was glad he had built the culvert over the stream several years back. He crossed the water without undue noise.

On the other side of the run, he turned right and drove westward for about three hundred feet, then stopped and cut the motor. From here on, saplings and brush made walking mandatory.

Boley opened the door of the vehicle carefully, swung to the ground, and relatched the door without slamming it. He removed nothing except the walkie-talkie.

A meandering path led away from him into the brush, following the banks of the run. The track had been created by dogs and various animals from the woods. Boley's family used it intermittently, especially after walnuts were down in the fall. Several large walnut trees were scattered throughout Boley's woods. One of the largest was in the direction of the saw's whine.

Boley moved quietly along the path, checking the ground frequently. He had occasionally encountered copperheads here. He had no relish for such a distraction today.

The view ahead became clearer as larger trees took over and the brush thinned. Then, seeing sky where this had previously been impossible, Boley's suspicions were confirmed before he even saw the men.

In the next seconds, he did see them: three timber cutters, working at the large walnut tree that once had blocked the view of the sky from where Boley stood. Two were busy with chainsaws, stripping away the smaller limbs. The third sat on a large tractor on the opposite side of the run. None of the three saw him.

For several seconds, Boley stared at the felled tree. The butt faced him, the crown pointing west, the trunk with its length along the upper bank of the run. He stepped backward quietly, then walked back to the jeep. He switched on the walkie-talkie.

"Neva."

There was a brief pause. The instrument cracked.

"Yes, Arly?"

"I was right. There's three of 'em in here. They've downed the big walnut along the run. Cuttin' her up right now."

"How did they get in?"

"Through Gib's. Took down a section of fence."

She made no immediate answer. He knew the reason.

Finally, "I don't like what that means, Arly. I always thought we got along all right with Gilbert and Helen."

"Neva, we don't know what it means. Not yet. Meantime, I want you to do this: call the sheriff's office. Tell 'em I've got some timber thieves at work over here. Tell 'em to pull in and block Gib Williams' lane."

"That might take a while, Arly. You know how the party line is this time of day."

"Use the CB."

"All right." Before she left: "Arly, you be careful."

"Don't worry. I'm staying right here until I hear from you . . ."

Boley leaned against the front bumper of the jeep. He stared down at the run. After a wait of about five minutes, the walkie-talkie rasped and Geneva's voice sounded again.

"Arly?"

"I'm here."

"I got through on the CB. Sheriff McKee is on his way over himself. Everybody else is out somewhere."

"You tell him where I said he should pull in?"

"Yes. He wanted to know why you said that."

I don't know, Boley thought. It just figures. "He'll find out," he said. "You say he's on his way?"

"He's supposed to be."

"All right. I know what to do, then."

"Arly," his wife said.

"Yeah?"

"I saw what you put in the jeep. I'll say it again: watch what you're doing."

"What else?"

"Nothing I can do, I guess." He heard her sigh. Then, "Arly, if you do shoot that thing, try to watch where you aim it. You know how Helen Williams is, always walking around the wood looking for plants to move to her own property. She's out more than she's in the house."

How likely is *that*, he thought, with all this racket going on. "I'll watch it," he said. "Got to go now. Keep tuned, in case."

He opened the vehicle and took out a shovel, an axe, and the gun. He made a bundle, with the gun between the tools to make it less noticeable, and clipped the walkie-talkie to his belt.

When Boley came out of the brush near the fallen tree, he was noticed by the man on the tractor. Boley nodded to him and leaned his tool collection against a big sycamore nearby. He scanned the activity slowly, with apparent interest, as though seeing it for the first time.

93

One of the sawyers stopped cutting and turned off his saw. Boley stepped over to him. He was a short, dark man. His rounded cheeks reminded Boley of a chipmunk's. "Hi," Boley said, raising his voice over the sound of the other saw. "Got a nice tree there."

The dark man was expressionless. "Yeah, we do."

From the corner of his eye, Boley saw the other sawyer become aware of him. The second man stared at him, then glanced quickly at the man on the tractor. He turned back to his work and went on.

"You buyin' at a good price?" Boley asked the dark man.

"We give good value."

It wasn't easy to keep his voice raised and also seem casual, but Boley tried. "Who'd you buy it from?"

The dark man took time to answer. Finally, he jerked a thumb over his left shoulder. "Man up there. Name of Williams."

The other sawyer stopped his saw. He sat on his heels and listened.

"That's funny," said Boley, dropping his tone to normal. "That tree's not his to sell."

"It ain't?" the dark man said. Boley could detect no surprise.

The other sawyer got up. He was only a little shorter than Boley, but he was heavier. He wore horn-rimmed glasses and a Massey Ferguson outdoor cap. His gray work shirt was heavily sweat-stained. "Whose tree was it?" he asked. From his accent, Boley placed his origin farther south. He also noted the use of the past tense.

"Mine," he answered. He let the short answer hang.

The two sawyers exchanged glances.

"Well, I don't know about that," the taller man said.

"I do," Boley said.

"We cut down one walnut up closer to the house yest'day," the dark man said. "We was told we could cut this'n today."

Boley looked at them without replying.

"That was Williams'," the tall man said casually.

"You'd better look at something," Boley said, pointing behind them. "Take a good look at that fence."

The two men turned and looked back up the edge of Boley's grassy field to a place where a corner of the snake fence had been opened. The locust rails had been pulled apart and scattered to make room for the tractor to come through.

"I don't know about where you came from," Boley said, "but around here, fences are used to divide property."

The dark sawyer shook his head. "We was told to go ahead and make that hole. Said the fence was put to keep the cows from comin' in where they didn't belong."

Before anyone else could speak, a harsh voice cut in. "Doc. Jack. Get back to cuttin'. We'll be here till Christmas if we don't get on with it."

Boley looked up. The third man was still sitting on the tractor, but he had decided to take a hand.

"I don't think there'll be any more cuttin' here unless I say so," Boley said. "Maybe you haven't been listenin'."

The man on the tractor was built much the same as Boley. He had a mass of wiry, curly brown hair and a thin-lipped mouth. His right cheek was distorted by a wad of chewing tobacco. He was wearing a dirty white T-shirt, stained khaki slacks, and heavy work shoes. Boley guessed his age to be in the early thirties. He stared at Boley with contempt. "I been hearin'. None of it says that tree was yours."

"That won't take long to prove. We just go talk to Gib Williams."

"Talk all you want. We got work to do." He raised his voice. "C'mon, you two. Get the lead out."

"Okay, then," said Boley.

He walked back to the sycamore and picked up the carbine. He worked a shell into the chamber, but left the safety on. He turned around and took a position where the other three were in the narrowest field of fire.

One of the saws had started again. "All right!" Boley shouted. "Knock it off!"

He had their attention. The taller sawyer shut off his saw. "That makes a difference," he said.

The man in the tractor spat over the left side of the machine. "Like hell it does. The tree's down. He can't put it back up. Go ahead."

Boley looked at the dark man. "You know who the worst fool in the world is?"

His short opponent hesitated, then nodded. "Maybe."

"Who?"

"Anybody who'd give an argument to a man holdin' a gun."

Boley grinned. "You win the stuffed teddy bear." He looked across to the tractor. "Some people are smarter than others."

"Maybe," said the man on the other side of the run. "But you needn't think you'll shoot me and get paid for that tree. No way."

Boley looked at the dark man again. "Takes a lot of convincin'."

The sawyer shook his head. "No. He's already give money for it to them other folks."

Boley shifted his attention again. "That right?"

"That's it. She's paid for. You want money, you collect from them. We don't pay twice."

Boley lifted the gun and stabbed vaguely at each of them with the muzzle. "I think we'd better take a walk. Let's go see Gib Williams."

The tall sawyer laid down his tool. "Better do what the man says, Jack." He looked at the third man. "Hal, you done all the arrangin'. Let's go get this settled."

The man on the tractor shrugged. He reached across the run. Boley held the gun high above his head, gathered his muscles, and charged down the bank. He leaped over the water, landing easily.

Jack looked at him and the gun. He looked pointedly at Boley's feet. "Maybe some people ain't as smart as others around guns, either." Boley reddened, but said nothing. As they started up the field toward the fence, Jack spoke over his shoulder. "You won't see this Williams, anyway. He ain't there."

Feeling that he'd been led into something, Boley gave them no satisfaction. "Oh? Where is he?"

"Dunno."

"Is his wife there?"

"Yeah. She is. She's the one Hal paid."

"All right. We talk to Helen, then."

The dark man went on, "She's the one that told us to take down the fence and get that tree."

Boley listened, but said nothing. He had decided they were trying to confuse him. It could be sorted out when McKee arrived.

The group walked through the gap where the snake fence had been pulled apart to let the tractor through. Boley conceded to himself that the lumberjacks could have been misled, because most of the land on the other side was pasture. Gilbert Williams' house, an old, two-story white frame, stood about two hundred feet away. It had a modest yard on all sides, set off by a low chain-link fence. There was a small garden in the back, beside a boarded-over "dug" well.

There were two poplar trees in the front yard for shade. A heavier stand of trees ran along the fence line to Boley's right as they came into the property from the rear. A walnut tree larger than his own had stood there. It was now cut down, only the stump remaining.

The driveway into Williams' property was between the house and the trees. At the rear of it stood two large, flat-bed trucks. Walnut logs were piled on the bed of one truck higher than the cab, secured against shifting by heavy chains. The other truck was empty. Just waitin' for my tree, Boley thought.

He looked around, noting that the brush had been slashed and beaten down where the first tree had been cut up and skidded over the flat-bed. Then he observed that a third truck, a one-ton stakebody, sat in front of the others. For hauling the tractor, he decided, when he saw a portable ramp leaning from the tail of the truck to the ground.

He was herding the three lumberjacks toward the back door of the Williams house when the sheriff's sedan pulled into the driveway and stopped, blocking access to the main road. The motor had barely stopped when Warren McKee climbed out.

"Boley," he called, "your wife says you've got a disagreement!"

Boley grinned. "Three of 'em. Caught 'em poachin' a big old walnut of mine."

The man from the tractor leaned against the metal fence. "Not our fault. We didn't know it was on his property."

The sheriff had walked closer. He was a spare man, deeply tanned. "Is that a fact? There've been a lot of walnut trees disappearin' around here when folks weren't home. Somebody's been gettin' 'em. The beavers aren't that good."

He walked to the three trucks and studied them closely. "Can't read the license plates for mud." He picked up a small cut branch and used it to rub mud from each plate. "Color's not West Virginia. Out of state."

The tractor driver, Hal, was not perturbed. "Things get pretty messy when you're off the hard road. What's the difference where we're from?"

McKee walked up to him and stared. "What I've just seen doesn't have to mean a thing, mister. Somebody could be doin' it to you and Boley both. We'd better have a talk with Gib Williams."

"I'll see if he's in," Boley said. He went to the back door of the house and knocked. It was opened almost immediately by Helen Williams.

"Is Gib here?" he asked.

"No, he's not."

"Any idea when he'll be back?"

Uncertainty showed in Helen Williams' dark eyes. She was a slender brunette in her early forties. Her face had almost a classic symmetry and her appearance was almost compulsively neat. She had never had children and her figure was still good.

"I don't have any idea at all," she answered. "He went over to his cousin Rome's—he didn't say when he'd be back."

Boley turned around. "Warren, we got us a problem. Gib's not here. Helen says he went over to Rome Allen's and there's no way of knowin' when he'll show up back here."

"It's a long haul over to Rome's," McKee said thoughtfully.

Boley turned back to Helen. "I caught these three woodpeckers makin' logs out of my big walnut tree nearest your back line. They claim they thought it was one of yours."

She leaned against the doorframe. "I don't know why they'd think that."

"Said they were told it was."

"Gib must have told 'em, then—I don't know a thing about it."

"One of 'em said that you were the one, Helen." He turned and indicated the dark man, Jack. "He said you showed them where they could take down the fence and go through."

"He's lying, then."

Boley looked at her steadily. She returned his stare unperturbed. He turned and walked back to the sheriff, motioning him off to one side, out of earshot.

"You heard that?"

McKee nodded. "I did. Any ideas?"

"Why don't we go over what we know about Gib and Helen? Take him first."

"All right," said the sheriff. "He's a bit older than she is, but not as much as he looks. Was a miner up until about ten years ago when that slate fall caught him. Been livin' on disability ever since because of what happened to his back. But—" he looked hard at Boley "—there's some that claim he can do more than he lets on. You live next, here. What do you think?"

Boley rubbed his chin. "Hard to say. The two of 'em are either good at stretchin' that disability or he's pickin' up some on the side."

"Does he keep her on a tight leash? I'd think it'd be hard to accept Gib, him havin' to wear the back brace and shuffle around. His disposition must be crippled, too."

"I couldn't say," Boley admitted. "He's not as sour as you'd think. He gets out and around."

"Changin' the subject," McKee said, "I think these three over there are at least some of what we've been lookin' for. Three things have bothered me: who's rustlin' walnut trees, how they know where to find 'em, and how they know when nobody's home."

Boley looked around, observing the debris left after Williams' tree had been cut up. He saw the deep ruts left by the trucks and the heavily ribbed tracks left by the tractor. As a user of heavy equipment, such things were familiar to him. He didn't expect them to tell him the truth about his tree.

"Why don't you get on the CB?" he said to the sheriff. "Have somebody call Rome Allen and get Gib back here."

"Good idea," McKee said. He walked toward his car.

Boley went back to the house.

"Helen," he said, "I understand you got a check for my walnut tree."

She looked at him in puzzlement. "They gave me a check this morning. I thought it's what they owed us for our tree."

Doc, the tall sawyer, spoke up. "We give you the money for your tree yesterday."

"To Gib, you mean."

"No, lady, to you."

Understanding smoothed her face. "Oh. I took it to give Gilbert."

Boley cut in firmly. "Helen, why don't you get both checks and bring 'em here."

She hesitated. He pressed the matter. "If there's two, one of 'em's bound to be mine."

She turned away from him and went into the house.

Boley addressed Hal, the tractor driver. "You wrote the checks. For how much?"

The other man made no answer. Finally he said, "What the hell, you'll see 'em, anyway. Three hundred for this one here. Two hundred for the one we just cut."

"Practically for free, both of 'em."

"You got big ideas, mister. It's what they're worth."

"I don't know what Helen'll do," Boley told him, "but I'm tearin' that two-hundred-dollar check up and you'll write me one for eight hundred. I just had all my walnuts assessed by Soil Conservation. Eight hundred's what that tree's worth."

The door opened and Helen Williams reappeared with two slips of blue paper in her hand. "Here they are," she said.

Boley looked at them. They were for three hundred and two hundred dollars, dated a day apart. He took them to the tractor driver and showed them to him.

"Is this your signature?"

"It is."

"And this company, Tapiola Lumber, is the one you work for?"

"Yeah."

McKee returned from his car, to Boley's relief—he wanted to go into the house but he hadn't wanted to leave while McKee was busy.

The sheriff was annoyed. "We got through to Rome Allen's. Gib's not there. He hasn't been there. Rome doesn't know a thing about him." He drummed his fingers on the butt of his revolver. "Know what I think? Gib's lit out for someplace and left Helen holding the bag."

"Why don't you think about it a bit?" said Boley. "I want to make a phone call that might give us a little more."

He crossed again to Helen Williams. "Helen, I want to make a long-distance call. Might I use your phone? I'll pay the charges."

She considered it. "Come on in," she said finally. "The phone's in the kitchen."

The telephone hung on the wall of a spotless kitchen. The room had only one bowl in the sink, but it had a dishwasher and a general air of efficiency. Boley leaned against the counter and lifted the telephone off the hook. As he had guessed, the party line was in use. He listened, then cut into the conversation. "Mary Ballard, it that you? This is Arlan Boley. I need the line for about five minutes for a long distance. Could I have it? . . . Okay. Thanks."

He had been busy locating an area code in the directory while he talked. He hung up the phone briefly, removed it again, then dialed the area code he needed, followed by the directory-assistance number.

The operator came on. "Directory Assistance. What city?"

He told her and she asked him for the customer.

"Citizens National Bank."

After a pause she read him the number, he thanked her, broke the connection, and dialed again.

A woman's voice with a pronounced regional southern accent answered. "Citizens National Bank."

"Bookkeeping Department, please."

In a few seconds, an older woman's voice with a similar accent answered. "Bookkeeping."

"Yes," said Boley. "My name's Boley. I'm calling from West Virginia. A Mrs. Gilbert Williams has endorsed a check for two hundred dollars over to me. It was made to her by Tapiola Lumber Company. It's signed by a Harold Lanham. I have two questions: is there enough money to cover the check, and has this Lanham the authority to sign it?"

One moment, sir."

In a surprisingly short time she was back. "Mr. Boley? The answer to both of your questions is yes."

"All right, thank you. Oh—one more question. This Lanham gave Mrs. Williams herself a check for three hundred dollars. She wants to know if her check and mine are both covered."

"Yes, they are." A note of exasperation came into the bookkeeper's voice. "Mrs. Williams should surely know that by now.

The company has never defaulted on any of its checks to her before, as often as she's asked us about them."

"I guess she doesn't like to take anything for granted," Boley said. "Thank you ma'am."

He was whistling between his teeth as he walked to the back door. Helen Williams was sitting on the top back step. He sat down beside her.

"I talked to the lumber company's bank," he said, looking slowly around the yard.

She turned and looked at him. "What about?"

"The two checks you let me have."

"I don't understand."

"Just wanted to know if they're good and if that Hal over there is allowed to sign. They're okay." He wasn't watching her face. He had always liked Helen, although he had always been wary of Gilbert.

"Well, of—" she began. "Oh, I see. I thought there'd be no question. Gilbert seemed to trust them."

"I wonder why. Because these guys show up with three big trucks and some equipment? Gib never seemed that ready to take anything at face value."

As he talked, he was cataloging: trumpet vine on the side of the house, lilies near the fence by the paved road, trilliums (he remembered) growing near the snake fence separating his land and theirs. None of these had grown on the Williams property until the last two years.

He looked up and called the sheriff. "Warren, when did somebody start sneakin' trees out of this county?"

McKee, leaning against the trunk of the sedan, considered the question. "Year before last, I'm pretty sure."

"Then I think I can answer how they knew where to find trees and when to get 'em. And these three you have here are at least part of the outfit."

"Well, sure, you caught 'em at it."

Boley nodded. "Yeah, but they claim not to know it was my tree. They put it on Helen, here. But she says they're lyin'. —Only they're not."

He turned to her. "Helen, you're always out in the woods. You're out locatin' walnut trees, isn't that right?"

She made no reply.

"When you bring back somethin' like that trumpet vine, you've really been fixin' it in your head where there's a walnut tree, haven't you? The plant you bring back is just a cover-up. It hasn't any more meaning than an excuse to be out in the woods. When you know where the tree is, you pass the word to somebody like this Lanham, telling him just where to find it. After they get that tree, he sends you a check, doesn't he? It's been goin' on for about two years. That's how long trees have been disappearin'."

The look she gave him was pure innocence, overlaying outraged indignation.

"All this time we've been neighbors, Arly Boley, and now you say a thing like that about me! There's no more truth in you than there is in those three there."

He was not disturbed. "That bank I called must be liars too, then. Said you've had more than one check from this Lanham here."

"They must mean Gilbert. I never did, until now."

Boley looked around casually. "Where is Gib, anyway?"

"I already told you."

"He's not there, Helen. They haven't even seen him," the sheriff said.

Boley looked at the tractor driver. "Lanham, you got any ideas of Williams' whereabouts?"

The driver opened his mouth, reached in with two fingers, pulled out his wad of tobacco, and tossed it aside. "No. Why should I?"

"You've done business with him," the sheriff said. "You're on his place."

"That don't make me his nurse," Lanham answered.

Boley walked over to the sheriff and took his arm. They walked several yards away from the others, where they could talk in low tones without being heard.

"Warren," said Boley, "I have an uncomfortable feelin' about Gib."

"I think he's in this up to his eyeballs," the sheriff answered, "but it doesn't make me uncomfortable."

"I think he's here somewhere."

"You might be right," the sheriff agreed. "But I can't do anything about it. I'd have to have a warrant, because I haven't heard one solid fact tyin' him to this."

103

"I don't think I'm gettin' through to you," Boley said. "I think it would take more than a warrant to find Gib."

The sheriff eyed him attentively. "Such as?"

Boley waved a hand at the beaten-down brush where the first walnut tree had been cut up, at the chips and scraps, at the ground churned by the tractor's belt. "It might take some hand labor or some of my equipment."

McKee stared at the disturbed earth, then he lifted his head and looked first at Helen Williams, then at Lanham. "You do think of things, don't you, Arly?" he said quietly. "How about you gettin' me a glass of water out of Helen's kitchen while I think this over."

Boley nodded and walked to Helen. "Sheriff wants a drink. You mind if I get him one?"

Her upper lip curled. "I'll get it. I don't want anybody in my house that talks to me like you do."

While she was inside, McKee took off his hat and ran his fingers through his hair. "You said trees have been cut around here for about two years, Arly. I guess that's about right."

"Close enough. Now, about Gib-"

The sheriff held up his hand. "Let's hold that a bit."

The door opened and Helen came out with a glass of water. McKee walked over and took it from her. He took a swallow. "Good water," he said, holding up the glass. "Don't see any iron in that. Not like what used to come out of that old dug well over there."

"They drilled pretty deep for this one," Helen said. "Close to two hundred feet."

"That makes a difference," the sheriff said, then stepped back to include them all in what he had to say. "Now, Helen, and you three chainsaw jockeys, listen to me. Boley here has got it into his head that maybe Gib Williams has met up with what they call foul play. If that is the case, and any of you knows about it and didn't have a hand in it, you'd better realize that it can be bad for you. Innocent or not, it can be bad for you. Think about it.

"Now, while you're thinkin', I'll run through what I suspect Arly has put together. He thinks that this business of ripping off trees has been puttin' money in Helen Williams' pocket and she's decided she no longer needs any part of Gib. Instead, she has a thing goin' with one of you three sunbelters and she's arranged to skip out of here along with this next load of logs. Only Gib has tumbled into it and confronts everybody. In the ruckus, he comes out the loser."

A flurry of protests began, but McKee ignored them.

"Boley thinks Gib is planted over there where you all cut up Gib's walnut. He figures that the ground's been buggered up so by your tractor that nobody'd ever suspect a body was under there. He wants to dig it up and see."

The tractor driver exploded. "If he thinks that, give him a teaspoon and let him dig up every inch of it!"

"All right!" the sheriff shouted. "I told you how it looks! Anybody have anythin' botherin' 'em they want to get off their chest—if what I've said's the truth?"

There was no answer.

"Well," McKee said to Boley, "You might take that to mean that things ain't the way you figured. Of course, it's a little early for somebody to come out and try to save his own skin."

"Facts speak for themselves," Lanham growled.

The sheriff still addressed Boley. "Trees started disappearin' about two years ago. That's about the same time Williams got his drilled well and its pump. He was able to fill in that dug well and cover it. That tell you something?"

"Lumber-company money," Boley answered.

"Money that was bein' paid to Williams' *wife*. Does that tell you anythin'—knowin' Gib?"

"She cashed the checks somewhere else, or set up a bank account in her name somewhere else. A front for Gib."

"When you were inside on the phone, did you notice any other things that you might not expect?"

Boley thought.

"A dishwasher. A clothes dryer."

McKee nodded. "And, while Gib benefits, who'd you say those were bought for?"

"Helen."

"And I'll bet there's more things like that around this house if we'd look. What that says to me, Boley, is one word: partnership."

"Partners have fallen out—even killed each other."

"They have. But if they knocked off Gib Williams and lit out, their operation in these parts would be done. It is, anyway, but that's an accident."

Boley had been pyramiding the evidence ever since McKee had started, using the drilling of the well as a base. He had been mentally piling it on the removable cover of the old well. He moved away from the sheriff and headed for the garden.

McKee's voice trailed him. "Go ahead, Arly. You'll be savin' me the trouble. Go look in the old well and tell me what you find."

Damn, Boley thought, not so smart after all.

The well cover was neatly made and covered with aluminum sheeting. It fit snugly over the top of the old well.

Boley lifted the cover and set it on the ground. He looked into the well.

"Well, I'll be dipped," he said.

The well was filled in with dirt and rubble, but only to within five feet of the top. An old stool stood on the top of the fill. On it sat a man with uncombed brown hair, wire-rimmed glasses, and nondescript clothes that bulged oddly above the waist. The bulge was produced by a back brace.

"Gib Williams!" Boley said. "Hello, Gib."

"I got nothin' to say to you," the man in the well grumbled.

"I have plenty to say to you," Boley snapped. "For openers, you can have that wife of yours endorse that last check over to me. That's three hundred dollars. That, plus the one they tried to give me, will make five hundred dollars. The tree is worth another three hundred. I figure you're the one who ought to cough it up. You pointed them at that walnut in the first place."

The man in the well climbed painfully to his feet. "You'll play hell gettin' it from me, Boley," he said.

8

Come Down From the Hills
(1987)

This story is a real gem.

Arlan Boley eased his backhoe down the ramp from the
flatbed, cut the motor, and climbed off. It was early in the
morning in the dry season of late August, but the dew was
just starting to rise. Boley knew that the oppressiveness of the air
would pass, but he hated it all the same.

"You want me to do the first one along about here?" he asked. He
brushed at his crinkly blond hair where a strand of cobweb from an
overhanging branch had caught.

Sewell McCutcheon, who was hiring Boley's services for the
morning, walked to the edge of the creek and took a look. He picked
up a dead sycamore branch and laid it perpendicular to the stream.
"One end about here." He walked downstream about fifteen feet and
repeated the act with another branch. "Other end here."

Boley glanced across the small creek and, without looking at
McCutcheon, asked, "How far out?"

The older man grinned, the ends of his heavy brown moustache
lifting. "We do have to be careful about that." He reached into a
pocket of his blue-and-white coveralls and took out a twenty-five foot
reel of surveyor's tape. He laid it on the ground, stooped over to
remove heavy shoes and socks, and rolled the coveralls to his knees.

He unreeled about a foot of tape and handed the end to Boley.
"Stand right at the edge and hold that," he said, picking up a
pointed stake about five feet long.

While Boley held the tape's end, McCutcheon stepped down the
low bank and entered the creek. The dark brown hair on his sinewy

legs was plastered against the dead-white skin from the knees down. When he reached the other side, he turned around. "She look square to you?"

"A carpenter couldn't do better."

McCutcheon looked down. "Fourteen and a quarter feet. Midway's seven feet, one and a half inches. I don't know about you, Boley, but I hate fractions."

He started back, reeling up tape as he came. "Seven feet, three inches from her side. I'll just give her a little more than half, then she can't complain. Not that she won't."

He plunged the stake in upright at the spot. Then he waded ashore, went to the other boundary, and repeated the performance.

"That's the first one. When you finish," he told Boley, "come down just opposite the house and we'll mark off the second one."

"How deep?" Boley asked.

"Take about two feet off the bottom," McCutcheon said. "Water's low now. When she comes back up, it'll make a good pool there. Trout ought to be happy with it."

"I'll be gettin' to 'er, then," Boley said, going back to his machine. He was already eyeing the spot where he would begin to take the first bite with the scoop. He began to work within minutes. He had moved enough dirt with his backhoe in the past to know what he was doing, even with the added presence of the water that soaked the muck. There was also an abundance of gravel in the piles he was depositing along the bank.

When he judged that he had finished the hole, he lifted the scoop until it was roughly level with the seat. The he swung the machine around and ran it down the creek toward his next worksheet.

The pebble-bottomed stream, one typical of West Virginia, was known as Squirrel Creek. It divided two farms of nearly flat land at an altitude of between one and two thousand feet. On the eastern side was McCutcheon's well kept eighty acres. McCutcheon, a recent widower, planned well and worked hard, aided by his son and daughter-in-law. Both sides of the stream were lined with trees whose root systems kept the banks from crumbling and silting the creek bed. This was deliberate on McCutcheon's part, happenstance on his neighbor's.

When Boley came down opposite McCutcheon's white frame two-story, he cut the motor and walked over to where the farmer was sitting on the steps of his porch. The house was on a small rise, with a high foundation that would protect it in the event of an unusually heavy flash flood. Because of this, Boley had to look up a few inches to talk with McCutcheon.

"See anything of her?" he asked.

"Not yet," the farmer answered.

"Maybe this ain't gonna bother her."

McCutcheon rubbed his moustache. "*Everything* about this stream bothers that woman, Arly. One of the biggest trout I ever hooked in there was givin' me one helluva fight one day. I was tryin' to play him over to this side, but I hadn't yet managed it. Then, all of a sudden, outa nowhere came the old woman, screechin' her head off. 'What d'you mean, ketchin' *my* fish?' she squawks. And with that she wades right out into the water, grabs the line with both hands, and flops that trout out on the ground at her side of the creek. Whips out a knife I'da never guessed she had and cuts the line. Then off to the house with my catch."

"Well," said Boley, "it was on her half of the creek, wasn't it? Property line down the middle? That why you've been measurin'?"

"Oh, sure," the farmer replied. "I recognize that. But that's not the way she looks at it. Had the fish been over here, she'd still have done it."

"I'd better get at it while it's quiet," Boley said, mentally thankful for his own Geneva's reasonableness.

As he walked to his machine, he heard McCutcheon say, "She must be away somewhere."

Later, Boley finished piling the last of the scooped silt and rocks on the bank of the stream. McCutcheon would later sort out the rocks and use the silt in his garden.

Paid for his work, Boley put the backhoe on the flatbed and fastened it securely. He turned around to head out, when he glanced over the creek toward the brown-painted cottage on the other side. A battered red half-ton pickup was just pulling up to the front of the house, barely visible through the tangle of bushes between stream and house.

A rangy older woman with dyed jet-black hair jumped from the truck and began to force her way toward the creek.

"Arlan Boley!" she screamed. A crow's voice contained more music. "What're you doin' over there."

Boley put the truck in gear and pushed down the accelerator. He had no wish to talk to Alice Roberts. Leave that to McCutcheon.

Six days later, Boley and his family went into town. While Geneva and the two children were making some minor purchases for the opening of school, Boley went to the courthouse to the sheriff's office.

He had just finished paying his first-half taxes and was pocketing the receipt when he was tapped on the shoulder.

"Guess I'll have to wait 'til spring now before I can get you for non-payment," a voice said.

Boley recognized the voice of his old friend, the sheriff. "Hi, McKee," he said, turning. "You want that place of mine so bad, make me an offer. I might surprise you."

"No, thanks," McKee replied. "More'n I could handle." He nodded toward the clerk's window. "You payin' with what you got from Sewell McCutcheon?"

"Some. It took a little extra." He looked at McKee with curiosity. "What's the big deal? All I did was scoop him two holes in the creek for trout to loll around in from now on."

"You did more than that, Boley. You might have provided him with a fortune. Or part of one."

Boley nudged McKee's shoulder with his fist, feeling the hardness still existing in McKee's spare frame. "Don't tell me he panned that much and found gold."

"You're not far off the mark."

Boley's eyes widened. He noticed a tiny lift at the ends of McKee's lips and a small deepening of the lines in the sheriff's tanned face.

"Well, get to it and tell me," he said.

"Maybe you heard and maybe you didn't," McKee said, "but a state geologist's been usin' a vacant office here in the courthouse tryin' to see if there's a coal seam worth explorin' by that company that owns some of the land. Anyway, today McCutcheon walked in lookin' for him. Said he needed an opinion on an object in his pocket."

"And he got his interview?"

McKee nodded. "It seems he pulled out a fair-sized rock. First glance, could have been quartz or calcite. Kinda dull—but somehow different. This state fellow thought at first it was another pebble, then he took a good look and found it wasn't."

"So what *did* he find it was?"

"A diamond."

Boley had been half anticipating the answer, but he had tried to reject it. His jaw dropped. "No kidding!"

"No kidding."

"McCutcheon's probably turning every rock out of that stream."

The sheriff dipped his chin. "I'll bet. Geologist said it's what they call an alluvial diamond, and the probability of findin' more is very small. Said it was formed millions of years ago when these mountains were as high as the Himalayas or higher. Somewhere in all that time, water eroded away whatever surrounded this one, and it might have even washed down here from someplace else. Come down from the hills, you might say."

An odd feeling crossed Boley's mind. Several times in the past, fragments of an old ersatz folk song had made themselves recognizable at the fringe of an unpleasant situation. "Just come down from the hills" was in one of the verses.

"What's the matter," McKee asked.

"Nothing. How big is this rock? What's it worth?"

"A little bigger than the last joint of my thumb, not as big as the whole thumb. Worth? The man told McCutcheon there's no way of knowin' until it's cut. And it might be flawed."

Boley stared into the distance. "I'd better get on home and start seein' what's in the bottom of that run that goes through my property. Everybody in the county'll be doin' the same thing wherever there's water." He paused. "Or does anybody else know?"

"Only McCutcheon, the geologist, and the two of us," McKee said. "There's sort of an agreement to keep our mouths shut. You never

111

know who would get drawn in here, if the word got out. Don't you even tell Geneva."

"What's McCutcheon done with the thing?"

"I suggested that he should put it in a safety-deposit box."

"It's what I'd do. I hope he has," Boley said.

The quirk around McKee's mouth had gone. "You know Alice Roberts?"

"Miner's widow across the creek from McCutcheon?"

"That's the one."

"I've seen her. She evidently knows who I am. I don't think I want to know her."

"Not good company," McKee said. "I wonder if she's heard about this. Do me a favor, would you? Drop by McCutcheon's place before long. You have a good excuse—checkin' up on the job you did. See what you can find out, but don't let on you know."

Boley gave him a thoughtful look. "Seems to me you know a lot already."

The following evening, Boley left home on the pretext that he wanted to look at some land where he might be asked to make a ditch for a farmer who wanted to lay plastic pipe from his well pump to a new hog house. Instead, Boley went to McCutcheon's.

He found the farmer sitting alone on his porch. The sun had not quite set. His son and daughter-in-law had gone into town.

"Hello, Sewell," Boley said, walking to the foot of the steps. "Water cleared yet where I dug 'er out?"

"If it ain't by now, it never will," McCutcheon said. "Come up."

Boley went up and sat in a cane-bottomed rocker like the farmer's. "Ever since I dug it out, I've been wonderin' why you did that," he said. "After all, you have a pretty good farm pond at the back. Fed by three springs, stocked with bass and blue gills, isn't it?"

McCutcheon smiled. "That's right. Bass and blue gills. But no trout. Running water's for trout. I like variety."

"You put all that gunk on your garden yet?"

"Oh, yeah. We just took a bunch of rakes and dragged all the rocks and pebbles out, let the muck dry some, then shoveled 'er into a small wagon, towed 'er to the garden, and that was it."

Boley looked at the gravel drive leading from the house to the main road. "I guess you can bust up the rocks and fill in some potholes when you get more."

McCutcheon seemed uninterested. "I suppose. I have a small rock pile out there. Don't know what I'll do with 'em."

Boley decided that the other man was keeping his secret. He wondered if the son and daughter-in-law knew. And if they could keep quiet. To change the subject he said, "Anybody ever want to buy your land, Sewell?"

The farmer nodded. "Every now and then some developer comes by. Thing is, this isn't close to the lake and the recreation area, and they don't want to offer much."

"It's a good bit for the three of you to handle."

"Maybe it will be later," McCutcheon agreed. "That's when I'll think again."

Boley jerked his head toward the Roberts' property. "I'd think they'd get that over there for the price they want."

"Funny old gal," McCutcheon said. "Her husband was a miner, died of black lung. No children. He never had time to work the property. Thirty-nine acres, came down from his old man. Alice like to wore herself out years ago, tryin' to make somethin' of it, then gave up. Except she thinks the place is worth like the middle of New York City—*and* that the creek belongs to her, clear to where it touches my land. You understand any better?"

"I see the picture," Boley answered, "but I don't understand the last part."

"Neither do I," McCutcheon admitted. "How about a cold beer?"

"Fine," Boley said.

McCutcheon went into the house to get it. He had been gone for several minutes when Boley heard footsteps coming around the house from the rear. He turned and saw Alice Roberts at the foot of the steps. She began to talk in a loud voice. "So. Both of you'll be here together—the two of you who took that diamond out've my crick. And how many more we haven't heard about yet."

Boley stood up. "What diamond? I don't know what you're talkin' about, Mrs. Roberts."

She continued up the steps. Boley guessed her to be in her early sixties, but her vigor was of her forties.

"Don't you lie to me, mister!" she growled, sitting in the chair he had just vacated. "You know all about it. I saw you here the day it came out of the water. What cut is he giving you?"

Boley leaned against a porch post. "I'm not gettin' any cut of any kind, lady. I've been paid for diggin' some dirt and rocks out of the water for McCutcheon. I don't see where any diamond comes into it."

McCutcheon reappeared at the door, carrying two cans of cold beer. He gave one to Boley. "Alice," he said, "I didn't know you were here. Could I get you some cola?"

"The only thing you can get me is the diamond you stole from my crick."

McCutcheon glanced quickly at Boley, who continued to look puzzled. "There's some mistake, Alice. I never took anything of yours. Did you lose a diamond in the water?"

"No, I did not lose *anything* in the water," she snapped. "You found out a big diamond was in my crick and your crony fished it out. I want it."

"I made two fishin' holes in my side of the water," McCutcheon said. "I got some rich dirt for my garden and a heap of rocks. You can have every rock in that pile, if you like."

She got to her feet. "I'll take you up on that. There might be more diamonds in there that you missed. I'll go get the pickup." She went down the steps at a speed that awed Boley.

He turned to McCutcheon. "What was that all about?"

The farmer began to talk in a low tone. "Water's down more and she can get across on steppin' stones, so she'll be back in a hurry." He proceeded to tell Boley the same story McKee had. Boley did not admit to its familiarity. Instead, he said, "How did she find out?"

"Beats me," McCutcheon answered. "But if you don't want a bad case of heartburn, you'd better leave right now. I'm used to it. It won't bother me."

"The diamond—"

"Is in the bank."

Boley was unable to tell McKee about this for several days. He had necessary work at home, getting in apples from his small orchard. He was also getting in field corn for a very sick neighbor.

After a little more than a week, he went to the courthouse. On the walk outside he was stopped by a friend. Harry Comstock, a quiet, balding man with thick glasses, drew maps for Border States, Inc. Border States harvested timber and was as efficient as the businesses that got everything from slaughtered pigs except the squeal. At times the company leased land for its operations; at others, it drew on its own land. Some of their holding abutted the land owned by McCutcheon and Alice Roberts.

"Boley!" Comstock said. "Got a minute?"

"One or two."

"Won't keep you." Comstock squinted in the sun. "Didn't you do some work on Squirrel Creek for Sewell McCutcheon right recently?"

"Yeah. Scooped out a couple of fishin' holes for him," Boley said, hoping no more information was asked for.

"Well, you must have started something. Or maybe it's just coincidence. You know what happened yesterday? He came to the office and made a deal to buy fifty more acres from us to add to his land. All rights."

"Whereabouts?"

"Beginning at the creek and going east five acres, then back upstream."

"I'll bet it costs him," Boley said.

"Comstock shook his head. "Not too much. Stuff in there's mostly scrub. Company's been wishing this sort of thing might happen."

Boley began to speak, but Comstock went on. "What makes it *real* interesting is that wild old Alice Roberts came barging in about an hour later and bought twenty acres on the opposite side of the creek. Only hers is two acres west, the rest upstream. Again, all rights. What's goin' on?"

Boley looked blank. "Beats me. Did Alice Roberts pay for hers now?"

"In cash."

Boley studied the pavement. "That's the funny part, Harry. I can't give you any answers, most of all about that."

He went into the courthouse and sought McKee. The sheriff was in.

After McKee had closed his office door, Boley ran through all that had happened, including the recent land purchases.

"I figure what they're doin' is buyin' more land along that stream so they can hunt for more diamonds without Border States gettin' into it," he finished.

McKee's head was cocked to one side. "What it really sounds like is that Alice intended to go up there and buy land on both sides of the water and cut Sewell off. He beat her to enough of it that she didn't want to push, or she would have stirred up Border States."

"Oh, well," said Boley. "It's none of our business."

"I hope you're right," said McKee, his voice dry and astringent. "I wish you'd keep your eyes and ears open, anyway. When there's somethin' in dispute that might be valuable, I always feel that I might be on the hot seat. Somebody'll be in this jail out of this, is my guess."

The following morning, Boley had left home in his four-wheel-drive jeep to help an acquaintance assess the feasibility of gathering bittersweet from a difficult location in the man's woods. With autumn coming, the colorful plant was easily salable for decorations to tourists passing through town.

He had completed the trip and was starting home after returning the man to his house. Looking down the long corridor of trees before him he couldn't see the highway. The lane swung to the right for a few hundred feet before meeting the paved road. He slowed and made the curve, then stopped abruptly. The lane was blocked by a familiar battered red pickup. Standing beside it was Alice Roberts.

He climbed from the jeep. "Mrs. Roberts. What do you want?"

The woman was expressionless. "Mornin' Boley. I want you to get back in your jeep and follow me."

Boley considered several replies. He answered evenly, "I'm afraid I can't do that. If you have work for me, there are some people ahead of you."

"I never said anything about that," she rasped. "How do you think I found where you were?"

"I suppose you called, and my wife told you."

"I didn't call, but she told me." She moved aside and opened the truck door.

Boley stared. Inside, very pale and very straight, sat Geneva.

There was a movement beside him and Boley's eyes dropped. Alice Roberts was holding a double-barrel shotgun in her hands.

"Woman," he said, "shotgun or no shotgun, if you've hurt Geneva, I'll stomp you to bits."

"Don't get excited, Boley," she replied. "Nobody's hurt—yet. Now, you get behind that wheel and follow me."

Forcing himself to be calm, Boley did as he was told. He watched Alice Roberts climb into the truck and prop the gun between the door and her left side. Then she started, turned, and drove out.

Boley followed, driving mechanically. He paid little attention to direction or time. Rage threatened to take control, but he refused to let it. He might need all of his wits.

He wasn't entirely surprised when he saw that they had reached McCutcheon's farm and were pulling into the drive leading to the front.

The truck stopped directly before the steps to the front porch. With her surprising agility, Alice Roberts came down from the driver's seat carrying the shotgun, darted around the front of the pickup, and opened the other door to urge Geneva out.

Boley pulled up behind the truck and got out. He walked over to his wife and put his arm around her quivering shoulders.

"Arly. What's this all about?" she whispered.

"I'm not sure I know," he murmured.

"Quit talkin'!" snapped the woman. "Just behave yourselves and nobody'll get hurt. Now get up there."

She followed them up to the porch and banged on the screen door. "McCutcheon! You in there? Come out!"

There was no answer. She repeated her demands.

Finally a voice came faintly through the house. "Come on around to the west side."

Boley took Geneva's arms and urged her down from the porch, Alice Roberts' footsteps impatient behind them. They went around the house to the right. Waiting for them, leaning against a beech tree, was Sewell McCutcheon.

The farmer's eyes rounded with surprise. "This is more than I expected," he said. "Why the gun, Alice?"

"To convince you I mean business. If I pointed it at *you*, you might think I was foolin'. I hear these folks got two kids, so you'll think a bit more about it. There's shells in both these chambers."

"What do you want, Alice?"

"I want the diamond. I want to look at it. I want to hold it."

"We'd have to go to the bank. It's in a safety-deposit box."

Alice lifted the gun. "You're a liar, Sewell McCutcheon. How do I know? I went to the bank yesterday and asked to rent a box the same size as yours. And what did the girl say? 'We don't have a box rented to Mr. McCutcheon.' Now you get that diamond out here."

McCutcheon looked from one to another of the three. "All right. You go sit on my porch. I have to go in the house. You can't ask me to give my hidin' place away to you."

"I could, but I won't," Alice answered. "And don't you try to call anybody or throw down on me with your own gun."

McCutcheon's only answer was a nod. He went rapidly up to the side door and into the house. Boley led Geneva up to a swing that hung near the front end of the porch and sat down on it with her.

Alice followed. "If you're thinking about those other two who live here, fergit it. They went off down to Montgomery earlier." She leaned against a stack of firewood McCutcheon had put up to season.

After what seemed to Boley to be an interminable time, the farmer reappeared. He carried a cylindrical plastic medicine container about two inches long and an inch in diameter.

"We'd best go down into the sun, he said. "You can get a better idea."

He led the way down into the yard toward the stream, out of the shade of the trees surrounding the house. He stopped, opened the container, and shook something into his right palm. He offered it to Alice.

"Here it is."

She plucked it from his hand and peered at it.

"Why, it looks just like a dirty quartz pebble or some of them other rocks," she muttered. "This is a diamond? An uncut one?"

"It is. It's real," McCutcheon answered. "I can prove it, too."

She stared at it, letting the sun shine on it. "Well, some ways you look at it— A real honest-to-God diamond, pulled outa my crick! McCutcheon, all my life I've wanted one nice thing to call my own."

The farmer pulled at his moustache. "Well, Alice, I'm sorry for you, but it came off my property. It came outa my side."

She raised her eyes to his. "How about you get it cut? Cut in two parts. Let me have half."

McCutcheon reached over and removed the stone from her hand. "Alice, you've been too much trouble to me over the years. Threatenin' these people with a shotgun is just too much."

"Shotgun!" she yelled. "I'll give you shotgun!"

She raised the gun swiftly, reversing it, and grasping the barrels with both hands, she clubbed McCutcheon across the back of the head. He fell to the ground, bleeding.

Stooping, she pried his fingers open and took the stone from them. "I'm not gonna let you take it!" she cried, running to the creek. When she reached the bank, she drew back her arm and threw the diamond as hard as she could into the woods upstream from her house. "Now," she yelled, "It's where it belongs! I might be forever findin' it, but you ain't gonna get it!"

Boley retrieved the gun where she had dropped it. "Go inside and call the sheriff," he told Geneva. "Say we need paramedics for Sewell."

When the sheriff's car and the ambulance came, McCutcheon was unconscious. Alice Roberts sat by the creek, ignoring everything until they took her to the car in handcuffs.

Boley explained the morning's events to McKee, who had come with a deputy. The sheriff heard him out. "Sounds like we've got her for kidnapping and assault, at least."

Alice Roberts, in the police car, heard them. "Kidnapping?" she said. "They's only old empty shells in that gun."

McKee leaned in the window. "But they didn't know that, Alice."

To Boley, he said, "And don't you back off on the charge."

"I won't," Boley promised. "I'm just glad it's over."

McKee gave him an odd look. "If you think that, you've got another think comin'. Let's do today's paperwork, then come see me late tomorrow afternoon."

When Boley arrived at his office late the next day, the sheriff closed the door and waved him to a seat. "Things are pretty much as I figured," he said.

"How's McCutcheon?" Boley asked. "And what about Alice?"

"Sewell's not too bad." McKee sat down. "He's gettin' a good goin' over for concussion, but that's about it. Alice is still locked up, which is where I want her." He leaned across the desk. "How's it feel to be a cat's paw?"

Boley was startled. "There's some kind o' set-up in this?"

McKee sat back. "I'll run it past you. Some of this I can't prove and we'll just have to wait and see what happens. Anyway, you know same as I do that one of this county's big hopes is to attract people with money to buy up some of this land. Build themselves a place where they can come weekends or for the summer. The trouble is, we have only one good-sized lake and one nice recreation area. There are lots of other good places, but developers want to pick 'em up for peanuts.

"Alice Roberts, poor soul, has a place that looks like the devil's backyard. But it wouldn't take a lot to make it presentable, and it lays well. Sewell's place looks good. Given the right price, he'd quit and retire."

"I'm beginning to get an idea," Boley said. "McCutcheon decided to start a diamond rush, is that it? Where'd he get the stone?"

"You dug it out for him," McKee replied. "Until then, everything was just what it seemed. You dug two fishin' holes. Then he did find the diamond, and all that hush-hush commenced."

"I'd say he called Alice over and had a talk. Showed her how they could put on an act, building things up to her sluggin' him, so his discovery would really hit the papers."

Boley said, "So they bought that land from Border States hoping to resell and clean up. But where did Alice get the money?"

"Maybe she had some put back. But I'd bet Sewell made her a loan."

"The diamond. Is it real?"

McKee grinned. "It's real. The state man wouldn't lie about that."

"You want me to press the kidnap charge."

"I do. And I've had the hospital keep McCutcheon sedated, partly to keep him from dropping the assault charge. You hang on until I suggest you drop it."

Boley was still puzzled. "What about the diamond? She threw it into the woods. I saw her."

"You saw her throw something into the woods. Remember I said you might mistake it for dirty quartz or calcite? That's probably what Sewell let her throw away." McKee's amusement grew. "Another reason for keepin' her locked up—I want McCutcheon to have time to go over there and 'find' that stone again." He added a post script. "Or maybe they'll leave it as an inducement for whoever buys Alice's place."

9

Not Alone In Her Grave
(1988)

The original ending of this story has been included here for the first time.

Arlan Boley's telephone rang a few minutes after seven on a morning in late April.

"Hello? Boley?" a man's sharp voice asked. "Hope I didn't wake you up." His tone implied that he was confident that he had not.

"No," Boley answered. He recognized the voice, so he said, "But I don't want this coffee to get cold."

"Oh," the man paused. "This is Jim Grant. You tied up today?"

"Not yet. I am tomorrow, though. What's on your mind?"

"I got a couple of dead cows I need buried. Suppose you could come over here and dig me a couple of holes with whatever machine it takes? Backhoe? You know best."

Boley ran a hand through his crinkled blond hair and frowned. "What'd they die of?"

"Shot."

Boley's eyes widened. "Both of 'em?"

"Both of 'em."

"Who did it?"

"Talk about it when I see you. You comin'?"

Boley swallowed some coffee. "Soon as I finish eatin' and get the backhoe on my stakebed."

"I'll see you then." Grant hung up.

Geneva Boley's brown eyes were concerned. Their two children, Carl and Martha, were curious.

"Trouble?" she asked.

"Not for me." Boley glanced at the children. "Go on, finish your breakfast. School's not been canceled." He addressed all three. "Listen to my call and you'd know what it's about." He lifted the receiver and was pleased to find that the party line was free. He dialed a familiar number and was even more pleased to find that the sheriff was still at home. "Hello, McKee," he said. "Arlan Boley. You got a minute?"

"Nobody's beat you to it," the sheriff's dry voice answered. "What's on your mind?"

"Jim Grant just called. Wants me to bury a couple of cows. He says they were shot. I thought you'd be interested."

"Could be. Did he say who or how come?"

"No. He said he'd tell me later."

McKee considered. "Well, no matter. I have a suspicion about it, but we'll see what you find out. I might drop by Grant's later. Give me some time to work first." As an afterthought, he said, "I hope there was nothin' wrong with those cows."

Boley finished his breakfast, loaded his equipment, and told his family good-bye. He had long since recognized that it was profitable to provide service with heavy equipment to those in his West Virginia county who couldn't afford to own the machinery themselves. His work hours were uncertain, but he tried to strike a balance between his own needs and the appeals he received.

As he drove west along the ridge where he lived, he passed alternate pasture and wooded areas. The leaves of the trees were just beginning to develop, but there were more than enough white dogwood blossoms and pink blooms from redbuds to relieve the drabness of the woods. In the yards of the cottages, the forsythia were luxuriant in their yellow this year.

Boley kept thinking of the job: bury two cows. Two cows in one grave. Much to his chagrin, a line from an old pseudo-folksong went through his mind. *She's not alone in her grave tonight*—It was absurd to suppose that remembering the song meant trouble again. Lines from folksongs had before, but this was too trivial.

He thought about Grant. Not a rich man, but doing better than many. Most of his income came from Black Angus beef cattle. All of his 130 acres was spread across a broader ridge that intersected this one, and the greater part was in meadow and pasture. Several acres were devoted to tobacco. Close to the white seven-room, two-story house was an extensive garden.

Boley drove four miles further, turned right on another black-top road, then right again after a half a mile. He kept going until Grant's place came up on his left. He entered it on a gravel drive, continuing past the house to the barn, where Grant, no doubt hearing the stakebed, stood waiting.

The farmer was a big man in his early fifties, dressed in blue-and-white coveralls, a yellow tractor cap, and thick workshoes. His heavy face was grim. Boley pulled up in front of him and cut the motor. "Mornin', Jim. Whereabouts should I park?"

Grant stepped closer and looked up at him with grey eyes under bushy brows. Salt-and-pepper stubble on his long jaw suggested he had yet to shave this day. "Hello, Boley," he said. "Pull over any-place and unload. It's off that way about a quarter mile." He pointed east along the ridge where grazing land lay. "Just cut in here to the fence and follow along back of the orchard. While you're gettin' ready, I'll get on over and meet you there."

Boley slid from the truck. "Right—" then, as Grant was turning away "—a question came to mind on the way over. How come me? Don't you have a tractor?"

Grant stopped and turned. "I do. But it's got to go to the shop. Somethin's wrong with the power take-off. They're pickin' it up this afternoon."

Boley squinted. "Tough. Just when you're startin' to need it."

Grant turned away again. "It happens."

Boley opened the tailgate of the truck and set his ramp. He fired up the backhoe and ran it off to the ground.

To follow Grant's instructions, he had to avoid a three-quarter ton red pickup standing beside the barn. He idly supposed that either the dew had been heavy or Grant had been washing it. It was noticeably damp, and several occasional drops of water fell from the tailgate to the ground.

After skirting the edge of a modest orchard of apple and pear trees, he came to a wire fence. He followed this east for nearly two hundred yards until he came to Grant. Just past the farmer he could see the carcasses of the two Black Angus cows. He came close, stopped the motor, and climbed to the ground. "That's them, I take it."

Grant turned his head to the left. "That's them."

Boley walked over and looked. The closer cow looked as though she had gone to her knees before collapsing. The other had fallen with legs outstretched—her eyes were still open and bulging.

"Shot, you said," Boley remarked.

"That's right. Both of 'em through the forehead."

Boley looked. A clean hole just above the eyes and in the center in both cases. "What with, do you figure?" he asked.

"Deer rifle."

Boley nodded. "Could be. *You* sound convinced."

The corner's of Grant's thin mouth turned down. "That's what he'd use."

Boley made eye contact. The grey of Grant's eyes was that of heavy smoke.

"You know who?" Boley asked.

Grant gave a curt nod. "Lon Willis."

The name was no surprise to Boley. Willis owned a small place just to the east of Grant's. He was a widower, without children.

"He still complain at you?" Boley asked.

"Most of the time. It's not my fault he has more'n he can handle." Grant gestured with a big hand. "Come over here."

Boley followed him for several feet along the fence. He needed no prodding to see what Grant had in mind.

The wires of the fence had been pulled loose from two posts and had been bent forcibly until they nearly touched the ground. The dead cows, now on the wrong side, had crossed over here from the pasture, judging by hoofprints in the soft earth.

Boley gave Grant a questioning look. "Willis?"

Grant shook his head. "No. That one." He pointed to the cow with her eyes open. "She was a rogue, no two ways about it. This is what she liked to do best. So she'd coax some of the rest to come along."

Boley said, "Then they'd go over on Willis?"

"Sometimes. The last time, he threatened to shoot any that did it. Kept his word, seems like."

Boley felt that he should get to work, but his curiosity got the better of him. "When did this happen?"

A vague look came over Grant's large features. "Last night sometime—I don't know when. I found 'em this mornin'."

Boley stared. "You didn't hear the shots? From a deer rifle?"

Grant seemed uncomfortable. "I was over on Flicker Ridge, fox-huntin'. Probably happened then."

Boley grinned. He saw a vision of Grant and others sitting around a campfire, drinking and listening to their dogs run a fox. In the background, he imagined Geneva's caustic comments to him about the triviality of such a pastime.

Sobering quickly, he asked, "What about Millie? She didn't hear?"

Grant shook his head. "She wasn't at home. She went to see her sister up near Sutton—left yesterday early."

"Has Willis admitted it?"

"Not yet. I was over there, but I couldn't rouse him. He must be hidin' out, can't face me yet."

Boley hated to push the older man, but he had to say it. "You'll take him to court if he doesn't settle with you?"

Grant withdrew within himself slightly. "We'll see. Maybe. I got my own thoughts about Mr. Willis."

Boley's seriousness increased. "You ought at least to report it to Warren McKee."

Grant opened his mouth, but Boley went on: "Look, nobody dragged these cows here. See where the fence is broken down? See where they walked through, where the bodies are? They weren't headin' for Willis'—they were headin' your way."

Grant continued to look thoughtful.

Boley continued. "Willis probably saw it happenin' and hurried over. Shot 'em before they even decided which way to go. When you blamed him, was it just because of his threat? Or did you figure this the same as I just did?"

Grant rubbed his chin. "You're ahead of me, I must admit."

Boley slapped a fencepost. "Good. Now, if you get some law over here to back you up, you can nail Willis' hide to the outhouse wall. Make him pay."

Grant pulled himself out of a slouch. "I hate to disappoint you, Boley, but I don't want to do that. I don't want to fritter away my time in court. I got too much to do."

Boley was taken aback. "But you'll be losing money."

Grant nodded. "Yeah."

"Then, why—"

"The fence was broken down more'n once, remember?"

"Yeah."

Grant looked away. "How would I look in court? A cow out-smarted me? Not once, but several times? A cow smarter than me? A *cow!*"

Boley sighed. "It's your decision."

He looked down. On the ground was a heavy-duty staple gun, capable of bonding light wood or heavy fabric to heavier wood. A short, flat piece of steel was near it. He picked up the gun. "Is this how you fasten wire to your locust posts? Straddle the wire with one or more of these staples?"

Grant nodded. "Partly. I use regular staples and hammer 'em or more of these staples."

Boley put the gun down. "All right. That was a strong, smart cow. So where do you want me to dig?"

"Just about where they are."

Boley looked about. "Doesn't look to be near your well. Safe enough. What about Willis'?"

"Around the other side of his house. A good distance."

"Okay, then." Boley turned back to his machine, then stopped. "Tell me something, Jim. Was there anything wrong with those two cows?"

"Isn't shootin' enough—" Grant began. He stopped and his face went white. "You think it's faked? You think I might be coverin' up? Coverin' up anthrax or another serious problem?"

Boley eyed him steadily. "Just askin' a question we hadn't brought up."

Grant began to quiver. "Do you realize I'd never have called you if that was the case? I'd have just loaded 'em into my pickup—never mind how I'd heft two cows in there, but I'da done it—then I'da taken 'em over to the Stink Hole and dumped 'em down it. Nobody'd ever been the wiser."

Boley knew about the Stink Hole. It was in a ravine a few miles east of this ridge. Not exactly a sink hole, it was a deep pit created by a quirk in the rock strata. Uncaring inhabitants of the county occasionally disposed of dead animal carcasses and other refuse by dumping into it. He held up a hand, palm out. "I'm sorry, Jim. I should have known. I apologize."

"And that answers one of *my* questions," said a voice behind them.

Grant and Boley looked around. A few feet away stood Sheriff Warren McKee, a spare man whose tan never seemed to fade from one year to the next.

Grant frowned. "What brings you here, McKee?"

McKee smiled faintly. "Rumors. Satisfy my curiosity. What's goin' on?"

Boley kept silent while Grant went through a synopsis of the situation, finishing with: "Boley's also helped me see how I could make Willis look bad in court if I wanted to."

The sheriff shot a glance at Boley. "Did he? I'm glad to see he respects law and order. Not like Willis. Not like you, maybe, if I'm listening right. Did you say you'd report this? No." He stared at Willis' cottage about six hundred feet to the east. "I think I'd better go over and see Willis," he said.

"I don't think you'll find him," Grant commented sharply. "I'll bet he's off hidin' somewhere."

"Maybe," said McKee, walking away. "Even so, I might learn somethin'. Don't go away," he called back, "and don't bury those cows yet!"

He was gone half an hour. Boley and Grant discussed fox hunting, the chances of a good hay yield, and other small topics.

"You were right," McKee said as he approached. "Nobody there. What's his car look like?"

Grant looked at a rifle McKee was now carrying with a handkerchief wrapped around his hand, but he said nothing about it. "A two-door '81 Chevy. Light blue. Faded some."

McKee stood the rifle against the fence and noted the information on a memo pad. "I think we want to locate that gentleman," he said. "I heard he was gettin' harder to deal with since his wife died. Would you say so?"

"I'd agree with that, yes," Grant said.

"Place looks kept up pretty well," McKee went on. "Just like a woman planned it, inside and out. Maybe he's tryin' to keep her memory alive. Maybe that's why he threw a gut-fit when your cows came trompin' through."

"I'd not be surprised," Grant agreed.

The sheriff gave him a level glance. "You have pretty strong ideas, too, don't you?"

"If you mean that I believe in givin' it everythin' I've got and tryin' to do the best I can, yes," Grant said. "Of course, Millie's been a big help. Always done what I expect out of her. That good garden we got—she's followed every one of my instructions, and it's paid off."

"Well, you do mighty well, even when you relax," McKee said. "You raise fine beef cattle. With that and that showplace garden you mention, you and Millie live pretty well. Everybody likes Millie and envies you for havin' her." He paused. "As for relaxin', you win trophies about every year with those fox-huntin' dogs of yours."

"Good of you to say all this," Grant murmured.

"Nothin' but facts," McKee answered. "Let's leave Boley's machine here and all of us take a little walk." He picked up the rifle, again with the handkerchief wrapped around his hand.

Boley glanced at the gun. "Willis'?"

"I guess so. Came from his house."

They walked in silence until they came to the gate to the grazing land. McKee stopped and leaned on it, looking across the fields. "I see some car tracks," he said to Grant. "Yours?"

"My pickup."

McKee turned around. "Your pickup. Oh, yes. I saw it when I came in. Over by the barn door. Let's look at it."

As they walked to the truck, Boley noticed that McKee had parked his car blocking the lane.

They stopped beside the truck. McKee looked at it, then at Grant. "Still damp," he said, "but not as wet as it was when I came in. Why was is so wet, Grant?—And don't tell me dew. My car was out all night, and it wasn't all that wet a lot earlier than this."

"I gathered up a lot of manure late yesterday and brought it in for the pile. Washed the truck off just before Boley came."

McKee looked closely. "Most farmers keep a cart they tow around for things like that. Hitch it behind a tractor."

Grant waved a hand. "My tractor broke down. That's why I called Boley over to bury my cows."

Boley nodded. "No, you wouldn't want to waste time gettin' 'em into the ground, would you?"

McKee turned away. "Excuse me a minute. Got to put the gun away."

After putting the rifle into his car, he came back.

He stared at Grant.

"So you washed away the manure smell, did you? Sure you didn't drive over to the Stink Hole sometime last night?"

Grant lifted his head and inhaled audibly. "What do you mean by that? What for?"

McKee stepped to the back of the truck and opened the tailgate. When he did, a small recess showed on each side where the hinges went into the body. From the right hand one he extracted a small piece of what looked like a sausage casing. "My curiosity'll be the death of me someday. My wife used to tell me that when she was alive. I saw your wet truck when I came in and I never thought about manure. I took a look and I came across this. Doesn't look like manure." He held up his hand.

Nobody spoke.

"Let's go back to the cows," McKee said.

As they walked, he said, "You know, gossip can be useful, even if you have to be careful about believin' it. I heard about Lon Willis from time to time. What it mostly seemed to add up to was that he was lonely. Would you say that he was neighborly, Grant?"

"Sort of. Until his wife died," Grant said indifferently.

"I wonder if he dropped over when you were fox-huntin'," McKee speculated.

"I can't answer that," the farmer grumped. "Millie never said."

They stopped beside the dead cows.

"Those cows were shot, that's for sure," said McKee. "But they weren't shot with Willis' gun, I'd bet on *that*. It didn't have any shells in it, and it hadn't been fired. I think it might even have a little dust on it. Could be my eyes, though."

He studied the sky a few seconds, then: "Here's what I think," he said. "Boley, you were sharp about what you suggested to Grant. I think Millie didn't go to her sister's yesterday. I have a feelin' that when the fox-hunt was goin' on, she and Willis were bein' *real* neighborly. Then one of the fox-hunters came home earlier than either of them expected. Old situation.

"All of a sudden, there are two less people out here. Then the third one, the one that was left, got real busy. When he pulled in from the hunt, he probably saw in his headlights that rogue cow was up to her old tricks. So he came back out of the house, takin' his own rifle that he'd just used. He worked on that fence himself, finishin' what the rogue cow had started, shooed those two cows out, and shot them both.

"What next? He drove his truck up, laid a tarp by each cow in turn, slit 'em up the middle, and dressed them out, you might say. Put the lights, liver, and everything else in the pickup, then drove the load of guts to the Stink Hole and dumped it. Came back, and washed up early this morning. Only—" he said, holding up the thing that resembled a sausage casing "—he missed this piece of gut."

"You're getting pretty wild, McKee," Grant muttered. "What all this is supposed to mean, I don't know."

"I probably have the order of everything mixed up," McKee said. "Maybe the trip to the Stink Hole came last. Anyway, at some time or other the two bodies were brought out of the house and crammed into the cow carcasses."

"I'd have seen cuts that big," Boley objected.

"Yes, but—" McKee went to the post and picked up the stapler and the pieces of steel "—the cuts were closed with this."

"The staples would back out without something to anchor them," Boley said.

"This hunk of steel would crimp the ends if you held it tight on the other side of the cut," McKee pointed out. "If we look, I think we'll see it."

Boley had thought he wouldn't shudder again after the blowing up of the jail a month earlier. He was wrong.

Grant started to speak, but thought better of it.

"What were you goin' to say?" McKee asked. "Where's Willis' car? I don't know, but I'd guess you ran it way down the other side of the ridge where your grazin' land turns into timber, then you walked back. There're tracks there. We'll find out."

He reached to his holster and drew his revolver. He handed it to Boley.

"Keep this on him, and don't hesitate to use it. I got me a job to do."

He reached into his coat and drew out a sheathed hunting knife. "Found it on the seat of the pickup." As he stooped over the first cow, he said, "We're a lot alike, Boley. We both do things that other people can't or won't do." He ran his hand over the cow's stomach. "Here're the staples, the way I said they'd be."

He began an incision. "I wonder which of them this will be."

10

No Cradle of Pine
(1990)

This story was a favorite with one of the units fighting in Desert Storm.

Alone in the house on a warm afternoon in September, Geneva Boley mistook a sound on the T.V. in the next room and went to the carport door, thinking that her husband and Sheriff McKee had returned. That was when she saw the trio coming down the gravel drive from the paved ridged road.

The woman had altered her pace to that of a little girl, who appeared to be about twelve. The mother, around six feet tall with a large frame, carried a baby completely covered by a thin pink blanket.

"You lookin' for somebody?" Geneva called.

"Anybody'd let us have a drink of water and a place to set down," the woman answered.

Geneva pushed her light-brown hair. Why were they coming here? There were other houses on the ridge road closer than this.

Both the woman and the girl had pleasant, open faces surrounded by curly black hair. The mother smiled broadly, the child timidly. Geneva's neighborly instincts took over. "I think that could be arranged," she said. "Come in out of the hot sun." She held the screen door open.

She let the little girl pass first, but when the woman was about to enter, Geneva extended a hand and pulled back the pink blanket still covering the baby. "Forgive me," she said. "I'm so afraid it'll smother."

The woman took no offense. "The sun might be too much for him. He's only five days old."

Geneva reddened. The baby was covered for protection. She glanced up toward the road. "Where'd you park?"

133

"Didn't. We walked."

Geneva stood in the doorway, speechless. She barely noticed that the others had gone straight into the kitchen. The girl was sitting at the table, facing her. By her feet was a modest multi-purpose bag of blue plastic. The mother had pulled a chair away from the table and was seated with the baby across her thighs—the open blanket showed it to be sleeping peacefully. By the woman's feet was a large duffle that Geneva noticed for the first time.

"Did I understand you?" she said. "Did you say he's five days old?"

"That's right. Isn't it, Ruth Ellen?"

The girl nodded.

"But the hospital—"

"Wasn't in the hospital," the woman said. "Had him at home all by myself. Put me in mind of the old folks. Used to have their babies right out in the field, lay 'em in the shade, then go right on workin'."

Geneva came into the room and seated herself on a kitchen stool. She had never met anyone like this.

"Where are you from?" she asked.

The woman opened the blanket to inspect the baby's diaper. Satisfied, she adjusted the covers slightly. "Up near Franklin," she said.

Geneva stared in disbelief. "Franklin? That's about a hundred miles from here."

"A little more maybe. Not easy miles neither."

"And you walked it?"

"A good bit."

The girl spoke up, "We got a ride or two."

Geneva stood up. "What am I thinkin'? You asked for water. Sounds like you really need it."

She got two glasses from the cabinet and filled them from a jug in the refrigerator. The girl drank eagerly, the mother in small, mea-sured swallows.

Geneva waved a hand toward the ridge road. "Am I the only one you could find at home?"

The woman set her glass on the table, but kept her hand close. Water was still left.

"Didn't try," she said. "Your house looks nice. All that big stuff out back, your man must be a hard worker. Figured you'd be good people."

Geneva had never looked at her husband's heavy machinery in that light before, as evidence of affluence. "I don't know how good we are," she said, "but we try to treat everybody right." She glanced out of the window. "As for all that stuff of Arly's, it's not all ours yet. Bank's still got claim on some of it."

"Don't they all," the woman said. "By the way, I'm Lila Anderson. This here's Ruth Ellen."

"Geneva Boley. My husband's Arlan." She looked out the window again. "And he ought to be gettin' back here. He's had a call to look at some gradin' a man wants done." She turned to the Anderson woman. "Where you goin'?"

"Huntington. I got a cousin there."

Geneva shook her head. "Walkin'? That's maybe even a bit farther than you've come."

The big woman smiled. Her confidence was unshakable. "We'll make it."

"But with that little baby—"

The mother dismissed it. "He comes from good stock. I'm not worried." She studied Geneva. "Since we're talkin' about this little feller, I'll just ask now. I would have anyway. Miz Boley, how would you like to buy him?"

Geneva laughed uncertainly. "*Buy* him? Don't joke about a thing like that." She looked at the girl. "You wouldn't let your mother sell your baby brother, would you?"

The child stared at the table. "Nobody wants him."

Lila picked up on it. "That's not quite true. His daddy left us because he showed up. His own kid, too. Ruth Ellen wanted to have a little girl. And I need money."

In afterthought, she said, "I'd not be the first to put her baby out for adoption."

Geneva said, "I already have two children, a boy and a girl."

Lila's tone was persuasive. "Where would you be if something happened to one of 'em? Or both?"

"I'd just have to live with it."

"But what would your husband think if it happened? If he knew you passed up—"

"There's no reason why we can't have one of our own."

"Well then—"

Geneva changed the subject quickly. "Can you carry enough with you to make out? The baby? Ruth Ellen? You?"

"We've not come up short yet."

"This soon after deliverin'—don't you need pads? I could let you have some."

Lila's gaze was steady. "No problem. Anyway, I have another question."

Just managing to speak, Geneva said, "What is it?"

"If you won't take the baby, would you point me to somebody who might?"

Geneva hesitated. "I don't know. I'd have to think."

"All right. Take your time."

In spite of herself, Geneva asked the question. "How much would you want?"

Lila absently stroked the baby's head. "Can't put a figure on it. I think maybe five thousand at least. I seem to have heard that that's what some of them get. That oughta tide us over a little while now that Ray's gone and left us. Maybe I can get me a job, but there's still Ruth Ellen. I think five thousand dollars. More, if I could get it."

Geneva was about to respond when she heard the sound of tires crunching on gravel. She got up to open the door.

The sheriff's car was coming down the drive. He was bringing Arlan Boley home as he had promised.

"I'll run through it again," Boley was saying. "The leak in your basement is best got at from outside." He outlined digging down to the footers, waiting until a waterproofer did the treatment, then ditching and backfilling.

McKee gave him a quick glance. "How much?"

"Depends on what I run into. You know I won't rob you."

The discussion ended abruptly. As the car pulled up to the doorway, both of them saw Geneva making beckoning gestures.

McKee glanced at Boley, his face expressionless. "I suspect she wants us both." He shut off the motor.

"Hello, Warren," Geneva said to him from the door. "You and Arly come in, we have company."

Boley slipped his tall body from the car, ducking his head so that his crinkly blonde hair cleared the house-door frame. He heard McKee's shoes crunch gravel.

"Go on in," said Geneva. "Both of you . . ."

When Lila Anderson had finished her explanations again, at Geneva's urging, Boley and the sheriff sat looking at each other. Boley knew that his face wore a half stunned look. He knew that he was hearing the woman propose an illegal act. He wondered how McKee was taking it. McKee's well browned cheeks were relaxed, no muscles betraying his thoughts.

"I told her we weren't likely to take on any more children," Geneva said, getting conversation started again. "But maybe you have different ideas."

"No, I'd go along with that," Boley said, assuming an expression of sympathy for Lila's sake. "You say the three of you came all the way here from Franklin? Walkin'? That's around a hundred and twenty-five miles. Down Randolph, Pocahontas, and part of Green-brier counties, up some pretty steep grades at times. I have to admire the three of you."

"We got some rides," Ruth Ellen said once again.

"We had us a room in Marlinton last night," Lila volunteered. "Right after we started again, a big rig came by. The driver let us ride to this place, Levi, where this road up here commenced. That was as far as he was goin' in the direction we're headed."

Boley shifted in his chair. "How come you didn't just drop down through Virginia below where you lived, follow that way, then cut back west somewhere else?"

Lila answered without hesitating.

"Not so many cars go by, that way. More people live along the road the way we came."

McKee cleared his throat. "You might have found some people with money around Green Bank. Ones who work on the radio tele-scopes. You ask around there?"

Lila shrugged. "I talked to two or three. But I still got him you can see. They did give me a little money and fed us. Last people let us rest overnight."

McKee nodded toward Geneva.

"You heard Miz Boley's reaction, you want some other names I take it?"

Lila smiled. "I'd thank you. You know some?"

"This county doesn't have very many people with a lot of money. The ones with the most are the ones with summer places over by the lake, and most of them have left now. However, we do have some who are well off."

"If you'd tell me who and where they are—"

McKee lifted a sinewy hand. "It'll take some little thinkin'. Meantime, I'm goin' to have to ask you to let me do somethin'."

"I guess I could. What is it?"

The sheriff leaned forward, clasping his hands between his knees. "If you make any kind of a deal with anybody in this county over that little one, I'd be shirkin' my obligation if I didn't see to it that the other folks got a good healthy specimen."

"But he is!"

"I don't doubt you think so, Miz Anderson. All the same, I'm goin' to take him into town and have the hospital check him out. I think it should be pretty easy just now. For some reason, they're not over their heads, like sometimes."

Lila hesitated.

McKee said gently, "I can insist and do it, anyway. I'd rather we had no bad feeling."

Lila gave in. "In that case—"

McKee relaxed. "Suppose you stay here and chat with Miz Boley. Arly here can go along and hold him. He's a father, he knows how to handle 'em."

Lila's big eyes scanned his face. "All right."

"And one more thing," McKee said in afterthought. "I'd like to have Ruth Ellen come along. All that walk, she might be a little peaked. We'll have 'em give her a quick check, too. No charge to you," he added.

"You're bein' awful nice, Sheriff, but maybe—"

"Just tryin' to make sure that you and the little ones are all right while you're in this county."

The firmness in his voice was clear. Lila objected no further. She turned to her daughter.

"Ruth Ellen, you be sure and take that bag with the formula and the spare diapers." She smiled at Boley. "And if Mr. Boley needs help, you give it to him."

Geneva got up and went to the counter. "That reminds me." She took a pencil from a mug of pencils and pens and tore a sheet from a memo pad. She wrote quickly, folded the paper, and wrote on the outside. She came over and tucked it into Boley's shirt pocket. "Couple of things I need while you're all in town. I've marked it so you won't forget."

The baby whimpered slightly and Lila explored. "I'll have to change him before you go."

While Geneva showed her to a chair in the corner to do this, Boley removed the note and read Geneva's instruction: *Give to McKee*. He handed it to the sheriff.

McKee's eyebrows rose as he read it. He peered over to see if Lila or Ruth Ellen happened to be looking and passed the note back to Boley, who read it. *Could they tell you if he's only five days old? She wouldn't accept pads for the bleeding.* Boley refolded the paper and put it away again.

McKee nodded at it and said, "It's good you'll be lookin' after that little one, Boley. Never havin' had one, there's a lot I don't know."

In a dry tone, Boley said, "I've had two and I still have a lot to learn."

"Why don't we get in the car?" McKee suggested to him. "You sit in back. Ruth Ellen can sit by me."

In a few minutes, Lila came out with the baby wrapped in the pink blanket. Boley opened the right rear door and she laid the baby beside him. Ruth Ellen watched until her brother was safe inside, then she climbed into the front seat.

McKee backed and let the rear end ease into the downhill part of Boley's drive, straightened, then headed up to the ridge road.

He turned his head briefly toward the girl. "You know somethin', Ruth Ellen? Nobody's ever told me your little brother's name."

She was looking out of the window. Her head didn't turn when she answered. "David."

"David. A good name. A pretty good man was named that. Your mother or your daddy pick it?"

The girl turned her head and stared through the windshield. "She did. He never called him anything but *it*."

McKee reflected. "*It.* Now, how did he come to do that? Is there anything wrong with that little boy?"

"No," she asserted, then lapsed into indifference. "He just didn't want him. Nobody of us does. That's why Mom wants to sell him."

"What if I called your daddy and asked him if that was his decision, too?"

"You wouldn't know where to call. No more'n I would. He pulled out and left us."

"After David came along," said McKee. "Why?"

"Because of him. He was real mad, and he slammed out of the house and left."

"He didn't want a little boy? Most daddies would, I'm told."

Ruth Ellen shook her head. "He didn't want *any*—boy or girl. Said I was enough."

"He didn't like you? I can't believe that."

"He liked me, all right. He was always nice to me. He just thought the family was big enough."

McKee wore a puzzled look. "David shouldn't have been a surprise to him. Did he act surprised?"

"Yes."

"But he must have been blind all those months, sweetheart. Maybe you don't know—"

Boley spoke up. "McKee, she's a big woman. It could happen. It has happened—or so I've been told."

"Learn somethin' every day," the sheriff muttered.

He turned toward the girl again. Not sounding convinced, he said, "Are you sure you never heard your daddy say to your mother months ago, *You'd better get rid of it. You better not have it.* Anything like that?"

"I never heard him say anything."

"You say nobody wants him. That include your mother?"
"Yes."

The CB radio came alive with a break call. A woman's voice asked for McKee. The sheriff picked up the microphone and answered. "McKee here. Go ahead, Jean."

"It's Evans, Sheriff. He got run off the four-lane just south of town by a rig from Pennsylvania. You want us to set up a road block for the sucker or ask the state cops to get into the act?"

McKee debated the pros and cons of the situation on the radio. When they had nearly finished, he became aware that he had accelerated and was close to town. "Call the state cops," he said. "We might chase him close to the county line. Call the state cops. They could put a block at I-79. Sit tight. I'm comin' on in."

He signed off and spoke to Boley and the girl. "I have to stop at my office for a few minutes, but don't you worry. I'll be back with you before you know it."

In a short time, he was at the courthouse and into his parking space. He jumped from the car and went briskly into the building.

Boley yawned and stretched. "About twelve, are you, Ruth Ellen?" he asked.

"That's right."

"You have eight or nine interestin' years ahead."

"I guess."

"About the same age as my boy, Carl. He gets along with his sister, Martha. But there's more of a gap between you and David. You afraid he'd be an anchor around your neck while you're findin' out what it's all about?"

She turned her head and studied him. "I never did think about it."

"Never thought you might be the babysitter now and then?"

"There's not a lot of that up our way. I've done it already, now and then."

Puzzled, Boley said, "Is there somethin' about him you don't like?"

Her answer was unexpected. "He's a boy."

Boley was silent for a moment. "But you'll be seein' a lot of 'em from now on. You're a pretty girl, even now. You just think you don't like boys."

He was afraid of the answer he might get.

She looked at him steadily. "Well, sure. I'm not *weird.*"

"Well, then—"

"All this time, I get *promises.* From Mom. A baby sister. *How'd you like a baby sister? One of these days there'll be four around the*

141

house. Another little girl. I ask you! Somebody I could share with. A boy, I'd have trouble with. Not on the same band most of the time."

Boley said, "I'm havin' trouble. I was the only one."

"Well, you at least have two kids." Ruth Ellen pointed toward the courthouse door. "Isn't *he* even married?"

"A widower. No kids. Bad luck."

The courthouse door opened and McKee hurried out.

"Got back as soon as I could," he said, climbing back behind the wheel. "Now let's get over to the hospital."

They drove without conversation for the next ten minutes before pulling up before a two-story yellow-brick multi-windowed building that was clearly a hospital. The parking lot was large without over-whelming healthy green lawns, flowerbeds, and well-tended shrubs.

McKee parked in one of the limited spaces at the emergency entrance in the rear. "Everybody out," he said. "Fetch the baby, Boley."

With Boley carrying the baby and Ruth Ellen keeping a wary eye on her little brother, McKee approached the desk. The woman in white in charge of admissions eyed him dispassionately. "You have a problem, Sheriff?"

"Sort of. No real emergency. Just need a couple of favors. No insurance, but the county will pay."

The woman had not relaxed. "Give me an idea of what you want."

McKee beckoned Ruth Ellen over. "I'd like one of your interns to give this young lady a quick check. Nothing fancy. She might be close to exhaustion and not know it."

The woman picked up the telephone and punched some buttons. "Hello, is Doctor Jordan available? If he has a moment, ask him to come to Emergency. No, no crisis. He might welcome this one."

She hung up and looked at McKee. "The other matter? You did say a *couple* of favors?"

McKee indicated the baby. "This little codger I'd like to have get a pretty good goin' over. Might take a while. Got any space in Mater-nity? They say he's only five days old."

She took up the telephone again and spoke at length in a lower tone. Finally, keeping the line open, she addressed McKee. "Maternity does have room and Doctor Hall, one of our pediatricians, is here just now."

"Jack Hall? I know him."

"You're to take the baby up to Maternity and discuss this with Doctor Hall."

"What about this young lady?"

The woman pushed a pad and pen across the desk. "Just write out instructions for Doctor Jordan and have this gentleman give them to him."

McKee busied himself with the pen. As he wrote, he spoke, watching Ruth Ellen from the corner of his eye: "Doctor Jordan. This is Ruth Ellen Anderson. She's come a long way, around 125 miles, and she's walked a lot of it. She might be tireder than she lets on. Give her a good look, but I think she only needs a good night's rest at Mr. Boley's. Sheriff Warren McKee."

Boley noticed that McKee wrote rapidly. He seemed to be putting down more than he was saying.

The sheriff finished, tore off the note, and gave the folded sheet to Boley. "Now let's have David," he said, "and I'll take him upstairs. If you'll tell me how to get there, ma'am?"

When McKee came back, Boley was alone in a chair.

"Where's Ruth Ellen?" McKee asked.

"With the doc. He took her around the corner."

"You give him the note?"

"Yeah."

"You read it yourself?"

"I did. You think of everythin', don't you?"

"Nobody can do that, not even a computer. It's not impossible for twelve-year-olds to have kids. Lots of pioneer women weren't much older, if that."

He changed the subject abruptly. "I guess you're wonderin' why I'm goin' along with somethin' that's against the law. I want to find out, that's why. Then—"

Boley said quietly, "Your business. You tell 'em upstairs about Neva's question about his age?"

"I did. They'll give him a good goin' over. He'll be stayin' here overnight. If you and Neva can put up with it, let the mother and big sis bunk with you tonight. I'll get back to you tomorrow."

Boley shrugged. "We can make out. Maybe we can find out some more. I had a talk with the girl while you were in the courthouse."

"Learn anythin'?"

Boley told him, McKee paying close attention. Finally he said, "It helps. And maybe you do better with her than I do since you have kids. Suppose you talk to her on the way home. Along these lines—"

When he had finished, he said, "Now, get out of here and get Geneva those couple of things her note forgot to mention."

Ruth Ellen accepted David's absence with indifference. She slid into the front seat of the car without a word.

When they approached the edge of town, Boley leaned forward. "Ruth Ellen," he said, "one thing I don't understand is why your mother wants rid of David."

The girl shrugged. "We need the money."

"I don't doubt that. But there's a big gap between you and him. You'd think she'd want to hang onto him, as long as it took before he showed up."

"She doesn't want him."

"But you told me she talked about another baby to you for a long time."

"She did. A little *sister*. She told me what kind of crib she'd get for her, what kind of covers—all that stuff."

When she mentioned the crib, Boley's scalp tingled. A line from the old song: *There'll be no cradle of pine*. A sense of trouble arose.

"She must have sold you on this idea."

"You can say that again."

"But it didn't take with your daddy."

The girl gave a short laugh. "When they had that fight—the last one—I heard him say, 'I thought you took care not to let this happen.' And she said, 'What makes you think I didn't take care to *make* it happen?' That's when he really came apart."

"I don't get it," Boley said. "She seemed to want a baby pretty bad from what you just said."

"She didn't get what she wanted, did she? Okay?"

"It's like she never grew up," Boley mused. "Like if she can't have what she wants, she doesn't want it."

Ruth Ellen answered through tears. "She was tryin' to get what she promised me."

After this she refused to talk. When they reached the house, she burst from the car and rushed inside.

McKee called around ten the next morning. "Baby's been cleared," he said. "Bring 'em all in. My office."

Boley took them in his Jeep, leaving Geneva to put the house in order. When he parked at the courthouse, he said to Lila, "Leave your stuff here. Maybe McKee'll want me to give you a lift. In fact, I'll run you down to Route 60, if he asks me or not."

Lila's face had been drawn all morning, but she smiled. "You're a good man, Mr. Boley."

McKee's office was on the ground floor, not far from the front door. It wasn't large and the two chairs in front of the desk made it seem crowded. His desktop had numerous papers, but it gave a sense of order all the same.

"I'll stand," Boley said. "Or maybe I'm just extra."

"No, you stay," McKee told him. "I might need you to correct me."

He gathered some papers and arranged them before him. "Now, Mrs. Anderson," he began, "most important things first. The hospital called and they say David is in fine shape—no diseases, no drugs, no nothin'. Just a little baby, less than a week old."

"Then I can—" Lila began.

McKee held up a hand. "Ruth Ellen Anderson, a good healthy girl. Not even overly worn out from all that walkin'. No sign she's ever messed with the boys—if you read me."

"What a dirty way of thinkin'!" Lila burst out.

"It's nobody's business!" Ruth Ellen shouted.

"That may be," McKee said, unperturbed. "I apologize. Doctor Jordan apologizes. The question did arise: everybody was so anxious to get rid of the baby, whose was it? We had to eliminate one of you."

"Well, thank you for nothin'," Lila told him.

"In my job, I can't take a thing at face value," said McKee. He tapped a memo in front of him. "For instance, you said that some people did give you money instead of buying the baby. I naturally

145

wondered if that wasn't your real aim. Sort of a con game. Pay your way to Huntington."

"Think what you like. You will anyway," Lila snapped.

"True," McKee replied. "However, we now come to the real core of this thing. Yesterday, on the way to the hospital, I stopped here and set up a bunch of calls and fax inquiries to sheriff's offices in a number of counties both here in West Virginia and in Virginia. Franklin's close to Virginia, west of it in one way, north in another. I asked if they had any cases involving a very young baby." He riffled through some other pages, then looked at Ruth Ellen. "Young lady," he said, "when did you first see David?"

"When I came home from school the day he was born."

"Your mother told you she gave birth to him all by herself while you were gone?"

The girl looked down at the floor. "Yes, sir," she said, little more than whispering.

"Ruth Ellen, ever been to Harrisonburg, Virginia?"

She raised her head again and her voice regained a little volume. "Yes, sir. Ever' now and then."

"Takes about an hour, or a bit less, by car?"

"I guess."

"Sometimes your daddy leaves his car at home?"

"His pickup. Sometimes he got a ride to work."

"Thank you, Ruth Ellen," McKee said.

He turned to Lila. "None of these messages of mine turned up anythin'. Except one." He pulled out a sheet. "From Harrisonburg, Virginia. Seems some woman slipped into the maternity section of the hospital there about a week ago and made off with a baby. A little boy. Would you know anythin' about that, Mrs. Anderson?"

She stared at him in indignation. "I would not. Why would I steal a little boy when I'm trying' to have my own adopted?"

McKee changed tack. "It was suggested that David wasn't as young as you claimed because you're not bleedin'. You might have been for a while after delivery. I suggest that you never gave birth to David."

"And I suggest you mind your own business and get me back my baby."

"That's not about to happen. They won't release him without my say-so. I'm goin' to have him identified—and I'm bettin' on it. I'm also holdin' you for suspicion of kidnap."

He looked at Ruth Ellen with compassion. "We have to do somethin' with you missy. Maybe we can track down your daddy."

The child burst into tears. "But why would she do it? She didn't want a boy."

"Exactly," said McKee quietly. "She drove over there that day, somehow got in where the babies were, and just grabbed one. She was fixated on a little sister for you, but some kind of pressure didn't give her time to check.

"She took the wrong one."

11

A Break in the Film
(1953)

The author's first foray into the short story form won a special prize in Ellery Queen's *annual contest.*

M y family moved away from that town while I was still a kid. That was 25 years ago, and I've only been back once or twice since then. The place has changed, and I don't much care about going back, even if at the time it did just about kill me to have to leave there.

Sometimes I wonder about change. Old Time itself is the main thing, I guess. Time and death. Slow death and sudden death.

I don't want to go back, mostly because of the old Graphic Theater. Not that the Graphic made the town. Most of the town would have ignored the Graphic if it had been able to.

Every town has—or has had—a movie house like the Graphic. There's one right here, only instead of naming it Hippodrome or Grand or Bijou, they simply call it the Travers after the fellow who happens to own it.

You know what it's like: certainly not anything like a first-run or even like the best "neighborhoods." Strictly one cut above a dump. Nowadays there are carpets on the floors, and lights on the walls, and the seats have some stuffing (they're not plain hard wood, the way they used to be), but these places are all basically the same.

This was the Graphic, back when I was a kid: About the size of a large independent grocery store, but not so big as a supermarket. Hard seats, no wall lights, no carpets. So dark inside it hurt your eyes to come out into the street, especially because there wasn't any lobby. You paid your ten cents to Bessie Hawes in the little cubbyhole by the front door, she tore off a ticket and dropped it into a can, and you went in. The screen was on the front wall, and you walked past it and Joe Stockton, the piano player, and found yourself a seat in the gradually rising amphitheater. Up at the rear there was a booth that doubled in brass: half was the projection room, the other half an office.

I was about nine when I started going to shows at the Graphic, and it was a battle to get started.

"I don't know whether I ought to let you go to that place or not," said Mom, staring at me as though she thought there was more to this than just my wanting to see a movie.

"Practically all the other kids go. Tommy Stewart does. If he goes, it's all right, ain't it?"

"*Isn't* it. Well, now—It's just that I've always heard it was such a dirty place. And you can't tell what might happen there."

But back in those days everybody in town knew everybody else's business, and they couldn't find anything to say against George and Bessie Hawes. Not then, anyway. And since George and Bessie ran the show, and since I kept at Mom, she finally gave in to me and I started going every Saturday.

If you went to the Graphic much, you met two people for sure, and maybe a third. Bessie Hawes you couldn't help meeting; she was always selling tickets. Bessie looked sort of middle-aged to me then, but I guess she was only somewhere between 25 and 30. One of the first women I ever saw with short hair—short, red hair that stood out ever so slightly from her head. Just a touch of powder and a suspicion of rouge, but enough to make her one of the town's first flappers. Lipstick, too, of course. And she enjoyed life. Don't see how she could have, stuck in that ticket office till all hours, but she always had a smile for you. Always.

Maybe what I remember most about the old Graphic is the front of it. Six-foot bills on each side of the building, with some kind of violent action going on in primary colors. Overhead, another big bill hanging, a square one, with more action screaming from it. William S. Hart in *Wagon Tracks*. Or Jack Mulhall in *The Social Buccaneer*, or Art Acord, Antonio Moreno, Hoot Gibson, that crew. And there in that little ticket cubbyhole was Bessie Hawes, smiling. I remember that big poster flapping in the wind over Bessie's smile.

Joe Stockton, the piano player, was another one practically everybody knew. It was mostly because of his playing, I'm sure. Even in some of the better movie houses across the street, the organists sometimes fumbled it and were out of step with the film. Not Joe. He was always in there with something light during the comedies, like *Yes, We Have No Bananas, It Ain't Gonna Rain No More*, or *Barney Google*, and he really bore down on it for the westerns and serials. You hear all kinds of piano nowadays—boogie woogie, sweet and sentimental, honky-tonk—but the kind I'd like to hear again is movie-house piano. With Joe Stockton playing it.

Saturday mornings, before the show opened at ten, Joe used to stand out front, and a lot of us kids would hang around and fuss over him. At the time, I thought Joe was a good guy being nice to us. Since then, I'm not so sure. Joe was only of average build, but he had pretty, almost white, blonde hair and a complexion like an old-fashioned rose. I wonder if he didn't stand out there for the women to look him over. A gang of hero-worshipping kids wouldn't have hurt him a bit. And there was talk that he was quite a man with the ladies.

Joe dressed well, too, for a piano player. The styles changed fast in those days, but he kept right with them. Always up to the minute. I seem to remember a cigarette case, and that was in the days when most men either carried the pack plain or rolled their own. George Hawes remarked on Joe's clothes one day as he passed on his way to get the show started. "You must put all the money I give you on your back, Joe," he said, grinning. And because it was none of George's business, and Joe knew George knew it, Joe just smiled and shrugged. Then Bessie looked up from counting out piles of change and tacked on a postscript: "Joe'll amount to something someday. Anybody can see that. Won't you, Joe?"

I have always liked to find out how different machines work, and it wasn't long after I got to going to the Graphic that I decided to find out how the projector operated. So one Saturday I slipped up to the rear of the theater, nearly killing myself in the dark, and poked my head into the projection room. It wasn't much bigger than a

Pullman washroom. Just room enough for the two projectors, a small work table with a home-made splicing outfit and rewind reels, and George Hawes.

George looked down his long nose at me, but he didn't have a mean expression in his eye. All he said was, "It'll cost you an extra dime to see this part of the show." When I pulled out the dime, he laughed and said to put it back in my pocket and come on in, if I could find some place to squeeze myself.

Hardly anybody got to know George. They never saw him long enough. It was his theater, but he was up in the projection room all during the show, and in his little cheesebox office next to it before the show started. After the last showing at night, he stuck around to sweep up the candy papers, and sometimes he mopped the floors with soap and water and carbolic. Bessie helped once in a while, but usually she left at close-up time to go home and get to bed early, she said.

George was a pretty nice guy. Not good-looking, but appealing. He had a long face—long in all dimensions—and his light brown hair wanted to soar off the back of his head as far as his face went down in front, even though his hair always seemed fresh-cut. A thin brown mustache gave him some distinction.

I learned about the machines fast, because he was entranced by them himself. I found out how to thread the film, how much loop to leave so there was no tautening and snapping, how and when to strike an arc with the carbons, how to splice and get the show going again after a break. All that I learned because George was delighted that somebody else wanted to know. He loved the movies and everything about them.

Finally, he said, "You're a big help to me, Jeff. I feel I can step out of here once in a while without worrying. Can't stay in here all day, you know. Tell you what: You come around anytime you want to and Bessie'll let you in free. Only thing I ask is, don't make this place a hang-out. You're welcome company, but your folks won't thank me if you're down here more than you're at home."

The bargain stuck. If Mom and Dad ever got ideas about not liking what I was up to, they never let on. I guess nothing bad ever rubbed off George Hawes onto me. I don't think there was any bad to rub off.

As I say, George loved movies. At least he loved westerns, action pictures, serials, and comedies. The sticky and the complicated stuff was not for him. Keep it across the street in the other houses, was his philosophy. His favorite was comedies. He always doled out generous helpings of Our Gang, Harold Lloyd, the chimpanzee Joe Martin, Felix the Cat cartoons, Ben Turpin, Harry Langdon, the Al Christie comedies (with the bone figures under the dialogue), the Hal Roach productions, Mack Sennett's stuff—all that. The titles alone would double him up, especially the take-offs on the more serious shows: *Donkey, Son of Burro; Riders of the Kitchen Range; The Three Must Get Theirs.* They were funnier to me because George found them funny.

Early in the summer of the year when we moved from town, I was watching a William Duncan serial through one of the portholes of the projection room. The machine was whirring away, and Joe Stockton was giving the piano a good working-over, so I didn't hear anything at first.

Somebody said, "Mr. Hawes?"

I looked around. The door was open, and I saw a pudgy, dark-haired man standing in the doorway. I pegged him for a business-man by his stiff white detachable collar and cuffs. At that time soft shirts had only taken with workingmen and sports.

George squinted around the back of the projector. "Yes?"

"My name's Hurst. Could I see you in private? I have some business to talk about."

George glanced at me. "Jeff's not a licensed operator, so I can't— Oh, well, he's good enough, sure he is. Jeff, can you take her for a bit while this gentleman and I go into the office?"

I nodded.

"All right." He stepped around to the door and I squeezed around to the right of the projector. The reel in it had just started. "Anything goes wrong, you knock on the wall."

Just before it was time to switch to the other machine George came back, alone.

"That," he said as he checked my threading on the new reel, "was an offer to buy this place."

I doubted I'd like this Hurst as well as I did George, just from the little I'd seen. I said, "You going to sell?"

He didn't answer until the new reel had started and he was cranking on the rewind. "You don't make up your mind that quick, Jeff, on things like this. Right now, I doubt it. He wants to put in a cut-rate men's clothing store, he says. There's enough of them in town, and not enough entertainment." He slowed his cranking for a moment. "It was a good offer, though. Maybe too good."

I asked him what he meant, but all he said was, "If you'd seen as many pictures as I have, you'd know that somebody who offers you more than a thing's worth is up to something."

I couldn't argue with him. He had the voice of authority. I went home not long after that.

The next week, when I went up to the ticket window to get Bessie to pass me in, she looked up and said, "Oh, Jeff. I want to talk to you. Let the rest of them go in first. D'you mind?"

I hung around until I was the last one. She motioned me over and put her face close to the hole in the glass.

"I want you to do something for me, Jeff," she said, low and sort of excited. "George has a chance to sell this place and make a lot of money. But he doesn't want to do it. I've tried to talk him into it and he won't listen to me. He might pay some attention if somebody else said the same thing. He likes you, Jeff. He might make up his mind if you talked to him. Would you, Jeff?"

Wouldn't listen to Bessie? I looked at her and, even in the early summer heat, she looked a picture. If I were only a little older—

She was saying, "He wouldn't have to give up theater work. He could afford a bigger and better house, show better movies, if that's what he wants. It would be a step-up. A big step."

But—*me* convince him? A kid?

"He seems to have some sort of prejudice against Mr. Hurst, Jeff. I don't know why. The Hursts are lovely people. Mrs. Hurst does get herself talked about, it's true. They say she's a little fast. And George fusses every now and then about the little bit I do, myself. But . . . Well, here I'm keeping you outside when you want to go in. Just talk to him, would you, Jeff?"

It wasn't easy; George didn't give me much opening. But I did finally get to ask him, as naturally as I could, if he'd decided to sell.

153

He was very casual. "No, Jeff," and he went on threading the projector as though there were nothing more to be said.

I thought a minute. "I'd sorta like to see you get a place like the Imperial, Mr. Hawes."

"Not my type. If I owned a house like that, I'd have to play the kind of shows they do. This suits me fine, here."

"I hear this Mr. Hurst's made you a good offer." (I hadn't, really. Just guessing from what Bessie said.)

"Yeah, and you know what I said before."

He started to say more, but then he stopped and mopped his face, which was wet with sweat in that hot little projection booth.

"Go get me a piece of ice to suck on," he said to me.

I went over and opened the bottom of the water cooler which he'd installed outside the door of the booth. But he'd forgotten to fill it with ice; there was only warm water in the ice section.

"You didn't put any ice in it today," I called.

"Well, get the ice pick and chip some up and fill it, would you? Then bring me a little piece of ice."

I ducked into George's office and reached up on the door jamb where he kept the ice pick stuck in the wood. It was a sharp pick with a stout, square, steel handle. You could really put a drive behind it and make the chips fly if you wanted to.

I got George his ice from the little icebox nearby and popped a piece into my own mouth. By that time, I'd forgotten all about the business of selling the Graphic to Hurst.

I remembered it later in the day. Going down the street, I ran into Joe. Someone else had been filling in for Joe on the piano that day.

"Hi, Joe," I said, surprised. "I thought you were home sick."

He took a minute to place me.

"Oh, hi, kid. Naw, I had some business."

"They sure miss you up at the Graphic."

He grinned a little. "Anybody could pound 'em out good enough for that dump."

"Not like you, Joe." Then I thought of Hurst. "Suppose Mr. Hawes sells out, like they're trying to get him to? What'll you do then?"

When he grinned this time, it was sort of to himself. "I'm not worried, kid. Old Joe'll get along. Might even sell clothes for Hurst."

It wasn't but a couple of days when there was trouble at the Graphic. And a couple of days later there was more trouble. I got it in a roundabout way, so I decided not to believe it until George or Bessie said something about it.

When I showed up in the projection booth the next week, I could see that George wasn't his usual self. It could have been the heat, because the summer was working up to a scorcher. But it proved to be something else.

"Jeff, I'm glad to see you!" he almost yelled, grabbing me by the arm. "Come in here and get on these machines. I've been getting film breaks right and left, and it's just bum threading, that's all it is."

"Yeah?"

George was one of the few guys still left in the Twenties who did his swearing by initials.

"H., yes! And who could thread right if he had to put up with all I've had to put up with the last few days?"

"What's wrong?" I could already see he had his loops too small for the next reel. I started in adjusting.

"That g.d. Hurst, that's what's wrong! Tuesday, a fellow comes in here from the Board of Health. Inspection, to see if I keep a sanitary place. Says somebody — he wouldn't say who—had complained that the floor was filthy, that he'd seen rats running around the place. Now you know, Jeff, that's a g.d. lie! This inspector had to admit, even if there's nothing fancy here, that I do keep it clean."

He stepped outside and fished a piece of ice from the cooler and came back talking around the ice in his mouth.

"As if *that* wasn't enough, on Thursday a guy from the Fire Department comes and says somebody's written them complaining that the Graphic is a fire-trap. Well, now, that concrete floor's not gonna burn. There's no fancy carpets to go up like across the street at those other places. I keep fire extinguishers handy, too. Even the film nowadays is safety film and won't go up in a flash, the way it used to. Why, what in h., I even use a white wall for a screen, and that's something else that won't burn! I told him all that. Oh, I told him good! Ended up, I have to put lights over the Exit doors. Well, that won't break my pocketbook."

"Anyway, they backed down, huh?"

"Oh, yeah. I'm not worried about any of that. It just gets me. I know Hurst is behind all this. He's trying to wear me down, make me sell."

"You know he is?"

"It's as plain as the nose on your face, Jeff. I've seen this same sort of thing, right there on that screen, a dozen times over. Next thing you know, he'll come around and he won't offer me as much as he did the first time. Just wait and see. But let me tell you, Jeff, the son-of-a-gun will have to burn the Graphic down around me to get me out. I can stand it as long as he can."

Neither of us was paying any attention. I was still checking the machine, and George was stooping over the film can under the table. There were several reels still in the can. Neither one had his eye on the door.

All of a sudden George said, "What in the —" just as I caught a flicker of something out of the corner of my eye. I looked up quickly. George stooped still farther and grabbed something out of the can in a hurry. He threw it on the floor.

"Some stupid—" he shouted, and stamped down hard. I watched for him to take his foot away.

It was a cigarette butt.

"If that hadn't been safety film, I'd have been cooked," he growled; and he stepped outside fast. I looked, but all I could see was the dark. Whoever had pulled this poor excuse for a joke, or whatever it was, had gone. Even when George came back, baffled, and asked me, all I could say was that I hadn't seen who threw it. But, for some reason, I remembered that butt.

That afternoon I was in Camp's Drug Store getting a soda when Mr. Hurst came in and pulled up the wire-legged stool beside me. He didn't know me from Adam, so I don't know why I said anything. Because I felt sorry for George, I guess.

"Mr. Hurst," I said.

He looked at me, sort of surprised.

"Yes?"

"Mr. Hawes won't sell the Graphic to you. Don't you know that? Why don't you leave him alone?"

He stared at me, then his face got kind of dark.

"I don't have troubles enough! Now I have kids trying to tell me my business! Didn't you ever hear kids should be seen and not heard?"

I was a little scared. Such a cowardly looking guy, I'd thought, and here he was turning out anything but. I quickly sucked up my soda and left.

Three or four days later I ran into Charlie Lester, who was in my grade in school, and he was asking me how last week's chapter of the serial came out. I told him. Then he said some funny things.

"Them Haweses is as good as the show, anyway."

He lived right next door to them, so I let him talk.

"Mostly we don't know they're around," he said, and I could see he was watching something in his mind. "But last night, late—I don't know the time, but it was late, because they woke me up—old lady Hawes musta just come in. First thing I knew, old George lets out a yell about where's she been? A woman's got rights, she says, or hasn't he heard about woman—woman suffer—suffer—well, something—hasn't he heard about it yet? Sure, you got rights, he says, but I've been hearing things, let me tell you. Why do you always leave the show before I lock up? he says. Tell me that. I have a right to some friends, she says. And what have you heard, anyway? I've heard plenty, he yells. But I always thought you could be trusted. Now I'm not so sure. You'd rather believe the lies? she asks him. Lies? he says, and he tamed down some. Well, now, he says, I see it clearer. It's just some more of the Hurst's scheme, he says, sort of talking to himself. She doesn't say anything to that. I better not catch him spreading this stuff, old Hawes says. Let him watch his own back yard, from what I hear. He'd better mind his tongue about mine."

Charlie stopped and looked me over.

"Well?" I said, "What else?"

"That's all. They shut up then. At least, that's all I could make out."

Next Saturday was the final chapter of the serial, and I went down to the Graphic as usual. It was one hot day. I remember it for the heat as much as anything.

Bessie looked pretty wilted and burnt-out when she passed me in. For the first time, I didn't think she was pretty. She wasn't smiling, maybe that was the reason.

"Go ahead, Jeff," she said, in a heavy voice. "When the last brick of this place falls to the ground, I'll be here selling tickets and you and George will be running the projectors. How's that seem to you as a future?"

I would have put an arm around her, the way I did to Mom when she was down in the dumps, but the booth was in between. I just went on in.

I looked to see if it was Joe at the piano. The playing seemed a little ragged. It was Joe, so it must have been the heat that threw him off.

George had his shirt off and was down to his BVDs. Nowadays he'd be in his shorts, period, but then that was as far as he felt he could go and stay decent. He was sucking ice and mopping his face. Even his mustache had little watery beads on it, and his face glistened with sweat.

He didn't bother to talk, just nodded and waved me to come in.

I looked around for something to do, but there wasn't anything. So I started watching the show through the porthole.

"This is a bum print they sent us this time," said George. "Film's old and rotten. A lot of splices already. We can look for it to break almost any time."

"Like me and the Graphic," I said.

George was a little startled. "What's wrong?"

"Pop told us last night he's been transferred. We're moving out to Chicago by the end of summer. He's been made some kind of superintendent or manager. I don't know. I don't care. I don't want to go."

George reached over and slapped me on the back. "There are lots worse things, boy. You'll get over it."

Then he leaned over and squinted through the porthole. Was that Hurst coming in the front door, in that short burst of sunshine? As hot as I was, I wasn't sure of anything. It might even have been Bessie.

I forgot about it in the next minute, because there was a brittle snap and a sort of flapping. The film had broken. George and I acted together. I jerked the ONE MOMENT PLEASE slide over into position and threw it on the screen, while George teased the film out of the projector and went to work on a fast splice. He had the emulsion scraped, the cement on, and the patch made before somebody else could have realized what happened. In almost no time, we were back in operation.

When we had finished, George was dripping sweat, and so was I.

"Take her a little bit, Jeff," he said. "I'm going out in the alley and cool off. Then I'll spell you."

He left. I kept one eye on the screen and one on the film unreeling in the projector, if you can believe it. It can be done. Everything kept going all right, so I relaxed.

Then I got thirsty. I stepped to the cooler and drew some water. It was warm. I opened the ice compartment. No ice. All melted.

I stepped across to the office quickly and reached for the ice pick.

No ice pick.

I went and looked in the little icebox. Ice, but no ice pick.

Disgusted, I started back to the booth.

All of a sudden, down front, Joe came down on that old beat-up piano with a jangling discord. It sounded like he was tearing the thing apart. I must have jumped a foot.

Kids were out of their seats all over the place. Somebody yelled, "Something's happened to Joe," and somebody went out the front door fast. The exit door to the alley opened and shut as somebody else either went out or came in. A hullaballoo started.

I did the only thing possible. I cut the machine and threw on the house lights.

Then the noise really got going. Kids were milling and shouting all over the place. George and Bessie were right in the middle of it, trying to shoo them out in orderly fashion. I left the booth and elbowed my way down to see what the trouble was.

Joe Stockton lay over the keyboard of his piano. A lot of the white keys were red. Out of the back of Joe's neck stuck the handle of the ice pick.

After a while the only ones there were George, Bessie, me, and the cops. George tried to ease me out, but the cops wouldn't let him.

They were asking questions, and George was bellowing.

"Who did it? That Hurst, that's who! He can't get me out any other way, so he murders my piano player to give the Graphic a bad name and get my license revoked!"

One cop, a leather-faced old guy with stripes on his sleeve, looked at George and shook his head.

"Maybe they do that in the movies," he said, "but I want to hear something more practical."

"He didn't do it himself," amended George. "He's too smart for that. He hired it done."

The cop turned to Bessie.

"Was anybody in here except kids?" She started to talk, but he went on. "Don't lie. I know that on Saturday afternoons you usually get 100 per cent kids."

Bessie gulped and nodded.

"That's what I thought," said the old cop.

Then George sort of collapsed.

"I was the one," he said. "I found out Joe was bothering Bessie here. My wife's a good woman, but Joe wouldn't let her alone. And this g.d. heat, I guess I just went crazy and stabbed him."

The cop looked satisfied.

"That's more like it. That makes sense."

So they took George away. It was like in one of his favorite movies, where the hero kills the villain to save the heroine's honor. And that's the way the papers wrote it up the next day.

As I say, we moved away by the end of the summer and I've never had the urge to go back. For one thing, there's a big cut-rate drug store where the old Graphic used to stand.

And life isn't as simple as in the movies George went for. It can be darned tricky.

Because I still remember the cigarette butt George fished out of the film can. It had lipstick on the end of the paper. Bessie almost never smoked, but there weren't any other grown women in the Graphic that day, so she must have been the one who tried to get rid of George. And she'd have succeeded, too, if she hadn't forgotten the film was safety film.

Of course, I can't prove that part. Any more than I can prove that Bessie'd been the one who complained anonymously to the Board of Health and the Fire Department when she thought Hurst was trying to buy the Graphic. She thought the pressure would force George to sell.

And when that didn't work, Joe looked even better to Bessie. A man like Joe could take her away from George and on up the ladder. Joe had a drive, she figured, that was missing in George.

I guess that's why George confessed. He must have thought that Joe wouldn't fall in with Bessie's plans and so she'd killed him—the woman scorned or the woman wronged. And maybe George felt responsible for driving Bessie into the whole thing. I don't know.

I do know George had nothing to do with Joe's death. The truth was pretty simple. Joe was playing around with Mrs. Hurst. She was even fool enough over him to give him money and little presents. Well, you know how gossip goes in a town. The gossip about his wife got to Hurst, but he didn't know just who the "guy at the Graphic"—as the rumors put it—was. Hurst's offer to buy was just an excuse so he could hang around the theater and smell out the identity of the guilty man. When he found out it was Joe, Hurst grabbed the ice pick he'd seen in George's office, and he let Joe have it.

How'd they find out all this? So simple, it's silly. People in the early Twenties weren't as fingerprint-conscious as today. Hurst just forgot to wipe the handle of the ice pick.

In some ways, we've changed nowadays. Progress, I guess you'd call it.

12

When Are People Going To Learn?
(1954)

Based on a real crime in Charleston, West Virginia, this story was written ten years before a similar case in New York stunned the nation.

T he murder, brutal and shocking though it was, seemed to be simple and straightforward. Harry Cooper and Dave Floyd went downtown on a warm evening in May, looking for Patrolman Jack McCoy. It should have been time wasted, for Patrolman Joe McCue was the man they really wanted, but they did not know that. A week earlier, McCue had given testimony which had sent their buddy, Jim Turner, to the State Pen for ten years. Neither Cooper nor Floyd was long on either brains or temper, and in a few days' time they had fumbled McCue's name. When an acquaintance (who was unaware of the purpose behind the question) told Floyd that he must have in mind Jack McCoy, whose beat was on the fringe of downtown, it was good enough.

Half a block from Main Street, McCoy was strolling along with little to occupy his attention. It was five minutes before eleven, and the next fifteen minutes would see crowds of people on the street when the various movies closed. He gave little notice to the two six-foot men in dirty T-shirts and blue jeans who approached him. He was five feet eleven, himself, and an ex-infantryman. Besides, these two did not seem drunk or disorderly.

When Cooper and Floyd came even with McCoy, they stopped. Cooper asked McCoy if he was Jack McCoy. When the patrolman admitted it, they moved in. Cooper landed a punch on the left ear of McCoy which threw him off balance. Floyd stepped in and jerked

McCoy's gun from its holster and threw it as far as he could down the street. McCoy swung his nightstick at Cooper, but Floyd sidestepped, closed in, and wrenched the club away from him. It joined the gun, far down the gutter.

As both Cooper and Floyd moved in, the first of the movie-goers began to appear. McCoy's attackers hit him several hard, vicious blows which doubled the cop in agony. Then Floyd, realizing that help might arrive for McCoy, tripped him and stepped back to leave the field to Cooper. A crowd gathered quickly.

Before the horrified, fascinated eyes of twenty-two persons, Harry Cooper beat Patrolman Jack McCoy nearly to death. It was revolting to watch. Although most of the spectators were men, nobody came to McCoy's help. Floyd had taken off his belt, a two-inch-wide piece of leather, looped it around his hand, and stood there swinging the massive bronze buckle in front of the crowd's noses as they watched the beating. He said nothing: his intention was obvious.

Inevitably, the word got to the police. In a few minutes two patrol cars arrived. Surprisingly, neither Cooper nor Floyd offered much resistance, and they both were placed under arrest without further incident. It appeared that their rage had spent itself in the fight. An ambulance came for McCoy very soon after that. He was rushed to the hospital, but he died of internal injuries an hour later.

With Cooper and Floyd under lock and key, and so many witnesses, it seemed simple and straightforward. It was only after a number of statements made by witnesses were read that something else became apparent . . . .

In a worn and grimly neutral office in City Hall, Detective Lieutenant Walter Dean stood looking out of his window, waiting. His broad back was turned to his secretary, Louise Moran. He was talking to fill in time.

"City's sixty-some thousand now, and not standing still. All this beef about juvenile delinquency and wanting us to read the riot act to parents. That's been done. Read the riot act to *every* adult would be more like it. Kids pay more attention to other adults than they do to their parents. When are people going to learn?"

The intercom hummed and said, "Mr. Emery is here."

Dean stepped quickly to the desk and flipped a switch.

"Send him in."

He nodded to Louise. She moved to her own desk in the corner and sat down at the typewriter with the noiseless keys.

The door opened.

The man in the doorway was about average height and weight. His most noticeable features were a long, straight nose and small, flat ears. His eyes and hair were brown and unexceptional. His forehead was already lightly creased, although he seemed to be only in his middle thirties.

Dean extended a hand.

"Mr. Emery. Glad you came down. You met Mrs. Moran the other time, I believe."

Louise Moran's poker face relaxed briefly into a smile, then went back to the strict neutrality which fifteen years of police experience had taught her.

Emery looked hesitant.

Dean retired behind his desk and waved to a chair.

"Sit down, Mr. Emery."

Both men sat, and began studying each other, Emery warily, Dean shrewdly. Dean leaned back.

"You're wondering what this is all about, I take it, Mr. Emery."

"Well, naturally—and since I have to take time off from work—"

"It's this McCoy affair, as you may have guessed. We need another statement from you."

Emery's brown eyes showed bewilderment.

"I've already told everything I know. I signed one statement, only yesterday. Don't you have that?"

Dean stroked his prematurely bald head absently.

"Yes, we have that statement, Mr. Emery. Right here on my desk. Trouble is, complications have come up, and we have to do some of this over again. So, if you don't mind, we'll do a run-through from another angle."

"Anything I can do—"

"Good. Now: I'll ask you questions, you answer, and Mrs. Moran will put it into proper form as we go along. Just answer to the best of your ability—and don't be surprised at anything I ask you."

Emery shifted uncomfortably. Dean pulled a pack of cigarettes from his pocket and pushed it across the desk, following it with a desk lighter. Emery accepted the offer and lit up. He seemed more at ease.

"Very well. Now, Mr. Emery. Your full name?"

"Herbert Martin Emery."

"Age?"

"Thirty-six."

"Height?"

"What's—"

"Please, Mr. Emery. Part of the information. Height?"

"Five feet nine."

"Weight?"

"One hundred and fifty-six. That's a month ago, but I stay pretty much the same."

"Close enough. Occupation?"

"Foreman for Jefferson and Robinson Roofing Company."

"That means you go out on most of their roofing jobs?"

"That's right."

"Indulge in any sports?"

"I golf a little. Swim a little when the weather's right. Bowl all season, during the winter."

"Very well. Where were you on the night of May twenty-sixth?"

"At what hours?"

"Nine to eleven-thirty."

Emery answered without hesitation.

"From nine until eleven I was with my brother, Calvin, at the Strand Theater. It was a war picture, and our wives didn't want to see it, so we went together, Cal and me. After we left the show, we started toward Cal's car."

"It was parked on Sixth, just off Main. We saw this fight, these two thugs beating up Officer McCoy, and we went by to have a look. When it was all over, we went home, and Cal and I had a couple of beers in my kitchen while we told my wife, Virginia, and Cal's wife, Emily, all about it. And that's all."

Dean nodded.

"That's the general outline. Let's get the particulars. You say you saw the fight and went to watch it?"

"That's right."

"You were there all the time? You didn't leave?"

"Well, we didn't get there right when it started. They were trading a few when we noticed it. Then we saw the officer go down, and we went closer to see what happened."

"Did you leave the scene of the fight at any time?"

"You mean me? Or Cal? Or both of us?"

"I mean you, particularly. And your brother."

"Neither one of us left until the ambulance pulled away with poor Officer McCoy."

Dean looked at the ceiling, then at Emery.

"Did either one of you have a hand in this affair?"

Emery seemed shocked.

"No, sir! Besides, with that hulking redheaded thug standing there with that wicked-looking belt—no, we didn't mess into it. Let somebody else be a hero, not me."

"Did you see anybody else get into it?"

"Nobody but the three of them. Of course, some of it was pretty bad, like when McCoy was getting kicked. I looked away a lot of times, so maybe I missed something. You might ask Cal. Maybe he saw something I didn't."

Dean leaned forward.

"Did you *hear* anything?"

Emery's brows contracted in puzzlement.

"Hear anything? What, for instance?"

"Anything at all. You tell me."

Emery shook his head.

"Not a thing. Only the noises they made while fighting and Officer McCoy groaning."

"Did any of them say anything?"

"The two thugs were doing a lot of cursing. I couldn't repeat it. That kind of stuff doesn't stick with me, and I've forgotten it all."

"What about McCoy?"

"Well, he was groaning."

"Groaning. That's all? Just groaning?"

"That's all I remember. They hardly gave him a chance to do anything else."

Dean nodded. He reached down with his right hand, slid open a desk drawer, and pulled out an 8 x 10 glossy photograph. He handed it to Emery.

The picture showed the head and shoulders of a blond boy of nineteen or twenty. There was nothing extraordinary about the picture.

"Recognize this boy, Mr. Emery?"

Emery studied the picture and frowned.

"I've seen him, yes. He was watching the fight, too. I think."

Dean took back the picture.

"We have his statement that he was there. Any idea where he was standing in relation to you, Mr. Emery?"

"Let's see—Cal was on my left—why, yes, he was right beside me, on my right."

"Did you notice this boy doing anything, Mr. Emery?"

"No. No—he was just standing there, the way I was. He didn't get into it at all, as far as I know."

"Did he *try* to get into it at all?"

"No—well, now, wait a minute. Maybe he did. Yes—yes, I recall now, he did make some kind of a move, but the fellow who was beside *him* on the other side kept him from getting mixed up in it."

"Do you remember what the boy, or this man beside him, said?"

Emery shook his head.

"No. Not a thing. There was so much confusion, I wouldn't know."

"Anyone try to stop the fight?"

"No, sir, nobody. I guess everybody was afraid of that fellow with the belt."

"The man who kept the boy out of it—do you know him?"

Emery thought carefully. He pulled at his right ear.

"Seems I should. He's sorta familiar."

"Would his name be Ben Rowe, do you remember?"

"Ben Rowe! That's right! That's it!"

"You're sure?"

"Oh, yes. I used to be in grade school with Ben Rowe. That was a long time ago and I haven't seen much of him since. He's put on weight, and his hair's thinned. But that's who it was—Ben Rowe."

167

"All right. Let's get this established. This boy—his name's Tom Stone, by the way—tried to interfere in the fight, and Ben Rowe prevented him. Is that right?"

"Yes, sir. That's right."

"But you say you don't remember what was said?"

"I'm sorry. I don't."

"Very well. Did you see anyone else in the crowd you recognized?"

"Two or three people. There was Art Smith. And Lew Young. And Bessie Blair and Myrtle Fisher—they were together."

"Your brother, Calvin, what's his work?"

"Don't you have that down?"

"We have one statement he's made, and we're going to get another. But we'd like to have you tell us."

"Well, he's a rigger foreman, over at the mill."

"He works with heavy equipment, moving it around. Is that right?"

"That's most of it."

Dean glanced at a small desk clock.

"Excuse me a minute, Mr. Emery."

He pushed a lever on the intercom.

"Reese."

"Yes, sir."

"Time for Stevens to make his call. Tell him, would you?"

"Right away."

Dean leaned back.

"Little job I almost let get away from me. Let's see, have we covered everything?"

He sat in thought for a moment.

"I guess that's all, Mr. Emery. Mrs. Moran, will you round this off and bring it over for Mr. Emery to sign?"

"Yes, sir."

Dean offered Emery another cigarette. It was refused. He took one, himself, lit it, and sat with one arm across the back of his chair.

"So it was a pretty bad fight, was it, Mr. Emery?"

"It was that. I don't think about it any more than I have to."

"I'm afraid you're going to have to think about it a lot, before this is over."

"Will they want me as a witness?"

"Possibly."

Emery grimaced.

"Some of that I don't *want* to remember."

"But you probably *will* remember it pretty well. I think you'd better get used to the idea."

Louise Moran got up from her typewriter and brought Dean two copies of Emery's statement. He handed the original to Emery, keeping the carbon himself. He glanced through it quickly.

"Take your time, Mr. Emery, and be sure to read it carefully. However, in brief, it tells us a few facts about yourself, then goes into your activities on the night of the fight, tells how you didn't get involved in it, the persons you recognized, and what you did or did not see or hear."

Emery grunted and read the paper carefully, stroking his nose with one finger as he read. Meantime, Dean looked through some other papers on his desk.

Finally Emery put the statement down.

"That looks to be what I told you. You want me to sign?"

"Please. Mrs. Moran will notarize your signature, where she has provided for it."

Dean handed Emery a pen, and he signed quickly and nervously. Dean gave the paper to Louise Moran. Standing beside the desk, she leaned over and carefully wrote in the necessary words and signature, finishing by impressing the paper with a large metal seal.

Dean took the statement and placed it on his desk in a folder with several other papers.

Emery got to his feet.

"You'll not be needing me for anything else, then? I ought to be getting back—"

Dean smiled humorlessly.

"Oh, yes, I will, Mr. Emery. This is only part of it. Please sit down."

Emery sat down again slowly, bewilderedly, as Dean took another paper from the folder.

"There is something you should hear, Mr. Emery. This is a sworn statement made by Mrs. Elizabeth Blair. I'll read you parts of it." He began to read, and his voice gradually gained bite as he read. "'The fight had already started when Mrs. Fisher and I came by. The officer was taking a terrible beating. In no time at all there was a crowd around, mostly men. Among them I saw Herbert Emery and his brother, Calvin. While the officer could still speak, he said to the crowd: *'I need help. I order you all to help me. Help me, and arrest these men.'*"

He looked up. "Do you remember that, Mr. Emery?"

Emery shifted uncomfortably.

"Well, it seems as though maybe—"

"I'll read some more. 'The officer almost begged a couple of times. Then he commanded. But nobody moved a muscle. That big man with the belt watched them, but not a one went to the policeman's aid. It was awful. Most of these men were able-bodied. I know, especially those Emerys. There was one light-haired boy who did try to break into it, and maybe if he had, some of the others might have joined in. But the man next to him—not Herbert Emery, but another one—grabbed him and said, *Stay out of it. Let them fight it out.* And before long it was too late.' That would have been Ben Rowe who did that, who said that, wouldn't it, Mr. Emery?"

Emery was looking at the floor.

"I guess so. I don't remember exactly, but I guess so. Yes, he did grab the kid."

Dean put the paper down and took up another.

"Statement by Mrs. Myrtle Fisher. Again, just parts of it. 'Saw Arthur Smith there . . . the Emerys, Herbert and Cal . . . a lot of average men, but none of them weaklings. Not physical weaklings, but certainly moral weaklings. It would only have taken two or three like the Emerys and some of the others to have stopped the fight . . . . One man, just a boy, really, did try, but they wouldn't let him . . . . At one time the policeman tried to sort of name the men in the crowd deputies, but nobody accepted the responsibility . . . . I thought the human race had climbed higher than it seems to have done.'"

Emery said, without looking up, "She's just sticking by Bessie Blair. Both of 'em just a pair of lying gossips."

Dean raised his eyebrows. He replaced the Fisher statement and took up another.

"That so? Here's one from Tom Stone. That's the boy who's mentioned. 'At first I thought it was just another fight. The one guy wasn't mixing in it. And I don't like cops too much, myself—always thought they picked on people a lot. But when I saw how it was, and how this cop tried to get help, and then when the kicking started, that was too much for me. I wanted to stop it. But when this guy in the crowd stopped me and I saw how the crowd was no help, I slipped off and called the cops. Only by then it was too late.'"

Emery looked up and fixed his eyes on the wall to the right of Dean. His voice shook a little when he spoke.

"Looks like Ben Rowe's in a spot, doesn't it?"

"Ben Rowe?" Dean snorted. "Yes—Ben Rowe—Arthur Smith—Lewis Young—James Cox—Terence Miller—Calvin Emery—*Herbert* Emery. You're all in a spot. Every one of you. And a damned tough one, at that."

"Cal—me—? Where do you get that? Just because Bessie Blair and Myrtle Fisher made some spite remarks, you can't say—why, Ben Rowe, maybe, is in trouble, yes. He wouldn't let that kid get into it, but the rest of us—"

"The rest of you didn't do a thing. I know. I have your sworn statement to that effect." Dean leaned forward. "I have your brother Calvin's, and he admits *he* did nothing. Lew Young admits the same thing. *And that's just the point, Mr. Emery.*"

Emery paled. "I'm a peaceful man, Lieutenant. I don't want to get mixed up in—things like that. I keep out of them. I want to see these two fellows punished, sure. I've given you two statements, and I didn't have to come forward at all. But I want to see those two thugs get all that's coming to them. Then you act like this, like I had a hand in this man's death. Like it was my fault."

Dean looked grim. "It *was* your fault. You *did* have a hand in it. McCoy, as an officer of the law, commanded you men to help him keep the peace. None of you men accepted the responsibility. So McCoy died."

"It's easy for you to talk, Dean. You weren't there with a six-foot thug in front of you swinging a murderous belt. You'd have done the same thing, unless you're a fool."

Dean nodded. "If I'd been there alone, I might have done the same thing. But *you* weren't alone. There were several able-bodied men there. You and your brother, at least. Your own statement makes it clear that neither of you is broken-down, physically."

Emery said nothing. Dean went on, savagely.

"A year ago, a case a whole lot like this happened. The victim, a small man, was beaten and crippled for life by a two-hundred-pounder twice his size. Sixteen people saw it happen, and nobody lifted a finger. *That* one made me sick, Emery, sick to my stomach!" He slammed his hand down on the desk. "But we couldn't do a thing, then, to the crowd, even though they were as guilty as the animal who did it! There's no law, you might be happy to know!"

Emery glanced at him triumphantly. "Then you're only bluffing on this one, too."

"Oh, no. Ohhh, no! This time, there *is* a law. McCoy, as an officer, commanded help. Your refusal lays you open to arrest and prosecution."

Emery managed a sneer.

"I've always heard it said that killing a cop would be the worst thing you could ever do, that the rest of 'em would get you, no matter what. You're out to rope in all you can get!"

"Yes, by God, I am! Not because McCoy was a cop, but because he gives us the only chance under law to pin the responsibility for this sort of thing where it belongs."

Dean got to his feet and put his knuckles on the desk.

"Ever think of yourself as an accomplice, Emery? As an abettor? As an accessory?"

Emery could not meet Dean's glare.

The lieutenant flipped the switch on the intercom.

"Reese, is Stevens back?"

"Yes, sir."

"Send him in."

As Emery stared at the door, it opened, and a policeman in shirt sleeves came in. He carried a folded paper in his hand. He brought it to Dean, who glanced at it, then slapped it down on the desk.

"There, Mr. Upstanding Citizen Emery, is a warrant for your arrest. You'll have lots of company before we're through, too. The only thing I can say is—and it breaks my heart to say it—we can't name you an accomplice, or any of those other things. But we can get you for a misdemeanor. Six months in jail's the worst we can do. Aren't you glad?"

Emery stood up.

"I'll call my lawyer."

"You do that. You start worrying about the thousand dollars bail it'll take."

Emery's courage was obviously rising.

"It's political, Dean. Political. The City Hall crowd's doing this as a stunt, to show the public how alert they are cracking down on law-breakers. But you can't fool the public. They'll know."

Dean scowled, shaking his head. "It was my idea."

Emery snorted. "But you couldn't make a move without the OK of everybody from your captain, through Chief Randall, on up to the Mayor. Don't try to tell me you could."

Dean gave him a contemptuous glance and looked away.

An icy anger settled on Emery's face. He said nothing more, but walked quickly to the door. Stevens followed him. The door shut behind them.

Dean sat down again. He looked older and infinitely more tired—within seconds. Louise Moran was now looking out of the window.

Without turning, she said, "It's a big order. It's never been attempted here before."

"I know. A political stunt," he said. "It could be political suicide for some of us."

"You have civil service."

"Yes. Civil service." He lit a cigarette wearily. "That doesn't protect your wife and kids from our good citizens when they decide to close ranks and shut you out. That won't keep me from being a target—the kind of target which gets shot to bits the first mistake I make from now on."

He exhaled raspingly. "I'll make you a bet, Louise. Emery'll get to trial, right enough. They can indict. But if he's convicted, I'll buy you a new hat. Every man on that jury will be just like Emery—and you just won't catch twelve average men convicting *themselves!*"

"You're so sure," she murmured. "Why try, then?"

"I don't know," he answered slowly. "I just don't know. I can't help it, I suppose."

13

Your Word Against Mine
(1955)

Another Ellery Queen *prize winner. The theme of this early courtroom mystery is so contemporary it might have been written today.*

Defending counsel Roberts looked up from his notes as Assistant Prosecuting Attorney Sutherland got to his feet.

The ceiling fixtures in Intermediate Court cast a yellow light over the dark walnut courtroom. The tall windows were gray blanks as the last of winter dissolved in slow, monotonous March rain. The tiled corridors outside were sharp with carbolic smell, but in the overheated room a heavy odor of damp wool mingled with a bitter whiff of wet overshoes and umbrellas.

The spectators' benches were packed.

Roberts, watching his small, bald, ferret-faced opponent gather himself for his closing remarks, found the day and the situation in league against him. *You can't snoop out all the surprises. But what to do about the one they pull out of the hat, as in this case? What to do?* He knew that he must expect Sutherland to hit it hard. It had to be hit back. *Can I make it come through?* A sneeze at the rear of the courtroom reminded him of the cold he was developing, another weight to be added to the pressure on his brain.

Be sharp, Roberts, be sharp. Sutherland's already used one or two of your tricks against you.

The defense lawyer looked at the child, hoping to surprise the malice that must be there, that must show itself, if only once—hoping that the jury would see it, too, when it did show. But her face was placid and innocent. He looked at her father. That craggy, ashes-colored face was no graven image. Anger and hatred ebbed and surged there, giving way to satisfaction as the prosecutor prepared to unmask the devil before the jury.

Roberts ignored the jury. He would get to them all too soon. He glanced at his client, Arthur Bradshaw, instead. Bradshaw—like his antagonist, the little girl—was utterly serene. His banner of prematurely white hair was smoothly brushed. His pink skin was unmarked save for the crow's feet of humor at his blue eyes. All his lines were finely cut—face, hands, and even the bones of his legs and ankles, as Roberts knew. Bradshaw personified dignity. The thing at issue was the integrity of the dignity.

And Roberts looked at himself. *It's all very well for Sutherland. He can be a machine if he likes. Strip another man to his bare bones, and if you've never had to open your own heart you won't mind it. My trouble is that I have too much heart. Wouldn't Bradshaw be better off if I didn't have an eleven-year-old girl myself?* He thought back to the clear, windy day at the beginning. Both he and Sutherland had indicated to judge Weaver that no sequestering of witnesses was requested. The jury was impaneled and ready to listen, and it was time for opening remarks. His mind's ear again heard Sutherland's dry, dusty voice addressing the twelve attentive jurors . . .

"Ladies and gentlemen of the jury [Sutherland said that first day of the trial], we are here to try a man accused of contributing to the delinquency of a minor. This is a case which I am most distressed to prosecute, because I am aware of the regard with which this community has held the defendant, Arthur Bradshaw."

Attempting to trump my ace already, Roberts had thought.

Sutherland had rubbed his bald head in affected embarrassment. "But in this life we cannot always do the things we should like to do. I am sure that my opponent, Mr. Roberts, would like it better if our positions were reversed because, as some of you may know, while I am unmarried, he is a father. His natural inclination in this case must be to prosecute, not defend.

"I feel a great responsibility in this case. A responsibility to Virginia May Tucker—to her parents—to everyone in our community. For this could be a crime against any child in town, not just Virginia May Tucker. The defense counsel's child, for instance. Or *your* child." He threw one arm out in Bradshaw's direction, but did not mention him by name. "So, I want you, friends, not to look upon me as a prosecutor in this case, but as a defender—a defender of the things we all cherish most: our homes, our families, our children. Think to yourselves, ladies and gentlemen: Have you ever regarded the Prosecuting Attorney's office as your defender?"

Sutherland had paused to wipe the sweat delicately from his palms. "Now, I do not wish you ladies and gentlemen of the jury to imagine that I intend to introduce evidence to show Arthur Bradshaw is the man who has been trying to lure other little girls into his car—the man the police have hunted for months.

(*No, damn you*, Roberts said to himself, *but you can play on their prejudices. Who hasn't read about that animal?* Then he remembered his own Bessie and the constant worry that she might not heed his and June's warnings.)

"The evidence we shall introduce is concerned only with the question: Did Arthur Bradshaw make advances to the Tucker child, or did he not? You must consider this, and this alone. If you are satisfied that he did—and we shall attempt to prove that he did—then you must find him guilty as charged.

"We shall attempt to show—"

After a time Roberts had been on his feet himself, facing the jury for his own opening. He knew exactly how he had looked standing there—six feet two, broad shouldered, high-cheekboned, one lock of black hair falling boyishly over his left eyebrow—a picture of the clean young defender of the wronged. A picture Roberts had tried to preserve over the years.

But he always forgot this picture when he began to speak. It never failed to surprise him, when he spoke to a jury, that these people were no more than his own neighbors. The owlish banker, Martin—foreman of the jury—was like Joe Hazleton, the insurance man who lived across the street. The pleasant-faced brunette in the second row could be a sister of the soda fountain girl in the neighborhood drug store. The stocky man sitting beside her could double for the meatcutter in the supermarket. These were just people, bent on seeking an answer as best they knew how. And he had spoken to them as people, not as an audience. *If I'm to save or break a man by talking, I can't be a performer, I must be a communicant. I must communicate with these twelve people.*

"I must confess to you, ladies and gentlemen, that in his opening speech Mr. Sutherland has given us all something to think about—especially me. And he has shown me that I ought to look at this case not only as an attorney, but as a father. For, as Mr. Sutherland has said, in so many words: What if this were *your* child? That is a terrible question to have to answer.

"Ladies and gentlemen, terrible as that question is, I must ask you to try to answer one equally terrible. What if you stood in Arthur Bradshaw's place?"

He had paused a moment, to let it sink in. *That's one for our foreman to think about.*

"By that question, ladies and gentlemen, I do not mean the familiar one: What if I were sitting there, on trial for murder—or some other crime? The question, rather, is: What if it were I, about to see my whole life wrecked, my good name torn to shreds, by someone's false testimony? For, ladies and gentlemen, is it not more terrible to strip a man of everything he is, and then let him live, than to take his life?

"I shall attempt to show, beyond question, that my client's life is as unblemished as you can expect any average man's to be—probably more so. Such a man is inevitably the target of people who cannot tolerate the good among us, who must continually look for flaws in them. It is a tribute to Arthur Bradshaw that I have had dozens of offers from persons who want to testify for him. I could fill this court-room with such character witnesses. If a time should ever come when I were on trial, I should be proud to have so many plead to speak on my behalf. Some of these people will tell you their stories later ... "

Roberts leaned against the table toward Bradshaw.

"Look again. Do you see anyone here who might have a grudge against you?"

Bradshaw said calmly, "But I have never given anyone cause to have a grudge."

The lawyer reddened. "That's not the point! People bear grudges whether you've given them reason or not. All they need is imagination. And the more well-known you are, the more they imagine. Someone like that might have used the Tuckers to set you up. Now, will you at least try to help me? Will you please look?"

Bradshaw scanned the courtroom.

"I don't see anyone who might fit your description."

Roberts leaned closer and spoke in intense undertone. "One thing Sutherland might do is to have someone swear that you've tried this sort of thing before. If you saw anybody here who might say that, it would help me to have some background on him."

"I don't see anyone."

Roberts thought: *So, if it comes, it'll catch me flat-footed. Well—*

The voice cut through their conversation: "Will Virginia May Tucker come to the stand?"

As the child rose and made her way to the stand, Roberts stared in surprise. *The first witness? No warm-up, no preliminary witnesses?* He hardly heard them getting the child to affirm the truth of her testimony. *Is Sutherland hitting for the deepest impression by putting the child first? Or does it mean that he has no supporting witnesses— as Bradshaw said?*

The child should make a good impression . . .

There was nothing falsely angelic about her features; they were only a little better than plain. Her light brown hair, which would later be mouse-colored, tended to be straight, but no false crimps had been put into it. Carefully placed barrettes caused it to fall softly, just far enough back from her face to create an image of placidness and honesty. Her blue print dress was faded and mended; but it was clean, and the needlework was neat.

The prosecutor spoke gently. Roberts said to himself: *He sounds like an old uncle played by a ham actor.* But juries weren't drama critics. It was always effective.

"Now, Virginia May, tell these ladies and gentlemen, how old are you?"

"Eleven." The childish voice was faint.

"I'm afraid not many of us heard you, honey. Try to talk a little louder."

"I'm eleven years old. Last June."

"And you live with your mother and daddy, do you?"

"That's right."

"And go to Sunday School?"

"Yessir, at St. John's. Nearly every Sunday, except sometimes when the weather's bad."

The prosecutor reached into his pocket and pulled out a small book.

"Do you recognize this, Virginia May?"

"Yessir. That's my New Testament. I got it for not missing Sunday School a single time for six months."

Roberts rose and addressed the judge. "Your honor, this is a pleasant interlude, I am sure, but I hardly think that we are here to find out how well the child knows her catechism. I suggest this testimony be stricken and such questioning be left to her Sunday School teacher."

Sutherland smiled ironically. "Your honor, I think it unfair to assume that the defendant has a character, while this little girl has none." He turned to the jury, held out the Bible, shrugged, and smiled again. Roberts fought to keep from reddening at the pantomime criticism: *What manner of adversary is antagonistic to a child's religion?*

Judge Weaver, a very short, very hairy, very gray man, glanced from beneath shaggy brows at both attorneys. "You have a point, Mr. Sutherland. The testimony may stand. However, I suggest you get on with your case."

Sutherland nodded and turned to the child. "What grade are you in at school, Virginia May?"

"Fifth. Miss Kincaid."

"Have your schoolteachers ever tried to teach you right from wrong?"

"Yessir. All of them. Miss Temple, in the fourth grade, was *always* going on about how we ought to do this and that."

The prosecutor rubbed the side of his face, then the top of his head, a picture of discomfort. "Now, Virginia May, I want you to tell these people exactly what happened on October 8th. Don't be afraid. Just speak out."

The child folded her hands in her lap and began speaking to the judge. "I was—"

Judge Weaver interrupted her, speaking quietly. "You must not turn to me, my dear. Those people over there won't be able to hear you. Speak to them."

She turned to the jury. "I was downtown that day, and I guess I got interested in looking in the dime store too long. All at once I saw by the clock at Moore's Jewelry that I'd better be getting home. So, I went to the bus stop and was waiting there. I guess a bus had gone just before that, because I was the first one there."

Sutherland interrupted tenderly. "You were standing there alone, honey?"

"Yessir. By myself. Well, I wasn't there very long when this car drove up and stopped. It was a blue car, all nice and shiny and clean. I guess it wasn't new, but it did look nice. The man in it leaned over and opened the door and called to me. He said: *I'm going east, little girl, and I'll give you a ride if you want.*"

"And you got in with him right away?"

"No, sir, not right away. I'd been told not to. I knew it was wrong, but I thought about being late. And I'd always thought that bad men were dirty and ugly. He wasn't. His car was pretty, and he looked nice. So then I got in."

"And what happened, Virginia May?"

"We started off. He asked my name and how old I was and things about school. He told me that I was a nice little girl. He asked me where I lived. He acted real friendly. Then, when we got to Plum Street—that's about five blocks from home—he started asking me if I wouldn't like to have a box of candy, all for myself. He said he had one there in that little place in the front of the car. He opened the little door and showed me. I said, well, maybe I would. Then he said was I in hurry to get home. I said, yes, I was. He said my mother wouldn't mind, let's go for a ride, say out to Media Park. I said no, I had to get home. He kept coaxing, and the next thing I knew we were going right past the street where I live. I told him about it, but he didn't seem to hear. When I said it again, and he didn't stop, I reached over and turned that key there on the dashboard and pulled the key out and threw it on the floor. The motor quit and he had to stop the car to reach down for the key. I jumped out of the car real quick and ran home. It was about four blocks back by that time. My Mom and Dad were there and I looked scared, I guess, so they got it out of me what had happened. Dad got awful mad, and he found out who it was after I gave him the license number of the car. And that's all."

Prosecutor Sutherland pulled at his nose. "Would you know the man who gave you the ride if you were to see him again?"

"Yessir." She stood up and pointed at Arthur Bradshaw. "That's him."

Bradshaw shook his head and smiled ruefully to Roberts.

"Poor child," he murmured. "To misuse her this way, so young."

Roberts did not reply. He listened intently.

Sutherland spoke to the child again. "Virginia May, what fraction of a pound is one ounce?"

She puzzled, worrying her lower lip with her teeth. "One-eighth?"

He smiled gently. "No, it's one-sixteenth."

"Oh."

He leaned toward her. "Now, honey, another man wants to ask you some questions." He nodded to Roberts. "Your witness."

Roberts approached the stand almost gingerly. *This could blow up in my face any minute,* he thought. He looked at the unsmiling, slightly apprehensive little face. *She could be my own little Bessie. No, not Bessie. Think of her as Joan, the two-faced one from the next block, the liar and the trouble-maker, the one who runs back and forth with the she-said-this-about-you tales.*

"Virginia May, I am glad to find that you are so good about going to Sunday School. Do you know how God looks upon people who don't tell the truth?"

"Yessir. They're sinners. He punishes them."

"You don't want to be a sinner, do you?"

"No, sir."

"Then we don't need to worry about anything you tell me."

The child looked at him skeptically. "No—sir."

"Have you any brothers or sisters, Virginia May?"

"I have a brother that's older and a brother and sister that're younger."

"Four children in your family, then?"

"Yessir."

"What does your daddy do?"

"I'm not sure—"

"What is his work?"

The prosecutor jumped to his feet. "Your Honor, I object! There is a deliberate attempt here to create prejudice against a man who is less fortunate than others!"

Roberts turned to the judge with surprise stamped on his face. "Your Honor, such reasoning had not crossed my mind. I should be the first to affirm the thesis that all men are equal in a court of law. If Mr. Sutherland had listened to my opening, he would now realize that this is the very point I want to make in this trial. My present object is different. May I proceed?"

"You may proceed."

Roberts addressed the girl again. "I'll ask you again, Virginia May, what is your daddy's work?"

"He's a foreman on the night shift at the Iron Works."

"What time does he go to work?"

"Three in the afternoon."

"Do you see much of him?"

"Mostly on Saturdays and Sundays. He's usually asleep when I go to school, and he's gone when I get home."

Roberts turned to the jury and said only, "I see." He paused.

Then he said, "Virginia May, what day of the week was October 8th?"

She hesitated. "Why—it was a Thursday, wasn't it?"

Roberts stepped quickly to the table where he had been sitting and picked up a calendar he had spread out there. He returned and showed it to the child. "Thursday is right."

He turned and showed the calendar to the jury, giving them time to look it over. Then he rolled it up swiftly.

"Thursday, October 8th. Is that a school holiday?"

She made no answer. He leaned closer.

"Virginia May, was there a holiday that day?"

She looked at Judge Weaver. He nodded sternly. "You must answer, child."

A small voice: "No, sir."

Not asking her to repeat, Roberts said, full-voiced, "You say it was not a holiday. Why were you downtown, then? Why weren't you in school?"

Her hands twisted. "Mom asked me to go down to buy some things for her."

"Oh, your mother asked you. I see. That would make it all right."

"Yes—sir."

"Your daddy wouldn't have any reasons to be angry, then, if you came home when you were supposed to be in school? Not if your mother had asked you to go shopping downtown?"

"No, sir. I guess not."

"By the way—you weren't carrying any packages when you got into Mr. Bradshaw's car, were you?"

"No, sir," she said quickly. "I couldn't find what my mother wanted."

"All right, Virginia May, I won't ask you any more questions. That's all."

He turned and walked away.

Bradshaw whispered to him, "I'm glad you weren't too hard on the poor little thing."

Roberts frowned. "She's a chronic liar. And her lying can ruin you. I'd like to shake her until her teeth rattle."

"I still feel that you should have let me discuss this thing with the child and her parents. It might never have come to this. That little one will remember this all the rest of her life."

Roberts leaned closer to Bradshaw and spoke earnestly. "Right. I *want* her to remember it. If she's not headed off right now, there's no telling . . . Look! you never had any kids. Sure, you've worked with boys for years, but you see only the good side of them. Kids can be the worst liars on earth. But we have to be careful to handle this one just right. If she goes to pieces in front of the jury—"

Prosecutor Sutherland's dusty voice said, "Will Alfred Tucker take the stand, please."

Roberts settled back and studied the child's father as he took the oath. Short, burly, with mouse-colored hair shot with gray and a seamed skin robbed of color by a lifetime of sunless foundry work, Tucker faced the court defiantly.

The prosecutor leaned toward him.

"Your full name, please."

"Alfred Charles Tucker."

Sutherland glanced at the jury. "Ever mistaken for Alfred J. Tucker?"

Tucker snorted. "The head of the bus company? Are you kidding?"

"What is your occupation?"

"Just like my kid said—foreman at Moore Iron Works."

"What are your hours there, Mr. Tucker?"

"Three to eleven—the night shift."

"That doesn't give you much time with your children, does it, Mr. Tucker?"

"No. Hardly any."

"But in spite of that, you think your children ought to be brought up properly, is that correct?"

"That's right! I'll have none of my kids hoppin' from one gutter to another. If they're not brought up right, it'll be no fault of me and Sade."

"By the way, Mr. Tucker, your wife isn't here to testify because she's so upset by what happened that she's in bed under a doctor's care? Is that correct?"

"Yes."

"Now, Mr. Tucker, you've heard Mr. Roberts suggest that you pay very little attention to your children. Is that true?"

Tucker's face darkened. "That's a lie! Sure I'm not around much because of my hours at the Works, but when I'm home it's the kids first and other things second."

Sutherland coughed. "I'm sure of that, Mr. Tucker. Now, suppose you tell us what happened at your home on October 8th."

Virginia May's father frowned. "It was about 2:30 in the afternoon. I was getting ready to leave for work. I'd just picked up my lunch box when the front door bangs open and Ginnie comes running in, all out of breath. It's not time for her to be out of school, and she doesn't look so good, so I ask her what's wrong. She tells me about this guy giving her a lift and trying to pull some funny stuff on her. This makes me see red, and I'm all for going to look up this guy, but she says he drove off in a hurry. And, anyway, she remembers his license number. So, I tell the cops and give 'em the number. So after a while they ask the kid to identify this guy and his car, and that's it. That's him, all right."

Sutherland glanced at the jury. "Did you ever know Mr. Arthur Bradshaw? Ever work for him?"

"Never laid eyes on him before in my life. Read in the papers about him from time to time, but hardly enough to remember."

"Anyone in your family, or your wife's family, ever know him before?"

"No sir. Not a one."

Roberts got to his feet. "Objection. Such matters would be pure hearsay on the part of the witness."

"Sustained."

Sutherland smiled. "Very well. But you *did* have Arthur Bradshaw's license number."

"That's right. The kid gave it to me. That's the way the cops found him."

Sutherland smiled again. "Your witness, Mr. Roberts."

Roberts opened with a calm he did not feel. "You're a foreman at the Iron Works, I believe you said, Mr. Tucker?"

Tucker's animosity was ill-concealed. *You say I didn't take care of my own kid! You're on the side of this Bradshaw! We'll see.*

His answer was a growl. "I am."

"You work eight hours as a rule, exclusive of overtime?"

"That's right."

"Heavy work?"

"It takes a man's work and then some."

"Takes lots of sleep?"

"It does at that. I don't usually roll in before midnight, and it's 10-11 next morning before I'm up."

"What time did you get up on October 8th."

"I don't remember for sure. About 10 or 11, like I said."

"Did you see Virginia May before afternoon?"

"No, not till about 2:30."

Roberts became almost apologetic. "Mr. Sutherland implied that I cast doubt on your responsibility as a father—that I thought you paid little attention to your children. He misconstrued the questions that I asked your little girl. I realize that you only have limited time to give your children, and I think this jury should realize it. That *is* right, isn't it, that you have only limited time?"

Some of the antagonism left Tucker's face. The harsh lines relaxed.

"Yes, sir. Like I told him, I do the best I can in the time I've got."

"But, of course, Mr. Tucker, in the very little time you do have at home, you let the children know their father's around."

"That I do. They'd run all over their mother if I didn't make them toe the mark."

"You're strict with them, then?"

"I am. I'm not ashamed of it. Those kids'll be brought up right."

"In what way are you strict, Mr. Tucker? How do you discipline your children when you feel they need disciplining?"

"I tan their hides good. A taste of the belt works best of anything I know."

Roberts nodded gratefully, and the last trace of Tucker's antagonism vanished. "By the way, Mr. Tucker. Your daughter Virginia May said she wasn't in school the day all this happened because her mother asked her to go downtown. That's so, of course? Her mother did ask her?"

"I guess she did, if Ginnie says so."

"Oh, I see, you haven't checked with Mrs. Tucker," Roberts said worriedly. "I see . . . Mr. Tucker, what if Ginnie *hadn't* been asked to go downtown that day? By your wife, I mean?"

Tucker glowered. "You mean what if she'd cut school? Why, I'd have blistered her—" He stopped suddenly.

Roberts turned away. "That's all."

He sat down and glanced thoughtfully over his notes. A glimmering of Sutherland's still-to-come attack was beginning to appear. *Can I head him off? Or neutralize it if I can't head him off?*

Roberts was still turning the matter over when Sutherland said, "We intend to call no more witnesses, Your Honor."

Roberts stared in disbelief, unable to fathom Sutherland's motive. But it would help. It gave his own planned opening move a legitimate excuse.

"Your Honor," he said, rising, "the defense is unprepared for such a brief presentation by Mr. Sutherland, I must confess. If Your Honor please, I should like a fifteen-minute recess to confer with our witnesses."

Judge Weaver bobbed his gray head. "Court will take a fifteen minute recess."

After the recess seven witnesses in succession took the stand and testified to Bradshaw's high character. Some had known him since boyhood. They said that Arthur Bradshaw was a wealthy man of fine family who had devoted most of his life to youth work; that he had built the city's playground program nearly single-handed; that he had been a leading vestryman of his church for 26 years; that he had held office after office in charity and civic drives, all without compensation; that he had been on the board of directors of the YMCA; that although he had no children, he had been happily married for almost 30 years; that he wasn't ever known to drink; that he had never been charged with anything more serious than a ticket for overtime parking.

The prosecution found no loopholes. The witnesses were unimpeachable.

Roberts was about to call his eighth witness when Judge Weaver leaned over the bench.

"Mr. Roberts, how many character witnesses do you have?"

"Twenty-two, Your Honor."

"I think that fact should be noted. However, I think it unnecessary that the jury hear them all. I shall limit you to one more witness of this type, as I am permitted by law. I am sure you understand."

"Yes, Your Honor."

"You may proceed."

The eighth witness hammered home the spiritual side of Bradshaw's character. This one, Bradshaw's pastor, one of the city's most prominent clergymen, likewise could not be shaken by Sutherland's respectful probing.

The judge glanced at the clock. "Gentlemen, the hour is getting late. Court will recess until 10 o'clock tomorrow morning."

Roberts had begun the next day's session by calling a schoolteacher, Anna Temple, to the stand. She was an excellent witness, with a firmness of manner and tone that overlay the appearance of innocence her small size, round face, and wide eyes gave her. Her hair was a pale red—not a deep enough shade to warn off the unwary.

Roberts was matter-of-fact. "Miss Temple, what is your occupation?"

"Schoolteacher."

"At which school?"

"Walnut Street."

"What grade do you teach?"

"Fourth."

"Have you ever had Virginia May Tucker as a pupil?"

"Ginnie Tucker was in my room last year."

"What sort of student would you say Virginia May was?"

"What I would call average." Miss Temple had glanced at Sutherland, who was rising from his chair, and her green eyes flashed. "By that, I mean that she was neither very dull nor very bright. She was like so many of the rest of us." And the prosecutor sat down again, choosing to smile.

Roberts smiled, too. Then he went on: "How would you characterize her ability to learn, Miss Temple? Did she memorize readily?"

The answer was emphatic and precise. "She did *not* memorize readily, Mr. Roberts. Virginia May had to work for the things she learned."

Roberts' next question was more a plea for advice. "Miss Temple, would you say that Virginia May Tucker was a well-adjusted child?"

"Not altogether."

"Why do you say that?"

"Oh—for instance—she often made a fuss about some possessions of hers being 'missing.' She would tell me this not in private, but before the whole class. *Someone took my ruler.* Or, *My box of crayons is gone, and somebody's got it. Somebody, somebody*—you know? So we'd stop class and look. Invariably, the missing object would be found in her own desk."

"Have you any idea why she did this, Miss Temple?

Sutherland's quick "Object!" was suppressed by the teacher's equally quick, "I'll leave that to a psychologist, Mr. Roberts."

Judge Weaver looked at Sutherland. "Does the prosecution still object?"

Sutherland waved handsomely. "We withdraw the objection, Your Honor." He had suddenly decided not to tangle with the red-haired Miss Temple.

Roberts asked carefully, "How was Virginia May's attendance record, Miss Temple?"

"Very poor during the year I had her. One more absence without a legitimate excuse, and she would not have been promoted."

"These were mostly willful absences, not for illness or other permissible reasons?"

"That is correct."

"What reasons did she give you for these willful absences?"

"She made up fanciful stories and stuck to them."

Still carefully, Roberts asked, "You mean Virginia May lied to you when she did wrong, and stuck to her lies?"

"About her absences, yes."

Roberts said gently, "She lied to you, and stuck to her lies. That's all, thank you, Miss Temple." He looked at Sutherland. "Your witness."

Sutherland's cross-examination was obvious. Lying was a common trait in children, Miss Temple admitted. So was rebellion at confinement in schools. Yes, even the finest children sometimes rebelled and lied sometimes. Yes, otherwise, Ginnie Tucker was a well-behaved child. Yes, Miss Temple had taught other children who were far bigger headaches. And so on.

Roberts merely said: "I now call Ethel Kincaid."

Ethel Kincaid was another teacher, but tall and bony with iron-gray hair and quick, black eyes.

"What grade do you teach, Miss Kincaid?"

"Fifth."

"Which school?"

"Walnut Street."

"Do you know Virginia May Tucker?"

"She's one of my pupils."

"Tell us what you know of her."

"Well, I've been sitting back there listening to Anna Temple. I see no need to add to or change anything she's said. Of course, I haven't had the child in my room for more than a few months, so perhaps I'm being unfair."

"But, in general, you confirm Miss Temple's testimony?"

"Yes. Of course, the absences—maybe it's too early to tell. But there does seem to be a trend—a definite trend already."

Roberts glanced aside. The child's face was expressionless; her father's was mottled in anger.

"Now, Miss Kincaid, please tell me what you remember about October 8th and what Virginia May did on that day."

The teacher's features drew together in concentration. "It was a beautiful day, as I recall—real Indian summer. I remember the leaves on the maple by the schoolroom window were beginning to fall, and the class seemed far more interested in watching them than paying attention to me. The Tucker child had come in that morning very listless. It was particularly hard to keep her attention. Late in the morning I noticed that she had her head pillowed on her arm. She said she felt sick, and I sent her to the school nurse. The nurse reported that she had no temperature, but of course was to be excused if she said she was not feeling well. I wrote a note to Mrs. Tucker and sent Virginia May home."

"This was about what time, Miss Kincaid?"

"It was around 11."

"And that was all you saw of Virginia May that day?"

That's correct."

"And she was back in school next day?"

"Yes—and quite a different young lady," said Miss Kincaid dryly. "As chipper as you please. Completely recovered."

Roberts turned to the jury, raised a knowing eyebrow, and smiled. "Your witness," he said to Sutherland.

Sutherland approached the stand, looking thoughtful. "Miss Kincaid, Miss Temple has testified that in her class last year Virginia May was just an average student. What she learned was by experience, not by memorizing. Is that your impression, also?"

"Substantially, yes."

"Now, Miss Kincaid, you said that on the day in question this child appeared to be ill, so that she had put her arm on her desk and pillowed her head on that arm?"

She answered calmly, "That is correct."

"You also said that you sent the child home. You mentioned no one's accompanying her. Are we to infer that she went alone?"

Miss Kincaid drew herself up. "She insisted on it. Begged us not to call her mother, as her mother might be frightened. Since there was no sign of anything seriously wrong with her, and she lives so very near the school, I allowed her to go home alone."

Sutherland threw up his hands. "What kind of teachers do we have who let a sick child make her way along the public streets *alone?*" He walked away. "That's all."

As Miss Kincaid retired to her seat, face flushed, Roberts arose. "I shall ask Arthur Bradshaw to take the stand."

The buzz in the spectator's section had not yet subsided when Bradshaw, a striking figure, was sworn in and sat down. The light gleamed on his fine white hair.

"Mr. Bradshaw," said Roberts quietly, "please tell us what happened on October 8th."

Bradshaw spoke in a clear, controlled voice.

"Certainly. I assume you want detail bearing only on this—incident. I was downtown that day, buying two footballs at the Sports Center. The city playground touch-football league was just getting under way, and replacements for two old footballs were needed. I bought them and was starting to take them out to Jack Shields, our activities director, when I saw the Tucker child standing on the corner. She looked rather woebegone—worried-looking, I thought. I hate to see a child unhappy, so I stopped and offered her a lift. She accepted. We talked of a few general things. When we reached a point about four blocks from where she lives—as I know now—she asked me to let her out. I did. Why she got out there, I don't know. That evening the police came to question me, and the next thing I knew I was charged with this—this offense."

"Mr. Bradshaw, let's get this clear: You say that *you* stopped the car to let the child out?"

"Yes. As soon as she asked. But, as I say, I have no idea why. At the time, I assumed she lived near where she asked me to let her out."

"Is it true that you offered her candy?"

Bradshaw smiled. "Oh, yes. I always carry a box or two in the glove compartment. I've never met a boy or girl who doesn't like candy. She took some, too."

Virginia May jumped to her feet. "That's not true! That's a big lie, and he knows it! I didn't even touch his old candy!"

Judge Weaver rapped sharply, and Alfred Tucker pulled his child back to her seat. The judge looked at Tucker and spoke evenly: "Sir, your child's testimony has been heard. Please restrain her. I will not have this sort of thing in my court!"

"Yes, Your Honor." Tucker's expression wavered between embarrassment and indignation. He muttered fiercely to Virginia May, who shrank back defiantly.

"Why, that's all there is," said Bradshaw, spreading his hands slightly. "The incident was so trivial that I almost forgot it. If the officers had not come to my house so soon afterward with a warrant—on this ridiculous charge—I would not have remembered it at all."

Roberts gestured to Sutherland. "Mr. Sutherland?"

Sutherland walked slowly around Bradshaw, looking him up and down. Time ticked by as he looked. Finally, he spoke. "Mr. Bradshaw, your witnesses would have us believe that you're a living saint. You'll pardon my curiosity. I've never seen a saint in the flesh, and I want to remember you. Answer me this question: Even assuming that you've led the blameless life they say you have, have you never heard that men can change in their ways? In their later years?"

In his seat, counsel for the defense closed his eyes. *Here it comes.*

Bradshaw replied courteously. "I certainly make no claim to being anything but human, sir. I have heard of what you say, yes. As far as it would apply to me, it is untrue."

Sutherland leaned close to him, "Can you prove that?"

Roberts was on his feet. "Objection, Your Honor, Mr. Bradshaw is not required to prove the truth or falsity of such a gratuitous allegation."

"Sustained!" The judge was not young, either.

Sutherland said suddenly, "What's the license number of your car, Bradshaw?"

"23309—no, 233084J."

Sutherland smiled. "Not easy to remember, is it?"

Bradshaw reddened slightly. "Not under circumstances such as these."

Sutherland turned toward the jury. "*Virginia May remembered it!*"

Defending counsel Roberts looked up from his notes as Assistant Prosecuting Attorney Sutherland got to his feet and turned to the jury to make his summation.

Roberts jerked his thoughts back from the past with an effort. Days of this, and now it was approaching the climax.

He looked at Bradshaw's face, hoping to find in its calm a release from his own worries. But the serenity and confidence he saw there only caused him to reflect. *Doesn't he realize? Is it real—or only pose? In a few minutes from now, Sutherland can . . .*

Sutherland began. "Ladies and gentlemen of the jury, you may wonder why the prosecution had its case so very simple. The reason is that it *is* a simple case. That being so, why should I complicate it for you?

"We have here a situation in which there are no direct witnesses for either side. We have only the testimony of an innocent little girl on the one hand, and a grown man who has lived the best part of his life on the other. No other person, adult or child, was present. No person saw Virginia May get into Bradshaw's car, no person saw her get out—or, at least, no one has come forward so to testify.

"You have listened to a great many witnesses giving Arthur Bradshaw, a wealthy and prominent man, glowing character references. You have heard attempts to darken the character of the young victim, to make her out a chronic liar, and worse—a shameful heaping of insult on injury! All this adds up to a *complete* attempt on the part of the defense to make a case. You may ask yourself *why?* The People's case is simple and direct. We have complete faith in the integrity of this child, and her good, hard-working parents, without a great parade of witnesses. And so, I think, have you."

Sutherland pursued his original attack along several variations of this theme of simplicity, with flanking references to the iniquity of middle-aged men who prey on the young. It was clear that he was depending on the brevity of his speech and the innocence of childhood to carry the day.

Then the moment came that Roberts had been dreading.

"I want to call your attention to one further fact," said Sutherland. "You will recall that this man Bradshaw was traced by the police because little Virginia May remembered his auto license number. You will recall that this was no simple number—Bradshaw himself had trouble remembering it! Ah, but perhaps this child is a mathematical genius, a prodigy with figures? Hardly! When I asked her what fraction of a pound one ounce is, you heard her answer, 'One eighth.' Besides, both of her teachers have said—witnesses for the defense, mind you!—that Virginia May is a poor memorizer. *What better proof of her story can anyone ask than that she remembered a complicated license number?"*

With that, the prosecutor sat down.

Now that he had actually heard it said, Roberts felt relieved. The die was cast. The question was: Whose version would the jury believe—Sutherland's or his?

He faced the jury, his expression as grave as he could make it. "Ladies and gentlemen, I repeat what I said in my opening: In these times there are far too many assaults on the integrity of blameless men who have a lifetime of good works behind them. This is the thing which faces us here. I will say no more about Mr. Bradshaw's character. You saw the caliber of people who testified to it; you heard what they had to say about him. Let us get down to cases.

"Mr. Sutherland has accurately stated that we have no witnesses to what took place in Mr. Bradshaw's car on October 8th. But we have had ample testimony as to some other significant events of that day. You have heard the child's teacher give sworn testimony that she sent Virginia May Tucker home because of an allegation of illness that was not borne out by the school nurse's examination. You have heard Alfred Tucker, her own father, testify that Virginia May did not arrive home until 2:30 in the afternoon—although she was sent home from school at 11 in the morning. But the child says her mother asked her to go downtown to do some shopping. Did Mrs. Tucker send a sick child downtown shopping? Obviously not. Then it must have been Virginia May's own idea to go downtown. But if she was not feeling well, why didn't she go straight home? I don't have to point out to you, ladies and gentlemen, the almost embarrassing contradictions in this child's testimony.

"You have heard both of Virginia May's most recent teachers testify as to her unreliable character—her lying; her record of unexcused absences. You have also heard Alfred Tucker admit that he deals out violent punishment to his children when they do wrong. Do you begin to see the truth?

"Is it not clear that Virginia May Tucker deliberately faked illness that day, and without her family's knowledge went downtown to window-shop or go to an early movie, after which she drove home through Arthur Bradshaw's kindness—and then realized that she was getting home too early, that her father had not yet left for work and would want to know why she was home before school let out? Wasn't she counting on the long slow bus ride, with frequent stops, to get her home after her father's car had left? Didn't the speedier ride in Arthur Bradshaw's car destroy this plan of hers? *Don't you see that Virginia May invented this fairy tale about Mr. Bradshaw to divert attention from her own misconduct and to avoid punishment by the father she feared?*"

He scowled long and hard at all twelve of them. "Ladies and gentlemen of the jury, Mr. Sutherland has made much of the fact that this child, a poor memorizer, remembered a complicated auto license number. I ask you to think: *Isn't it far more likely that she made a special effort to remember that number just so her story would sound more convincing to her father?*"

Roberts paused, then said with weary repugnance, "Perhaps she also sought to gain attention as children just entering adolescence sometimes do, by the device of accusing an adult man of wrongdoing. An unpleasant thought; but ladies and gentlemen, the defense did not make this case unpleasant."

Roberts thrust the clean, sharp lines of his face forward. "I tell you, ladies and gentlemen, I am a father of a child—a girl—the same age as this one. Had I not been convinced of Arthur Bradshaw's utter innocence, I would never have undertaken his defense."

The jury deliberated the rest of the day. Someone took Virginia May out of the courtroom, and she did not return. Her father sat stiff in his chair, doggedly seeing it through. Sutherland spent much of his time in conversation with the bailiff near one of the windows. The judge was busy going through a mound of papers. Bradshaw methodically read a packet of letters he had brought with him.

Roberts occupied his time organizing an army of notes he had made for an auto theft case which was pending. Concentration was intermittently difficult. At one point, the jury requested a transcript of the evidence. *What do they want to know? Aren't they convinced the child has lied? Or did I slip up somewhere?* He glanced at Bradshaw, calmly reading business letters. *He's the one who should be wondering. Does he still think it can't happen?*

The day wore on. Finally, it was clear that the jury would have to be locked up for the night.

Bradshaw leaned over and whispered to Roberts, "What do you think?"

Roberts shrugged. "I try not to." He stood up. "Not very successfully, I'm afraid."

The morning was sunny. The courtroom was jammed. At 10:25 a.m. the jury filed back into the jury box.

Judge Weaver leaned across the bench, his hands clasped. He addressed Martin, the foreman.

"Have you reached a verdict?"

Martin's owlish face assumed a look of exhausted pique.

"No, Your Honor, we have not."

The judge considered. "Mr. Martin, do you think that by further discussion the jury can arrive at a verdict?"

"We do not, Your Honor."

"How are you divided?"

Martin looked in Bradshaw's direction. "We stand eight to four for acquittal. This has not changed for nine hours. We were up all night."

Judge Weaver pursed his lips and nodded. Then he leaned back. "Very well. The jury is dismissed from this case . . . . The others— please report back here at the usual time tomorrow morning."

The courtroom was quiet. There was no sound of either gratification or sympathy.

The spectators drifted away in knots of twos and threes. Alfred

Tucker, in a glowering group of friends and relatives, muttered with Sutherland. A number of Bradshaw's friends came up to express regrets and leave.

Roberts sat there alone at the table, packing papers in his brief case. He looked ten years older this morning—far more worn than he had looked the night before. His hands were trembling a little.

"What's next?" It was Bradshaw, bending over him anxiously.

Roberts looked away. "They'll ask for a new trial."

"But I thought you couldn't try a man twice!"

"There was no verdict, Mr. Bradshaw."

"You think that next time—?"

Roberts laid the briefcase down and buckled it shut. Then he rose and looked directly into Bradshaw's eyes. "There won't be a next time—for me, I mean."

Bradshaw frowned. "You're quitting? You don't think you can beat them?"

Roberts said slowly, "The best thing you can do right now—and I should have insisted on it before I took the case—is to see a psychiatrist."

Bradshaw's face went bloodless suddenly.

Roberts said, "Four people on that jury didn't believe the kid lied about you—even though they might well have believed that she lied about other things.

"Well, Bradshaw, they were right. I didn't see it till I got home last night.

"Bradshaw, both you and the girl made it clear that you didn't let her out near her home. She said she had to make you stop. You said you stopped where she asked. But it wasn't *near her home.* All right. Maybe somebody on the jury thought of it. I thought of it—too late—and that's why I don't want to go on with this. I'm a father, remember. Next time, Sutherland will think of it.

"Bradshaw, if that child wanted to avoid being punished by her father, it wasn't necessary for her to lie about you. She wasn't that close to her home. *She could have stayed away from her block until she was sure her father had gone to work.*"

14

The Touch of a Vanished Hand
(1992)

This story placed ninth in Ellery Queen's *readers' voting.*

"This is the photocopy I received," Porter said, holding the manuscript in his blunt fingers. He laid it on the mahogany chairside table by his right hand. His intense blue eyes looked calmly at Peter Richter across the restored, high-ceilinged Victorian room.

"And here is the original." Richter leaned across the fireplace, extending the pages with a hand all knobs and taut flesh. His face seemed to Porter to be one huge freckle crowned by thinning, unruly straw hair.

Porter held the original script close to the copy. The title pages both read "Strifeless Victory by Emma Porter." He leafed through pages at random and cross-compared.

"They appear to be identical," he said, extending the original to Richter.

"You read the story?" his visitor asked.

"I did."

"What is your opinion?"

Porter rubbed his coarse moustache with his left thumb. "Some questions first. Since Emma is no longer here to tell me, how did you get this?"

Richter perched on the edge of his leather chair. "As I told you in my letter, I do literary research—"

"Yes." Porter's tone resonated and overcame Richter's nails-on-blackboard, screaky voice.

"In the mid-70s, I was invited to conduct some sessions on my subject at the Seneca Writers Conference. There was a workshop on the short story at the same time."

He warmed as he saw that Porter was giving him complete attention. "At one of my discussions, a very pleasant woman dropped in, although she was not registered. She spoke to me afterward and introduced herself as Emma Porter, attending the story workshop. She had found my talk interesting, she said. I was gratified. I sometimes drift when I talk, and it can be heavy going for an audience."

"But she put you at ease," Porter remarked.

"Yes, she did."

"Did you two talk very often?"

"Just that one time. I might have forgotten her, but George Billings, who did the workshop, wrote to me later, enclosing this manuscript and asking me to confirm a Willa Cather influence he thought he saw in the text."

Porter brought his stocky frame upright in his chair. "Willa Cather? Quite interesting."

Richter waved a jerky hand. "It might have been, but Billings was killed in a plane crash the next week, and the manuscript found its way into limbo until three months ago."

"When I found it among a pile of miscellany, I almost discarded it, but then I thought that the author might want it."

"After all this time," Porter remarked.

Richter's freckles became deeper-hued. "As I said, I felt guilty and thought the author should have her work back."

"Fortunately," he added, "the Seneca people are like pack rats when it comes to records."

"But," said Porter, "we've only had this house four years. Our move must have caused some confusion. Didn't you think it wasn't worth it, after all?"

Richter lifted a hand. "It's the way it is with research. Once started, you can't quit."

Porter looked up at the marble mantel between them. "Seneca Conference? About as far back as those pictures."

Richter's gaze followed Porter's. At each end of the greenish marble mantel stood a color photograph in a brass frame. On the left was a picture of a younger, deep-tanned Norman Porter. On the right was the likeness of a laughing-eyed, round-faced woman with thick, greying brown hair.

"Emma Porter," murmured Richter. "Just as she was on the day we talked."

"You wouldn't have known her after the eighteen-wheeler rolled over on her little Mercedes," Porter said heavily.

"I'm sorry that this makes it so difficult for you."

Porter took two minutes before continuing. "The story in the papers read: 'Emma Porter, widely known as best-selling author Irmalin Porterfield, was killed today when . . . and so on and so on. Is that when you found out who she was? Or did somebody else tell you? Did you get the idea then?"

Richter stammered. "You make it sound like—"

Porter cut him off. "What do you want out of this *Mr.* Richter?" He held up his copy of the story. "Don't tell me you're offering to give it to me. I won't buy that."

Richter pulled himself together with an effort. "Well, you see, I have expertise in the literary field. I suspect that you haven't, if you'll forgive my saying so. I thought we might help each other."

Porter stared, saying nothing.

Richter went on, "This manuscript is worth more today than it was when she wrote it. Even if Irmalin what's-her-name was selling then, she wasn't as widely known as she is now. I have contacts—"

"She had an agent," Porter cut him off. "His contacts might be better than yours."

Richter rubbed the back of his neck. "Who is her literary executor?"

"I am."

"Did she leave any unfinished manuscripts?"

"Four novels in various stages of progress."

"How will you handle them?" Richter pushed.

"Finish them and sell them, perhaps. Maybe donate them to the university for their files. That's for the future."

"Did you say *finish them*, Mr. Porter?" Richter looked about him. "This is a restored Victorian mansion, isn't it, Mr. Porter? How high is this ceiling?"

"Thirteen feet."

"The mantel, there—faux marble?"

"Genuine, from Italy. I have twelve stained-glass windows, among other things."

"And you've had it four years. Restoration and furnishings didn't come cheap."

Porter nodded. His mouth twitched at the corners.

Unnoticing, Richter went on. "It must have cost a lot of money, Mr. Porter. But I understand that Irmalin Porterfield commanded a lot of money from books, TV rights, screen rights. None of my business, but who paid for all of this—this house and what's in it?"

Porter's smile was grim. "Both of us. First, we got the house for a song. Then—well, let's go back to a little before the Seneca Conference. Our lawyer called us in one day. The IRS was getting tough on joint accounts. On survival, a spouse had to prove, to the last penny, that he or she had contributed equally to a joint account. So he advised us to divide our property down the middle, giving each the same worth. And that is when, so the IRS could not quibble, Irmalin Porterfield's identity was made known to a limited number of persons. It would make her bankable talent clear."

"And," he went on, "I ceded certain of my stocks to her at that time. What we did with our money was each one's own judgment. We always acted in harmony, however."

Richter sat, not commenting.

Porter picked up the photocopy. "Now, this story. It might be hers. She did go to Seneca. She never mentioned this, however. I don't believe it's hers."

Richter stirred. "What makes you say that?"

"Little things I won't discuss unless I have to. Above all, it's just not her voice."

Richter, unable to control himself, lifted his upper lip. "Are you a judge of literature?"

"I've read all of her books, plus the unfinished ones."

"Writers do sometimes produce uncharacteristic work."

"Perhaps. And perhaps you found this story by someone else altogether, realized what had happened to Emma, and put a new title page on it. It's not handwritten."

Richter tried a conciliatory tone. "I assure you—Look, Mr. Porter, I could take this, do an in-depth analysis, and we'd both benefit from simultaneous publication. Why should you care? You seem to have plenty of money."

Porter stared at him. "Integrity."

Richter fidgeted in his chair. "Integrity? Believe me, in spite of your suspicions, I've not tampered with this. My credentials—"

Porter leaned forward. "Your credentials stink. As soon as I read this thing, I had a trace run on you. You've been accused of plagiarism in scholarly circles three separate times. Can't you stand on your own feet?"

Richter jumped up, clutching the original of the story.

"I'll get it published in spite of you, Porter. All you are is a moneygrubber, sanctimonious in the light from your stained glass. All she meant to you were the dollars earned."

Porter also rose. "Since you paint that portrait, I'll live up to it. You try to do what you talk about, and all of that money will fall on you and squash you like a bug."

Richter rushed to the front door and jerked it open.

"Ram it and jam it!" he shouted.

He tried to slam the door and break the etched glass in it, but Porter, anticipating this, managed to get there in time. He eased the door shut, but let it close with audible firmness.

Porter sighed. He walked slowly back to the living room, opened the drawer in a small writing desk, took an object out, and closed the drawer.

He crossed to the marble mantel and stood by the photograph of the woman.

"Hello, Sis," he said. "Just made a new acquaintance, didn't you?"

He moved to the center of the mantel and set up the picture he had taken from the drawer. It showed a white-haired woman with high cheekbones and a patrician nose. Her mouth wore a Mona Lisa smile.

"Hello sweetheart," he said, emotion underlying the words. "I didn't know your spelling had improved so much, years back. But you always managed our money well."

He walked across the room to the steep stair that rose to the second floor. Halfway up, a stained-glass window shed a warm glow on the oriental runner on the treads. At the bottom of the stair, a heavy, gilt-frame mirror hung on the wall.

He looked into the glass.

"Hello, Irmalin Porterfield," he said.

15

The Seeds of Murder
(1955)

Is it nurture, or is it nature?

Ellis, the private detective, pointed a long finger at the sheaf of typewritten pages he had just laid on the desk in front of Kendig.

"Your man's all in there. Everything. We've really done you a thorough job, gentlemen. I repeat, he's all there."

"How much would you like to bet?" I said.

My question was out of place, but it startled Ellis. He had almost leaned back in the metal chair, but it brought him forward, his shrewd deep-set green eyes snapping.

"Well, now, Doctor Carter, you're not being fair. You haven't read it yet." Then the expression on the detective's ellipsoid face relaxed. "Well, of course, the thing that made you gentlemen call on me . . . I forgot."

I think my colleague Kendig was a little annoyed. He usually is when the lines begin to appear in his plump face.

"I'm sure your report is as thorough as you say, Mr. Ellis," said Kendig. "Your agency was highly recommended."

Ellis inclined his head, his domed forehead gleaming. "Thank you, Doctor. We did try to do a job for you." He glanced at each of us searchingly. "Maybe you'd like to ask some questions before you read this?"

Kendig's brown eyes gleamed behind his glasses. If he were as impatient as I, there were two of us fighting to keep calm.

"I believe we might have one or two." His voice was calm and even. "Don't you think so, Harry?"

I studied the end of my cigarette. "I have one question." I leaned over and flicked ash as I spoke to cover up any undue emotion. "You remember, Mr. Ellis, we gave you a name: Iris. What did you find out? Who is Iris?"

Ellis took a drag at his own cigarette. "Gentlemen, as far as we're concerned, there is no Iris. I knew how you'd hammered at that when you gave us this job, and we've been extra-careful. Wallace doesn't know any Iris now, and we can't find that he ever did know any. And that means that we not only know the names of all the girls in every neighborhood where he ever lived, but we've been through the rolls of every grade he went through in school."

Kendig pulled at the tip of his left ear. "What was his mother's name? Full name?"

"Anna Marie Trumbull was her maiden name, changed to Wallace on marriage. No Iris among either the Trumbulls or the Wallaces." His wide, thin-lipped mouth quirked briefly. "And none of his toys or possessions was ever named that, either."

Kendig looked at him with interest. "An original notion which we didn't suggest to you, Mr. Ellis. May I ask if such service is customary?"

"No, Doctor. But with two psychiatrists for clients, I thought a fancy touch would be right up your alley."

I thought to myself that I'd like to get Ellis maneuvered into an analysis some day. Aloud, I said, "What did you find out about young Wallace and his mother?"

"First off, the old lady's dead. You know that?"

We both nodded.

"I'd bet Bill Wallace's life's been a lot brighter since that happened. It was natural causes, by the way. Cerebral hemorrhage." Ellis tossed this last out casually.

Kendig showed no emotion. I hoped that I did not, either.

Ellis glanced quickly from one to the other of us. Then he shrugged.

"Nothing would've surprised me, is what I mean. When you read what I've written, you'll see. I guess he's had one long fight of it through his twenty-two years—twenty-one of them, anyway. She died a year ago. She beat him often, lots of times without much excuse. She ran off all his friends. He never had any pets, that goes without saying. She made him take odd jobs to earn money when he was a kid, and she took all the money for herself. Didn't need it, either. When her husband died, seventeen years ago, she was left pretty well fixed. And as for young Bill and girls—you can guess."

He stopped and looked at us again. "Maybe this fits in with something you've uncovered? I mean, I read somewhere about mother fixations and all the trouble they cause."

Kendig said carefully, "What you've told us is very helpful, Mr. Ellis. I'm sure your report will be even more helpful."

"Thanks." He was still watching us, looking for some reaction. It was hard for me not to show one, even if people do say I remind them of "a strong, silent Westerner."

I've never tried to live up to that reputation, and it comes hard when I have to be impersonal.

"Phil," I said to Kendig, "I imagine Mr. Ellis must be wondering when we're going to pay him."

"No, no, Doctor," Ellis said. "It never crossed my mind. I'll send you a bill at the end of the month. You needn't be in any hurry. I never had any question—"

Kendig reached for a pen. "The University's credit is good, I'll grant. But Doctor Carter and I are paying for this. You know nothing about *our* credit."

Ellis protested more. "No, I wouldn't take it at this time. Haven't figured up all of the expenses. Let me send you a bill."

Kendig laid the pen down deliberately. "I like to get things settled, Mr. Ellis. If your agency hadn't been recommended as extremely honest, I'd be certain you had something unpleasant in the back of your head."

Kendig outclasses me in many ways, but sometimes he can miss the obvious in ordinary matters. "I think the only thing Mr. Ellis has is curiosity," I said.

Ellis's work evidently had thickened his hide over the years. He did not redden or show any other sign of being flustered. "Well, now, Doctor Carter, I'm human. Sure, I'm curious. But when I'm asked to do something, I do it. If the customer doesn't want to elaborate, that's his business. If I get too nosy, I lose customers. It's not smart to lose customers."

Kendig crossed his arms. "I hear a certain amount of claptrap about detectives respecting confidences, even under extreme pressure. Is there any truth in it?"

Ellis spread his hands. "I'm still in business. Would I be, if I didn't know when to keep buttoned up?"

"Phil," I said, "we're going to publish, anyway."

Kendig looked foolish momentarily, then covered up. "Certainly, Harry. But perhaps we won't include this one." He stared at me for a moment, then looked at Ellis. "Mr. Ellis, I think we'll take a chance. You'll tell no one what you hear?"

"Doctor, when I go out that door I'll have forgotten it. That's a promise."

I smiled. "You'll not forget this, Ellis. Maybe officially. But not personally."

Kendig got up and walked across the office. First, he locked the door. Then he went to the safe and removed several reels of tape. He ended at the tape recorder, placing one of the reels in the machine.

"Mr. Ellis, these tapes were recorded two months ago. They have been played back only once since they were made. Doctor Carter and I have avoided them in order to keep open minds." He fiddled with the machine, "Doctor Carter and I have been experimenting with hypnotic regression, using some of our students as willing subjects."

"Phil, better keep the discussion nontechnical. We don't want to seem to be trying to put one over."

"Sorry. To translate, Mr. Ellis, we have hypnotized some of our students and have suggested to them that the date is such-and-such in the past—say, April 10, 1939. The student relives his experiences, and we note them."

Ellis leaned forward, interested. "This is real? They don't feed you a line?"

"We think not. Their accounts are perfectly consistent with the age level of the time suggested."

"Sounds like you're on to something."

"It's nothing new," I said. "Several good men have tried it and reported on it. We've been looking for some original line to follow."

Still working with the recorder, Kendig said, "This tape is William Trumbull Wallace's. We have suggested that he is age twelve. I'm going to skip the portion where we hypnotize Wallace. Take my word for it—he *was* hypnotized."

As he spoke, I saw again the tall form of Bill Wallace stretched out on the couch—big and sturdy as a forest giant, dark, tightly-curling hair—but big, sad eyes and a cleft chin. A woman wouldn't have a chance: he'd either have to be worshipped or mothered.

I heard my own voice coming from the speaker: *Bill, you know what day this is, don't you? It's March 26, 1949.*

He answered: *March 26, 1949. Yes.*

Tell us about it, Bill.

I'm coming home. Coming up the front walk.

What kind of walk, Bill?

Brick. The sidewalk out along the street is cement. It's brick from the house to the street. Laid in squares, the bricks turned a different way in every other square.

Ellis nodded in agreement. He'd seen that walk.

All right, Bill. What kind of day is it?

"It's a pretty day. The sun feels good. Gee, I hope winter's really gone. There's a few crocuses along the walk, ready to open, it looks like... Now I'm on the front porch, taking off my overshoes.

Why overshoes, Bill?

Huh? Mom—Mother—said to wear 'em. Said the ground's still muddy, even if the snow is gone.

All right. Go on, Bill.

Now I'm going in and hanging my jacket in the hall closet...

Hello, Mother... No, I didn't leave the overshoes by the front door. Here they are, on the closet floor. I scraped 'em clean, too... But Mother, I'm not very late! I came straight home, I only lost a minute or two helping Mr. Townsend get his storm door off. I held the door steady while he pulled the pins on the hinges... Why, yes, he did. He gave me a dime. I thought it was too much, but he made me take it... No, I've still got it... Aw, couldn't I keep it this time? My old pocketknife's sprung—look, I'll show you—and I'd like to get enough to buy a new one! Lots of times, when I'm doin' something for somebody... But I can't fix it. I've tried. Well, I was *careful. I've had this one*

four or five years, I guess... Oh, all right! Here's the darn dime...
What're we having for dinner, Mom-Mother?... Oh... Oh, sure, I like
potato soup all right. It's just... Could we maybe have sausage some-
time? I like sausage... Oh—yeah. I'm sorry. I forgot it upsets you... No,
no, forget I said it. I don't want you to be sick just on account of me...
Now, look, Mother, I don't want you to. Please!... Huh? Today? Nothin'
special. Just another day... Well, now, wait. I forgot. Doctor Redmond's
been talkin' to me about joinin' the church... Well, he says I am old
enough, and that it's a sort of responsibility. And that's like you always
say, I better be watchin' my responsibilities. Anyway, if I go and study
at the church one night a week from now until... Aw, Mother, why not?
But I am old enough! I know what I'm doin'!... Well, no, I've never
pledged any money at church, yet. Aw, I don't think they can make me
sign up for any definite amount... I'd just give what I could. A nickel a
week, like now... It wouldn't? I think you've got the wrong idea,
Mother... Now, I didn't say that. No, I didn't say you lied. Anybody can
make a mistake. Maybe you're mistaken... Anyway, I want to join. I
like St. Matthew's. I like to go there. They treat me nice... No, I never
said you didn't. I wasn't even thinking it... But I am gonna join... Yes, I
am... What if I tell Doctor Redmond you won't let me?... Oh, yes, I
would, if he wanted to know what I had decided to do... I wouldn't go
right to him, but I wouldn't lie about it... Mother! You use that belt on
me for this and God'll punish you!... You're mean to me, and you won't
let me come unto Jesus like He said! He said forbid them not. He did! I
try to be good, I try hard, and when I want to be extra-good, you won't
let me! No, you won't! You won't!...

Kendig turned the volume down and looked at Ellis, who had
been listening intently. There were only a few more feet of tape left,
and the sound on them was unintelligible.

"You get the idea, Mr. Ellis."

Ellis nodded and wiggled a finger toward his report.

"It fits." He leaned back in his chair. "You know, that's a pretty
good recall."

"Ellis," I said, "it's not just recall, as you probably think of it. For
that period, he *was* a twelve-year-old again."

Kendig rewound the tape and slipped another one on.

"Let's see what you think of this, Mr. Ellis."

I tried to see which one he was using. "What's this one, Phil?"

"This is Terry. I thought we'd better use a warm-up."

I turned to Ellis. "Terry is a different subject. A girl, Edna Terry. Please listen carefully."

Ellis looked at me as though he thought we had sold him out. "That name wasn't in your instructions. We didn't come across any Terry girl."

"You shouldn't have," I said, casually. "She has no bearing on the case. Another subject, entirely."

The recorder began to speak. Kendig was talking:

Edna, listen carefully, this is very important. Today is June 14, 1963...

Ellis' reaction was all I'd hoped for. A slap in the face would have had the same effect. He muttered, *"Three years from now?* For the love of—!"

Kendig waved him to be quiet.

June 14. Why, yes. Yes!... This is the day! It's a beautiful day... There are the birds; morning light's pure gold... I wonder if he's up this early, too? Oh, Bob, Bob! Four hours until 10 o'clock! Mr. and Mrs. Robert C. Stone... What? Oh, no, Mother, don't fix me any breakfast. I don't think I could eat a bite... Strength? Who needs strength? I could live on air today... You're sure everything's ready for the reception? Did Mrs. Black ever send over the extra punch cups? I've been so excited, I didn't notice... I wonder where Bob's going to hide the car? He said for me not to worry, Frank Hughes and that crowd would never find it... Well, I'm not so sure. That Frank can think up more things... I wonder if I'll be like Betty McCulley when I'm supposed to say, I do? *She was so meek and mousy all through the ceremony, up to that point, and she practically shook the rafters when she said it. If everybody hadn't been crying so, she'd have brought the house down... Mother—try not to cry, will you?... You're not really losing me!...*

Kendig shut it off.

"I think you get the idea, don't you, Mr. Ellis?"

Ellis' jaw was slack.

"You're kidding!"

"No."

"It was framed! It was somebody rehearsing for a play. Or you fixed it up to throw me off."

Kendig went on working with the machine. Unconcernedly, he said, "It's the genuine article, Mr. Ellis."

"We'd give anybody an affidavit," I said.

"However," said Kendig, staring at me through his glasses, "there are different points of view."

He picked up another roll of tape and fitted it into the machine.

Ellis looked at me uneasily. "I thought I had both feet on the ground. Now—"

Kendig started the machine. "Gentlemen, we return to young Wallace."

My voice came out of the speaker:

Now, Bill, you feel quiet and relaxed?

Yes, I feel fine.

All right. We're going ahead now, to September15, 1965. Got that? September 15, 1965.

September 15, Yeah... What a day! Boy, am I tired! I'm going to need glasses at this rate. My eyes...

Bill, I don't get you. Where are you?

Huh? Oh—getting out of my car. I've got it parked in the drive-way.

Driveway? Where? Where are you living?

Why, at my house. You know. You've been there. Just a little place. Well, you never did come back after that first time... Not all the place a man could want, but we'll have a better one some day... I hope.

What kind of car? What does it look like?

Car?... Oh, just a Chevy... Last year's... Two-door. You remember the ads...

All right, Bill. I'll shut up. You were going into the house.

Yeah... Door still sticks, a little... Wish I could remember... Oh, hi, Iris...

I didn't dare look at Ellis' face.

Oh, just another day, chasing columns of figures. Thank God for the IBMs, or it really would have been one for the books. I think I'll have a quick one... Look, let's not get off on that again. This is my house, too, and if I want a drink, I'll take one... You don't have to like it. If you'd married a drunk, it would be something different. You've never

seen me anything but sober, have you? . . . Well, have you? . . . All
right, don't admit it . . . That's what I like about you. You expect me to
admit what a heel I am every five minutes, but you never admit
anything. Hell with it . . . Well, now I feel a little better. Where's the
paper? . . . What? Who? . . . No, thanks. Tell 'em to look for another
boy. Tell 'em to hire themselves a full-time accountant . . . I should
keep books for Dwyer's Confectionery in my spare time! . . . Well, sure
I appreciate your trying to line it up, but life's just too damn short. I
don't get out enough as it is. Work all day and spend all my spare time
keeping the place up . . . Don't know why you fussed about it when I
wanted to hire out the painting. We'd have got it done a lot quicker,
and I wouldn't have used up so much of my vacation . . . Well, maybe
having my own office would give me more money to hire things out
and maybe it wouldn't . . . What do you do with all the money I give
you? Save it? Sure, maybe a day'll come when we need it, but I figure
we need some of it every day . . . Oh, hell, I'll take the pup for a walk .
. . Here, Mike. Here, boy. Come on, Boy. Here, Mike . . . Iris, do you
know where Mike is? . . . Well, all right, but you can give me a civil
answer about where my dog is. I know you don't like him, but I do . . .
What? WHAT DID YOU SAY? . . . Just for a bunch of dahlia plants?
With the mattock? You hit him with it and then had the garbage man
haul him off? . . . NOW YOU LOOK HERE, Iris . . . You don't let me
have a life of my own. You hoard all our money so it's no good to us.
You want me to work twenty-six hours a day because you're greedy for
more. And then, because an animal gives me a little affection, you . . .
I'M SICK OF YOU! SICK OF YOU! . . . LET ME GET MY HANDS ON YOU,
YOU . . . NO, YOU WON'T GET OUT OF IT . . . SCRATCHING WON'T
HELP . . . GO ON, CHOKE, DAMN YOU . . . CHOKE . . . Iris. Iris! . . . Oh,
my God . . .

Kendig turned and snapped the switch. Ellis' face was greenish-white. The back of my shirt was clammy.

Kendig clasped his hands and stared calmly at the detective. "That's Iris."

Ellis shakily lit a cigarette. "And we don't know who she is. No way to warn her! Damn it, there must be somebody we missed!"

Kendig shook his head. "Not necessarily."

Ellis looked at me in appeal. "You mean, he hasn't even met her yet?"

I said, "We don't know that."

Kendig spoke carefully, "It's not so fantastic as you might think, Mr. Ellis. Iris might be a name which has caught his fancy. We are inclined to think—or I am, at least—that these 'future' manifestations are traumatic, and—"

"Stick to two-bit words, Phil," I said. "No sixty-four dollar ones, remember?"

He readjusted. "What I mean to say is—we know, from the subject's past history, that his childhood was unhappy because of his mother's influence. You confirmed that yourself. We also know that questions about *specific* things in the future—his house, his car, you recall—drew only vague answers. Young Wallace was explicit only about things which are projections of what he has on his mind at the moment."

Ellis grimaced. "What things on his mind!"

"Doctor Carter is a little more the romantic than I am. He refused to dismiss these 'futures' as rationally as I do."

I looked at Ellis and smiled without humor. "If I could make money at it, I'd go back to farming."

Ellis considered each of us in turn. "Well, which is it: Did he look into the future, or didn't he?"

Kendig put his clasped hands behind his neck. "He did not. I'll be glad to go over it in more detail, if you like."

I got up to unlock the door. "Ellis," I said, "*it doesn't matter.* Don't you see: *If he did see the future, somebody's got to watch for Iris. If he didn't, the seeds of murder are there, anyway.*"

AUTHOR'S NOTE: *So far as details are concerned, the cases described in "The Seeds of Murder" are wholly fictitious. However, the scientific experiments which suggested the plot are absolutely true. For further information please consult pages 472 and 473 of "Science," Volume 119, Number 3093, issue of April 9, 1954, where the experiments are reported by Robert Rubinstein and Richard Newman of the Department of Psychiatry, School of Medicine, Yale University.*

16

The Impossible Theft
(1964)

The hand is quicker than the eye in this "locked room" mystery.

Robert Chisholm's palms were faintly damp. He had less confidence in his ability to persuade than in the probability of his accomplishing the theft. Still, he hoped that theft would be unnecessary.

Donald Tapp looked up at him sardonically as he turned the second key to the double-locked room.

"Robert," he said in a voice that had been hoarse all his life, "you still haven't told me how you found out about my collection."

Chisholm's shrug was the smooth, practiced action of a man who knows and controls every muscle. He permitted his smile to be open and frank, instead of the faintly diabolical one which his lean face wore on certain occasions.

"I told you," he said. "A mutual friend. He just doesn't want to be identified."

Tapp reached around the metal doorframe and pressed a switch. Fluorescent lights hesitated, blinked, then came on.

He pursed his thick lips. "Mutual friend? I don't advertise what I own. There is always a clamor to have such items as these placed in a museum. Time enough for that when I'm dead." He studied Chisholm quizzically. "Would it have been Perry?"

Chisholm became poker-faced. "Sorry, Don."

Tapp still waited before ushering him into the room.

"Robert, I haven't seen you in—how many years? Even though we played together as boys and went to school together—clear through college. Now you arrive in town for a convention and after all these years you look me up. I'm delighted, Robert, delighted. I don't see old friends much any more. Chiefly my own fault. But, Robert, you arrive and make small talk and then, in the middle of it, you ask to see the collection."

Chisholm said, just a shade too casually, "If you'd rather not—"

Ask yourself, Don, he thought; *when you were a kid and somebody asked "Whatcha got?" you'd always hide it, make a big secret of it.*

Tapp stepped away from the door, lifting a stubby right hand. "Come in and look. I'll be honest and say I'm particular. Not everybody can get into this room. But you're an old friend. At least, you were never grabby like the other kids."

If you only knew, Chisholm thought, entering the strongroom which Tapp devoted to his collection of rare historical documents.

It was a windowless room, about 12 feet by 20, lighted only by two rows of fluorescent tubes overhead. The only door was at the end of one long wall. To the left, on entering, the wall was decorated with a large rectangular mirror in a gilded frame. The borders of the glass itself were worked in elaborate scrolls and tracery. Ranged against the two long walls and the far end of the room were nine exhibition cases, four along each wall, one at the end. The cases were of beautifully grained wood, with glass tops.

Tapp beckoned Chisholm across the room.

"We'll begin here." He snapped a switch on the side of one cabinet, and the interior became evenly illuminated, showing a frayed yellowed paper on a background of black velvet.

As Chisholm bent his lean shoulders to look at the descriptive card, Tapp began to explain, "The last page of a letter by James Garfield. Identity of recipient unknown, but signature authenticated. Can you read it? It says, *As to your wish that I make a Fourth of July address in your community, this would give me the greatest pleasure. I must defer my answer, however, because I feel that there is some prior commitment which I cannot identify at this moment. Should this prove to be only faulty memory, I shall be pleased to accept . . .* Of course, when you realize this was written just prior to that fatal July 2, it makes for interesting speculation, doesn't it?"

As Chisholm murmured an appropriate reply, Tapp switched off the light and moved to the right. "In this cabinet I have a receipt from William Tecumseh Sherman to Braxton Bragg for money that Bragg asked Sherman to invest for him in San Francisco in 1854, when Sherman was in the banking business. The accompanying letters have great historical significance."

Chisholm stared with a fascination he did not need to pretend as Tapp led him from case to case, showing him exceptionally valuable documents signed by George Washington, Abraham Lincoln, Andrew Johnson, Alexander Graham Bell, John C. Fremont, William H. Seward, and Carry Nation. This last brought a chuckle from Tapp.

"Simple, isn't it? *No truce with Demon Rum! Carry Nation.*"

He snapped off the light in the eighth case and turned toward the last one, at the end of the room. He paused and glanced at Chisholm.

"Robert, what was it you told me you were doing these days?"

"Area man for Shaw and Pontz Lock Company." Chisholm reached toward his left lapel with supple, slender fingers and tapped the identity tag which was stuck to his coat by the adhesive on the back of the tag. "The convention is one of hardware dealers. I'm showing a new line of passage sets."

Tapp shrugged off a faint air of perplexity. "Well! Let's look at my prize exhibit." He illuminated the last cabinet.

In it lay a scrap of paper no bigger than the palm of the average-sized hand. It was even more yellowed than the other documents, the ink slightly more faded. It was charred along the top edge.

Tapp said nothing. Chisholm bent to look closely.

"Some kind of register or ledger?"

"That's right. From an inn."

"Three names. James—Allen? Samuel Green. That one's clear. But Button Gwinnett?"

Tapp rubbed his stubborn chin with his solid-fleshed left hand. The tip of his broad nose wrinkled in amusement.

"You're amazed, Robert. Yes, the rarest of all signatures in United States history. Your amazement is justified. But it's genuine, I assure you—absolutely genuine."

"But how did you—? Where did you—?"

Tapp shook his head. "When I am dead, all information on these documents will be released to the museum which will inherit them. In the meantime, that information is my secret."

Chisholm glanced around the room. "I hope you have these well protected. And adequately insured."

"Both, you may be sure."

"What protection, Don? This interests me, since I'm in the lock business." He bent over the case containing the Button Gwinnet signature.

"I'm satisfied with it," said Tapp bluntly.

"Are you?" Chisholm drew a key ring from his pocket. It bristled with keys—and other odd-looking objects. His supple fingers gripped something which Tapp could not see, and he inserted it quickly into the lock on the edge of the glass top. Something clicked and he lifted the lid of the case. "You see?"

Instantly a clamor began somewhere in the big house.

"I see. And do you hear?" Tapp gave his old friend an exasperated look. "Come on. I'll have to shut off the alarm."

"Might I remain here, Don? I'd like to look some more. I promise I won't touch anything."

Tapp shook his head. "Nobody looks unless I'm here. But if you don't want to come with me, you may stand by the door, outside, until I come back."

After Tapp had locked both locks from the outside, Chisholm stood by the door thinking about the strongroom. All the cases were obviously wired to alarms. He had seen no wires. This meant that the wiring probably went through the legs of the cases, where it would be difficult to reach. Did each case activate a separate alarm, or trip a separate indicator, to show exactly which cabinet a burglar had attacked? Probably.

And the mirror on the left wall? What was a mirror doing in a room of this sort?

Tapp came bustling back, his chunky frame still radiating annoyance.

"Now, Robert," he said, unlocking the door for the second time, "I ask you, *please* don't try to sell me any locks—not this time."

"We have some things which would help you, if you'd let me demonstrate," Chisholm said, as he began to scan the room closely on re-entering.

"All right, all right—but show me a little later. In my den or in my office. Of course, I'm always interested in improving my safeguards. But not just now."

Chisholm moved slowly from case to case, keeping up a running conversation to distract Tapp's attention. But he could discover nothing other than the alarms and the puzzling mirror. There were, of course, the two locks in the door—which would be impossible to jimmy, or to pick. Then two tiny air passages, high in the end walls, protected by a fine, strong mesh caught his roving eye; but he dismissed them as irrelevant.

Finally he straightened and looked directly at Tapp.

"There's a lot of money represented here, Don."

Tapp nodded soberly. "I'd hate to tell you how much, Robert."

"And you'll put even more documents in this room, won't you?"

"If something good comes along."

"This, of course, means that you have the money to spend."

Tapp's expression grew pained. "You're being a bit ingenuous, Robert. Of course I have the money."

"Have you ever considered putting some of that money into something more worthwhile?"

Tapp grinned without humor. "I should have known there was more to this visit than a chat with an old friend. Now comes the touch. How much do you need?"

Chisholm shook his head. "The need isn't mine, Don. It's Green Meadows Hospital. A check for $50,000 from you would put their new equipment drive over the top."

Tapp grimaced. "Green Meadows! I've heard their pitch. A corny one, too. Green Meadows—even the name's corny. No, thanks, Robert. Why did you have to spoil our first meeting in years?"

Chisholm said seriously, "I don't consider geriatric problems corny, Don. Are you sure you just don't like to think of the kind of future any one of us might have to face? Look here: I've contributed $20,000 myself, and believe me, it'll hurt for a while. If I could give twenty, surely you can give to charity.

"It would be a deduction on your income tax return."

"Thanks. I know all the possible deductions upside down and backwards."

"Is there any way I can reach you on this, Don? Could I tell you some details of their program—"

Tapp shook his head firmly. "No way at all—not even for an old buddy. Especially not for an old buddy. I can't stand corn."

Chisholm's eyes narrowed, and his brows slanted up in a manner familiar to many people who had met him.

"All right, Don. You won't listen to a rational argument, so I'll make you an irrational proposition. Is your gambling blood still what it used to be?"

Tapp's smile was grim. "If it's a sure thing, I'll still bet."

"Would you bet a check for $50,000 that I can't steal something of value from this room?"

Shock and amazement crossed Tapp's heavy features. "Why, that's idiotic. I won't listen."

Chisholm held out a restraining hand. "No, wait. You have complete confidence in your safeguards. Let's see just how good they are. I don't know a thing about them except there are locks on the door and alarms connected with the cabinets. Yet I am willing to bet I can beat your system."

Tapp pondered. "There's nothing in the world which can't stand improvement. But $50,000—"

Chisholm pressed on. "Here's what I propose: shut me in this room for fifteen minutes—no more. In that short time I guarantee to steal one of these documents—*and get it out of here in spite of all your safeguards.* If I get that paper *out* of this room, you'll make the contribution to the hospital."

"And if you fail? What is your stake?"

"I'll guarantee to increase the efficiency of your safeguards one hundred per cent."

"That's hardly worth fifty thousand."

"I own a quarter interest in my company. I'll assign it to you."

Tapp eyed him shrewdly. "You seem pretty confident."

"I might be betting on a sure thing, Don, the way you like to do. Or I might be willing to take a bigger risk than you."

Tapp mused, "Fifteen minutes. And you have to get it *out* of the room by the end of that time. You know, I could just leave you locked in here."

"No, you must come and let me out. But I must agree to let you search me or put any reasonable restrictions on me until it's absolutely clear that you've lost."

"When do you want to do this?"

"Right now."

Tapp studied Chisholm speculatively. "Chisel—remember how we used to call you that?—when we were kids a lot of the others had contempt for me because I wouldn't take chances. I've done pretty well in life because of caution. But don't be misled: I *will* take a risk. I'll take this one."

Chisholm smiled broadly, but this time his smile had a Mephistophelian look. "Fine. Shall we begin?"

Tapp held out his wrist silently and they compared watches.

"Fifteen minutes from the time you close the door," said Chisholm.

Tapp went out. As he pushed the door shut, he called through the narrowing crack, "Not that I think you have a snowball's chance, Chisel."

The door had scarcely closed before Chisholm was examining the mirror on the long wall with minute attention. He would have to proceed as though it were a two-way mirror, with only a thin layer of silver. He doubted that this was true, but he could not ignore the possibility. Finally, he located what he was looking for: a circular loop in the border decoration on the glass. The glass within the loop looked subtly different.

His smile grew even more diabolical. He quickly stripped the convention badge from his left lapel and pasted it over the circle in the glass.

He then turned swiftly to the cases, taking out his keyring. Before he started to use it, he took a pair of thin rubber gloves from another pocket and put them on. Then, at a pace only a little slower than a walk, he went from case to case and opened the locks, which he had studied while looking at the documents the second time.

When he had lifted all the lids, he laughed at the thought of nine alarms ringing simultaneously in Tapp's ears, or nine position lights flashing at one time in Tapp's face. He then went from case to case and reached inside each. All his movements were swift. Most of them were intended as pure misdirection.

Finally, he had what he wanted. Now all he had to do was to make sure—doubly sure—that he was not being observed. To provide a cloak, he removed his jacket and slipped it over his shoulders backward, with the back of the jacket hanging in front of him and concealing his hands. His fingers made several rapid movements beneath the protection of the jacket. Then he suddenly reversed the process and put the coat back in its normal position.

He looked at his watch. Only eight minutes had passed.

For the remainder of the time Chisholm lounged against the doorframe singing slightly ribald songs in a clear, but not overloud, voice.

Precisely at the end of fifteen, first one, then the other of the door locks was opened. The door itself, which was covered with a paneling of steel, swung back.

As Tapp stepped in, his glance already darting around the room, Chisholm clapped him lightly on the back.

"I hope you brought the check with you, Don."

Tapp half turned, and Chisholm felt a hard object bore into his ribs. He looked down. Tapp had shoved a pistol into his side.

"I have the check, Chisel, but you're going to earn it—if you get it at all. Step back."

Chisholm obeyed.

"Now, go over there to the opposite wall and sit on the floor by that first case. Fine. Extend your arms so that one is on either side of the leg of the case. Very good."

Chisholm, from his position on the floor, saw Tapp take a pair of handcuffs from his pocket. Warily, the shorter man approached him.

"Wrists out, Chisel. Good."

Tapp leaned over and snapped the cuffs on Chisholm's wrists. The tall diabolical-looking man had not ceased to smile.

"A lot of trouble, Don, just to find out what I did take. A lot of trouble to keep me from confusing you even more while you look. But I'll be glad to tell you without all this melodrama."

"Just be quiet, Chisel," Tapp said calmly. "If you aren't, I'll slug you with the butt of this gun."

"Violence wasn't in our agreement, Don."

"You were not completely honest with me, Chisel. After you put all your misdirections into action, the hunch I'd had about you came out into the open. I remembered your hobby when you were a boy. I made one phone call to a local convention delegate I happen to know, and he told me you still practice your hobby. You're still an amateur magician, aren't you, Chisel?"

Chisholm shrugged. "I do a little routine to catch the buyer's attention, then I work it into a sales talk for our products. It often helps."

"Spare me," Tapp muttered, peering into cases. His face darkened. "You lied to me, Chisel. You said you would take only one document. I count three of them: the Garfield letter we read, the Seward I mentioned, and the Button Gwinnett."

"I didn't lie," Chisholm replied calmly. "Figure it out for yourself."

"Misdirection again." Tapp turned and stared at him, but it was clear that his thoughts were elsewhere. In a moment he turned back to the cabinets and carefully lifted the velvet in the bottom of each. He found nothing.

He stood in thought for a few more minutes.

"The Garfield and the Alexander Graham Bell are the same size, and so are the Seward and the Lincoln. The Button Gwinnett doesn't match any, but it is *smaller* . . ."

Once more he went from case to case, this time lifting each of the remaining documents. When he had finished, he was smiling. He had found two of the missing papers carefully placed beneath others of the same size. He restored the Garfield and Seward documents to their proper cases.

"That leaves only the Button Gwinnett, Chisel. But this was what you had in mind all along. It's obvious. And if you're worth your salt as a magician, its hiding place won't be obvious. So let's eliminate the commonplace."

Tapp went over the cases carefully, first lifting out all the documents, then each piece of velvet. When he had replaced everything, he closed and locked the cases. Then he dropped to his knees and inspected the undersides of the cabinets.

He found nothing.

He walked to each end of the room in turn and reached up to the tiny air passages. The mesh in both was still firmly in place, and he could not budge it at either opening.

Then his eye caught the mirror.

"Oh, and another thing—" He walked to the mirror and stripped off the convention tag. "You're a sharp fellow, Robert."

Chisholm laughed. "Was my guess right? Closed-circuit TV? Did I cover the lens?"

"You put a patch on its eye, I must admit."

"No two-way mirror?"

"I considered it, but with several receivers on the TV, I can be at any one of several places in the house. A two-way mirror would only restrict me."

He walked over and stood in front of Chisholm. "Two possibilities still remain. One is that you might have slipped it into my own pocket at the door. So, I'll check that out now."

He searched through all his pockets, but found nothing which had not been in them before.

He now stooped and unlocked the handcuffs, but made no move to take them from Chisholm's wrists.

"Drop the cuffs there, get up, and go to that corner," he said, motioning with the gun to the bare corner farthest away from the door.

Chisholm obeyed. When he had moved, Tapp inspected the area where the magician had been sitting.

"All right. Now take off your clothes—one garment at a time—and throw them over to me."

Chisholm complied, beginning with his coat jacket, until he stood completely stripped.

Tapp went over each item minutely, crushing cloth carefully, listening for the crackle of paper, inspecting shoes for false heels and soles and the belt for a secret compartment. From Chisholm's trousers he extracted a handkerchief and an ordinary keyring. In the pockets of the coat jacket he found a larger collection. The inside breast pocket yielded a wallet and two used envelopes with jottings on the back. The outside pockets contained the unusual keyring, the rubber gloves, a nearly full pack of cigarettes, a crumpled cigarette package, a ballpoint pen, and a rubber band.

Tapp examined all these things with intense concentration. In the wallet he found money, a driver's license, a miscellany of credit and identification cards, and a small receipt for the purchase of a shirt at a local department store. He searched for a hidden compartment in the wallet, but found none. He then shook the cigarettes from the pack, but neither the pack itself nor the individual cigarettes was the least out of the ordinary. Replacing them, he then smoothed out the crumpled pack. Several items inside it he dumped on the top of one of the cases: a twist of cellophane; two wadded bits of brownish, waxy-looking paper; a fragment of wrapper from a roll of peppermints; and part of a burned match. He snorted and swept this trash back into its container.

He drew in his breath with an angry hiss. "All right, Chisel, let's look *you* over. Turn around. Raise your arms. All right, now sit down on the floor and raise your feet."

"Nothing on the soles of my feet except dust from the floor. You should clean this place oftener," said Chisholm, leaning back on his arms.

Tapp's only answer was a growl.

"Have you checked the ceiling?" Chisholm asked

Tapp looked up involuntarily. The ceiling was bare.

"See, you wouldn't have thought of that, would you?" Chisholm mocked.

Tapp leaned against one of the cabinets and aimed the pistol at Chisholm's midriff.

"Chisel, playtime is over. I want that Button Gwinnett back."

"Or else, eh? You forget a number of things. We haven't yet established whether the paper is in this room or out of it. We haven't exchanged your check for $50,000 for the stolen document. I haven't even put my clothes back on. And, incidentally, I give you my word: the missing paper isn't in my clothing."

Tapp tossed the clothing to Chisholm. "It doesn't matter. You're going to tell me where that piece of paper is."

Chisholm began to dress. "How do you propose to make me tell? Shoot me? On the grounds that I broke into your house to steal? A respected businessman like me—steal? If you killed me, then you'd never find your paper. If you only wounded me, I'd refuse to talk. So where are we, old friend?"

Tapp said grimly, "This bet of yours is just a stall. Once you get out of this room you'll take off with that signature to certain other collectors I could name. Why else won't you admit who told you about my collection? Only a handful of people know about it."

Chisholm was tempted to yield on this point and reveal to Tapp that it was the district manager of Tapp's own insurance company who had mentioned the collection to him in strict confidence. Had he not wished to show even the slightest sign of weakness, he would have told this.

"The whole thing was strictly honorable," Chisholm said. "This stunt was my own idea."

"And my idea," said Tapp heavily, "is to lock you in here without food and water until you return that paper. When you finally get out, I could always claim that I thought you had left the house and had locked you in without knowing."

Chisholm shook his head. "I had more respect for you, Don. If you did that, you'd either have to leave the other documents with me— and risk my destroying them—or take them out and have their absence disprove your story."

Inwardly, Chisholm was beginning to have qualms. If Tapp should abandon reason in favor of a collector's passion, as he seemed about to do, anything might happen. The best course was an immediate distraction.

"How do you know," he said challengingly, "that the paper isn't *already* outside the room?"

Tapp snorted. "Impossible!"

"Is it, now? There is a small trick I often do at dinner gatherings *which depends entirely on the victim's being too close to me to see what my hands are really doing.* I move a handkerchief or tissue from hand to hand near the victim's face, then throw it over his shoulder when my hand is too close for him to see exactly what I've done."

Tapp said warily, "But at no time were you outside this room."

"I didn't have to be."

Suddenly Tapp understood. "You mean when I came in!" He moved back and reached behind him to open the door. "Stay where you are." He stepped out and pushed the door shut again.

Chisholm waited tensely.

The door opened to a pencil-wide crack. "There's nothing out here, Chisel."

Chisholm answered evenly. "I didn't say there was. But if you'll use the brains I've always given you credit for, you'll realize that I don't *want* to steal your precious piece of paper. If I had, why make the bet? Let me out of here and give me the $50,000 check for the hospital, and I'll tell you where the Button Gwinnett signature is."

A silence followed his words. Seconds dragged by. Minutes.

Finally Tapp spoke. "You swear that this will end here? That you won't even tell anyone about this incident? I used to think your word could be relied on, Chisel."

"I'll swear on anything you name."

"That won't be necessary." The door opened wide. "Now, where is it?"

Chisholm smiled and shook his head. "First, the $50,000 check."

Tapp eyed him shrewdly. "I don't know that the paper is out of the room. I don't owe you anything unless it *is* outside, and you're still *inside*. But you agreed to tell me where it is."

Chisholm kept smiling. "I'll swear again, if you like. The paper is outside the room, according to the conditions of our bet."

Tapp studied him. "Very well, come up to my den and I'll give you the check. You have my word that I'll keep my part of the bargain. Now—*where is that paper?*"

Chisholm stepped to Tapp's side and clapped him affectionately on the back. Then he held out his right hand.

"Here."

As Tapp snatched the document from him, Chisholm fished in his own jacket pocket. He took out the crumpled cigarette pack, opened it, and shook out the contents.

"Remember the convention badge I stuck over your TV camera lens? Such badges are only strips of cardboard coated on the back with a permanently tacky adhesive—the way surgical adhesive tape is coated." From the cigarette pack he took the two scraps of brownish, waxy paper. "That gave me the idea. It's easy to obtain tape with such an adhesive on *both* front and back. This brown paper protects the adhesive until it's peeled off, making the tape ready for use. In this case I kept a small bit of such tape in my pocket, removed the Button Gwinnett signature from the cabinet, exposed the adhesive on one side of the tape, and stuck the Button Gwinnett to that exposed side. Then I made the other side of the tape ready and palmed the whole thing."

Chisholm repeated an earlier gesture. A look of comprehension spread over Tapp's face.

"When you came into the room at the end of the fifteen minutes," Chisholm explained, "I simply put the Button Gwinnett paper in the one place you couldn't see—*on your back!*"

17

The Stone Man
(1986)

This story started as just a title.

P ete Bender never thought of the phrase "living rock" as a
literal one, although he had heard it and understood it. It was
the medium in which his father had made his life's work, as
had other ancestors. Pete, himself, had planned his life to carry on
the tradition.

Four other men worked for him, but for Pete the tradition and his
line were about to end. With one of his tools of the trade, Bender had
slain his wife, who had never presented him with a child of either sex.

Bender, a spare man with a lean face, intense blue eyes, and jet
black hair, did not fit the image of Hercules as a stonemason. Perhaps his wife Marie, a hoydenish type only one generation away
from France—as Bender was from his own native soil—had brought
this on herself.

"You build fine houses for the rich," she was fond of saying. "But
do you bid on the fancy buildings for the city government? The
exclusive clubhouses? The bridges in the city parks? No. What's
wrong with you?"

Pete sipped his wine and bestowed a faint smile. "Aren't you
living comfortably?"

"Comfortably, yes. Excitingly, no!"

Anyone could have written the script from then on. It ended on
the day when Marie and Pete arrived home late within minutes of
each other. Pete was sorting his tools at the back of his truck when
the red Ferrari stopped to let Marie out. It roared off as she teetered
in Pete's direction.

Bender eyed her with disgust. "What is it?" he said, biting off the words. "You're not worth enough for him to see you to the door? Or can't he look me in the face?"

She tried to toss back her hair, but the effort was too much.

"Not afraid of you," she muttered. "You wouldn't make two bites for him."

Pete was holding his favorite knapping hammer. He hefted it. "That one, he wouldn't have any teeth to bite with."

Marie tried to focus her eyes on the tool. "You know somethin'? Long time ago, you cut yourself a hunk of granite and stuck it in your chest. Where most men have a heart. No blood in you, either. Just water 'n a sludge of granite dust."

"A home," Pete growled, "what kind of home have you ever made for me?"

"Who could make a home outta . . . maus—mausoleum?" She swayed, spilling words. "I need to be warmed."

Once Pete had wanted to create for her something beyond anything a man ever made. He remembered this now and mentally saw it washed away like a sand castle by the sea. Warmth he had provided, to excess. Suddenly, it was all too much.

His arm came up, almost unbidden, and he hit her with the flat of the hammer. Four times, each blow on a different side, her head turned with the force of every stroke.

When he stood over what was left, he passed his right hand over his face and groaned. Then he went into the house to the telephone.

To his surprise, his call was answered.

Gathering his will, he said. "This is Bender. You'd better call the police. I've just killed your whore."

"May I fill your glass again, judge?" Arthur Price asked, gesturing in the direction of his visitor's right hand.

Judge Whiteman stirred in the depths of the leather chair. "I'd like that, Art."

Price, a successful lawyer still some years away from becoming an institution, walked across the family room to his bar. "Have I told you we're thinking of a new house?" he said casually.

Judge Whiteman, a John Doe sort who donned distinction with his black robe, looked about him. "Hunting a place to spend it, is that it? I'd be satisfied with this, myself."

Price added water and ice to the scotch. "It's been quite comfortable, but frame has always bothered Anne. New paint job every few years, this and that. She'd like for us to go to stone."

"Lower upkeep, I'll agree," the judge said, accepting the glass. "Initial outlay—you can afford it, I'd say. Who would do your stonework?"

"That's the problem," Price said, sitting in the companion chair opposite. He smoothed his graying hair. "You're about to sentence the man I'd hoped to get. I'll probably have to hire somebody from out of town. There's nobody else anymore."

Judge Whiteman sipped. "Bender? He didn't operate all by himself. Get his crew. They might come up with somebody to head it."

"I thought of that, but they feel that they'd need someone with Bender's business sense and eye for the finished product."

The judge mused. "A pity that his father had to die twelve years ago. That old Italian—" He paused. "Or was he Austrian? He changed his name before he came here. Could it have been Benda? Or Bendt? No matter."

"As you say, no matter," the lawyer said impatiently. "What sentence are you going to give Bender?"

Judge Whiteman stared into his glass. "I haven't made up my mind yet."

Price consulted his own drink. "It's a pity to make a talented person's services unavailable to the public. Under the circumstances, I might have done just what he did."

The judge looked up. "I have never explored what I think you're hinting. But why not? Other judges have done it."

"It might not be too popular."

"With whom? the judge asked. "Oh, with Jules Vernet, the wife's brother—of course. And maybe with that hunk of sleaze who precipitated it all. I wonder why Bender didn't split *his* skull? Can you think of anyone else?"

"Some of the unpredictable public. Those who've seen Marie Bender's picture but never knew her."

Judge Whiteman thought it over. "I try never to let the public influence me. Still, careful thought seems to be indicated."

Judge Whiteman had called two persons into chambers before he sentenced Pete Bender for the murder of his wife, Marie. One was Bender himself; the other was Jules Vernet, a wide-shouldered, barrel-chested worker of wrought iron. Where Bender's darkness ended at his hair, Vernet was black of eyes and beard, as was his scowl.

The judge, now robed, was, to his visitors, the unquestioned embodiment of the law. He looked first at Vernet, seated on his left.

"I have requested both of you to be here," he said, "because what I intend to say in court will be unusual. Mr. Vernet, I don't want you in there unprepared because I don't want you upsetting the dignity of my court."

Vernet's milk-white skin flushed. "I respect the law, Your Honor."

The judge rubbed his chin. "I'm sure you do. All the same—"

He turned to Bender. "What sentence are you expecting?"

Bender shrugged, expressionless. "Not for me to say. You're the judge."

"Mr. Vernet. Any opinions?"

The red was fading on Vernet's cheekbones. "I'd throw the book at him."

Judge Whiteman nodded. "Understandable. She was your sister."

He clasped his hands and looked down at them. "The evidence would indicate that Mr. Bender acted in a moment of blind rage, after some provocation. He should, of course, have checked himself. He is not known to be a violent man, according to those familiar with him. Unfortunately, the penal system in this state has no outlet for his talent, even in hard labor.

"On the other hand, when Mr. Bender is sent to prison, this community will lose the services of a very skilled person. True, he has been well paid for those services. And one way of looking at his incarceration is that the citizens of this state will be paying handsomely to keep him locked up, his talents no longer available for anything constructive.

"In recent years," he continued, looking up, "the courts have taken a careful look at certain criminals: hit and run killers, embezzlers, perpetrators of various types of involuntary manslaughter, and others. They have decided that justice is better served by allowing them to remain outside prison, dividing their time between continuing with their normal lives and devoting their energies to public service. This permits their families to survive and society to benefit."

The judge looked directly at Bender. "I have decided that this is what I shall require of you, Mr. Bender."

The stone contractor's voice was husky. "Thank you, Your Honor. It's better than I deserve."

"And *that's* the understatement!" Vernet roared. He leaped from his chair and started for Bender. "I'll kill him now and take my chances!"

Judge Whiteman had anticipated this and had already pushed a buzzer. The rear door burst open, and two husky guards rushed in. Vernet had barely reached Bender before they seized him and dragged him aside.

"Mr. Vernet!" the judge snapped. "Now you see why I wanted this private session. Set him in that chair again," he directed.

When things had quieted, Judge Whiteman addressed the room in general. "I'll now finish this discussion. Mr. Bender will be permitted to take up his business again. But, there are two things he is required to do, and others might be added later."

"First, the county wants to build a small nondenominational chapel in memory of its citizens who died in the Korean and Vietnamese wars. They prefer that the material be stone. You will undertake this contract. Your men will be paid. You will not. Your efforts will be a public service. When this is finished, there might be more."

"Second, you are to build a memorial obelisk for the woman you murdered."

"She's already buried, with a good headstone over the grave," Vernet interrupted."

"The column will be set in one of the divider islands in one of the cemetery drives," the judge said. "It will be an honor, sir."

He turned back to Bender. "You will be given a sketch of the obelisk. You will be furnished with the materials you specify. You are to do the entire erection of the column yourself. There are certain rules you must follow."

"Anything you say," Bender agreed.

The judge continued, "You will be permitted to lay the pavement around the base at your own pace. However, you are to construct this column with stones no larger than ten inches long by six inches in each of the other dimensions. These stones can be irregular. You may lay only one stone a month. The last act will be to fix a simple bronze plaque to face the column. It will read 'Marie Vernet Bender, February 17, 1943-June 6, 1973.'"

"When you complete the column, your sentence will be served."

Bender had listened attentively and with growing interest to the conditions of his sentence. From the moment of his arrest until an hour ago, something had been dying within him. Not to be shaping stone would reduce him to zombie status. Now he would be at least almost whole again. He truly mourned for Marie—the Marie of the day they married. He privately felt that the Marie he had killed had enough memorial already.

"I have some questions, Your Honor," he said.

"Go ahead."

"For this column—what kind of stone?"

"Sandstone, limestone, granite—it makes no difference."

"I should have said, 'which style.' "

The judge frowned. "Dressed quarried stone." He studied the stonemason. "Are you trying something, Bender?"

Bender shook his head. "I'd have preferred rubblestone, but I'll follow your directions, Your Honor."

"Rubblestone!" Vernet snorted. "Plain old fieldstone. Even now, he hasn't any respect for her!"

"I'll make it so that even you will be proud of it," Bender said.

"That's another point," Judge Whiteman interrupted. "Mr. Vernet will be one of three inspectors of your handiwork. He will be critical, but fair. We shall see to it that he is."

Bender whistled between his teeth. Then he said, "Is the column to be hollow or solid?"

"Solid."

Bender's eyebrows raised.

"Are these requirements unsatisfactory?" the judge asked. "If so, I have an alternate sentence ready. It's the customary type."

"Quite satisfactory, Your Honor," Bender said, avoiding looking at Vernet. "At least, to me."

After Judge Whiteman had pronounced sentence in open court, Pete took steps to adjust his life to the new pattern imposed on it. He cleared the house completely of any influence Marie had ever imposed on it. This done, he found himself living in austere surroundings. He coped with them temporarily by closing rooms he did not immediately need and generated cash by selling discards. Vernet attempted to claim some of these things, but Bender ignored him.

In quiet moments, he made calculations about the column. It was directed to be no less than three feet square at the base, tapering to a point no fewer than six feet above the ground. He was allowed to extend the square at the base or increase the height if he wished.

When he had finished his estimates, he understood the judge's stipulations. He mentally bowed to the jurist or to his advisor, if one had been involved.

The construction, at one stone a month, would last twelve years. He grinned. Unless—

There was no specification about the mortar.

He could use as many or as few stones as he wished, provided the workmanship was sound and pleasing to the eye.

His feeling of elation diminished. He knew that his pride of workmanship would not let him take absurd shortcuts.

He decided to count on eleven years, at least.

The adjustment to a changed life was not easy. Bender found himself in places where Marie had been favored, many of them not in the least cheap or tawdry. In the large, the congregation of his church shunned him, preferring to forget the teachings of their Leader. In the end, Pete found religious acceptance by a mission doing no-questions-asked work in the lower stratum of society.

He did not look for friendship and companionship. His workers had not changed loyalties, and there were enough friends and acquaintances who remembered with disapproval Marie in her later years.

He had intended to begin on the memorial, both as a start to freedom and as a renewal of his personal bond with stone. Before he could do more than order a supply of sandstone from local quarries, Arthur Price had approached him about his new house.

Bender studied the plans before him on his work table.

"A well-designed house," he said. "It will be a pleasure to work for you, Mr. Price."

"You don't see any problems?" the lawyer asked, running a long finger down the edge of the table.

"Oh, no. You'll find us very acceptable. One thing: you don't need us to lay up the block for your foundation or inner wall. After all, the stone is the facing on the block. It might cost you less to have somebody like Miller Brothers do the block. We can do it all, of course, but we get along with the Millers. It's your money."

Price stood absorbed in thought.

Bender smiled. "Take your time, Mr. Price. Give me an answer later. We have plenty of other work, I assure you."

"I'm thinking of Zimmerman as the main contractor. Any ideas?"

"Good man. I don't know his feelings about me. We'll see."

Price rapped the edge of the table with his knuckle. "Well, if it's all right with you, I'll see about Miller Brothers."

"Sure." And good public relations for you, thought Bender. You'll be running for something someday. Spread it in lots of places.

The mistaken thought also came to him that Judge Whiteman was directing work toward him, to help him remain a useful citizen.

He frowned. In his mind's ledger, there was enough debt already.

The county was stalling on the memorial chapel, still arguing about small points in the design.

As soon as he realized this, Bender went to the cemetery, located the spot intended for the memorial, and measured it off. He arranged with the superintendent for removal of the sod for the base of the column. Then, when the grass was gone, he returned, dug and smoothed the ground, and poured footers.

The next day, he came back with boards he had sawn for the frame and installed them. Then he took the cornerstone he had already cut and dressed and carefully laid it, wiping away a small amount of excess mortar when he had finished.

It looked small and inconsequential, a token beginning of something a trifler would never complete. In Pete's mind it was different. Each stone would remind him of what he had done.

The base of the monument took him eighteen months. His first thought was to fill the center with concrete, without stone, but he feared the effects of expansion. A faulty job would tie him to this project for too long a time.

Price's house was long since finished, to his and Judge Whiteman's satisfaction. The memorial chapel construction was into its second month.

The nineteenth month of the obelisk had come, and Bender had laid the first stone of the second course, tapering the edges of the outer face.

The day after it was laid, he received word from Judge Whiteman's secretary that the three-man inspection team would be looking at his work. Bender asked to be present.

The request was a surprise. Bender knew that previous inspections had been made, but he had never attended and no comments had ever been made to him.

He arrived at the cemetery at ten in the morning. His ex-brother-in-law and two other men were already there.

Vernet looked at him when he walked up, then at the other men. "I guess we can start now," he said. He addressed Sheets, a weather-beaten general contractor. "Why don't you look at it first, Bill?"

Sheets glanced apologetically at Bender. He clearly viewed inspecting one stone as a waste of time. He walked to the monument and bent over, peering at it.

"Looks like a good job of layin' to me," he said.

"Not lopsided? Is it good and firm? Go on, Bill, shake it," Vernet prodded.

The older man, looking even more sheepish, leaned over and began a half-hearted push at the stone. As mild as his effort was, it was too much.

The mortar crumbled, and the stone fell to the ground.

"Well, would you look at that!" Vernet bellowed. "Bill—you saw that. So did you, George. That's shoddy workmanship if I ever laid eyes on it. Did you ever think you could get away with this, Bender?"

Bender's mouth was set in a thin line. "It's been tampered with. Never in my life have I set a joint that didn't hold."

"Would you listen to him," his ex-brother-in-law hooted. "That was the story of my sister's marriage: cheap, skimpy, tenth-rate . . ."

"I'll re-set it this afternoon," Bender said. "If it's not like the Rock of Gibraltar tomorrow, I'll quit my business."

"You won't quit until the whole job's done," Vernet roared, shaking a big finger. "And you won't put it back until next month. It counts as another stone."

"But—?"

"Another stone. Ask the judge."

Bender glanced at the other two men. "Hey, you guys, you know me. You know my work. Ever know me to do anything like this?"

Both of them avoided his eye. Sheets muttered that anyone could have an off day. "You'd have caught it next month, I'm sure, Pete," he finished.

Bender said nothing. He picked up the stone and drove off with it, thinking hard all the way.

When he reached his supply shed, he went to the materials that had been specifically furnished for the construction of the column. He ignored the stone pile but headed for the bags of sand, lime, and cement. He put samples from each into separate small bottles.

An hour later, he was at Vernet's place of business. He found the man in the workroom where he shaped the wrought iron. A hanging lamp in the last stages of construction was getting attention.

"What do you want?" the heavy man demanded. "You come here whinin', wantin' me to get you off the hook?"

"Not me," Bender replied. "I just took samples of some of my materials over to Elementals Labs for analysis. It wouldn't be too hard for some switching to have been done. And I think it happened."

"You lookin' at me?"

"Not necessarily, Jules. But you have to admit, I might think I should."

Vernet picked up a hammer and hefted it. Bender wondered if he was going to work with it or was making a threat. "Yeah, I can understand. To me, you'll always be a bastard. Marie was my kid sister, and you could have done a lot of things other than killin' her."

Bender looked about him. Several large charts illustrating different styles of calligraphy were taped to the wall. "What are those? You taking up fancy writing on the side?"

The change of subject surprised Vernet. "No. I got a contract for puttin' rails on fancy balconies on a house for Dave Grinstead. They want alternate initials worked into 'em, his and hers, to match their handwriting. I got these for study and practice."

"All right," Bender said. "I'll put it this way: I don't think you'll use spot welds when you put initials into Grinstead's rails. Do you think I'd do cheap work on Marie's monument?"

Vernet gave him a long look. "No, Bender, I don't think you would, believe it or not. I don't know what the lab will tell you, but I've not touched your stuff. But that doesn't let others out."

He turned to lay the hammer down, then he glanced back at Bender. "Or maybe somebody had it done."

Later, Bender learned that powdered chalk had been substituted for his lime and a mixture of barytes, carbon black, and a trace of cement (for odor) for his cement. He got rid of the bags and put his own materials in their place. The problem never recurred although once, two years later, the entire upper surface of the older construction was soaked with an oily substance that prevented new, water-based mortar from adhering. Bender restored the surface with paint thinner and a wire brush, then laid the next stone successfully.

No incidents ever occurred on his private jobs or with the chapel.

The years passed without any other bother. Once a fresh bag of cement set up a month after being received. Since Bender still used his own supplies on the monument, this was no problem. He did suspect that water had been injected into the bag with needles, but he returned the bag without comment and got a fresh bag.

Four years after Marie's death, Bender met an attractive blonde, Louisa Trubar. She was twenty-eight, born in Slovenia, Yugoslavia, but a resident of Maryland since early childhood. She and Bender met at a beach in Virginia, found they were decidedly compatible, and married. The union was happy, and their first son arrived fourteen months after the wedding.

Not long after the wedding, Bender met Sheets, the contractor, on the street.

"Hey, Pete," the older man said, thumping him on the shoulder. "I hear you got something nice at home now. Congratulations."

Bender thanked him and they made small talk.

"How's your ex-brother-in-law taking it?" Sheets asked.

"Hasn't said a word," Bender replied. "Hardly his business, is it?"

"Well, no," Sheets admitted. "He's of Corsican descent, isn't he? Aren't they supposed to harbour grudges?"

"I don't know. Are they? Louisa's people had a hard time in World War II, but she's not about to cut down any Germans."

Sheets spat into the gutter. "I could never figure out if he was madder at you or Judge Whiteman over your sentence. He had his back up with the judge even before that, I guess you know."

"No, I hadn't heard."

"I guess it came to a head while you were waitin' for trial. Jules' father had bought a nice piece of land out in Overbrook, before Jules was born. About five acres. He kept it up, but he never did anything with it. When he died, Jules inherited it. He had his own place, so he figured it for an investment. So it would have been, if any new industry would be wanting to move a small unit here.

"At the same time, the school board was starting to think about a new grade school, but they were unaware of this land. Judge Whiteman knew what they wanted, and the Vernet land was well situated, so he talked them into considering it. They ended up getting it."

"But didn't Jules get a fair deal?" Bender asked.

"Oh, yes, but you know the Board can use eminent domain. They did. Jules didn't get anything like he might have otherwise. He couldn't dicker. He's pretty bitter about it."

Sheets added an afterthought.

"I heard rumors about commission."

Bender grimaced. "I don't even want to guess who got it."

Eleven years and seven months passed, and the memorial was finished except for setting the paving and fixing the plaque.

Bender, now a father of two boys and a girl, worked harder on the last day's stonework than he had on any part of it. This was the pavement around the base, where he was permitted to work at his own pace, ignoring the number of stones. He worked with a steady rhythm, truly enjoying it and realizing that it had been worth doing.

I destroyed a person, he thought. Not a nice person. But I had no right to make that judgment. Maybe this was the way to make me realize it. God, forgive me. Then this other thought: Marie, forgive me.

The pavement completed, he went home. Next week, the plaque would be installed.

The next day, he drove by the site to have a look, to see if any changes should be made.

As he wound his way among the headstones, the columns, and the occasional small tombs, something seemed odd. The general panorama was changed somehow. Bender could not explain the feeling.

Then he rounded the last turn before the three-sided island where the monument stood.

Had stood.

Nothing was there except a barren square spot surrounded by a larger area bare of everything except sand. A shower of stone chips and chunks of mortar covered the grass and part of the cemetery drive.

One of the cemetery workers was shoving the debris on the paving into piles with a pushbroom.

Bender, shaken and unbelieving, climbed from his car and walked over to him.

"What in God's name happened here?" he asked.

The workman, a short, sinewy man in navy jeans and khaki work shirt, slowed his effort without stopping completely.

"City. Couple fellows come by with a big pickup and some sledge-hammers. Busted 'er up but good, flung it all in the truck, and hauled it away."

Bender knew the man was not involved, but he had difficulty restraining himself from physical assault.

He finally calmed down. "But why?" he said.

"You better go see Keller," the man answered. "They showed him some paper. I never saw it."

Bender wasted no more time but went to the superintendent's office. To his relief, Keller, who was in charge, was in.

The superintendent was an average-sized man with a long face. He wore striped coveralls and a railroader's cap, from which gray hair straggled. He was sorting work slips when Bender came in.

"Hello, Pete," he said. "Guess I don't have to guess why you're here. Sit down?"

"No, thanks," Bender said. "How come, Sam? You know how many years' work have gone down the drain?"

Keller leaned back. "I do. Can't tell you how sorry I am. But they came here with a fistful of papers, and there was no way to argue."

"Papers? What kind?"

"An order from Judge Whiteman that the monument was to be torn down. It had been inspected and found in a deteriorating condition."

"Deteriorating?" Bender shouted. "That shaft would have stood up to a nuclear bomb!"

"Woulda said so, myself, " agreed Keller. "But they had a copy of an inspection report, and deteriorating's what it said. Signed by Bill Sheets, Jules—"

"I know who signed it," grated Bender. "And the shaft's gone, so I can't stuff the lie down their throats."

He stood cursing under his breath. "Not that it matters, but what did they do with the stone?"

Keller rubbed his chin. "Probably took it to use in the base for the cut-through between First and Clark."

"No good to me, anyway," Bender said. "I'll have to start all over."

"Maybe they won't ask that of you," Keller remarked.

"But they will," Bender growled. "You can count on it, they will. I should have seen this coming, years ago. I heard a legend when I was a kid. A guy in hell, rolling a rock up a hill. Just as he got to the top, it always rolled back down. That's what they set up."

When he left, he went home. His chest felt as though it contained the stone that Marie had said it did years ago.

When he entered, his house was empty. That suited him because he wanted to be alone for the moment

He began by calling Sheets.

"Bill. Pete Bender. What's this about a bad inspection report on my monument?"

Silence met his question. Finally Sheets spoke. "Pete, I'm not sure I heard you right. Inspection report? What inspection report?"

"The one that made Judge Whiteman order them to tear down Marie's column. The one you three clowns signed. And don't give me any innocent crap. A guy saw a Xerox of the thing."

"Pete, I swear by anything you want to name that I don't know what you're talking about. I never even saw such a thing, let alone signed it."

"You swear?"

"I swear."

He hung up, his hands shaking and his thoughts racing. The actual work on a new column was small, measured by time consumed and labor done. Its weight on his spirit was of the Earth itself.

His memory went back to the time he had seen Vernet about the earlier bad inspection. He replayed the scene—the business with the hammer, the calligraphy charts—

Forgery would not be too difficult for a man with a good eye. Signatures—easier on paper than in iron—?

A rage began to build in him, the sort of thing that had not happened for nearly twelve years.

Bender went to his home workshop, looking for his knapping hammer. He was unable to find it.

He left the house and went to his business storage and tool shed. He searched for the hammer, but it failed to turn up even there.

"The bastard's own tool," he growled. "Better yet, I'll use that."

Before he left he picked up a pair of heavy rubber gloves, worn when smoothing large areas of mortar. He threw them into his car and drove to Vernet's house.

There was no answer when he rang the bell of the sprawling ranch-style dwelling. He was not surprised. Vernet was childless, and his wife spent much time on community projects.

He walked to the rear, to the neat aluminum shed where Vernet worked. The door was locked, but Bender was surprised to find no deadbolt or guard. On a chance he took from his pocket a multi-function tool that contained a key chain, pocket knife, and other useful implements. He opened out a sturdy nail file and applied its point to the lock. In seconds he had it open.

Vernet's workroom was a collection of articles in various stages of construction. Bender went through them, looking for a hammer. He found a small sledge, considered picking it up but decided to wait until he had determined how to confront Vernet.

As his attention wandered, a new thought began to build in his mind. It had not been Vernet who had conceived his punishment in the first place. In fact, his ex-brother-in-law had been antagonistic to the judge, as Sheets had said. And Vernet had made vague hints when the poorly laid stone had been found.

Bender noticed that he stood by a telephone extension, with a directory beneath it. He picked up the directory, found a number, and punched it in.

After one ring, a woman's voice answered, "Judge Whiteman's office."

"Is Judge Whiteman in?"

"I'm sorry," the woman said. "Judge Whiteman will not be here during the next three days."

"Is he in town? I'd like to reach him."

"You might try his residence. I don't believe he's away."

Bender thanked her and hung up. This was better than he hoped. Whiteman was a confirmed bachelor, living in his family's spacious old house. If he were there, he might be in a relaxed mood, less alert to possible trouble.

Bender put on the gloves and carefully edged the hammer onto a newspaper, then wrapped the tool in the paper. He did not want anyone aware of what he carried, least of all the judge.

It took only twelve minutes to drive to the judge's house, a large, red brick, ten room, two story on a hillside overlooking the city.

A five acre lot surrounded it, well maintained by a crew that came once a week. A cleaning woman gave the inside minute attention bi-weekly, but the judge employed nobody else. He dined out.

Bender walked to the steps leading up to the wide porch spanning the front of the house, the wrapped hammer tucked awkwardly under his left arm.

He mounted the steps and crossed the porch, trying to organize his approach. It might be well, he finally concluded, to come to no decision until he saw a lead.

He rang the bell and waited. There was no response. He heard the chimes reverberating in the hallway.

His mind came alert. The sound was not muffled. The door—

He looked closely at the door. It was open about an inch.

But no one had responded. Perhaps the judge was in the yard.

Bender walked around the house and looked as closely as he could among the numerous trees and bushes. No person was visible.

He returned to the porch. The door had not moved. He decided to go in.

He pushed the door open and stepped into a deep hall carpeted with a long red Oriental runner.

"Judge Whiteman," he called.

No answer came, and no sound of movement was heard.

He explored several of the rooms leading off the hall without encountering anyone. Then, in the last room on the right, he found him.

In his booklined study, Judge Whiteman was sprawled across his blood-spattered mahogany desk, his head beaten in, the floor beneath him a red horror. He was unquestionably dead.

Bender's first instinct was to turn and run as fast as he could. Then an inner compulsion caused him to look closer at the scene. It was because of that that he found it.

Behind the desk, its head drenched in blood, was his own hammer.

A grim smile crossed his face. "Trying for two for the price of one, eh, Jules? Well, I don't think so."

He unwrapped the other hammer and carefully exchanged it for his own. He then smeared Vernet's hammer equally and dropped it behind the desk.

He was pondering how to draw attention to Vernet as he climbed back into his own car. Suddenly he lost interest in that for the moment.

"My God!" he said, his hand arrested in the act of inserting the ignition key. "I almost made it *first* degree this time."

Lowering his head, he vowed to restore Marie's monument, no matter what time limits were required.

18

Shattered Lamp
(1988)

"Yes," said a neighbor therapist, "people do abandon loved ones."

Mark Bell stretched his right hand up from the bed toward the crossbar that spanned it. He closed his fingers on the triangular attachment hanging down that was nicknamed "the trapeze." With a powerful lift, he pulled himself upright. There was no assist from his legs. They were as dead as last summer's weeds in mid-winter.

He was not thinking of metaphors. With his left hand, he was working his legs around to the point where he could lower himself into the wheelchair. As he had done on more than two thousand other mornings, he cursed the bullet that had put him in this position.

When he was in the chair and had finally maneuvered his heels onto the footrests, he considered his next move. He decided in favor of the motor. Manual propulsion could follow breakfast this morning.

Bell had often been thankful that he and Elsie had bought this house before the accident. Everything was on one floor, except for the recreation room in the basement. His bedroom, bath, and another bedroom converted into his workroom were at one end, flanked by the garage across the house's front.

He guided the chair to the bathroom and switched on the light. The pastel blue of the tiles was beaten into submission by the stainless rails and grips protruding from every vertical surface.

Every time Bell faced this room, he wished for someone to blame for his condition. Neither of the two possibles had survived, and realism convinced him of the futility of hating the dead.

A bank robber and a cop. He would never know which one.

Eventually, all of the morning necessities out of the way, he left the bathroom shaved, combed, ready for breakfast. He had decided on scrambled eggs, bacon, and waffles that could be heated in a toaster.

The all-white kitchen adjoined the bathroom. As soon as he wheeled in, he checked the coffee maker. Cold. Inside, second-hand grounds.

Must be sleeping late, he thought as he disposed of the waste and prepared the machine. He wondered if she was beginning some illness. No sign of it the night before.

He started the eggs and bacon in a big skillet, then wheeled to the refrigerator to get the waffles from the freezer side. The shelves were filled, but even a methodical search revealed no waffles.

Surprised, he rubbed his stubborn chin with long fingers. Someone had been forgetful. Perhaps, he thought as he closed the door, she had put the rest of them into a freezer bag to save space. Better ask her.

He cut back the heat, left the kitchen, and wheeled across the long living room to Elsie's bedroom door. It stood partly ajar.

He tapped lightly with his knuckles and pushed the door open, expecting to see her curly dark hair stirring on the pillow, her small head starting to turn. Instead, he saw a neatly made bed and an empty room.

"Elsie?" He spoke in a low tone, then louder. "Elsie?" No answer.

He backed, turned, and looked in the other bathroom, then in the guest room at the rear of the house. Both of them were empty.

The stairway to the basement opened near the guest bedroom. Bell opened the door and called loudly down the steps. It was futile.

He closed the door and ran his right hand through his sandy hair. His hazel eyes were narrowed in perplexity.

As he sat there, the clock in the entrance foyer struck eight. Elsie did not usually leave for work before nine forty. If she had only gone to the supermarket, she would not have made her bed yet.

He wheeled back to the kitchen and opened the garage door. The only car inside was his own. But he had not heard the overhead door go up or down.

He reached into the garage and flipped a switch. The overhead door rose with a noise that could not be overlooked.

The drive was empty.

Bell could see a touch of frost on the grass. The October air had a bite in it. He put the overhead door down again and closed the one from the kitchen.

He tried to remember when Elsie had come in the evening before. It was around five fifty, her usual time. She had entered from the garage, so he must have assumed...

But her car must have been in the drive. Then, sometime while he slept she went out of the front door and around the house. The drive had a small slope, as did the street for the length of the block. She had only to release the brake to be virtually out of earshot before starting the motor. He could not have heard.

Why?

Bell rationalized: something had to be done very early. Several hours extra work. Something had to be finished before the ordinary work day began. She had probably left around daybreak, trying her best not to disturb him.

His eyes softened. She had always been considerate, never more so than in the past six years.

He had never been able to persuade her that she had no guilt for placing him in the situation that had caused his paraplegia.

"Don't I still love you?" he often said. "Don't I appreciate everything you do for me? Do you think I don't know how supportive you are? Where would I be without you?"

Her big, dark eyes would fill with tears at the memory of his quickness and his strength, cut down in one immutable moment. Yet she had never let him sink into despair and self-pity in all the long time of readjustment.

He shrugged. He would know when the time came. Better to get on with the day's routine.

Yet, with ten o'clock barely past, he was in his workroom, staring at a large, unsullied sketch pad. No line had been drawn for the preliminary studies for the next children's book he was to illustrate. The text had charmed him, but now the harmony he needed would not come.

The telephone rang.

"Mark Bell."

"Hello, Mark. This is Karen, Galleon Travel. Is Elsie there?"

"Sorry, Karen, she isn't. She hasn't come in yet?"

"Not unless—no, that's not likely. I came in early myself."

Bell decided to sit on it. "She left here with time to spare. Maybe it's car trouble."

The woman at the other end sighed. "And welcome to the club. Well, it's just that she has a scrap of information about a departure time that I need. I'll get it another way."

"Karen," Bell spoke quickly before she could hang up, "has Elsie been carrying a bigger load lately?"

"Not that I know of."

"I just thought she might be. She's seemed preoccupied at times."

"It's not impossible, but we keep in pretty good touch."

He thanked her and hung up.

Then, in succession, he called the garage where she took her car and the emergency rooms of the two hospitals. No, he was told, her car was not in the shop, nor had it been. Both hospitals said that no woman of her name or description had been brought in.

Neither the city police nor the sheriff's office had any report of an accident involving her car.

He made one more call before noon. Any more would be blowing things out of proportion, he decided. He phoned her sister, Dorothy, a four hour drive away in Ohio.

In answer to his discreet questions, Dorothy, a large, placid woman, told him that she had not seen or heard from her sister in recent weeks. She considered Elsie unlikely to arrive unannounced. Bell hastened to reassure her that the call was unimportant, no more than a need to get some information quickly when nobody could locate Elsie momentarily.

When he finished the call, Bell stared out the window, totally unaware of the light gilding the edges of the leaves. He was becoming aware of the lies he had been telling in cover-up. Cover-up of what? Had anyone, even in this house, been lying to him?

Early in the afternoon, he tried to report her as a missing person, only to be told by the police that he must wait two more days.

"Be honest, mister," said the woman who had taken his call, "you'd feel pretty silly if she came in this evening—wouldn't you?"

"What if she's been kidnapped?"

"Do you have any evidence of that? Any demands?"

"Not a bit," he confessed.

"Then there's nothing we can do. If you still have the problem day after tomorrow, call back."

He gave up, went to the basement on the chairlift, and worked out with his exercise equipment for an hour.

On the following day, Bell considered the first thing he knew anyone would ask: had she left him?

He told himself that this was unlikely. She had not taken her suitcase, and her clothes seemed to be undisturbed. Her briefcase was missing, but that could have been in the car.

He had never heard rumors of any other man. Certainly, faced with the radically different domestic life of the past six years, she had abundant reason to be tempted.

In recent months they had begun to discuss having a baby. It was not physically impossible, and life had stabilized enough now. Would she have sacrificed something so fulfilling?

The thoughts chased themselves around in his brain through the long day while he waited in vain for the telephone to ring or a door to open.

He resisted turning on the living room television. At the far end of the room, near her bedroom, was a double-length davenport where Elsie liked to lie while she watched her favorite programs. Its emptiness mocked him.

Somehow, he got through a second bad night and into morning.

When he finally thought that someone would listen, Bell made a call to the police. This time, he did not call Missing Persons.

"Yes. My name is Bell. Mark Bell. I'd like to talk to Sergeant Adams."

"Sergeant Adams?" The impersonal voice on the telephone hesitated. "Would that be Ben Adams?"

"That's right. Don't tell me he's not with you any more."

"No, sir. It's Lieutenant Adams, now. And you want to talk to him?"

"Yes."

"A minute. I'll see if he's available."

A short interval. No Musak. A faint flurry of noise, then a resonant baritone. "Lieutenant Adams. What can I do for you, Mr. Bell?"

"I need some help. Do you remember who I am?"

"Maybe. Fill me in."

"The time Officer Train was killed by a bank robber six years ago—?"

Adams' tone became more personal. "*That* Bell. I thought you might be the one. The last time I saw you, we had a talk when you were in the hospital. How're things?"

"Pretty good, up until two days ago. Then my wife disappeared."

"Oh. Tough. Have you reported this to Missing Persons?"

"I tried, but it was too early. It didn't sound like I'd do much good with them anyway."

Bell envisioned raised eyebrows when he said this.

"Don't sell them short," Adams said. "They know their business. Try again."

"Well, maybe. But, look—you don't owe me, and I don't owe you. Would you give me some time and let me lay it out? Then you decide, and I'll go along with it."

Adams said, "Hmmm," then was silent. He came back on in several seconds. "When can you come in, Mr. Bell?"

"Could you come here? Two reasons. One, you'd get a better picture of things. Two, I'm a paraplegic. I can make it, but it would be a great favor if you came here."

Some discomfort came into Adams' voice. "Sorry, Mr. Bell. I never knew how you came out of that mess. All right. Sit tight, and I'll make it this afternoon. Now—I'll ask you a favor. I'll bring along somebody from Missing Persons. Okay?"

Bell swallowed. "Okay."

"Good. Now, what's your address?"

At a few minutes past two, the front door chime sounded. Bell found two men on his doorstep—Adams, little changed since they had last met, and a tall, young black man.

"Come in," he said.

Adams, a near six-footer with high cheekbones, close-cropped black hair, and a poker face, nodded. "Hello, Mr. Bell. I'd like you to meet Detective Riggs, from Missing Persons."

Riggs topped Adams by an inch. He had a completely round head, was light brown with a thin, straight nose and thin lips. The hand he extended was long; his grip was firm, but not challenging.

Bell showed them into the living room. Adams and Riggs elected to sit at one end of the long davenport. Bell wheeled to face them across the walnut coffee table.

Adams glanced at Riggs, then at Bell.

"Mr. Bell, I want to give Riggs some background on your situation here. I waited until now so that you can correct me when I'm wrong. Okay?"

"Go ahead."

Adams addressed Riggs. "A little over six years ago, somebody decided to knock off First National's mall branch. We don't know how many. Only one, maybe. Possibly three."

Riggs nodded. "I read about it."

"Mr. Bell and the holdup guy came out of back doors of the bank and a shop next to it at the same time. Also by coincidence, a cruiser was just seconds away when the alarm went off, and Officer Train was out of the car, waiting. Mr. Bell had a few steps' lead on the holdup man. He caught on—got confused—turned to go back— and both the thug and Train opened fire. One of them shot Mr. Bell in the back. With their next shots, they killed each other."

"The thing I remember most," Riggs said, "is that they had no way to prove who messed up Mr. Bell."

"That's right. Both Train and the thug got off only two rounds. Both guns were the same caliber. The slug from Mr. Bell was too distorted to be useful. There was no doubt where the second rounds went. The missing first round was never found."

"What about direction and angle?" Riggs asked.

"Not much value. Mr. Bell was turning to go back. He *could* have been hit by Train—but he couldn't remember which way he turned. Train's partner was busy looking for the wheelman—if there was one—and he didn't see most of it." Adams looked at Bell. "Right?"

251

"As near as I can tell."

"The two of us got acquainted when he was in the hospital. I was assigned to sort out what had happened. After all, this man here *could* have been in on the heist in some way. I did find out that he was in the mall to deliver prints of some of his pictures to a book shop for a promotion. His wife had a blouse on layaway at a shop next to the bank. When she heard he was going to the mall, she asked him to pick up the blouse. It checked out. He was off the hook."

"I was," said Bell, "but Elsie put herself on one when she realized how it happened. I've had an uphill fight getting her off it. I was going to the mall anyway. She didn't send me there."

Adams and Riggs exchanged glances.

"She's had enough on her hands, helping me to come back as far as I have," Bell went on. "I never knew how strong she was, physically and psychologically, until I had to turn my life around. The things she helped me with—the everyday things you take for granted—"

His voice trailed off.

Then he rocked them.

"I gave two reasons for wanting you here. There's a third. I haven't killed her."

He could see them searching for words.

Adams cleared his throat. "Why should we suppose you had?"

"When a man's wife 'goes away' and isn't seen again, isn't he suspected of killing her? Isn't it often the truth?"

Adams' poker face was back in place. "It's happened."

"Not this time," said Bell. "I'd like the two of you to go through this house and walk over my lot and satisfy yourselves that she's not hidden or buried here."

Adams rubbed a big hand along the arm of the davenport. "We'll take you up on that. First, you tell us what's happened, the way you see it."

Bell leaned forward to relive his agony. Before he started, Riggs took out a pocket recorder, laid it on the coffee table, and started it.

When Bell finished, Riggs spoke up.

"Does anyone know yet that your wife has disappeared?"

"Not to my knowledge. I told Karen at Galleon that she had gone to Ohio on a family emergency. Elsie's sister Dot, thinks that Galleon sent her to Chicago on a rush job to negotiate a hot package deal.

Would it help if the truth were let out?"

Riggs flipped his right hand. "Hard to say."

He looked directly at Bell. "However, when the lieutenant gave me the preliminaries, I called your neighbor, Mrs. Disch, across the street, and asked her when she'd seen your wife last. She saw her come home and park on the drive three nights ago. Next morning, the car was gone, just like you said. I told Mrs. Disch that you had misunderstood the date when your wife was to go away on business, and you were further confused when she hadn't called you. I think she was satisfied."

Adams cut in, his baritone voice neutral.

"Mr. Bell, when you were in the hospital six years ago, Dr. Lenhardt was your doctor, wasn't he?"

"I had several, depending on what was needed."

"I understand. Who is your family doctor?"

"Laird is my doctor. Elsie goes to Carroll."

"Then, if she should go to a hospital, she'd ask for Carroll?"

Puzzled, Bell said, "Yes, but they'd probably call me first and have me arrange it."

"Not necessarily," Adams replied. "Might I use your phone?"

Bell pointed. "Take it in my workroom. First door on your right, past the kitchen."

Adams got up and left. Riggs glanced down.

"Attractive rug, Mr. Bell. Don't often see short pile in a lot of homes."

Bell slapped the arm of his wheelchair. "This rolls easier on it."

"Nice place you've got here."

Bell laughed. "You should see the mortgage. If both of us weren't pulling in decent money, we'd not be here."

Riggs' eyebrows rose. "You didn't get a settlement?"

Bell shrugged. "From Drew, the thug at the heist? No way. Why should the city, when it couldn't be proved who did it? They did contribute medical costs for the first year, after insurance. They felt some obligation because Train should have waited to open fire."

"About your wife, Mr. Bell, I should warn you that it will be assumed that she just decided to leave you."

"I realize that," Bell conceded, "but I refuse to believe it. When two people love each other, it just doesn't happen."

Riggs sighed. "I'm only two years into this, sir, but I could tell you stories you'd find hard to believe."

A door opened while he was talking, and Adams came back.

"Stories you wouldn't believe?" he said. He sat down. "Any story you've got, I've got ten to top it. Anyway, I got through to Dr. Carroll. Lucky he's my doctor, too, or he might not have talked to me. To his knowledge, she's not in any hospital in the area. That includes Shadowlawn."

Riggs' eyebrows went up again. "I might not have thought of that one right away. It could have been a breakdown."

"Not in any to *his* knowledge," Bell said.

"Well, yes. But something more," Adams went on, leaning forward. "She doesn't have cancer or any other horror."

"Doesn't have—?" Bell snorted. "Well, of course not! She'd have told me."

"Don't be so sure." Adams said. "Some people would do just what she might have done. When they find out, they run. Why? To spare their partner agony? To hope to outrun it? Who knows?"

"I appreciate your thinking of this, don't get me wrong," Bell said. He spread his hands. "Look, here's our situation. I'm over the worst of my problems and am living with the way things are. I have all the contracts I can handle, and I sell my other paintings for good money. Elsie's freer than she has been for years, and she's the backbone of the travel agency. And we hope to have things even better."

He paused. "We'll be having a baby in the next year or two, I'd not be surprised."

He saw their incredulity.

"Do you mean—" Riggs fumbled.

Bell smiled. "Sex? Oh, yes, it's possible. Not easy, but possible."

"Mr. Bell," Adams said in a soft voice, "you have more spirit than anyone I've met in a long, long time."

"Thank you. Now—how about proving that I haven't killed my wife?"

"All right," said Adams, getting to his feet. "Tell me the layout, and Steve and I will check it out."

Bell gave directions. When he had finished, Riggs said, "One question. She took no suitcase. Any makeup, stuff like that, missing?"

Bell shrugged. "She had three of everything. Who knows?"

Adams and Riggs went slowly and carefully through Bell's end of the house, getting a rapid education in how he had to live.

Riggs eyed the bathroom. "The poor sonofabitch. Wouldn't you hate to put up with this?"

Adams was testing the sturdiness of a section of railing. "Wouldn't you hate to be the one to have to supply what he doesn't have?"

In the workroom, Riggs carefully looked through a rack of paintings and a folio of charcoal illustrations. "This guy is good."

"If you say so. I could live with any of it, I'll say that."

No comments on his bedroom. Kitchen and dinette admired for cleanliness and order. Nothing out of the ordinary anywhere.

The garage. Riggs: "She took her own car, so that must be his. How can he cope with it?" Adams: "Hand controls, special modifications. You ought to look around more. You'd flip if you saw how some of these people make out. Load their wheelchairs, cruise around just like you and me."

Dining room across the front of the house, living room behind it. Nothing obvious either place. Riggs: "One or both of 'em has a good eye." Adams: "Or paid for good advice."

Guest room. A blank. Wife's bath. Neat, but crowded with accessories. Adams: "Like the man said, three of everything."

Elsie's bedroom. Riggs eyed a long bookshelf running above the head of the bed. "Lot of poetry here. This I can relate to."

Adams, stooping, was peering under the bed. "It takes all kinds. I'll come by in ten years and see if you still say that."

"I'm wondering if she had any diaries."

Adams straightened. He had not even found dust. "How'll we know? Our man says she took a briefcase."

"We'll know if we find any."

Riggs leaned over, glancing along the books. "Frost, Sandburg, Masters, Housman, Dickinson, Shakespeare's sonnets, Tennyson, Keats, Shelley—"

"Quite a collection. What's it tell you?"

"A good mind. I haven't covered 'em all. I suspect there'll be some good moderns here."

"No sugar and spice? No heavy perfume stuff?"

Riggs shook his head. "A piece of paper sticking up from the Shelley—" He leaned over and slid the book from the shelf. Opening the volume, he glanced idly at the pages and the poem spanning two of them, "When the Lamp Is Shattered." He read the paper.

"Anything?"

He passed it to Adams. "To her, maybe."

It was a sheet from a blue memo pad. Adams read, from a clear, flowing hand:

"One times two
Is true
Two plus one—
One's undone"

"What would you call it?" he asked Riggs.

"New math," Riggs answered, laughing.

Adams pocketed it, thinking. "Put the book back. Let's get down to the basement."

Ten minutes later, they came upstairs again. Bell sat where he had been, waiting.

"You can give yourself quite a workout down there," said Adams. "I'm impressed. Maybe I'll drop in now and then."

"I'll be happy to share," Bell said. "You might have to wait your turn."

"Nothing new." Adams turned to Riggs. "Steve, why don't you walk around the place? Call me if you find anything." He eyed Bell. "Especially if anything's been sodded."

When Riggs had left, Adams, seated again on the davenport, said, "I think you told it straight. However, there's something you might consider."

Bell's pulse began to increase.

"All right."

"It's not going to be easy. Suppose we take a look again at what happened six years ago. That hood, Drew, decides to pull that bank heist. Was he alone, or were one—two—more in it with him? If he was alone, he had to make his grab, get out to his car, and be long gone before we could get moving.

"After it all went down, we did find a two-door Pontiac that had made the stolen vehicles list that morning. It could have been left by Drew or by his wheelman, who thought the scene was too hot for him to be moving at all.

"Complication. Points to another accomplice. Drew came out carrying a shopping bag, supposed to be full of x amount of money. Bank never did release a figure publicly, but told us about thirteen thousand. Trouble is, the shopping bag was empty. How come?"

"Possible answer—Drew had an accomplice on the scene. Accomplice has identical shopping bag. In the confusion, they switch. Are you with me?"

"No problem."

Adams smiled without humor. "Don't worry. I don't read you as the accomplice."

"Here's where it gets painful. Were you and your wife getting along when you were shot? An honest answer."

Bell's temples pounded. The pain was almost intolerable.

"Why, yes . . . We've never had any differences . . ."

Adams sighed. "Well, maybe not. Now—you're going to want to kill me, but control yourself—suppose your wife set you up."

He almost screamed back. *"Set me up? Why?"*

"She's the only one who can answer, if you can't. She wanted you out of the way. Who knows? She's the one who switched bags. She had the money all this time. Now the third man has turned up and wants his cut. Maybe he's been doing time and just got out. She takes off to give him his split. How about it?"

"Not a word of truth! I know her too well—"

Adams pushed it. "Maybe you're wondering about her part of the money. She's had six years. She could slip in a little bit here and there, and you'd never notice. She makes good money, and that would be a good cover-up."

Bell strained in his chair. "If any of that is true, why did she stay with me? Why did she help me fight my way back?"

"Maybe she knew that, if you got to thinking, you'd put things together. Maybe she was sorry for what happened. Maybe it gave her good cover. Who knows?"

Bell wheeled his chair close to Adams' feet. His hand hovered near the motor's controls. The policeman sat without moving, not watching what Bell might do.

"Think, Mr. Bell," Adams said. "As I remember, she wasn't local. You told me you'd met her on a vacation in Ohio and married her in two weeks. How much did you really know about her?"

"Enough. Her family were good, middle-class—"

"That can go either way. Be fair. Think about it. Missing Persons will give you a break, anyway. They'll be on your side. Just realize that there might be surprises."

Bell lifted his hand and laid it on the arm of the chair.

The door opened, and Riggs came back inside.

"Not a thing. You seem to be clean, Mr. Bell."

"Thanks," Bell growled.

Riggs looked at Adams. "What happened to sweetness and light?"

"Out to lunch," Adams answered.

Riggs turned to Bell. "I'll need a description of the car and the license number. It would help if I could have a picture of her."

"We have some pictures that were just made for the church directory. I'll get you a wallet-sized one. The car—"

When they had finished, a still-shaken Bell showed Adams and Riggs out. He had expected hope and reassurance. He was left with doubt and depression. How could police live with never-ending suspicion and cynicism?

Adams was driving. Riggs studied him thoughtfully.

"What did you do in there while I was outside?"

"Gave him some pain reliever."

"Come again?"

Adams gave him a side glance. "Something for you to remember, even though you won't want to. A lot of people—a *lot* of people—will pull out and leave somebody who needs them. From abandoning a baby to ones like we just left. They can't take it any more."

"Even if they love the one they've left?"

Adams shrugged. "Makes you wonder, huh?"

Riggs pulled out the paper he had found in the Shelley collection. Adams had returned it to him. "The poem next to this was

'When the lamp is shattered
The light in the dust lies dead—"

"That makes some sense. But, if she wrote this paper herself, what did she mean?"

Adams grinned. "It's what's behind this."

"Huh?"

258

"You're the poetry expert. And I figured it out."

Riggs studied the verse. Irritated, he muttered, "So, give."

"The last line. 'One's undone.' Read that, 'I'm undone.'"

"How?"

"Two plus one."

"Three?"

"Yeah. She's pregnant."

"He didn't say anything about that."

"He doesn't know," Adams pointed out. "But she is pregnant. Carroll was so glad to let me know she doesn't have cancer that he let slip what she really has."

"Bell seems to think they both wanted that."

"Yeah, but it takes two. Suppose you put in nearly six years raising an adult-sized baby—a pretty self-reliant baby, but not completely independent. Then suppose you forget and let down your guard a time or two, and you find yourself with two infants in your future. And you're not psychologically up to it. What do you do?"

Riggs considered. "Face up to it. Or go for an abortion."

"Just what I'm sure she did—go for the abortion. She probably went somewhere in Ohio. She might come back, but don't bet on it."

Riggs reflected on this. "And what you gave him to think on is so tough that the truth won't cross his mind?"

Adams grinned again. "Until he starts to see the holes in it."

"Holes?"

"Beginning with the fact that the police cruiser showed up only by happenstance."

"What choice will he have?" Riggs challenged.

"My story makes her an adversary," Adams said. "The truth might be that she has just discovered her breaking point."

Riggs spoke softly, quoting:
"'Naked to laughter
When leaves fall and cold winds come.'"

"What's that?"

"The last lines of Shelley's poem."

"How did he know?"

19

That Man's Moccasins Have Holes
(1987)

Eleanor Sullivan, late editor of Ellery Queen's Mystery Magazine, *wrote: "Stories that depend on dialogue as much as this one are seldom as successful. It is, we think, a rare treat." This story placed third in* Ellery Queen's *reader's poll in 1987.*

C alvin Slaughter sat on one of the concrete benches before the county courthouse. It was nearing nine in the morning and he was glad of it. The sun of early autumn was above the hilltops, but there were tatters of morning mist remaining to be dispelled. His navy-blue windbreaker still felt good.

Slaughter was a compact man of average height, with a physical hardness acquired by years of working underground. Early detection of black lung had forced him out of the mines and into an undemanding job as a night security guard at a plant manufacturing plastic houseware. His lungs gave him no trouble there, but the demands of his small farm sometimes reminded him of his mortality.

His grey eyes searched the few walkers on the street, but the man he wanted was not in sight. He pushed back his grey tractor cap, crossed his arms, and stared at his heavy shoes.

"Mornin', Cal," a nasal voice said from behind and to the right.

Slaughter half turned as a thin man in grey coveralls came around to the far end of the bench and sat down. "Hello, Floyd," he said. "Glad you could make it."

Floyd Amick rubbed the end of his sharp nose with the back of his right hand. "Had to see what it was that couldn't be discussed over the phone." His dark eyes gleamed in the slanting light. "Or at your place or mine."

Slaughter sat erect. "Just seemed best that it be someplace like this. I had to come into town, anyway. You probably did, too."

Amick nodded.

"How're things with you?" Slaughter asked.

Amick cocked his head. "How do you mean? We're all well enough, if that's what you want to know."

"Glad to hear it," Slaughter replied. "What I should have said is, how're you makin' it?"

"We're gettin' by."

"Pretty much on your feet again?"

"You might say. The walkin's a little unsteady, I have to admit." After studying Slaughter's face momentarily, Amick said, "How's it with you?"

"About like you just said," Slaughter replied in a dry tone. "Only we might be the ones about to be off our feet."

"Oh? How so?"

"You heard about Cam?" Slaughter asked, referring to his son, Cameron.

"Oh, yeah. Turned a tractor over on him. How's he doin'?"

Slaughter ran a big-knuckled hand along his jaw. "More's broke than's not. At least, it seems like it."

Amick dropped his gaze. "That's tough, Cal. Any idea how long he'll be laid up?"

"A good while. A good long while."

"Is he covered?"

Slaughter nodded. "Some, but I doubt it'll be enough. If it'd happened while he was at work, State Compensation would've helped. It happened at home, not at the mine, and that's a difference. Premiums for what it'll probably end up costin' would've eat him and us up."

Amick looked up. "It will, anyway, won't it? They get you comin' and goin'."

Slaughter fixed a steady glance. "It looks like a good market for potatoes this year, and we got plenty. I was countin' on makin' good money with 'em before this happened. Now I don't see how I'll be able to get 'em all in. More'n we can handle."

"Hire it done."

A small pebble rested at Slaughter's right foot. He picked it up, placed it at the end of his thumb, and flicked it away. "Can't get nobody."

"Arlan Boley's a fair man. He'd get over with one of his small machines and do it for you."

"I dunno, Floyd. All I can think of is the cost."

"But you'd get some return—"

Slaughter's gaze became so intense Amick found it hard to meet. "There's another thing that might help us, Floyd."

"What's that?"

"It's why I wanted to meet you here, away from everybody else. I need help, Floyd. How about could you pay me back the money I loaned you a little over a year ago?"

Amick's face assumed a guileless expression. "Don't see how I could do that, Cal."

"It wasn't easy for me to do it, either, when that flash flood wiped out that good bottom land and most of your crops. But I did it. Two thousand dollars."

"I know."

"Never asked you for a note to cover it, either, Floyd. Figured your word was good enough between us."

Amick turned his face away. "Yeah. Well, I just can't do it, Cal. I'm sorry."

Slaughter kept his attention on the other man. "Bruce still workin' at Riverside RV's?"

"Good steady job."

"Glad to hear it. With us, not only is Cam's accident costin' us, but he's not bringin' in any money to help keep the family goin'."

"That's hard," Amick admitted.

"That's why I'd like you to turn around and help us, Floyd."

"Well, I don't see how."

"What about sendin' Bruce over after work to help us get the taters in and sacked?"

Floyd leaned his pointed chin on his hand. "I could ask him. But don't get your hopes up. He's pretty tired when he gets in."

"Not too tired to come over now again to fish for bass in the pond I got out back."

"Yeah, well, he's got to unwind, y'know. Fishin's not work."

Slaughter turned his head and spat into the grass, which was still covered by a heavy layer of dew. "Think I'd better post that pond. We'll probably be needin' them bass."

"Seems a bit unneighborly, but I see your point."

"I think not takin' care of your debts is unneighborly, Floyd. Seems to me that what you take in from the weldin' jobs you do out in your shed, plus some of what Bruce makes, you oughta manage to set aside a bit for what you owe."

Amick shook his head. "We're still not doin' so good with the land. Barely enough for our own selves."

"I know that. You notice I didn't mention it."

"Well, then, you got some idea."

Slaughter considered. Finally he said, "That's not the way I was brought up. Get what you owe off your back first was the way I was trained. That way, if you need help again, you're more apt to get it."

He got no answer.

"I see you got one of the dish TV antennas," he said.

Amick's thin face reddened. "Yeah, I reckon we're entitled to it, if we want."

"How many times did you cinch up your belt so's you could get it?"

"None of your affair, Slaughter. Life's hard enough. You bitchin' about us gettin' a little pleasure out of it?"

"No, but I reckon there's plenty would agree with what I'm thinkin'."

Amick's face was expressionless. "Neither you nor anybody else runs our business."

Slaughter's remark was mild. "Feel that way myself. I never attached one string to that two thousand. Except that it was a loan."

Amick started to rise. Slaughter went on. "I had occasion last week to go past that little ravine between your place and Paxton's."

Amick sat down again. "Oh?"

"I saw what looked like an almost new wash machine in there. On your side of the fence."

There was a chill in Amick's voice. "Are you spyin' on whatever we do? Do I have to teach you to keep your nose to yourself?"

Slaughter's tone remained mild. "A man can't help seein' a thing that's right in front of him. Doesn't look pretty, but maybe the sides of that ravine need bolsterin'. It's your property."

"Damn right it is!" Amick growled. "That machine's there because Lucille and Bruce's Pearl decided we needed a new one. They won't take the old ones on trade nowadays."

Slaughter watched the other man intently again. "I always thought Bruce was pretty handy about electric and plumbing. Was it too much for him, whatever's wrong?"

"I think he could have—" Amick began. "It's only two years—I think them women just want a *new* thing every now and—" His chin thrust out and his day-old stubble was evident. "Anyway, it's in the family and that's where it stays. You hear me?"

"Loud and clear," Slaughter said. "Gettin' back to the loan, do I understand that you're not goin' to pay me back?"

"Not until I get good and ready. Maybe never."

Slaughter turned away. "I could sue," he remarked quietly.

"Go ahead and try," Amick snapped. "What'd be your evidence? What's on paper? Your word against mine."

"Yeah," Slaughter said. "I said *could,* not that I *would.* More'n one way to skin a cat."

"Are you threatenin' me, Slaughter?" Amick growled.

"I didn't think I was," Slaughter replied. "However, I will say that, from this minute on, things between your family and ours will never again be what they used to be."

Amick got up quickly. "We'll never notice the difference."

He strode off, his heels sounding loudly in the quiet air.

Slaughter remained, thinking. He had not truly expected to get the whole two thousand but he had thought Amick's sense of decency would cause him to make some kind of offer.

He wondered how he could have been so blind for so long.

He could see Maxine out in the potato patch with a hoe when he drove up to the side of their six-room cottage. Their place was on a wide ridge. On it, they had an extensive garden for their own needs, with large plantings of blueberries, squash, and potatoes for marketing.

He slid from the car and walked out to her. "Max," he said, "you hadn't ought to be doin' that. Not with your back the way it is."

She straightened and pushed back her fading red hair. He was happy to see a spark still glowed in her green eyes. The humor lines hadn't been replaced by clefts of bitterness.

"I can hold up as good as you can," she said.

"That doesn't say much," he replied.

"Get what you went for?" she asked.

"Some," he answered. "Hardware store's out of duct tape. Be in next week."

"Did you stop to see Cam?"

"I did. Didn't get to talk to him. He was asleep."

Maxine surveyed the work she had done. "I'd better get inside and start on lunch."

"That sounds good," he said. "It'll give your back a rest. However, my appetite's a little short, so far. Just fix me about half as much as I usually eat."

"You feel all right?"

"Never better."

He sensed skepticism, but he didn't care. As she headed for the back door, he went into the small aluminum shed nearby where he did repairs.

When he was sure his wife was in the house, Slaughter took out the key to a locked drawer in his supply cabinet. Maxine would tolerate no guns in the house. This was where he kept the .38 he was permitted to carry on his security job.

He unlocked the drawer and slid it open. The gun, unholstered, lay inside. A box of bullets was beside it. The gun wouldn't be armed until just before he left for work.

Slaughter opened the box and took out three bullets, placing them beside the gun. He stood there, thinking. Then he walked to the door and looked toward the house. He could see the top of Maxine's head as she bent over the sink. A spasm crossed his face.

He returned to the drawer and rolled one bullet back and forth with his forefinger. Then he picked up another and hefted it in his hand. Finally he returned all three bullets to the box. He pushed the gun to the extreme rear of the drawer, then slammed the drawer shut. He locked it and tested it, as though it might come open from a life of its own.

"He ain't worth *that!*" he muttered. "He'd win all the way, and Cam would lose the most. I'm not gonna let it happen."

The following Sunday, Calvin and Maxine Slaughter went to church, as was their custom. They sat six rows from the pulpit. This was also customary.

As they waited for the service to begin, Slaughter wondered if the Amicks would be present, third row from the back. He resisted turning around to find out.

The service proceeded as it did on most Sundays, eventually reaching the point where members of the congregation were encouraged to name persons ill or in other distress who could be mentioned in prayer.

"—and Bernice Morgan," the minister was saying. "Are there any others?"

Slaughter rose to his feet. "Preacher, I'd like to offer a prayer for a member of the congregation."

"Fine, Calvin," said the minister. "Just tell me the name and I'll include it."

"You misunderstood me, Preacher," Slaughter said. "I'd like to be the one offerin' the prayer."

The minister's eyebrows rose. He occasionally requested certain reliable members of the church to give prayers, but this type of request from the flock was seldom made. However, he couldn't refuse.

"Very well, Calvin. This is a fine spirit you're showing. I'll call you at the proper time."

Maxine leaned close when Slaughter sat down. "Is this for Cam? The minister can do it good enough to suit me," she whispered.

"Not Cam," he murmured.

"Then who is it?"

He made no answer.

"Let us pray," intoned the minister, launching into a long generalized exposition of the many weaknesses and vicissitudes being encountered by his flock, by the nation, and by the world. He prayed for the forgiveness of sin, for the salvation of the wicked, and for everlasting peace. He then prayed for the help of those named by the congregation.

"And now, Lord, one of our members, Brother Calvin Slaughter, wishes to beseech you in behalf of one of our members," he said.

Slaughter got to his feet and bowed his head.

"Oh, Lord," he said, "I know that we have been instructed to pray in secret, but I've tried that, and it's come to me that if I pray this one time openly it will come to others to pray also for a member of this congregation who sorely needs Your guidance and redemption. And he does need these things from You, Lord, because he is a sinner who tests the patience and understanding of those around him."

"In this world, Lord, a saying has come down to us from our red brothers who were known more by our forefathers than by us. It goes something like this—that we must not judge a person until we have walked a mile in his moccasins. The man I pray for, that man's moccasins have holes in them."

"I'm minded, Lord, that Your Son has told us to lend and expect nothing. I've tried to do that, Lord, but the man I loaned to laughs and sneers when I ask him for help. If he only couldn't pay I'd be content to ask You for help, because I trust You. But I'm not strong enough for just that. This man mocks me as a fool. I pity him, but I have to call him to Your attention."

"I know, Lord, that You are aware of my family's misery and how it looks to get greater. We accept Your will, whatever it is, in all of this. But this man, Lord, who wastes *my* substance, I pray that he be chastised so that he realizes he needs to ask for forgiveness."

Slaughter paused for breath. He heard the minister clear his throat. He gathered his strength and went into his conclusion.

"Lord, I suspicion that you knew I meant to do this. I have been bein' prompted to do what I didn't mean to do—name his name. But if others are to pray along with me for his redemption, I have to name him. I guess that's what You want me to do. So, all right, before You and this congregation I name him. Floyd Amick—the man I loaned good money when he didn't know where to turn. I leave the forgivin' to You. I'm too weak. I can't."

About to sit down, he finished. "Amen."

When he stopped, a thunderous silence gripped the church.

Hurriedly, the minister called for the final hymn. It was sung very much off-key. "I didn't know any of this," Maxine hissed into Calvin's ear. "I don't know whether to be proud or humiliated."

"Just hang in there," he murmured.

When they turned to go, the Amicks were long gone. The Slaughters tried to leave early, but the bulk of the congregation had the same idea and departure was slow. At the door, the minister gave Slaughter a searching look. "That was quite a prayer, Calvin," he said. "I'll have to give it considerable thought."

"Same as I did," Slaughter responded.

At the foot of the steps, a man somewhat better dressed than most waited. Slaughter recognized him as Charles Braxton, president of the local bank. He came forward as the Slaughters reached the ground.

"Mr. Slaughter, Mrs. Slaughter," he said, concern showing on his round face. "I had no idea. If you find things too difficult to handle, come in and we'll work something out. It won't be hard on you, not hard at all. You've had a savings account with us, haven't you?"

"Still do," Slaughter replied. "It's down a bit."

"Well, don't you worry. We want to help you."

After he had gone, a short, pink-cheeked man, also well dressed, gripped Slaughter's arm. He was Arthur Franklin, head of the principal building-supply and hardware store.

"Cal," he said, "gettin' a thing like that out in public does everybody good. Keeps the rest of us from bein' trapped. That critter *must* have a white stripe up his back. As of tomorrow, he gets no more credit from me. Nor from anybody else, once this gets around."

He narrowed his blue eyes. "You never ask for any, do you? Well, if you need to, we'll lend a hand."

When Slaughter finally escaped numerous well-wishers, he found a man keeping pace with him on his left. It was a few minutes before he recognized the man, who was not in uniform. "Why, hello, McKee," he said, "hardly knew you. Max, you remember Sheriff McKee."

The sheriff, a spare, well tanned man, exchanged formalities. "I've been in church with the rest of these folks," he told Slaughter. "I've heard what you prayed, Cal. I'm glad you did that, instead of goin' out and shootin' him."

"I thought about it," Slaughter said. "Then I realized I couldn't see what good it would do."

"More people ought to think like that," McKee said. Then his tone changed. "I've been hearin' what people said to you a bit ago. It's a good spirit. So I'll make an offer, too. If there's anythin' out at your place that needs doin', I'll send a couple of boys over to help. There's some in jail right now that're harmless and need to be kept occupied. What do you say?"

"It's a generous offer. I'll call you."

"Now there's another thing," McKee said. He stopped walking. "A lot of resentment was stirred up against Amick this mornin', and there'll be more. He's apt to find it hard to live around here and he won't like that. Hear what I'm sayin'?"

"I hear you, Sheriff."

"He might hunt a chance to throw down on you. Like when you're on night security. Who'd say it wasn't someone tryin' a break in?"

Slaughter made no answer.

"If it was the other way around, I'd be worryin', if I was him," McKee went on. "Somebody said you beat him bad in a turkey shoot."

Slaughter nodded. "Two years ago. By a considerable distance."

"Anyway, watch your back," the sheriff warned.

"I will. Which raises another matter."

"Oh?"

"Self-defense."